D1329683

THREE LIVES FOR THE CZAR

Three Lives for the Czar

STEPHANIE PLOWMAN

1970
HOUGHTON MIFFLIN COMPANY BOSTON

C.3

FOR MY MOTHER
F.D. 1 and 2,
and C.C.

— *BL*

AUG 1 8 '70

CONTENTS

PROLOGUE

They tell me that on a winter night, with the snow drifting down, and the street lamps now so few that they do little to illuminate the darkness, you can still stand staring across the unsullied whiteness of the Nevsky Prospekt and believe —at, say, that traditional hour of magic, midnight—that nothing has changed. Or you can gaze across the broad reach of the frozen Neva towards the Winter Palace, and the Admiralty—the outlines remain superb and beautiful.

But the dream, like all dreams, dies at daybreak, when the sad grey light comes slowly, as if reluctantly, and all is frozen silence save, perhaps, in a narrow channel of the Neva, where in a mild winter the icefloes rumble and grind against each other as the ebb sets out towards the Gulf of Finland.

Poor Petersburg, once the city of Pushkin—*I love you, city of Peter's creation, the Neva's majestic flow, her granite banks—the troops of infantry and horses, the tattered remnants of victorious banners—the gleam of bronze helmets shot through in battle—*

Also the nightmare city of the novel written by Bely a few years before the war—the people all ghosts in a ghost-like city, they have lost their souls, and live in a cold hell of frozen canals and inexorable straight avenues, where it is always winter; yet it's only a temporary hell, itself rotten and condemned. *Mist, moss, mess,* said Bely. First the mist came out of the Baltic, next the storm, and all will be destroyed.

Or did the destruction begin on that fine autumn day in 1894?

A young Russian army officer watches
the inexorable rush toward revolution
under the rule of Nicholas II.

I

'Dwindling indeed'

THE AUTUMN DAY had been clear and sunny, unlike most late October
days in St Petersburg, they had told the French visitor. Usually there
was fog, with rain in the air, mud and slush underfoot.

Yet he could not have chosen a worse time for his first visit to
Petersburg, alas!

No need to say that, thought the Duc de Saint Servan-Rézé. Even if
he had been told nothing of the news from the south, had not attended
the special prayer of intercession in Kazan Cathedral, he, a foreigner,
speaking no Russian, would have known something was badly wrong.
The groups of people standing at street corners would have been
enough, a clerk reading aloud a bulletin to an odd little group—workmen in blue blouses, an old-clothes seller (why did all the old-clothes
sellers seem to be Tartars?), a street pastry-cook with his pasties and
pancakes, a flower-seller, a wet-nurse in national costume, blue because
her charge was a boy. The wet-nurse was crossing herself and crying.
Yet, because of the brightness of the clothes (everyone in Petersburg
appeared to wear some kind of highly-coloured uniform) the scene
lacked reality. You thought only of people on a stage-set—opera,
perhaps, or ballet—acting, miming grief and consternation. Any
moment they'd start singing.

He had seen the little group just before noon, standing at a spot on the
Neva embankment directly opposite the Peter and Paul Fortress, with
its soaring slender gold spire crowned by an angel bearing a cross. And
because it was noon the cathedral clock, brought from Cologne in
1760, played instead of the hourly hymn *Kol Slaven*, the National
Anthem.

'*God Save the Czar—*'

It had brought a sudden silence to the city.

It was quite dark when, at half-past eight, the Frenchman, escorted

9

by a young officer, drove down the Nevsky Prospekt again, to the Znamenskaya Square and the Nicholas Station. They drove in silence until the carriage stopped, and then the young officer said jerkily: 'I keep forgetting, sir, that though this is your first visit to Russia, you know His Majesty well.'

'I've met him several times in Denmark.'

A bell rang as they began to walk through smoke and sulphur fumes along the platform. '*Pervi zvonok!* That's the first of three, sir. Fifteen minutes' warning.'

Whorls of steam and lamplight, green third-class compartments, yellow second, first blue.

'Here we are!' said his companion. 'Through sleeping car to Sebastopol, sir!'

'Monseigneur—'

His valet, looking as morose as Dante in exile.

'If the gentleman would tell me how I can find out what's become of Monseigneur's linen—'

'Ah, that will have been sent down in good time, sir. The *provodnik* —the coach attendant—will have it.'

A second bell. An enormous guard in black, belted blouse and fur cap strode past calling, '*Vtoroi!*'

'Five minutes,' said the young officer, and then many people were shouting, there was tremendous agitation along the platform. The lieutenant went very white. 'An extra paper,' he said. 'Excuse me, sir, while I get one. It can mean only one thing.'

He shouldered his way through people sobbing, crossing themselves.

'Get in, Michel,' said the Duc. 'There's nothing we can do.'

People were kneeling in prayer on the platform.

'I can't say, Monseigneur,' remarked Michel, 'that I'm happy about Mademoiselle living in a country smelling so odd—cabbage soup and sunflower seeds, they tell me—but at least the people seem to take religion seriously.'

'Ah, yes, enough crossing of themselves before ikons at the frontier station to satisfy even a Breton.'

Michel remarked he couldn't say the Russian kind of ecclesiastical architecture appealed to him. He would not fancy worshipping in a building that looked more like an outsize cruet than a church.

'Wait till you see the Moscow churches. They look more like cacti than anything else, Mademoiselle says.'

The lieutenant came running back through the crowd, just managed to come alongside the compartment, and called out, 'Yes, the end—' The Duc could hear nothing else, for at that moment there was an explosion of steam, the engine whistled mournfully, and the train was off.

He stood staring out at the agitated groups, until the express, gathering speed, had left the station. Then only telegraph poles slid past, uncertainly lit by the smudges of light from the train. Beyond them darkness covering a flat, featureless plain, a country wholly unknown to him, only two of its people familiar, his son-in-law Alexander and the gigantic Czar who had made him his friend and something of a confidant. He abruptly moved from the window and crossed himself.

Suddenly he was aware of the appalling heat in his compartment. He had been warned of this feature of Russian trains, but had not found it too unbearable during the journey from Virballen; possibly, he thought, his feeling of oppression and anxiety was partly to blame for this suffocating sensation. He summoned the conductor, who luckily spoke a little French, and said he wanted his window opened. The conductor's eyes almost started from his head. 'Such a thing is never done!' he cried wildly. 'It must be done!' said the Frenchman with Breton stubbornness. 'These are double windows—take one of the panes out! I'll be back in ten minutes.'

In the corridor he stood staring out at the dark forest; no need to steady himself on this train, for the gauge was wider than any other in Europe and the line was dead straight. His son-in-law had told him how in 1842, when Nicholas I had decided to build the line from St Petersburg to Moscow, there had been so many arguments among the engineers laying out the route that the Czar had seized a ruler, traced a straight line on the map between the two cities, and had ordered, 'You will lay the track along this line and no other!'

So thank a dead despot and a government's fear of invasion by rail for a straight line and an extra broad gauge which made for smooth-running train journeys and—

Here an elderly Russian general in his dark green tunic began making his way along the corridor. A high-ranking officer because his epaulettes were fringed.

How the fringe on those epaulettes danced—

Because the general was lurching.

Ill?

Or drunk?

If he were drunk, one should look away. On the other hand, if he were ill—He'd speak French, presumably—

'You are not well, I think. If you will tell me where you are going, I'll—'

'Thank you,' came a breathless voice. 'If you would give me your arm—to the dining-car.'

'Will they be serving dinner now?'

The old man smiled faintly. 'You're a foreigner, I see. In Russia, especially on trains, there are no specified times for eating. We eat when we're hungry.'

'But why not go back to your compartment, and send your servant for something? You're not well, and—'

'The truth is that after hearing the news I don't relish being alone with my thoughts,' said the general.

'Ah!' said the Frenchman. 'Obviously we've both made the same mistake—reserved a compartment, only to find the solitude unendurable. Shall we therefore join forces?'

'I warn you that I am already slightly drunk. Probably I'll become more so. In which case I shall talk—endlessly. I always do when I'm the worse for drink.'

'Come, does that matter? I am a Frenchman on my first visit to Russia; there is no need for you to identify yourself to me, so whatever you choose to say—'

'You are as considerate as all your countrymen, and so I accept your offer, sir. In any case, I shan't bore you for long. I'm going only as far as Tver, three hundred miles south of Petersburg.'

'Before we reach Moscow, then—'

'Oh, yes. Damned dull journey all the way. You're wise to make it at night; Baedeker tells you to do that, doesn't he—*as little of interest is passed on the way.* Are you going beyond Moscow?'

'To Livadia.'

'Kharkov, Sebastopol, then a carriage drive,' said the general bemusedly. Then came a reaction. 'You were *summoned?*'

'Too late, I fear. I reached Petersburg yesterday to see my new grandson for the first time. My son-in-law's in attendance at court and he'd mentioned to His Imperial Majesty that I was coming to Russia. The Czar said he would like to see me; the telegram came at midday, and then, of course, after I'd boarded the train, this tragic news—'

'You're still going, though?'

'Ah, the Embassy got in touch with me this afternoon to ask me to go whatever happened.'

The general abruptly burst into tears. 'Our Czar—now we must speak of him in the past tense, he is dead and we must live. Do you know how we announce a death in Russia—*He had bidden you live long*—'

The Frenchman decided to get him back to his compartment, and sit with him as he ate a meal. Despite his grief, he ate voraciously—a soup he said was called *stchi*, made of cabbage, with bits of meat floating about in it, followed by veal cutlets. It was deftly served by a smiling little waiter with a shaved head and hairless face. 'Tartar,' said the general, finishing his cutlets. 'All the waiters on trains and in the station restaurants are Tartars.'

'That's a sad comedown from the hordes of Genghis Khan.'

'Ah,' said the general, 'being Moslems, they're clean—'

The inoffensive descendant of a race synonymous with barbaric cruelty took the last plates away. 'And now,' said the general, 'let me try to thank you for the way you've helped me to recapture my mental equilibrium after this frightful news.'

Hitherto his French had been faultless; for the first time he appeared to have chosen the wrong word. His companion said tentatively, 'Surely not frightful! Unexpected, tragic—yes, a thousand times, but not as terrifying a thing as—as—'

'As the atrocious murder of the late Czar's father thirteen years ago? My God, I knew such misery then, I felt I stood in the ante-chamber to Hell—Yet, believe me, sir, I didn't feel *then* this ghastly uncertainty about the future of my poor country. What's going to become of us all?'

'Surely this reign is beginning in circumstances more auspicious than any in the past century? You may laugh at me, or be angry that I should lecture you on Russian history, but I think my facts are right— that the late Czar succeeded in circumstances of complete horror; that *his* murdered father became Czar during the Crimean War; that when Nicholas I succeeded there was a rebellion; while Paul was murdered to make way for Alexander I.'

'Ah, the circumstances of the accession!' said the general impatiently. 'Are they as important as the character of the Heir?'

If he had been clearer-headed, he would have seen a sudden watchfulness appear in the grey eyes regarding him. 'I don't know much about him,' said the Duc, 'but at least he's not a child, is he? He's in his mid-twenties, and not an idiot!'

The general gave an extraordinary barking sound, half derision, half despair. 'He's retiring, modest, and a dutiful son—that's all most people know about him—by God, that's all there *is* to know about him! One look at that vacant face of his is enough!'

'Faces can deceive,' said the Frenchman. 'Think of any Englishman you know. He's completely banished all trace of emotion, and you might think him incapable of any feeling. But it is not so.'

But the general was not listening. 'I've no doubt,' he was saying furiously, 'that at first there'll be those who'll blame his father for not giving him training and experience in government matters, but I can tell you that if at any time the Czarevitch had shown the slightest inclination to take a real share in the government, his poor father, especially in the last few months, would have been overjoyed.'

'I remember that he said to me once that he disliked that impossible, spoiled old woman, the Queen of England, too much to imitate her attitude to her heir.'

'Exactly—but *this* heir wasn't interested. He's held precisely one public office. Two years ago ministers suggested he might be the chairman of the committee to supervise the construction of the Siberian Railway. His father agreed it *might* make him grow up, though he wasn't really hopeful. I was in attendance when the request was made. "Do you know what you're asking?" said the Czar. "He's still a boy —his judgments are those of a mere child. He's never grown up—all he wants is to be amused!" Well, that's the only brand of government with which he's been officially connected—God help us all if he fancies himself as an expert on Far Eastern affairs on the strength of it! Otherwise he's never been more than "Nicky"—timid little Nicky, self-effacing, passively obedient little Nicky, always treated like a little boy because people can't help it, he looks so much younger than his age, and he's so short, too. Talk of the Romanovs for the last century, and you think of great tall strapping fellows, as imposing as you like. This one seems to belong to a different race, doesn't *look* like a Czar. Always walks on his toes, being self-conscious about his appearance. Keeps looking over his shoulder with a—a kind of apologetic smile.'

'And you think he knows he hasn't the qualities necessary for an autocrat?'

'I'm sure of it.'

'Then—referring again to my scanty knowledge of Russian history
—he's not the only son, is he? If I remember correctly, at the death of
Alexander I, the elder brother, Constantine, stood aside in favour of
Nicholas I—'

'You mean he could abdicate?'

'Well, it's been done before.'

'The Grand Duke Constantine was married to a Polish lady, who
had no wish for greatness. The new Czar's marrying someone very
different!'

'Ah, yes, the Hessian princess Alix. I'm afraid all I know of her is
that her strong Lutheran convictions at one time seemed to put the
marriage out of the question, and that she has been brought up largely
by her grandmother, Victoria of England.'

'Ah, yes, those religious scruples,' groaned the general. 'Well, she's
surmounted them now—or whatever you do with scruples—and I can
tell you what the next step's going to be. She's proud, you know, can't
bear the thought that people may be saying that she's changed her
religion only for reasons of ambition. So she'll let herself go entirely
overboard, she'll be more Orthodox than the Orthodox, more super-
stitious—though she'll call it mystic—than any old granny in the most
backward village. Then, as you said, she's been brought up by the old
Englishwoman, and takes after her in character—prim, obstinate,
narrow-minded, bent on domination. I'll tell you something—my
cousin's a diplomat, and a couple of months ago he was accredited to
Darmstadt, her home. The odd thing was that he found it hard to get
anybody to talk about her. Finally he got the old Marshal of the Grand
Ducal Court to unbend. He didn't say much—but it was enough! The
old fellow got up, waddled across the room, closed the door, then
whispered, "We shall all be pleased to see the departure of Her Highness
—*so self-righteous!*" '

'Wait a moment, though, you've already had one Czarina from Hesse,
haven't you—Alexander II's wife, your new Czar's grandmother?'

A sudden gust of wind rattled the steamed windows, came whistling
in through invisible cracks—possibly the reason why the general
suddenly shivered. His face looked ghastly in the jumping orange flames
of the lamps.

'We don't want another Czarina from *that* stable,' he said.

'Ah, yes, Alexander's wife wasn't strong, was she? Your Russian
climate didn't suit her.'

The general muttered, '*Bolezn Gessenskikh.*'

'I'm sorry,' said the Frenchman after a moment, 'I speak no Russian at all.'

'The Hesse disease—have you never heard of it?'

'No.'

'The women have a tendency to hysteria—' He brought his clenched fists down upon the arms of his chair. 'Why do you think his parents did all they could to stop the affair?'

He seemed on the point of bursting into tears again.

'It's high time,' the Frenchman said, 'that royal families began to show the ordinary common sense of a peasant. Would he expect his livestock to breed from a strain that's not healthy?'

'That's common sense,' said the general very loudly. 'Royalty's insulated against reality. I don't know if anyone's talked to the Czarevitch—I mean the new Czar—oh, my God!' And then, very abruptly, he slid over in his chair, and within seconds was snoring so loudly that the Frenchman did not need to call the waiting servant.

The best way for the extraordinary conversation to end, of course. By morning the general would be off the train with only the haziest recollections of what he had talked about.

'I wish I were as lucky,' mused the Frenchman, returning to his own compartment where the temperature was now bearable. Michel, waiting, good fellow, was dismissed. The hovering conductor was told he had done all he could to make sleep possible; one could not add wryly that an elderly general had quite spoiled all prospect of a night's sound rest.

One did not sleep well after hearing predictions of disaster for the country where one's adored daughter had made her home, particularly since the general's remarks had only confirmed what Avoye and her mother-in-law had said on the previous night in St Petersburg when they were trying to accustom themselves to the fact that soon there might be a new Czar.

'It was so much more pleasant,' the Princess had said, 'to accustom myself to the fact that soon there would be a new member of the Hamilton family.'

One hoped the new—first—grandchild, Andrei, had chosen a good time to be born.

There was that odd little contribution from Avoye. 'Once he's Czar,' she said drowsily, 'there'll be hundreds of portraits of him, great garish things in almost impossibly bright colours. But the more accurate would be a portrait in half-tones of grey, against a—a background of pale twilight, for his character's so vague, so elusive, so diffuse, all nuances —you can never define it in exact terms.'

The Duc had got up to take a turn about the room, a beautiful room, walls hung with tapestries over which strutted white peacocks, a perfect background to great Chinese vases of flaming scarlet porcelain, and a matchless collection of white jade. Curtains of dove-grey velvet shut out the October night.

'When I was informed by this dutiful daughter of mine that I was going to have a Russian son-in-law,' he said meditatively to Avoye's mother-in-law, 'my first thought was that I should read up some Russian history, after which the very strong image of a Russian Czar that became fixed in my mind was that of a Peter the Great—supplemented, of course, by my own knowledge of the ruling Autocrat. I could think only of a giant of a man, of ferocious energy, whereas—'

'Whereas now, Papa,' his daughter said, suddenly grave, 'you find the image is dwindling into that of a—a nervous little man with no willpower whatsoever.'

Which brought his musings in full circle back to a respectable Russian general getting drunk because of his fears for the country's future under a new ruler who lacked willpower. And nerve, said the Frenchman to himself. Far more important than mere cleverness. The late Czar was anything but brilliant, but he had plenty of common sense, and he knew what he wanted. And one of the things he did want was the truth. Ministers had to let him know the facts, unpleasant and brutal as they might be. He was remarkable, in that respect, as far as the majority of monarchs went.

Unless a ruler were as remarkable as the dead Czar, his life was one of essential artificiality, leading to a kind of two-way blindness, for while the monarch, living in an atmosphere above all unnatural, rarely saw matters as they actually were, so he—or she—was rarely *seen* with any realism. Kings and queens, mused the Frenchman, become legendary creatures in their lifetimes and the term can include monsters as well as gods and goddesses—

Only a small, restricted circle knows them, and a monarch's chosen circle—unless he's exceptional—is rarely outstanding for intelligence—

Or articulateness—so who'll be able to describe the character of the new Czar—?

And at last he was asleep.

In due course the Duc de Saint Servan-Rézé returned to the capital as one of the official French mourners at the Imperial funeral.

The Nicholas Station was very different now. No noise but that of muffled drums and then, outside, the immense square filled with a great black-clad crowd. Snow fell raggedly from a grey sky.

For the men an interminably slow march of four hours across the city to the Cathedral in the Fortress of Saint Peter and Saint Paul on the other side of the Neva for the lying in state; for the women court carriages painted black, the very handles wrapped in crêpe. In the second, the *fianceé* of the young Czar, tall (which was a pity as she overtopped her future husband), classically beautiful, but set-faced. No warmth or animation. '*Icily regular, faultily faultless, splendidly null*,' his son-in-law had muttered to him at Livadia. 'All very apt— Alfred, Lord Tennyson.'

'But, Alesha, may not the exceptional circumstance—'

'No, they say she's always like this, socially stiff and reserved as a turtle.'

'But admit someone's showing a complete lack of imagination here! She should go straight back to Darmstadt, and come back in the spring, to make an entrance in the sunshine! As it is, every old woman in the crowd will be talking of bad luck!'

'Haven't you heard, then? The marriage is taking place a week after the funeral—mourning's being lifted for one day.'

'What damned stupidity! Surely your Czar can rouse himself to countermand *this* piece of lunacy.'

It was impossible ever to find a private place to talk in during those frenzied hours at Livadia. A middle-aged baroness from the Baltic German nobility was bearing down on them; Alexander looked at him expressionlessly and said, 'It's the Czar's own idea; he doesn't want her to go back to Hesse, he needs her too badly.'

His words were overheard. 'The poor little Czar!' gushed the baroness.

Poor little Czar, thought the Frenchman. And this is the Autocrat of all the Russias, God help us!

He remembered the conversation as he gloomily watched the falling snow turn yellow beneath the procession. He was to remember it again a week later, at the end of the funeral ceremonies.

For the last time they had crossed the exposed bridge, shivering in the cutting wind, to enter the Cathedral in the Fortress. Thousands of candles flickered on so many brilliant uniforms that the effect was that of a wall of solid gold. The most sombre effect came from the women in their long black dresses, veils and trains. Cannon boomed outside, and the chanting of priests began. At first snow could be seen falling past the high windows, but before the giant Grenadiers lowered the coffin into the ancestral vault, the sky had cleared. The Cathedral had come as something of a surprise to the foreign representatives, who had generally expected a fortress church to be grimness itself. Instead, one received the impression that in normal circumstances the place was anything but sombre; there were always plenty of flowers, Alexander had said, while the tombs were splendid.

And, at the end, all eyes on the new Czar.

A small, slight figure, with indecisive movements, and an anxious, almost hunted expression in his blue eyes. When the funeral was over, he escorted his mother to her carriage, waiting at a side door and then, after another look at the tomb, which was being closed, he went out of the Cathedral by the front entrance.

He was alone now, and for a few seconds he hesitated on the steps— yes, there was the odd rising on his toes, the uncertain quick, backward movement of his head described by the general. It was almost as if he were dazed and blinded by the light—although the thousands of candles made the interior of the Cathedral far lighter than the grey November day outside.

And then the flags were lowered before him in salute, and the bands crashed out the finest of all national anthems; the Duc de Saint Servan-Rézé wondered what expression was on his face, or, indeed, if there were any expression at all.

He remembered the impression made on him by the new Czar during the audience he had been given at the Anitchkov Palace on the previous day, the first real conversation they had had together. He recalled, It was like standing in the presence of an empty place.

Now he found himself echoing the word his daughter had used on the last evening of the old reign—'Dwindling indeed.'

2

Measles and Lost Luggage

IF I, ANDREI HAMILTON, chose an inauspicious moment to be born in Russia, that same year, 1894, was scarcely a good year for my Uncle Raoul, Mother's only brother, to enter the Army in France. He was merely given sufficient time to realise how much he wanted to make the Army his career—and then, it seemed, the chance of a career was snatched from him.

Within a few years successive governments of the Third Republic were to carry out a systematic plan of anti-Catholicism where the Army was concerned. Uncle Raoul was a *Postard*—he had attended the Jesuit preparatory school in the Rue des Postes in Paris—and his family was Breton and Royalist.

Until 1905 if you were a Catholic the Army had no future for you, you were a member of a suspected, estranged minority, your efficiency hamstrung by political interference, your morale ebbing away in the knowledge that the government and a large part of the nation had no sympathy or trust for you. After this, affairs improved, but it had meant nearly a decade in the wilderness for many officers of brilliant gifts and selfless devotion, and France never recovered from the years the locust had taken.

Not that Uncle Raoul suffered as much for his religious and political beliefs as his father had done—Grandfather, in fact, had been one of the hostages—priests, policemen, Army officers—desperately defending themselves in the prison of La Roquette during the Paris Commune in 1871, and saved from the howling mob only when the Versailles troops broke through at dawn on the day all surviving hostages had believed must be their last. Often one forgot that he had undergone this experience; certainly he rarely, if ever, spoke of it. I myself heard him refer to it only once—in Petersburg, at the beginning of 1917.

He was Alain Xavier Anne Louis Arnaud Valentin de Lannion, Duc de Saint Servan-Rézé. When the Communards arrested him he had just returned to France after more than ten years' service in Algeria; refusing to serve the tawdry Second Empire in Europe, he had been more than content to be a soldier in North Africa, where France, he believed, had a civilising mission. His escape from the Communards made him fêted for a little while but then he was informed that he could have no hope of employment in the new *régime*. He decided that before retiring to Brittany to lick his wounds in private, the best way of forgetting what Paris had become was to pay a short visit to the last civilised capital in Europe—Vienna. On his second night there he dined early with some Austrian friends who insisted on taking him off to the first performance of the new Strauss opera, *A Thousand and One Nights*; what happened there can be timed with some minuteness, because of his lasting attachment to the Intermezzo at the end of Act Two of the opera. At this moment he was introduced to Elisabeth Francesca von Hohenems-Landeck, and before the year was out married her in a small Tyrolean church, the ceremony being performed by a Prince of the Church (the bride's Uncle Stefan), the bride being given away by a Prince of the Empire (her father), while to the ecstasy of the fanatically loyal Tyrolean villagers, the Emperor Franz-Josef himself attended in his capacity as the bride's godfather.

The marriage was blissfully happy. There were two children, my Uncle Raoul, born in 1873, and my mother, Avoye, born in the following year.

If ever in my childhood Grandfather felt I was becoming uppish, he could always bring me to heel with the comment, 'Consider the sole reason for your existence—measles and lost luggage!'

Actually Grandfather over-simplified matters. Another factor was my father's inheritance not only of the Scottish name of Hamilton from Jacobite ancestors taking service in Russia in the mid-eighteenth century, but also their looks—height, fair hair, grey eyes. More, he not only bore a Scottish name and looked a Scot, but English was literally his mother-tongue.

He arrived in Vienna as assistant military attaché in 1892; his mood was vile. Either the Russian or the Austrian railways—probably the Russian—had contrived to lose his luggage for him. Until the missing uniforms turned up, he had to exist in hurriedly-purchased civilian clothes, looking, he remarked gloomily, like a óne-man peace mission. He was also sure that it was going to be all work and no play for him— he'd been sent to Vienna at the wrong time of the year, he would be out of everything because in Vienna dancing engagements were made for the whole season, and he had come three weeks too late.

But then his luck turned. One of the other young men at the Embassy went down with measles, and asked Father to act as substitute. 'There's a French girl—she put me down for three dances. All I could manage to get—she really is astoundingly beautiful.'

So, because of the measles, for three times most nights Father waltzed with Mother, and the lost luggage played its part in bringing about my existence, because if Grandfather had seen his cherished Avoye smiling up with such brilliance at someone in *Russian* uniform . . .

Why do I spend so much time on the frivolous circumstances of my parents' first meeting? Because, I suppose, it is in such marked contrast to the way in which they parted from each other.

In any case, Grandfather remarked later, things might have been worse. He might never be able to stomach the fact that his son-in-law was usually addressed as Alexander Mikhailovitch, but it wasn't as if he were pure Tartar. In point of fact, Russian blood was non-existent in the family. Andrew Hamilton, after wanderings on the Continent after Culloden, had eventually turned up in Russia with his Austrian wife at the time of the Seven Years' War, commanded a regiment against Prussia, and was ennobled by the Czarina Elizabeth. His son was Stepan, one of the heroes of 1812, who became a field-marshal and prince, and was supposed to be one of the few people who knew whether Alexander I really died in 1825 or went off to be a hermit in Siberia. His wife was a member of a French *emigré* family.

Great-Grandfather Nicholas Hamilton married a Polish lady, and was killed fighting in the Crimea. In 1861 my grandfather Michael went reluctantly to the Paris Embassy, and provoked in Petersburg society the irritated comment—'These Hamiltons, always marrying foreigners!' Yet really he was marrying one of his own kind, for he married a Scotswoman.

Her name was Anne Hilarion, and she was the daughter of a Scottish colonel serving in India. In 1857 she was seventeen; for two years she had been completing her education, and she was looking forward to the following spring when she would rejoin her father, mother and small brother, aged four. Perhaps by that time they would have left Cawnpore, which they had never really liked. . . .

The father died in the siege that followed the outbreak of the Indian Mutiny. The mother and small brother survived a little longer.

It was known in England—eventually—that while all the men but four had died, the women and children were captives. It was known that Sir Henry Havelock and his Highlanders were marching under a burning sun to their rescue. They covered 126 miles in nine days and then came to the torrid, airless prison. Silent and empty. Then to a well in the courtyard. Silent too, now, but not empty. Not empty.

She wrote disjointedly in her diary: 'But it must have been quick. *Dear God, it must have been quick!*'

Then, underneath: 'But they were prisoners for days. They were murdered only when the rescuers approached . . .

'One shouldn't attempt to rescue prisoners, then. It increases their danger.

'Perhaps they were not so afraid as I dream. People say that when a cat has played with a mouse for some time, the mouse ceases to feel pain. Fear acts as an opiate.'

But then the dreadful details became known. Well-meaning people tried to hide them from her, but she said she must know. 'I realise now why friends wish to be present at the execution of a victim; with love, one must share.'

And so she read of a room ankle-deep in blood, walls gashed not as if men had fought, but low down, and in the corners, as if creatures had crawled and crouched to avoid blows. She read of strips of dresses tied round door handles, in a last attempt to keep the murderers out.

She wrote in frozen horror: 'Why do people speak of clumsy murderers as butchers? Butchers are skilled at their job.'

Someone brought her two relics she recognised; a locket 'with Ned's hair,' a torn prayerbook. She wrote something disjointed about, 'Too many mistakes—too much blind faith in loyalty.'

There was no money, and no relatives. She became a governess. She took the first post that she was offered, being in no condition to discriminate. She was employed by a family living near Kettering in Northamptonshire. Her employer, the widow of a wealthy manufacturer, disliked her, but kept her because she gave value for money. There were entries in the diary of a 'dull, hostile stare,' the unbecoming flush of rage on the heavy face if a visitor penetrated into the schoolroom and came back to praise Miss Hilarion's intelligence. She was never addressed except in terms of stinging rebuke, yet could not leave without a reference.

In 1861 the family went to Paris. It was hot, and the children were

23

bored by the exhibitions and spectacles to which their mother dragged them. They behaved badly, and the governess was blamed. 'It's not Miss Hilarion's fault!' a small voice said shrilly. 'We *love* Miss Hilarion!' ·

'What! Love a *governess*!'

The children were hustled out of the gallery; the governess was told to follow on foot, alone. 'I shall see you later. I think it's quite clear you must go—you're a disastrous influence.'

The governess stood white-faced, tearless. A voice said, 'You must forgive me for speaking to you, but you must have someone to talk with. You must forget what that magenta-faced hag said.'

'I believe one of Charlotte Bronte's employers expressed disgust because her little son said he, too, loved his governess.'

'What are you going to do? She intends to dismiss you, a young girl, left adrift in Paris, damn her.'

'You heard everything, then?'

'Yes. When the scene commenced I withdrew behind that very bulbous piece of statuary, feeling you would prefer not to have a witness.'

She turned. 'I was conscious of no one. I thought you were English, but from your uniform . . .'

'I'm Russian. And I was conscious of you from the moment you came into the gallery like—like a white rose accompanying an overgrown beetroot.'

The employer waited, fuming, until evening. The children stood wistfully, their noses pressed against the window, watching for the slim figure to come up the street with her quick, light step. Instead they suddenly ran to their mother, shouting: 'The Emperor of France must be coming to see us!'

'Look! There he is getting out!'

'Don't be silly! The Emperor has a big nose and very short legs!'

Their mother, panting, hurried to the window. 'It's a footman,' she said.

'I've never seen a footman dressed like that!'

'I've never seen a *carriage* like that!'

'You must not shout like this! Your governess has a great deal to answer for!'

The footman was accompanied by a maid with the air of an empress. They came from the Russian Embassy, carried a letter from the Ambassador's wife. To her great pleasure Miss Hilarion had consented to stay

24

with her for a few days; the maid would collect and pack her clothes. 'Clothes! She'll need different clothes for this new kind of life!' The maid smiled briefly: 'One dress in particular.' The children a week later wrote: 'We could not understand what she meant by this. Now it is clear—a wedding dress! Mamma says she does not believe you are being married, and in any case is sure he is not really a prince, but she would not be so angry if she did not really know it to be true.'

Again, I have a reason for relating this story, another favourite of my childhood. It made me believe too obstinately and too frequently in the possibility of all coming well in the long run, in the miraculous happy ending. To another aspect I did not give sufficient attention, although more than once I read my grandmother's diary. 'Too many mistakes—too much blind faith in loyalty,' she had written. And the description of the bloodsoaked room, and the slashes on the wall, and the summer heat beating down. It was dreadful, but it was history, it had happened a long time ago, and in a distant country, and the perpetrators were an alien race. One didn't feel personally involved in despairing calculations as to whether fear acted like an opiate.

A marriage that neared perfection lasted for eighteen years until the beginning of the attempts to murder Alexander II, when my grandfather threw himself between the Czar and an assassin's bullet. He was too badly wounded to be taken home, and was carried into a nearby house. My grandmother was just preparing to join him at Peterhof, and wore a dress of some lilac stuff. When she came to him, he could not speak, but his eyes smiled at her, and she sat beside him for hours. Her only sign of weakness was when the doctor asked her if she would like to moisten her husband's lips. 'I think,' she said carefully, 'my hand would tremble too much, and this would distress him.' At dawn they made her go and lie on a couch in the next room. At six o'clock the Czar returned and bent over the bed. My grandfather stirred, opened his eyes. The Czar knelt beside him. 'Sir, please tell Anne that it was a pretty dress,' whispered grandfather, and died.

So here we were, the Hamiltons, resident in Russia for a century and a half, yet with nothing racially Russian in us.

It was no doubt because of this that we all had such passionate love for St Petersburg, most un-Russian of cities, as the new Czarina Alexandra said, frequently and angrily.

Petersburg was a city whose population was never worthy of her, and when I think of Petersburg, I always think of an early summer morning, the population asleep, but the sky light, because in summer the nights are never dark in Petersburg. There are the great quays of pink granite, lined with dreaming palaces. A little breeze ripples the blue Neva water. I walk up from Suvorov Square and stand on the Troitzky Bridge, built to commemorate Alexander III's silver wedding, all cast-iron eagles and pylons of polished granite, and I look across the waves of the Neva to the slender gilded spire of the Peter and Paul Cathedral, crowned by an angel bearing a cross. There is something magical in the soft light and the wind and the water, an alchemy.

Petersburg is feminine on a summer's morning, serene, golden, with a brightness from sky and water, yet always a little breeze creeping across the squares and waterways to ruffle the hair and bring the scent of lime blossom from a hundred enclosed gardens, or of deep pine forests stretching down to the transparent waters of the bays and inlets of the Gulf of Finland. There are gentle gusts, little ripples of watery movement; soon, further along the bay, the fountains of Peterhof, bright in the sun, will fling their shining waters high into the air, in sparkling mist, diamond-bright; all is motion, and fluidity and grace.

And on a winter morning Petersburg is masculine, martial, a sentinel, but a sentinel from the past, when colour and splendour went with war. After the first heavy falls of snow, the sun rises late in a sky of brilliant blue, to show a city shining with a hard brilliance against a background of dazzling whiteness. The gold spires and many-coloured domes stand out as never before, clear and distinct. There are no rippling waves, no little breezes, for the river is frozen, solid ice, workmen are laying tracks for trams across to the islands and the Vyborg side. Petersburg is now a city of granite, stone, ice, the temperature falls below zero, but the atmosphere is dry, sparkling, there is exhilaration in the air, the blood seems to flow more briskly, at night the stars blaze down like white fire.

Such was the city in which I was born, and where my world came to an end, a city created by a giant—bestial as Peter the Great may have been, he was a Titan—to be a setting for a race of Titans, a backdrop of immense palaces, squares, expanses, splendour unimaginable to those who have never seen it. . . .

And the actors didn't fit the setting.

A setting for heroic drama, and the actors were miscast, and their lines, inept in themselves, were badly delivered; they didn't look the part, they didn't sound the part, it was as if Marie Corelli had written the libretto for *Boris Godunov*. And most of the time the actors missed their cues completely.

We always hated going back to Russia, my sister Alix and I, since it meant leaving much-loved relatives in Brittany and the Tyrol, both places we adored. It also meant having to cross Germany, and Germany we detested. Those journeys always had to be made stealthily, almost as if we were criminals, because if the Kaiser had known of the nearness of the descendants of his old friend Prince Eugen von Hohenems-Landeck (Great-grandfather detested him, but Wilhelm II airily assumed the old gentleman's monosyllables were caused by shy admiration), we should have been commanded to present ourselves. Sometimes we were unlucky; one of my earliest recollections is of a man laughing, throwing back his head as far as possible, opening his mouth as wide as possible, shaking his whole body, stamping with one foot. I was terrified. A year later we were in Vienna; Father had me in his arms as he gazed at Great-grandfather's most prized possession, the little Velasquez portrait. I took one look and burst into sobs. It was the man who laughed—the man who opened his mouth and stamped as he laughed.

'No, it isn't,' said Father. 'I don't suppose this poor devil ever laughed in his life, and if he did, you wouldn't see him. This is King Philip IV of Spain, who died hundreds of years ago.'

Great-grandfather gave a sudden exclamation. 'But the child is right! Look at the moustache—the extraordinary upward thrust! Upon my soul, I'd never noticed the resemblance before!'

'I believe Velasquez was his father's favourite artist—the inspiration for the moustache may lie there!'

But even when he was serious I found the Kaiser terrifying—I suppose intensity always intimidates children. Even when conversing on trivial matters, Wilhelm would, as it were, talk with his whole body, nodding his head, rocking from one leg to another, wagging his finger in the listener's face—which threatened to poke one's eyes out, since when he talked to—or rather, at—you, he practically stood on your feet, glaring into your eyes, punctuating his monologue with grunts of self-approval.

'What one dislikes most,' Great-grandfather reported to his own Emperor, 'is that one never knows what mood he'll be in.'

'What's he been up to now, Eugen? I take it that my god-daughter Avoye's been there? Did he expect her husband to kiss his hand?'

'If he did, sir, he was sadly disappointed.'

'Never heard of such a thing,' remarked the Emperor. 'They say I'm a stickler for etiquette, don't they, but, dear God, such a thought would never cross my mind. Still, that's the man for you, all vulgar ostentation. Do you remember, Eugen, when he invited himself to manoeuvres, and expected champagne? Beer was all he got. Well, what happened when Avoye was there?'

Great-grandfather relaxed. 'Actually, sir, it might have been worse —my grandson-in-law didn't knock the All Highest down as he swore he'd do if . . .'

'Good God, Eugen! What are you talking about?'

'I don't suppose anyone's told you, sir, but there's a new Imperial trick now—he thinks it funny to grab women's hands and squeeze them until they wince with pain, at which he guffaws, "Ha! Ha! The mailed fist—what!"'

The Emperor put down his knife and fork; Great-grandfather was sharing his frugal lunch. 'Incredible! I quite understand the feeling of the child's husband. I take it, however, that on this occasion . . .'

Great-grandfather laughed. 'Your godchild doesn't lack shrewdness, sir. She knows, of course, of that other nasty trick he has—wearing rings so that the jewels come on the inside, so that when he shakes hands . . .'

'I know, it's abominable. One tries to find excuses for the fellow— he feels he has to stress the vice-like grip of his right hand to compensate for that left deformed arm—but one gives up!'

'Well, sir, your god-daughter before leaving begged from me a collection of the most heavy, elaborate jewellery possible—you know there are things the English call *knuckle-dusters*? Well . . .'

'You mean the child went forearmed, her hands weighed down with heavy rings—all with heavy stones turned round . . .'

The two old gentlemen sat laughing happily together.

And so the long minutes spent as the Nord Express puffed slowly round Berlin were always loathed by us; at any moment we might be summoned to the presence of the All Highest and be bored or infuriated or embarrassed. Getting round Berlin took longer each year, too— always new suburbs, new blocks of flats, more dreadful statues. But if

28

we were lucky, as evening fell we knew that this time we'd escaped—
twenty-four more hours and we'd be in Russia. Not that this was much
consolation if the wind was howling outside, and the occasional peasant
was to be seen plodding sullenly forward, head downthrust against the
gale. Because at Virballen, the Russian frontier station, we should all
have to get out of our warm compartments; Russia, for military reasons,
had a railway gauge wider than that of Germany. So to grinding of
brakes, shrill blasts of the whistle, we stared out, grabbed fur-capped,
high-booted porters, dragged on coats, groaning, left the train—and
encountered the smell of Russia, sheepskins and sunflower oil and
cabbage soup.

You waited in deep depression for two hours. There is nothing so
hopelessly unromantic as a frontier railway station. One might read of
an exile returning home by ship or coach or on foot who rapturously
saluted his country by kissing its dear earth, but it would take patriotism
of a remarkable intensity to kneel down on the railway track at Virballen
and kiss the dirty cinders.

I never knew why one had to wait so long at Virballen. They wouldn't
even let you get on the train. But then, at last, there were the officials
in their green uniforms, saluting in the way so odd to non-Russians,
bending their heads downwards to meet the uprising hand, and the beds
were made up, you'd crawl into them; thirty or more hours of it, but at
least you could sleep some of those hours away.

Morning, drab scenery, endless flatness, pines, birches, poor roads
all mud or all dust, according to season, few villages or farms, horrible
to someone fresh from Brittany.

Alix and I were always in the depths of despair as we passed Gatchina,
then the first few houses of Petersburg. At times we felt that even a few
hours in the Kaiser's company might have been worth it, we'd have had
to come on to Petersburg a day later.

Often it was misty, fog coming in from the Gulf of Finland. Sometimes rain teemed down. It was drab, and the station again would have
the smells of sheepskin and sunflower oil and cabbage soup, and the
wind outside was raw and damp.

And then one by one the familiar landmarks would appear; with any
luck the silver bells of Peter and Paul would ring out the old hymn
Kol Slaven, there was the slender golden spire soaring into the sky, the
angel surmounting it, bearing the golden cross. *I love you, city of Peter.*
Yes, Pushkin had been right.

29

But Petersburg, we were so often told, was not Russia, so we didn't love Russia.

And we couldn't understand Russia, we were told, because we did not belong to the Russian Orthodox Church, remaining obstinately Catholic.

I think that possibly one can understand a country better if one's attitude is not purely emotional, if detachment and a degree of intelligence are components.

And no one can deny the element of deep gratitude in my family's feelings for Russia. Russia had offered sanctuary and a livelihood a century and a half before, when the countries of the West presented the bleakest of faces. Czars had given friendship as well as favour. My family did not forget its debt to the monarchy or to Russia—but until some years after I was born it appeared there was only one creditor, for the Czar *was* Russia. It might be argued that it was because we were un-Russian in truth and belief that our doubts began to grow.

3

'Senseless dreams'

BUT A FAR MORE exalted couple did not share my family's objective affection for Russia, even though, as Grandfather remarked during his second visit to Russia in 1895, in view of Catherine II's morals it was hardly likely that the Czar was any more Russian by blood than Father was. And even if he maligned Catherine, the original stock of the Romanovs had been diluted almost out of existence. Yet—'Because he's something of a biological freak,' said Grandfather; courtiers put it more discreetly, talking of, 'A strange alchemy of ancestry'—the new Czar was completely Russian in character, dreamy, introspective, with a mystical resignation which made him follow life rather than try to lead it, all the while meekly accepting the superhuman task God had given him.

My father said one day: 'He's a throwback to the original Slavs who asked Rurik the Varang to come and rule over them.'

'And who's his Rurik?' asked Grandfather.

'It used to be his father, of course, the giant who could tie pokers in knots, the man of supreme self-confidence. He still has a filial piety amounting to superstition, he means to keep on his father's advisers, to follow his father's policies.'

'Absurd. You need a strong man to carry out a strong policy, Alesha. Surely he doesn't flatter himself that he's the man his father was?'

'Oh, anything but! In what I can call nothing but a fit of puerile reverence for his father's memory he's proclaimed that he, the supreme head of the Russian Army, will never take a rank higher than that of colonel—the rank he achieved during his father's lifetime.'

'I must pass that on to Raoul. Well, what's he doing now, apart from carrying out acts of ancestor-worship reminiscent of the Far East? Wobbling uneasily in his new-found freedom?'

'Oh, no. He's dominated now by—er—a female Rurik. It's odd in a way—the rôles of husband and wife are reversed, *he* has all the charm, *she* has the willpower. He knows this. He also knows she has had a far better education than he has, and he confuses being well-educated with being intelligent. It's a confused relationship—he feels he's her mental inferior, yet she gives him a kind of hysterical adulation. Avoye says that to hear her talk of him, you'd never guess. . . .' Father broke off suddenly. 'From the sublime to the ridiculous—did Avoye tell you about the blacklead?'

Mother had already been received several times by the young Czarina; why, she could not understand at first, because it was soon very obvious that the Czarina did not like France at all. It was largely a matter of temperament; the Czarina could not understand the French mind, she had no sense of humour whatsoever, and spoke with deadly seriousness of French 'immorality' and 'frivolity'. She also spoke French badly. Eventually Mother came to the conclusion that she was summoned so frequently for two reasons; she, too, was still learning to speak Russian, and the Czarina, who was extremely self-conscious, wanted practice in speaking Russian with someone whose command of the language was little better than her own. ('I told her it's the rage to talk Russian with an English accent, but she wouldn't have it—she's a perfectionist.') Secondly, the Czarina was in a continual state of outrage at the luxury and indolence she encountered every day, and had to have another foreigner to confide in.

'And *faute de mieux* it's me,' said Mother.

'That's it,' said Father. 'You're a substitute for her illustrious grandmother—I've noticed the strong resemblance myself.'

'You won't make jokes about Victoria in her presence, will you?' asked Mother, looking alarmed. 'She's the only woman the Czarina admits to be her superior.'

On Mother's second audience, the Czarina, who to quote Father, had been as reserved as a turtle on their first meeting, said suddenly, 'You must have noticed many differences between Russia and France; I know I was amazed at the contrasts between Russia and England. Only imagine, no Russian servant knows how to blacklead a grate properly! Shining grates—such as all the grates at Windsor are—seem absolutely non-existent in Russia!'

She went on talking about the horror of the discovery as if she had stumbled upon some unholy religious rite; Mother, thinking silently, 'Dear God, she'll find there are worse differences than this!' realised that the bad condition of the grates had become something of an obsession. 'I wanted them done every day—I told one of the maids to

32

do this, and she said it wasn't part of her work. Eventually they sent a man to do the job, but he didn't have the faintest idea how to set about it. Do you know, Princess, I had actually to show him *myself* how to blacklead a grate!'

Father had hailed this *dénouement* with a shout of laughter; Grandfather took it more seriously. 'Incredible!' he said austerely.

'Poor thing,' said Mother. 'She's in a very difficult position, of course, not knowing anyone or anything, but expected to know everything and everyone. And she's not very clever when it comes to conversation.'

'Alesha doesn't seem to share your pity for her.'

'For two reasons,' said Father. 'Personally, because I can't endure priggish self-righteousness, patriotically because I think she'll be a disastrous Czarina for Russia.'

'I am *sorry* for her!' Mother persisted. 'She might have been very different if the last Czar hadn't died so unexpectedly. You see, she's been Czarina almost from the moment she entered Russia. If there had been a period when she'd had to bend that stiff neck, to obey, to submit to being told what she must and what she must not do! But almost immediately, she's Czarina, accountable to no one, subject only to an adoring husband.'

Father said with sudden seriousness, 'It's *her* attitude towards her husband that scares me—for Russia's sake. It's a kind of obsessive jealousy.'

'She *is* jealous of anything that deprives her of her husband's company,' admitted Mother. 'He belongs to *her*, not to Russia. She never intends him to neglect his duty—she is far too much the conscientious German for that—but her conception of that duty is so limited and narrow! He can give audiences to people in the armed services, he can even give a reception so long as it is absolutely necessary for reasons of state—but she bitterly resents anything else that keeps him from her, and she'll cut all the "duties" to a minimum.'

'Oh, yes—he reads aloud to her each evening, doesn't he, and even an affair of state can't keep him from the cosy *tête-à-tête* by the fireside, with the Czar reading Marie Corelli.'

'Who is this Marie Corelli?'

Mother shrieked with laughter. 'Papa—you must read her books and find out for yourself!'

'Thank you,' said Grandfather grimly. 'From your tone I'd rather not.'

Mother was frowning suddenly. 'This German temperament beneath

33

the superimposed English upbringing . . .' she began. 'I feel there's a craving for *affection* beneath the suppression. I am more than ready to *give* her affection, for she's so lonely, poor thing, but I feel I couldn't give her the affection she wants; it's not—not an affection on equal terms, it's affection with flattery, dependence—I can't give that.'

'You know,' said Father, 'I begin to think I married a very intelligent woman.'

Mother said: 'I *can't* give hysterical adoration.'

'Of course not,' said her father, 'because you're too intelligent and honest, but there'll be others without your integrity.'

'This,' said Father under his breath, 'is one of the reasons I think she'll be a disastrous Czarina—*married to this Czar.*'

'A Czar tied so firmly to her apron-strings,' said Grandfather.

'As no Czar has ever been before!'

'So the situation seems to be this. We have a Czar so devoted to his wife that her word is law with him. She prides herself a great deal on being strong-minded, but in fact, because of her craving for uncritical affection and admiration, she will be unconsciously influenced by anyone unscrupulous or foolish enough to give her this flattery and apparent devotion. So therefore real power in Russia will rest with the sycophants, the emotionally immature who lead the Czarina, who leads the Czar . . .'

'Have you ever seen her smile?' asked Father suddenly.

'Once,' said Grandfather, 'and grudgingly at that. Even so, I was amazed. Because of that tightness about her lips I'd almost come to believe that she was physically incapable of smiling. That painful earnestness—'

'And, dear God,' exploded Father, 'always so conscious of the fact that with *her* high sense of duty she will always know precisely the right thing to do! "*I* am Czarina, *I* am devout, *I* am right!" The air of tension, constraint!'

Mother said laughing: 'Poor Alesha—he thought at first that the chilly attitude was reserved for him personally.'

'True, I can now take cold comfort from the fact that my reception was the rule, not the exception, that there's always the forced greeting, the tight compression of the lips, the putting of that impenetrable distance between you, but it's a poor outlook for Russia, isn't it, when everyone's made to feel an intruder, an outsider, when everyone's chilled, disheartened, discomfited? She listens abstractedly as if what

34

you're saying isn't worth listening to; if she speaks it's in a whisper, scarcely moving her lips, as if you're not worth speaking to. You can almost hear her sigh with relief when you beg leave to retire.'

'Poor thing,' said Mother. 'She hates giving audiences.'

'In that case she shouldn't have married a Czar. She knew what to expect. Do you realise, incidentally, how often you've called her *poor thing*?'

My mother's mother—whom, for purposes of identification, I shall call Grandmère—came to Petersburg in the early autumn of 1895; her letters to Uncle Raoul, together with one written by Grandfather, round off the picture of the Czar and Czarina during this period.

'. . . and so I was presented, went between two *immense* Cossacks guarding the study door, and then I was making my curtsey to this small, slight young man. Great charm, an almost feminine delicacy. A manner of extreme simplicity—and my first reaction was to feel sorry for him. Not because of the simplicity—nothing could be more simple than the Emperor's* manner, and yet, despite the immense tragedy of his life, one's reaction to him is *admiration*. I think in the case of the Czar the pity is roused because although his conversation shows intelligence, it also exhibits, even more strongly, a weakness, a lack of self-confidence, a feeling of personal inadequacy, that acute awareness of physical unimpressiveness which Papa has remarked upon.

'His voice is low, a little muffled. A great part of his charm is that—unlike his wife—he seems so very glad to see you. And then, suddenly, you begin to have doubts. Why? I cannot explain it—it would take far more than my powers of analysis and description to do this. His character is far more complex and baffling than that of his wife, partly because it is so negative; for example, with *her* you immediately feel she is remote from you, but with him it's not so positive, it's a *gradual* realisation that you haven't come close to him after all.

'(Your father, of course, puts it more robustly: "You can't get to grips with him because he's a slippery character!" I seek for the *mot juste*—complex, vague, elusive, shifting. Your father answers with derision, "Elusive—a polite way of saying slippery, as I said! Shifting? Rather say shifty!")

'Are there other reasons for my feeling of pity? Yes. Because I think he is a very scared young man—scared by the fantastic power of the

* For all my family 'the Emperor' was, of course, the Emperor Franz Josef.

35

Autocracy. And because I believe that though he is never consciously deceitful, weakness and moral cowardice will give every appearance of deceit. Alesha says he hates saying or doing anything that will produce unpleasant results in his presence—lacking imagination, he is not disturbed by pain or mortification suffered out of his sight. He therefore allows ministers to think they have obtained his approval—and then they find a day or so later that he is following a completely different policy. Presumably, says Alesha, when he decides to dismiss a minister, he will talk to the unfortunate man in the most friendly and flattering manner, the poor wretch will return home radiantly conscious of the favour and confidence of his sovereign—and within an hour receive a curt message of dismissal.

'Papa says that the kindest thing to say about him is as negative as his nature—that he suffers from *les défauts de ses vertus*, that he'd be a good private citizen just as he's a good son, a too-good husband and, from all accounts, in a few months, will no doubt be a good father. Like Charles I and Louis XVI, he adds.

'It is, of course, true, alas, that lack of will cancels out all other assets.'

'Your mother still insists on regarding the Czar with pitying sympathy. So does your sister. He is the type for whom women *do* feel a kind of protective pity; he would do very well as an English curate in a genteel parish populated chiefly by wealthy old ladies; he is more at home with women, children and priests than with men. Fresh sighs of pity from your mother and sister. *I* say they should be feeling sorry for Russia. There are, after all, a hundred and sixty million people dependent on him.

'Your mother took tea with the Imperial couple yesterday. She returned still perplexed by *his* baffling character, talked of impenetrability, charm, immaturity, intelligence. I feel the intelligence is overrated, that it's a slow nature unable to grasp for a long time what another person would see at once. This lack of intelligence also covers what she would call lack of imagination—he will, I fear, never be able to read between the lines of the careful ministerial reports he'll get served up to him.*

'Alesha says he abhors any discussion of general questions and doesn't believe that other people should take the initiative in any conversation,

* Here Uncle Raoul wrote later in the margin, *As at the time of the Khodynka Field disaster.*

introduce a new topic. "We are there merely to answer questions." He says, furthermore, that the Czar's mental timidity, negativeness, is due only partly to his lack of self-confidence—it also stems from what I suppose one might call politely his strong vein of Christian resignation. (More like the fatalism of the Mohammedans, in my opinion.) He (the Czar—not your brother-in-law, thank God!) feels any kind of personal initiative verges on blasphemy; either you're opposing the Higher Forces that direct the course of events or you're guilty of sinful pride in believing your puny efforts can assist the Omnipotent. He has a conscientious sense of duty towards his throne and his country, but unfortunately if there's a conflict of loyalties the country always loses. There was a good demonstration of this the other day.

'The various *Zemstvos*—local councils—of Russia had sent in congratulations to the new Czar on his accession. You may remember that at the time of his father's death I travelled for a time with a bibulous old general who got off the train at a place called Tver? Tver, it seems, is something more than a nondescript station on the way to Moscow, it's a place with something of a name for independent thinking. So in their message of congratulation they slipped in the hope that the voice of the people might be heard in the new reign . . .

'Each *Zemstvo* sent a delegation to Petersburg to offer the Czar the traditional bread and salt (on gold and silver plates that must have sent the local rates soaring!) They were admitted to the Throne Room in the Winter Palace, and lined up by the Minister of the Interior. I, the recipient of a gracious invitation, stood by Alesha's mother, who told me the ceremony would serve a double purpose—congratulations both on accession and on marriage.

'Unfortunately, the new Czarina disobeyed the old tradition of wearing white—she was swathed in black crepe and a long veil. Immediately there was whispering among the delegations (kindly translated by Princess Hamilton). "This—after coming to the capital in mourning!" "She came to us behind a coffin—she's surely brought misfortune with her." "Wedding bells mixed with funeral tolling— that's bad luck for everyone!" Her Imperial Majesty's expression wasn't of the kind to dispel these murmurs, being very much of the coffin-lid variety.

'Well, they presented the bread and salt, and the Czar began to read his speech of reply—a formality, I thought, the usual routine thanks for the loyal sentiments which had been expressed. But then the attitude of

37

the various delegations amazed me. Instead of the bashful smile, there was either bristling or cringing. "What's wrong?" I whispered. "He has said," the Princess replied agitatedly, "it has come to his knowledge that in the last months there have been heard in some assemblies of the *Zemstvos* the voices of those who have indulged in the senseless dreams (that's where he raised his voice) that the *Zemstvos* could be called to participate in the government of the country. He is going to maintain the principle of absolute autocracy."

'By this time the Czar had finished speaking, had withdrawn. Slowly we made our way out, just behind the excited delegations. In the square outside crowds of people were waiting. An old woman called out to a sturdy man just ahead of us (again the Princess translated for me), "My son! Have you really seen the Little Father?" He replied: "A little officer came out; in his cap he had a bit of paper and began mumbling something, looking at this bit of paper. All of a sudden he shouted out, 'Senseless dreams!' We understood then that we were being scolded for something or other, but we don't know why he should bark at us like that." '

On the first day of September 1895, Grandmère wrote: 'Well, you are now an uncle for the second time, and a few weeks before we expected. However, the household is enraptured because your niece arrived on August 30—the feast day of St Alexander Nevsky. She is to be called Alexandra, and the Czarina has asked if she may be godmother . . .'

At the end of October, she wrote: 'The first long outing for little Alix, who's been granted an audience by her godmother. The Imperial couple are now living in the Alexander Palace at Czarskoe Selo, about fifteen miles to the south of St Petersburg. It was built by Catherine the Great for her grandson, Alexander I; it's little, it should be entrancing, but, alas, the Czarina has "improved" it. Alesha says it was the epitome of elegance and charm, but the eighteenth-century furniture and paintings have been relegated to the storerooms, to be replaced by stuff ordered from an English firm called Maples; there is heavy mahogany woodwork everywhere, and an assortment of what the Czarina calls "cosy corners". The reign of Catherine has given way to that of Victoria. The boudoir, where we were received, is mauve, mauve, mauve . . . Photographs everywhere—an unsmiling portrait of Victoria taking place of honour.

'We took Andrei with us. The Imperial couple were delighted with their godchild, but both kept looking almost hungrily at her brother. They are both hoping that the child expected in November will be an heir.'

But it was a daughter. In Petersburg and out at Kronstadt the guns began to fire in the grey mist—300 rounds if the child were a boy. But after 101 they fell silent.

'A girl!' said Grandfather. 'Inevitably the poor creature will be called Victoria.'

'She can't, Papa; the Russian Church doesn't allow names that don't exist in the Russian language.'

'Then it will be Alexandra.'

'I don't think so—the name's considered unlucky in the Romanov family.'

'Oh, that's another unfortunate coincidence, isn't it?'

In the event, the new Grand Duchess was christened Olga, carried to the ceremony on a cloth-of-gold pillow, dressed in lace robes lined with pink silk. Her fine baby hair was cut and the fair little snippets were rolled in wax and thrown into the font. According to Russian superstition, a child's future happiness would be shown if the wax sank— Olga's, auspiciously, sank immediately. But in any case, no one was likely to have doubts as to the future of a baby robed now in silver, invested by her father with the Order of St Anne in diamonds, taken back to the palace, as she had come, in a coach of glass and gilt drawn by six snow-white horses, each led by a groom in white and scarlet livery and powdered wig, the whole escorted by a guard of Cossacks.

Such a fine, bonny baby, too—the picture of health. And the parents were young. Everyone's spirits rose. Soon a boy—big and strong and healthy like his sister.

But first the Coronation in Moscow.

4

'Difficult ceremonies'

'I believe we should regard all these difficult ceremonies
in Moscow as a great ordeal sent by God.'
The Czar to his mother, before the Coronation

THE CORONATION took place in May 1896 in Moscow. Alix was left
behind in Petersburg, with our French grandmother to look after her,
but I went to Moscow in the care of Grandmother Hamilton; Mother
was in attendance on the Czarina, and Father would be appearing in two
rôles, as part of the cavalry escort, and, after the actual Coronation, he
would join the oddly mixed little group of people treated with special
honour—the descendants of those who had saved the lives of Russian
sovereigns, from the Ivan Susanin who had saved the life of the first
Romanov to those who, like my grandfather, had saved the life of
Alexander II.

The Coronation impressed me greatly, and to read the long descrip-
tive letter written by Mother to Grandmère, and the accounts sent by
Grandfather to Uncle Raoul, brings back those curiously vivid
memories of sight and sound that I think only a young child can have.

At two o'clock on May 25, the Czar's formal entry began. The sunshine was brilliant. We sat on a balcony overlooking the street; looking
down I realised I would never have guessed that the world—let alone
Moscow—could hold so many people.

First the squadrons of Imperial Guard cavalry.

Cossacks in red and purple.

The nobility of Moscow.

On foot the Court Orchestra, the Imperial Hunt, the Court footmen.

Higher Court Officials.

And then the Czar.

They had told me he would ride a white horse the nails of whose
shoes would be silver. I think it must have been this that had made me
imagine that the man riding the horse would be someone altogether
bigger, more magnificent than the person who had spoken to me dozens

of times. I think I expected him to look like all the Chevaliers Gardes rolled into one.

Instead of which, in his isolation, he looked slighter than ever. He wore a simple army tunic, his face was waxen, drawn with excitement, he rode with his right hand held stiffly at the salute. I peered down at him, speechless with disappointment. I wanted to say, 'Such a *little* man!' but I knew I shouldn't, and, in any case, it was very stupid, I realised that. I had known what the Czar looked like. But I suppose I had thought confusedly that being crowned would add a cubit to his stature. In any case, he shouldn't have been so pale. If I were Czar, I would be smiling at people, turning from side to side to look at them. I wouldn't look scared to death.

'He looked *frightened!*' I said in outrage.

Everybody said no, no, *serious*—as he should—but not frightened.

'Here come the coaches,' said Grandmother Hamilton hastily. 'Look for Mother.'

The Grand Dukes—immense, formidable men, all of them—and the foreign princes were passing and already the sound of carriage wheels was drowning the noise of hooves.

The gold coach of Catherine the Great, with the Dowager Czarina bowing, smiling, even though her dark eyes were bright with tears.

'Poor darling!' said our hostess. 'She must be remembering her own coronation—so few years ago!'

'But she smiles,' said her husband. 'She *smiles*. Whereas—' He shrugged and pointed.

A second gold coach, also drawn by eight white horses. Inside it the Czarina. As she leaned from left to right to bow the sun shone blindingly on the diamond necklace at her throat. She wore white, she was marvellously beautiful, she was pale and tense, she did not smile.

A whisper from my hostess, 'Like marble!'

Other coaches and then, smiling up at me from a background of white satin cushions, Mother. According to Grandfather's letter, I began to bounce up and down on the balcony. 'Isn't she lovely? Isn't she lovely?' Some people standing below, hearing my shrill voice, looked up and laughed agreement. 'Yes, yes, little *barin*—her smile is like the gift of a big silver coin!'

I forgot my earlier disappointment.

Mother managed to get away that evening, long enough to see me to

bed and hear my prayers. Grandmother sat on the other side of the
bed.

'The Czar looked miserable,' I said with the infinite tactlessness of the
young. 'Isn't he looking forward to tomorrow?'

'I don't know about the Czar,' said Mother, 'but I'm not.'

'Why, Maman? Beautiful coaches—white satin cushions—'

'They don't feel beautiful, darling, they haven't any springs.'

'I know,' said Grandmother. 'Any bump in the road, and you feel
that every bone in your body is broken, don't you?'

'Yes, and the stuffiness! I don't think they've been aired since the
last coronation.'

'I don't think they were aired then. People were nearly fainting, and
the coaches swayed so much it made you quite sick.'

'Will the Czar be sick? He'll be in a coach tomorrow, won't
he?'

'You're a little monster—you sound as if you *want* him to be sick,'
said Grandmother.

'My God,' said Father, suddenly appearing, 'that would be the last
straw.'

'Isn't he going to *like* tomorrow, Daddy?'

'Well,' said Father, 'for a start, he has to wear on his head for hours
on end a heavy crown weighing nine pounds, and he's not looking
forward to that.'

I began piling books on my head to try to assess the weight. In an
undertone Grandmother said, 'Is it true he wanted a lighter crown to be
used in the ceremony?'

'Yes,' said Father. 'Impossible, of course.'

'After all, the crown he'll be wearing was made for Catherine the
Great. If a woman didn't object to the weight—'

'Ah, but what a woman!'

'Seriously, though, my dear, I hope all this doesn't leak out. You
know the mania people have for symbolism. Unequal to bear the weight
of the crown—'

The next morning was all blue and gold. From the grandstand
opposite the Red Staircase leading to the Ouspensky Cathedral we
watched servants laying down a red velvet carpet, and then the Imperial
Guard took up their positions. There was Father, wearing his tremendous helmet. Later Grandmother wrote in her diary, 'Andrei kept asking

me how much the helmet weighed, the working of his mind was obvious.'

Grandfather sat in the Cathedral gazing at the thrones, the Diamond Throne of Czar Alexei, almost solid with diamonds and pearls, and the Czarina's Ivory Throne, probably more comfortable, decidedly more elegant, brought to Russia in the fifteenth century by the heiress of fallen Byzantium, Sophia Paleologus.

Before the altar stood an effulgent host of clergy. My God, thought Grandfather, there'll be cramped living-quarters in Heaven if all that gathering go aloft. Still, he reflected, possibly it took all this *galère* to crown a man who was Emperor and Autocrat of all the Russias, Czar of Moscow, Kiev, Vladimir, Novgorod, Kazan, Astrakhan, of Poland, of Siberia, of Tauric Chersonese, of Georgia, Lord of Pskov, Grand Duke of Smolensk, of Lithuania, Volhynia, Podolia and Finland, Prince of Estonia, Livonia, Courland and Semigalia—where the devil was Semigalia? It sounded like something from the English book Andrei was so fond of, *The Rose and the Ring*—plus thirty-two other stated regions—Alesha had once written them down for him—apart from deliciously vague regions such as 'all the region of the north' and romantic titles like 'Sovereign of the Circassian Princes and the Mountain Princes'.

Throughout the Cathedral the scene was the same—so many precious stones, so much gold that the whole assembly seemed to swim and shimmer in unearthly, reflected, sparkling light.

And since the congregation stood in an edifice whose decorations seemed to an austere Breton to aim at giving the impression of being a gold and diamond mine combined, the effect was enough to make him feel his eyesight could never be the same again.

Outside, the procession was beginning. Long lines of priests. The Dowager Czarina, whose train was so heavy it needed a dozen men to carry it. And finally, under a canopy of cloth of gold, with ostrich plumes waving rather drunkenly at the top, the Czar and Czarina. He wore the uniform of the Preobrazhensky Regiment, and she, silver.

The quiet, almost diffident voice of the man kneeling at the altar, making a contract with God.

'—Thou hast chosen me as Czar and Judge of Thy people.

43

'—Thou, O my Lord and Master, make me skilled in the task which Thou hast set me—

'Grant me wisdom worthy of Thy Throne—

'—*So on the Day when Thou sittest in Judgment I too shall be able to render account without shame—*'

Mother's eyes were fixed on the Czarina. Her face was flushed, her lips compressed, she watched, listened with a concentration, an intensity that was almost ferocious, but there was no joy in her, no glory, no warmth. An expression of almost painful earnestness—

No intermediary between him and the Almighty, thought Grandfather as the Czar, anointed, crowned, a man set apart, prepared to enter the sanctuary, the only layman in his Empire to give himself Communion as a priest of the Church. This, even more than the Coronation Oath and the actual crowning, marked the climax of the ceremony. Mother felt she had never known such stillness. The hush was great enough before, but now it was as if no one was daring to breathe. This was one of the occasions when one could literally hear a pin drop—

And certainly the sound of a heavy golden chain falling came with almost shocking harshness, jangling the nerves.

What idiot—such a distraction to the Czar, who's tense enough— Oh, dear God, it's the Czar's own chain! Mother's thoughts raced.

The heavy chain of St Andrew, falling from his neck as he walked up the steps of the altar to take Communion.

Next time there's a coronation, thought Grandfather, it's to be hoped they'll have the sense to put down sound-muffling carpets all over the Cathedral.

Apart from the first excitements I disliked Coronation Day. After our first view of the Czar, we had to wait another five hours as the ceremony went on under the gilded domes of the Cathedral. Grandmother took me up in her arms, and I slept fitfully. It was very warm. I was hungry; luckily Grandmother had brought something for me to eat, and told me stories in a low voice until I dozed off again. Then I was jerked awake by the booming of cannons, the mad ringing of church bells, people shouting and cheering.

'It's all over! They're coming out!'

At the top of the steps two small figures, crowned, wearing mantles of purple and ermine. They looked small, tired, lonely. They bowed three times. The noise was indescribable—every bell in Moscow, and

44

there were thousands of them, clanged ecstatically. The sound of the bells drowned the noise of the guns—that came as a mere vibration.

No person in Russia today will ever hear that lovely heart-stopping sound again—the bells of Moscow ringing from every tower in the city.

The rest of the day dragged. I was taken home through the packed, cheering streets, and put to bed. No, I couldn't go out again. Yes, people *were* dancing in the streets, but it would all be much better when I was taken to the traditional feast at the Khodynka Field, and thousands of peasants would sing and dance before the Czar. No, I must not keep awake for Mother and Father; very possibly they would not be able to get away, for after the Coronation Feast there was the Coronation Ball.

Father and Mother prepared for the Ball. 'Have you spoken to the Czar today?' she asked.

'Yes; he told me his head ached—but he wasn't surprised, he'd always known the crown would be too heavy. I said boldly, "No need to worry about the chain falling, sir—people will soon forget it." "But I shan't," he said. Did the Czarina make any comment?'

'Alesha, she's all—all exaltation. "*Now*," she said to me, "*now I know Russia.*" She was too tired to do more than peck at all the stuff brought on the golden plates—in any case, she loathes rich foods—but afterwards she managed to snatch a little rest away from those Kremlin halls all hung with blue silk and the endless rows of gilt chairs, and she and I sat down and drank tea. I produced some of those English biscuits that she likes so much and talked determinedly about babies—she looked absolutely worn out.

' "You are very sweet, Avoye," she said at the end, "I felt quite exhausted, but am better now."

' "It has been a dreadfully long, tiring day for Your Imperial Majesty—" '

' "Ah, but a wonderful day, too! You see, I understand everything now. *He* has made a pact with God, Who has chosen him to be Czar and Judge—" And out it all came pouring, Alesha. The Czar has sworn to God to maintain the Autocracy and pass it on intact, the Autocracy that's not a privilege but a holy duty. The Czar is now a man apart, anointed with holy oils; his power is given him by God, and it's blasphemy for anyone to want to curtail it.'

Father sat looking at her, hairbrush in hand. 'That's heady talk over

45

a cup of tea and a plate of English biscuits,' he remarked. 'Did you find it impressive?'

Mother said, 'What impressed me most was the last remark she made: "You know how I dread public occasions—the difficulty I have in swallowing, in breathing even, the feeling I'm going to faint. Well, this was the greatest of all public occasions, but I didn't feel oppressed with thousands of eyes fixed on me, I didn't feel I was carrying an intolerable burden dragging me down, down—I was scarcely conscious of the other people. Avoye, I only knew my husband was making a promise to God that will make him a man set apart for the rest of his life." '

5

'The *Niemka* dances'

I DIDN'T sleep much that night because of the lights flickering against the wall of my room and the singing and laughter in the street; therefore next morning found me drowsy and quite ready to accept the idea of having a quiet day—especially since next morning we should be going out to the Khodynka Field* to see the Czar's gifts being distributed to his people. So I played in the garden under the great flowering lilacs and listened to Grandmother's stories, and was already sleepy when Father and Mother came to us for an hour in the evening.

They sat with Grandmother beside my bed and talked in low voices. I caught occasional phrases, but they conveyed nothing to me, but later that night Grandmother set down the conversation in her diary.

'Alesha is not at all happy about the arrangements for tomorrow. I suppose he's already got himself into hot water for voicing his misgivings.

' "It's a mad idea to use the Khodynka Field," he said tonight.

'I was surprised. "But why? It's always been used for popular entertainments—for race meetings and military reviews, too."

' "Exactly, Mother. In fact, the military have taken it over completely in the last few months—and do you know what branch of the military? The sappers. They've been using the place as their training ground."

'I was startled. "Trenches, you mean?"

' "Yes. I haven't been able to get out to have a look at the place, but even if the trenches are only shallow, if they haven't been filled in properly, a slight unevenness of the ground could be dangerous, couldn't it?"

' "Does the Czar know these engineers have been using the Field?" asked Avoye.

' "Oh, yes, I told him. He merely said he wants everything at the

* Now the site of Moscow Airport.

47

Coronation to be an absolute replica of what was done when his father was crowned. *Then* the gifts were distributed at Khodynka—"

' "Yes, they always are," I said.

'Avoye asked what kinds of gifts they were. Alesha laughed. "Tin cups enamelled and decorated with the Czar's initials and the double-headed eagle, filled with fruitdrops, the kind they call *ledenzy*, and a piece of gingerbread all tied up in a big red and yellow cotton handkerchief printed with a view of the Kremlin—that's all, but it's their memento of the Coronation, that's why it matters to them."

' "And it's not merely the gift," I said. "It's all that happens at Khodynka, the whole thing's arranged like a country fair, that's why Andrei will love it so. There'll be bandstands, open air theatres, roundabouts, greasy poles, acrobats, thousands of barrels of free beer, dancing, and then, when the Czar and Czarina arrive in the afternoon, there'll be a procession of decorated carts and figures—"

' "Yes," said Alesha, "when they arrive in the afternoon they come out on a high balcony of the Imperial pavilion to show themselves to the people. This is the people's day. As yet they haven't had a good view of their new Czar, most of them, Muscovites or peasants who've travelled for miles. Most of them have seen only the backs of the police and troops cordoning the routes of the procession. And it's to see the Czar that half a million people are going to jostle their way into the Field tomorrow."

' "Half a million!" Again I was startled. "Why, in 1883 there were two hundred thousand people at the feast, and I found that number frightening. I remember thinking that for the first time I realised the truth of the expression, 'A sea of humanity.' But half a million, Alesha! Are you sure?"

' "Yes, Mother. *That's* the reason, I've been told, that it must be Khodynka—it's the only place large enough to hold them all."

'Avoye said, "Half a million people! It will take an army of troops to control so many!"

' "Well, there are enough of those to hand!" I said with a feeling of sudden relief.

' "They're using a single *sotnia* of Cossacks," said Alesha.

' "A *sotnia*," said Avoye uncertainly. "That's a single squadron for half a million people? *With all the troops they have here!*"

'Alesha has inherited from his father several characteristics—usually exhibited when he is disturbed, as he was now. The habit of running his

48

fingers through that thick, fair hair. "More troops are unnecessary because of the miraculous precision of the planning for the occasion," he said violently. "The gifts have always been given out at various points in the Field to prevent congestion, but now they're going one better— they've put up barricades at the entrance, and then there are narrowing passages to turnstiles, and there the people get their gifts."

' "But narrow passages—!" I began despairingly.

' "I know, it makes it worse, doesn't it? An enormous crowd, blundering along those narrow passages—"

' "Surely," said Avoye, "there should be dozens of squadrons of Cossacks and police outside breaking up the crowd into small groups before they reach the entrances, and then—what is the English word?— *filter* them through?"

' "Maman," came Andrei's voice suddenly. "What is the noise?"

'Let this be some indication of our absorption in our discussion—we had not heard the sound that had roused the sleeping child. Now the sound was inescapable—voices talking, singing, the sound of many feet and the creaking of carts.

' "Let me see!" said Andrei. "Please!"

'So his father drew back the curtains, carried him on to the balcony, and we saw hundreds of peasants making their way along the street; women, bright-kerchiefed, riding in carts, men in their Sunday best, in magnificently embroidered blouses.

'There was a family party passing below us, and they looked up; the man, bearded, walking at the horse's head, bowed, and the women smiled.

'Andrei's shrill little voice called out, "Please, where are you going?"

' "To Khodynka Field, little master."

'Andrei became agitated. "Daddy! We'll be too late! I must dress, and we must go now!"

'We all laughed. "No, little master," called the peasant, "they will not let anyone into the field until eleven o'clock tomorrow morning, but we are going because we want to be sure of getting in soon—we have to decorate our cart, you see, so we go to sleep on the waste ground outside the Field, and then we shall be certain of getting in."

' "You will be in the procession!" Andrei was very excited. "Will you wave to me—give me a special wave?"

'They all laughed. Yes, indeed they would—all of them, bearded father, blue-kerchiefed mother, daughter with flaxen pigtails, and little

49

son of Andrei's age. Andrei was inclined to be jealous of him. "Why can't *we* decorate a cart and be in the procession?"

' "Will you know them again?" his mother asked. "They may be a long way from us."

' "Oh, yes, he's wearing that lovely bright blue blouse with the sunflowers embroidered on it," said Andrei, gazing slightingly at his father's uniform.

'And below us, under a night sky the colour of wisteria blossom, tens of thousands of people were already moving, singing as they moved, to make sure of their place in Khodynka Field.'

It was a perfect day when we drove out to Khodynka Field. Mother and Father were still in attendance, so I was taken by Grandfather and by Grandmother Hamilton. Grandfather was irritated—the organisers had made a mess of things, and arranged for the carriages of the ticket-holders to arrive at the Field hours too soon.

'Still,' he admitted, cheering up, 'better to sit here for hours waiting for something to happen than to be driven into premature dementia at the Embassy.'

The French Ambassador, Montebello, was giving a ball for the Czar and Czarina that night, and, according to Grandfather, 'Is behaving more like an old hen of an American woman married to an upstart Yankee millionaire than the representative of a civilised nation. A hundred thousand roses from the South of France. Tapestries and plate from Versailles and Fontainebleau. No, on second thoughts, it's the kind of vulgarity a Heliogabalus might have devised. I—'

There was a sudden clatter of hooves. Cavalry galloped past— Cossacks.

'Good,' said Grandfather. 'Obviously sense has at last prevailed. I saw Avoye for a few moments after breakfast, and she told me Alesha was asking the Czar himself to send more troops.'

More and more cavalry passed us. I craned out of the window. With any luck, Father himself might be there.

'They should slow down their pace, though,' Grandfather continued. 'Their officers must be out of their minds, permitting such a—'

'What is that?' asked Grandmother suddenly.

A very odd noise, at the same time shrill yet undulating. A thin noise.

'I expect,' I said with a sudden beaming smile, 'it's animals. They'll have animals there. Dogs.'

Neither of my companions said anything, but they had turned, and were staring at each other over my head. I was just about to gaze enquiringly up at them when another clatter of hooves took me to the window. I shrieked, 'Chevaliers Gardes! Chevaliers Gardes! And Daddy!' I waved frantically. And Father didn't notice me. He galloped past with the same fixed look on his face that the Czar had had on his entry into Moscow. His face was the same colour as Grandmother's ivory silk dress. He was almost unrecognisable. Still Grandfather said nothing. I thought he was angry because the Chevaliers Gardes, like the Cossacks, were riding so fast. Nearly in tears because of mixed disappointment and trepidation, I stared out of the window again. This time my attention was caught by something coming from the other direction—not fast, this time, but very slowly. Carts with tarpaulins over the top. More disappointment.

'Aren't they going to decorate their carts, then? And those nice people were going to wave to me—'

'You must sit down, Andrei,' said Grandmother evenly. 'Come, my darling, you'll get so dirty at the window.'

But my voice rose to a triumphant shout. I had seen a bright blue sleeve, with a sunflower embroidered on it. Father hadn't seen me, but I wasn't forgotten.

'They've remembered! Look, he's waving.'

'Sweet Jesus!' whispered Grandfather uncomprehendingly. 'Andrei, *who's* waving?'

'There—the nice man we saw last night. He—he's sort of hiding under the tarpaulin, but there's his arm sticking out and it's going up and down, waving to me.'

He dragged me inside and blocked the window with his body. He was talking to the coachman. 'Leave me here. When this—this procession of carts permits, turn round and take the Princess home. Come back if you can to pick me up, *but you must get the Princess and the child home.*'

He was gone. Grandmother held me to her; she was trembling violently. Because of that I was not angry, but frightened.

'Are you ill?' I whispered.

'Yes—yes. That's why we must go home and after a little while I must leave you and go out to—a hospital.' With a shaking hand she reached out and pulled down the blinds. 'It makes everything so dark and stuffy, but my head is aching.'

'Your mouth is all white, Grandmother.'

'Sit here close to me, my darling, and don't move and then I shall feel better.'

The carriage was dark now, as Grandmother had said, but not to dark for me, craning up worriedly to stare at her face, to see her lips moving silently, desperately, in prayer.

So, mercifully, all I saw of the Khodynka Disaster was a blue and yellow arm dangling from under a tarpaulin. Father saw much more.

There had been half a million people waiting at dawn on the waste land separated from the Field only by flimsy wooden railings—so much for the 'barriers'. They watched carts arriving loaded with the gifts, and they cheered. Then came wagons filled with barrels of beer—more applause. They saw the gifts being arranged on the distant counters, the barrels being rolled along the ground. They began to make confused, tipsy calculations, straining their eyes towards the counters and barrels, trying to estimate the vast throngs about them. Someone said in a loud, confident voice, 'There's not enough to go round. It'll be first come, first served.' Someone else said, 'Each first-comer gets a cow.'

People started to run. They rushed the barriers, began to blunder into the Field. The single Cossack squadron was swept away, lifted in the air together with their horses. The rest of the crowd, shouting, came on behind. The mood was still one of good humour, but any moving crowd looks frightening. The scared men behind the counters first pointed wildly towards the trenches—the crowd thought they were being waved on—then began to throw the gifts into the crowd, to get rid of them, and the uproar increased. Nobody could turn away, the pressure of the tens of thousands behind was too remorseless. Turnstiles, counters, booths, all went down. The walls of the 'narrow paths' disappeared.

Just beyond the turnstiles, before the Field proper was reached, was a trench fifteen feet deep, twice as broad, dug by the sappers. This had not been filled in—it had been thought that light wooden bridges where the paths ended would be adequate to carry the crowds. But now the paths had gone. There were thousands of people screaming along the brink of the pit, fighting madly to save themselves, then thrown down by the human torrent pressing behind them. They were thrown down, trampled into the mud, suffocated by those who within minutes were themselves felled, then crushed by trampling feet. And when the dead and dying filled the pit, and frenzied screaming men, women and children were borne on by the remorseless, unwitting tide behind them, there were other trenches—

Most of the bodies looked as if they had been pounded by a gigantic pestle.

The full number of victims was never published.

It would take a long time to remove so many corpses and mutilated, though living, bodies. Grandfather, eventually arriving at the field, found fresh panic. Among officials. The Czar would arrive before the corpses could be removed. He asked in incredulous fury, 'He's still *coming?* The "Feast" hasn't been cancelled?'

They stared at him as if he, too, raved.

There was no one he could reason with; Father with his squadron was placing broken bodies on hurriedly-improvised stretchers.

'But of course it must be cancelled!' said Grandfather.

'Cancelled? Unthinkable! What would people think?'

'*What would people think?*' he repeated in a whisper. After this all one could do was rescue work, searching for those who still lived, noting with a kind of stunned sickness that corpses were being carried to one side to be hidden with greenery and bunting.

At one point he met Father. Both were haggard scarecrows, filthy with drying blood and dust. They stared wordlessly at each other for a moment, and then Grandfather seized Father's arm. 'For the love of God, can't anything be done to stop the Czar from coming here? When he steps out on that balcony to bow to the people—who still live—there'll be corpses hidden not a hundred yards away from him! Does he want to start his reign with a reputation for callous inhumanity that—that—' He broke off, retching, as a Cossack came by with a child's corpse in his arms. It appeared to be of my age.

Father wiped some of the sweat out of his eyes. 'They're still going to your ambassador's reception too,' he said.

Grandfather straightened up. 'That I cannot believe.'

'It can't be cancelled—our most powerful ally can't be slighted—'

'Slighted! It couldn't be slighted—it's too damned keen on the Russian alliance.'

'A hundred thousand roses,' said Father. 'Tapestries, silver plate.'

'They're going to dance quadrilles,' said Grandfather, and broke off.

'Yes,' said Father, steadily, 'they will dance, and the lights will stream out from the windows, the music too, and you and I will still be here, I think—'

'But *he knows* what's happened, doesn't he?'

'He's been given a brief version.'

'Merciful God, that's enough! He's not a monster! Only a monster could—'

'Apparently his first reaction was to express a wish to retire to a monastery to pray.'

'Why in damnation isn't he here, doing what we're doing? It's what his ancestors would have done! Nicholas I went down among the people when there was cholera, Alexander II fought the great fire in Petersburg. But even so, penitence in a monastery would be better than this atrocious adherence to programme.'

'If he didn't come here, he's been told, it will be interpreted as condemnation of the authorities who planned—'

'Can't he think and feel for himself? As for Montebello's reception— will Avoye have to go?'

Mother went for just a little while. The red-eyed Czarina had begged her not to stay too long at the hospitals. Mother arrived late. The music floated out from brilliantly-lit windows. There was a little crowd in the street. One woman said, 'The *Niemka** dances.'

'Why should she care?' came the reply. 'She's used to funerals.'

* German woman.

6

'We should be above that sort of thing!'

IT WAS ETIQUETTE for a newly-crowned monarch to pay courtesy calls upon his older-established *confrères*, so after the Coronation the Czar and Czarina, with baby, went abroad on a series of State Visits. They visited the Emperor of Austria, the Kaiser, the King of Denmark. They crossed to Britain to visit the Czarina's grandmother at Balmoral; the visit, so long anticipated by the Czarina, was something of a disappointment. The Czarina's English relatives were dismayed at the change in her—'So proud and distant!' one said. The chief success was the baby—'Beautiful!' her great-grandmother kept saying, and the first newsreel photograph to be taken of royalty marked the visit.

And there was the most important visit of all—not to another crowned head, this time, but to Russia's ally, France, where the republican government went to almost ludicrous lengths to give a splendid reception to its powerful ally. For example, the visit being made in October, the famous chestnut trees in Paris were not in bloom; they were therefore covered with artificial flowers.

Mother had been in attendance on the Czarina in France, and she did not look forward to the journey back to Russia. Father was coming to Berlin to meet her, and they had both been commanded to present themselves to the Kaiser.

'At least,' said Father gloomily, 'we are spared two possible ordeals. It's not yet the depth of winter, so we shan't see Wilhelm merrily rolling generals in the snow, as has been witnessed in the past. And it's not his wife's birthday.'

'What does he do then, Alesha? Roll *her* in the snow?'

'My dear girl, don't you know? Every year on her birthday he buys her a dozen hats as a birthday present—awful things smothered with fruit, feathers, flowers, crosses between aviaries, orchards and greenhouses. He has them put on display in a reception room and he stands there complacently awaiting the compliments on his exquisite taste. "Ach, the All-Highest is an expert on all things, even on women's millinery!" '

'Well, we haven't to put up with that in Russia.'

'If we did, the boot would be on the other foot—rather, the hat would be on the other head. It would be the Czarina choosing hats for the Czar.'

Mother hurriedly changed the subject—as she often did, hating any difference of opinion with Father.

My parents loved each other passionately; everywhere my father was sent over the years—from the Caucasus to Siberia—Mother would follow him, hating every moment of the inevitable brief separations when he would go on ahead to make basic arrangements for us: I think the only time I heard them arguing was over the Czarina, whose way of life roused pity in Mother, anger in Father.

But even then there were times when Mother would say ruefully, 'Very well, Alesha, I'll admit that you're right in this case!'

And finally even Mother had to admit complete defeat. The Imperial Family was on its way to the Crimea by train. Mother was in attendance on the Czarina, Father, just back from the Caucasus, was equerry to the Czar; Alix and I were telling the two elder Imperial children, Olga and Tatiana, of our stay in the south. The Czar was listening, too.

'It was so nice *getting* there!' Alix was saying passionately.

We had gone south in the summer. For an entire day (the second of the journey) the train had made its way through an endless expanse of sunflower fields. The flowers turned their faces to the sun, that is, to the south. Therefore as we came down from the north and stared ahead, we saw mile after mile of moving yellowing-green, but when you looked back all you saw was tossing gold. This had, of course, fascinated us.

'And what did you like, Andrei?'

Even a child was never afraid of the Czar—unfortunately for Russia. Without shame I said, 'The black cherry jam and almond and pistachio tartlets for a start—'

'Yes,' said the Czar, laughing.

'—and the birds were fun too. White eagles, gold eagles, flamingoes, kingfishers—'

'It sounds wonderful,' said the Czar. 'I'm sure Her Majesty would like to hear it, too. We'll join her, shall we?'

But the tale lost excitement in her presence. She was extremely fond of us, and wanted us to be at ease with her, but one noticed even with her own children the atmosphere of constraint she always brought with her. The girls, especially as they grew older, were always subdued in her presence, far livelier when away from her.

But I think that what chiefly oppressed us on this occasion was the closeness and dimness of her sitting-room. She was expecting a baby, and had said before leaving Petersburg, 'I don't want staring crowds at every station I pass through!' So the orders had been given, and, to make doubly sure, any time we approached a station she had the blinds drawn. Even the quicksilver Alix found it difficult to rattle on about white eagles with black-tipped wings soaring over the enormous bulk of the Kasbek height which dominates Tiflis, or the foaming glory of April in orchards of apricot, cherry and peach. One couldn't with the sun and air and light so deliberately obscured. 'It was so *stuffy* and *cramped*,' she said afterwards. 'You couldn't talk about things flowering or flying, could you?'

We found ourselves reduced to an account of the Golovinsky Prospekt, the main street of Tiflis, and that sounded dull even in our own ears.

Flat as stale soda-water.

The train stopped.

'Are we supposed to stop here? It's only a little place, isn't it?'

'The provincial governor comes aboard here to pay his respects. Hamilton's seeing him.'

But the governor was not alone at the little station. Father came to knock at the door.

'Sir, there's a crowd of people here in their Sunday best.'

'Yes, but we stopped merely in order that the governor of the province—'

'The governor of the province, with the deepest respect, sir, begs you to come to—to a window where the blinds are not drawn.'

'Orders were given that there were to be no crowds!' said the Czarina violently. 'What was the governor thinking of, to disobey orders? No one was supposed to know—'

Father kept his eyes fixed on the Czar. 'No one was told, sir, but when it was learned yesterday that the governor would be coming to the station here this morning, people guessed. They put on their best clothes, and—'

'The police must clear the station!'

'Sir,' said Father to the silent Czar, 'they've been waiting all the night for just a fleeting glimpse of you. We can't send the police to hustle them off the platform! Sir, many of them have been kneeling since the train stopped!'

The Czar took a step towards the window. His wife's angry voice halted him.

'You've no right to encourage even indirectly people who're not carrying out our orders!'

From outside, the people, kneeling, began to sing, *God Save the Czar*.

Not looking at his wife the Czar went to the door. Father, saluting, followed him. A tremendous outburst of cheering, mingling with frantic cries of, 'Little Father! Our Little Father!' told us he was standing at the window, as requested.

'Your Majesty,' said Mother softly, 'shall I move your blind—just a little?'

The Czarina had been staring, set-faced, at the door. 'No, not an inch!' she said, turning—to find her little fair-haired daughter had crept to the window and was wistfully pressing her face against the slit between the blind and the window-frame. 'Olga! Don't let yourself be seen! We should be above that sort of thing!'

Mother whispered to us, and, gratefully, we crept away. Doubly grateful, in fact—we could escape that tense, darkened, stuffy room, and we, the children of a subject, could do what the children of the Autocrat of all the Russias couldn't do—we could look out of a window!

When our parents rejoined us, neither made any reference to the incident, but late that evening I awoke, thirsty, and heard a low-toned conversation going on.

'Yes, I agree, she was altogether in the wrong. The poor children, too! They were like little whipped dogs—"we should be above that sort of thing!" she stormed.'

'What did she mean?'

'Vulgarity, I suppose.'

'Vulgarity to win the people's affections? If she weren't his wife he'd be twice as popular. And wasn't she complaining to you the other day because of the public indifference to her?'

So the people came to the Czar, and the blinds were drawn to exclude them.

But at least on this occasion the police did not hustle them away, and there was no sound of shots.

That winter we went back to Petersburg, and Alix and I were taken for the first time to the ballet. Tchaikovsky—*Swan Lake*. 'Will he go on writing things like that?' asked Alix excitedly. The reply that he had died a few years before brought her to the verge of tears. But although I, too, was much downcast by the news, something else made an even more powerful impression on me. Imagine the Marinsky, the warmth of the darkness all scented by women's perfume and cigarettes, and then the sudden blaze of light between acts, showing the white, blue and gold of the decorations—and the fact that every man in uniform was on his feet.

'*Why* is Papa standing?' demanded Alix, craning about to see the cause.

'Everybody else is, too.'

'*Why?*'

'All officers have to stand,' said Mother, 'in case the Czar or the Imperial Family should be here.'

'But he's not—that's the Imperial box, you showed it to us, and there's all that electric light *glaring* down in it—anybody can see no one's in it.'

'It—it rather draws attention to it—all that light in it,' I said. 'That it's empty, I mean.'

Father looked down at me quickly, but said nothing.

'It's an awfully *big* box,' said Alix thoughtfully, 'and people are packed in everywhere. It's a wonder they don't try to sneak in—'

This time Father did speak. 'They couldn't. There's a guard with fixed bayonets surrounding it.'

'*Every night?*'

'Yes.'

'Although the Czar's not there?'

'Yes.'

Alix gave up, but I went on worrying.

The chandeliers blazing down every night on an empty box, men throughout the thickly-packed theatre on their feet out of respect—and no one there. Guards at attention with fixed bayonets—and no one there.

A brightly-lit box, and no one to see in it. The Imperial Family in the train—and the blinds drawn. Peasants on a dingy little railway station and splendidly-dressed officers in the most magnificent of theatres. And both coming to the same conclusion—'*They* don't like their people.'

And the daughter, who tried vainly to peer out from the gap between blind and window-frame? She would have loved to come to the ballet, as she told Alix, Alix being her closest friend. With Alix (and myself usually taking the unsympathetic parts) she acted innumerable scenes from history—and humbly allowed my sister to assume the chief *rôles*, 'Because you go to the theatre so often.' So Alix would borrow an old black velvet dress of Grandmother's and be Mary Queen of Scots on the way to the scaffold, although Mary Queen of Scots was Olga's own ancestress and Olga cried with greater depth of feeling over her fate. She was always haunted by it—the little dog following its mistress to execution, the attendants hurried away immediately afterwards, leaving the poor corpse to be plundered and despoiled by enemies.

'But the little dog was there!' said Alix. 'It must have *helped* her.'

Olga looked unconvinced. At that time her mother had a small terrier called Eira, a vicious little beast that spent most of its time lurking under the Czarina's sofa, emerging only to nip at any ankles that came close. A progress to the scaffold in the company of Eira would mean torture preceding execution.

The Czar would probably have been more than happy to take his daughters to the theatre, but accepted the fact that their upbringing was exclusively his wife's concern. Two or three times he arranged a treat; we children all trooped solemnly through the immense state and reception rooms of the Winter Palace, over parquet floors polished mirror-bright, past malachite pillars and doors of tortoise-shell embellished with gold, until at last we came to the theatre, and here we would sit for half an hour while attendants changed the drop scenes and turned on the various coloured lights. This the little girls called, in all seriousness, 'going to the theatre'. I remember that on one occasion Mother accompanied us; 'Maman didn't look at the stage at all,' Alix told Father afterwards. 'She looked at Olga all the time, and she looked as if she were going to cry.'

60

To me, Alix had whispered (while trying not to fidget at the 'theatre'), 'I think that Maman is really *sorry* for Olga.'

Olga looked across at us. The stage was quite empty. No actors, no music. Lights blazed down on a void—as in the Marinsky they illuminated the Imperial box.

'Isn't it *marvellous*?' breathed Olga.

Every schoolchild in the capital had either free entry or half-price tickets to the opera and ballet, and the Czar's daughters sat watching an empty stage.

By 1901 there were four little girls; Olga, Tatiana, Marie and Anastasia. Olga I knew best, for she and Alix were so close; they were a perfect contrast to each other, Olga with her wide-set blue eyes, golden hair, delicately flushed face, and Alix with Mother's magnolia skin and great glowing dark eyes. Alix was Olga's champion, all the more since Olga was supremely unaware that she needed protection. '*Why* can't she come out?' Alix would demand. 'Why can't she come to the theatre or the circus with us? And why can't she have a room of her own? I'd hate sharing a room with Tatiana.'

Tatiana returned Alix's coolness. She was a very beautiful child, eighteen months younger than Olga, dark-haired, slim, with eyes the colour of topazes. You would always think she was the eldest child— except, as Father remarked once, 'There was little that was childlike about her. She's her mother's daughter, isn't she?' One day Alix and I heard some Caucasian troopers muttering, 'You can see *she* never forgets she's the Czar's daughter.' Alix said, 'She'd like that, wouldn't she— but they didn't mean it kindly.'

The other girls called Tatiana, 'the Governess'. If they wanted a favour from their mother, Tatiana was the person to ask for it, being the favourite.

Marie, two years younger than Tatiana, was the picture of health, simple, warmhearted, with immense grey eyes. At one point the other girls called her Toutou, 'fat little bow-wow'; certainly she had all the gauche devotion of a bounding puppy.

And there was Anastasia, born in 1901, and given the name— breaker-of-chains, prison-opener—because in honour of her birth a pardon was issued to Petersburg and Moscow students who had been arrested after a riot. Anastasia was the *enfant terrible* of the family, a tomboy, a merciless mimic, full of energy and mischief, possessed of an ability to turn any solemn occasion into one of unquenchable laughter.

61

Anastasia was the child of whom thoughtless visitors said, 'She should have been a boy!'—and, with luck, never saw the expression on the Czarina's face.

These were the days when, although the Czarina disliked the idea of too many contacts between her daughters and the outside world, she had no secret motive for making the isolation absolute. There were, of course, long periods of time when we were not in Petersburg, when we went with Father first to the Caucasus and later to Siberia, where he inspected the garrisons, but as soon as we returned, the invitations would arrive and we would go either to the Winter Palace nurseries or out to Czarskoe, to the white, green-roofed Alexander Palace and the rooms on the second floor, all yellow and green, daffodil colours at that time.

I can remember talking to Olga of Siberia, not the details, but I know the overall impression I was trying to give was of the sheer *spaciousness* of Siberia, though I don't suppose that I knew that precise word at the time. Spaciousness, or, as Mother said I put it, 'You could take really long breaths and run for miles!' Meadows and steppes dotted with birch groves stretching endlessly away. The glorious smell of a pine forest in summer, strewn with raspberries, blackberries, clearings carpeted with strawberries, life everywhere in the forest, animals and green things and flowers growing almost man-high.

Olga looked rather wistfully out of the window. 'Is it only nice in the summer?'

'No—people say it's marvellous fun in the winter, too.'

'What are the *people* like? People are very interesting, aren't they?'

A boy can't often guess what a girl feels, but on this occasion I could follow her gaze. From the window she could see the palace gardens, the guard-house, and then, a little beyond, through the grille of the high iron gate, a street corner. It wasn't easy to see any people.

Within a few years she had schooled herself so that even such an indirect piece of wistfulness as this would never pass her lips. I think few other girls would have shown the good humour with which the Czar's four daughters adapted themselves to the life of family self-sufficiency decreed by their mother ('They can amuse themselves!')—no outside amusements, scarcely any outside contacts, tied to their mother.

This isolation had little effect in the case of the three younger sisters, who had no taste for learning, but as far as Olga was concerned, it was a tragedy. She painted well, was a magnificent pianist, had a gloriously

62

clear, soaring singing voice. As a child she had real intellectual power; Gilliard, the children's Swiss tutor, had the highest hopes for her, but the hopes were never fulfilled, the fine intellect was never sharpened, extended by the right teaching, the necessary competition. So she became Olga, the impractical one, always with her nose in a French or English book—and usually the books were censored by the Czarina. I don't think she ever realised how immature intellectually her sisters were, but she knew how her own intelligence was being blunted by isolation. Sometimes, despite that terrifying dutifulness shown by all four, because of that intelligence and honesty that was part of her, she would gently differ from her mother; independence of thought was dismissed by the Czarina as 'grumpiness', and no attention was ever paid to Olga's reasoning. She herself never persisted in maintaining her ideas, being essentially a humble person.

I think it might have been different if my sister had still been her closest friend; Alix was a great one for telling people to 'fight for their rights!' But by the time that affairs in Russia began to go badly wrong, the friendship had been broken.

But for my own sake I shall confine myself only to a few more memories of the years between 1901 and 1904. Tea in the Czarina's boudoir, mostly mauve, but with traces of green here and there—the walls crowded with crosses and pictures, all chosen for sentiment only, and clashing madly with each other. Sentimental paintings of the Annunciation, even more sentimental water colours of German and English scenes. A large photograph of Queen Victoria, whose protruding eyes followed one accusingly and stonily. To add to one's unease, Eira the terrier under the sofa. Everywhere tables covered with snapshot albums and ornaments—mauve enamels, bookmarks decorated with edelweiss in pearls, or bearing the swastika, that 'sign of eternity' as the Czarina called it, to which she was devoted.

I was always afraid of sending some of the *bric-à-brac* flying; young though Alix and myself might be, we could see there was all the difference in the world between this depressing, intimidating mauve clutter and the clear, flowing lines and colours of Mother's ivory and primrose room.

The Czarina talking about Tolstoy to Mother. Most of his philosophy was wrong, but in his view of the peasant, those simple, innocent creatures with childlike faith—ah, he was right there!

I gazed hungrily at the saffron buns always served for tea at the

63

Imperial palaces since the days of Catherine the Great. The Czarina had introduced a new delicacy—tiny vanilla-covered wafers called *biblichen* of which I was very fond. So were the children, but they were never allowed to ask for anything at tea.

There were great masses of lilac and orchids everywhere. Alix and Olga were having a literary discussion; Olga's English governess had read *Alice* to her, and Olga was rather shocked. The Queen's manner was so rude. And her Aunt Irene, who was married to the Kaiser's brother, had sent her a wonderful book—*The Princess and the Goblin*. Had Alix read it? Alix had, and Grandmother Hamilton—this was just before Father's mother died—had read her the sequel, which Alix thought was even better—*The Princess and Curdie*.

(But, Olga, when she read it, disliked it. It was horrible, she said—all the people believing dreadful lies about their king.)

'Have you any new ideas for dressing up?' demanded Alix next. 'What history lessons have you been doing?'

'We've been doing Edward I who was horrid—he cut off the poor Prince of Wales' head and sent it to the Tower of London.'

'No, we can't act that.'

'People are much better now than they used to be; I'm very glad I live now when people are so kind.'

'They're not kind everywhere.'

'No—it's horrible in Serbia, they've killed their king and queen. I'm so glad I live in Russia.'

'Show the Princess the present you made for Papa's Christmas gift,' said the Czarina.

Olga had embroidered a blue kettleholder for the Czar—a little kettle singing on the fire, and 'Polly put the kettle on' worked on it.

Mother expressed admiration. Olga whispered to Alix, 'I could make one for your Papa too! Would he like one?'

Alix said valiantly that though Father mightn't find much use for it as a kettleholder, he could put it on his desk and use it as a mat. Father, who was extremely fond of Olga, did better when the gift arrived. He wrote to say that he was hanging it on the wall as a picture.

But my chief memory of Olga as a young child will always be this. Four to five miles from Peterhof was a little rococo house built by Nicholas I. It had a rose garden, trees, a farm. The little girls loved going there for a picnic, especially at haymaking time when they would ride on the wagons and climb about on the haycocks. The summer after the kettleholder presentations there was another tremendous attraction— the farmer's wife was rearing by hand four kittens whose mother had been killed. Each Grand Duchess would be given a bottle of milk to feed the orphans.

Alix had a cold, so had had to stay at home. The children rode over on their Shetland ponies—but I had just mastered my first bicycle so I showed off to the farmer, and—showing off even more—talked in a lordly way about motor-cars. Father had just bought a 12 h.p. Panhard-Lavasseur, a menace of a machine with an engine which had to be started up like a primus stove, and which made the most fearful noises and explosions, threatening to shake the car to bits.

Olga lingered on for a little while. 'Papa would like to have a car,' she said, 'but he doesn't like to do anything about it because he'd have to dismiss so many people from the stables.'

But I didn't listen, I was telling the farmer how wonderfully our spluttering monster climbed, and eventually she went off disconsolately. And got lost.

The whole farm was in an uproar. Her sisters sobbed, the farmer's wife made them worse by declaring at five minute intervals that all there remained for her to do was to throw herself down the well, and I crept away feeling like a murderer. If she hadn't been snubbed, she'd have stayed with me.

'Please God, if You'll let me find her, I'll never be beastly to her again!'

God helped those who helped themselves. So I must think.

The kitten. The kitten was missing too.

Perhaps the kitten had run away, and she'd followed it.

I enlisted further help. 'Holy St Francis, let me find Olga and the kitten.'

Think, said Heaven.

Grandmother Hamilton used to read a poem that haunted Alix and me, Alix to the extent of knowing it all by heart. I remembered only isolated lines. Like *None but my foe to be my guide.*

My foe being the kitten. If he'd got Olga lost, he was my foe all right.

A kitten runs away. What does he do? *Ten to one he scrambles up a tree and can't get back.*

Beyond the corn and hayfields there were pine trees.

I set off at a run, past corn and hay, poppies, cornflowers.

As I neared the trees, I began to call, 'Olga! Olga! Don't be afraid! Andrei's coming!'

And at last a voice replying, 'I wasn't afraid, for I knew you'd come.'

Olga beneath the tree, where the kitten alternately wailed and spat from a branch. Olga smiling, and repeating, 'I wasn't afraid, for I knew you'd come.'

'Why on earth did you stay with the stupid thing? It's his own silly fault that he got there!'

'I know, but he's scared, and fond of me. I couldn't leave him.'

So much remembered now, and so little comprehended at the time. Alix and I on a June day in 1901, sitting in Grandmother's room as the guns began to thunder when Anastasia was born. Mother was in attendance on the Czarina. A few days later she came home, and I heard snatches of conversation between her and Grandmother. 'Yes, quite well—heartbreakingly disappointed at first, of course—'

Grandmother said something I could not catch, and then, in a voice heightened by despair, 'Dear God, does this mean we'll have to go through this degrading business all over again?'

I thought 'degrading business' meant an Imperial christening, and so thought it rather odd that Mother said, 'I shall have to tell her I can't leave the children for lengthy intervals—with Alesha away. In any case, he was so angry last time—'

It is best, perhaps, to quote here in explanation two extracts from the diary of Mother's own mother.

'—a very distressed letter from my darling. Alesha wants her to resign from her position at court, but she feels she cannot, for pity's sake. The grotesque series of pilgrimages to pray for an Heir has continued. Alain, of course, says that Alesha is completely right; Avoye must stop taking part in this grotesque lunacy—'

And two years later:

'The humiliation is now complete. After the birth of the fourth daughter, the Czarina came under the influence of a charlatan calling himself a "soul doctor", not a Russian, but a Frenchman from Lyons, Philippe Vachot, who teaches a mish-mash of herbalism, astrology, and "animal magnetism". When we were last in Paris, Alain talked to the official head of Russian police here, Rachkovsky, who was hideously embarrassed by the whole business. Alain advised him, "Dig into the quack's background, expose him—what else can you do?" Rachkovsky found Vachot had a police record—twice he'd been prosecuted for practising medicine without a licence. He started his career as a butcher's boy. The evidence was sent to Petersburg. It had two results. The Military Academy of Medicine in Petersburg (which has a good reputation) has been forced to give him a licence—and Rachkovsky has been dismissed. Reading between the lines of Avoye's letters, one grasps that there have been the most appalling hysterical outbursts—this trickster appeared on the scene when the Czarina was in despair after the birth of the fourth daughter—she clings to him like a drowning woman. He assures her she will bear a son—God help us, this has been the final humiliation, he assured her the birth was imminent, she accepted his word against that of all the doctors, preparations were made for the birth—all false hopes, the fruit of hysteria on the one hand, trickery on the other. Avoye thinks of the woman, the butt of cruel, derisive laughter; Alesha thinks chiefly that the throne has been made a laughing-stock.

'Despite all this, the infatuation continues. Vachot has been given a house close to the palace. She speaks of him as her "dear Friend"; she even said to Avoye yesterday, "He came to me today, looking so sad. He said, 'They are still trying to get rid of me, and I think they will succeed. But if I am sent away, you are not to worry—one day there will be another friend like me who'll speak to you of God.' " Avoye said the Czarina wept when telling her this—"It was so beautiful." '

No, we children knew nothing of this.

We were, however, conscious of Father's growing restlessness, though not of the causes. He hated being in Petersburg; he went on tours of duty to the Caucasus, Siberia—in 1901 he was actually in South Africa, having gone there with a friend, Feodor Soloviev, at the outbreak of war between the British and the two Boer republics. Nominally he was an 'official observer' attached to the Boer armies; with tremendous admiration and interest he watched the amazing fight put up by that race of Davids against the clumsy British Goliath—only this time Goliath won.

He was, I know now, intensely concerned by the backwardness and corruption that characterised the Russian army. He and Uncle Raoul were both agitating for a new approach, a recognition of the dominating rôle of artillery in modern warfare. In the summer of 1902 Father was asked to give a series of lectures at the Staff College—as he remarked with a grim smile, the invitation came because people thought he was 'safe'—he wore a Chevalier Garde uniform. The course of lectures was never completed. The first one—on the lessons to be learned from the American Civil War—passed off quietly enough, amid an air of general bewilderment. The second—on the Franco-Prussian War—brought a request that he would submit for scrutiny the text of all his future lectures. Father did so, was told alterations must be made. And deletions. 'This passage about the future rôle of cavalry—'

'I say there *is* no rôle—'

'Well! We can't allow that to pass!'

So Father, who in any case was an *aide-de-camp* general, with right of access to the Czar, asked for a special audience. He asked leave to give the lectures—unaltered.

The Czar listened to him, saying nothing, lighting one cigarette after another. Father made all his points. After a moment's silence the Czar got up and walked to the window; Father knew what that meant —in a few seconds the slight figure would turn, the low voice would say, 'It's been good of you to give me so much time, but I mustn't weary you—'

Dismissal.

Refusal.

Next day Father, riding along one of the small, willow-bordered Peterhof canals, met the Czar, coming in the opposite direction. The Czar seemed pleased to see him, said, 'Is this the new horse Andrei's been telling the children about? Turn back with me, so that I can have a proper look at her.' So Father turned back, and the Czar took a proper look at the new mare. Then the Czar talked about the collie dogs he possessed at the time, and an albino crow that had belonged to his sister when she was a child.

'Sir,' said Father, 'if I might have permission to resume our last conversation—'

'She had a tame wolf-cub, too,' said the Czar. 'It had been reared on a strictly vegetarian diet—'

'Sir, I give you my word it's not merely conceit on my part that—'

The Czar spoke hurriedly. His voice was so muffled that Father caught only two words—'unsettling' and 'unsafe'.

'But, surely, sir, it's even more unsafe to—'

The Czar abruptly stuck in his spurs and galloped away from him. And, this being Russia, a plain-clothes policeman darted out from behind one of the willows, produced his notebook, and said, 'Your Excellency, would you mind repeating the conversation you had with his Imperial Majesty?'

7

Pilgrimage to Sarov

IN NOVEMBER of that same year, 1902, Uncle Raoul came to stay with us.

'If you stay on into the New Year you'll be invited to a Court Ball,' said Mother.

'I loathe dancing.'

'You wouldn't have the option, darling; being a foreigner you'd watch, not participate.'

Grandfather, who joined us at the end of January, received an invitation too. 'I'm honoured,' he said, without any appearance of being delighted.

Uncle Raoul remarked as much. 'My good Raoul,' said Grandfather, 'you're not anticipating a riotously enjoyable occasion, are you—a jollification? Because once Her Imperial Majesty appears the jollification ceases to be jolly. That stiffness and pallor, that fixed stare that says so unmistakably and unerringly, "See how I am suffering, *meeting people* —" The constant martyred peering at clocks, showing her guests unmistakably that she is counting the minutes until—'

'I'm sure she'll be absolutely *gracious*!' said Mother indignantly.

'You'd better take a few blackleading lessons, just in case,' said Father.

'You're perfectly horrid, Alesha! Just because I've been away from home a few times—'

'I wish, sir,' said Father, 'you'd tell her to forget her loyal duty and remember her wretched husband and children. If this new idea comes off, this—this quest for Seraphim, it will take place in mid-July, sweltering heat—'

'A quest for Seraphim? My daughter is proposing to acquire part of the hierarchy of—'

'Oh, Papa, it's not funny, it's tragic. Seraphim is—was—a man.'

'Impossible. Seraphim is the plural of—'

'Grammatical or not,' said Mother, very flushed, 'he was a holy man born about—oh, a hundred and fifty years ago, who lived in the forest of Sarov with birds and animals as his chief friends. He had an immense bear who'd bring him a honeycomb each day, then lie across the threshold of Seraphim's cell—'

'Are you hoping to acquire an animated hearthrug, Avoye?' asked Uncle Raoul, bursting out laughing. 'Unless—Wait a moment, though! Wasn't this Seraphim mixed up with the extraordinary story that Alexander I didn't die in 1825?'

'That's the man,' said Father. 'Officially Alexander died at Taganrog, but there's always been a rumour that instead he slipped away dressed as a beggar, to spend the rest of his life as a hermit in Siberia. Certainly before he left for Taganrog, he saw Seraphim, and—'

'Light,' said Grandfather, 'probably a false light, is breaking. Does the present Czar contemplate a similar step?'

Father said dryly, 'The driving motive in the entire ludicrous business comes entirely from the Czarina, who's contemplating anything but abdication; in a sense she plans the reverse.'

'Not planning to seize power à la Catherine, surely? As a—Oh, I see what you mean.

'I can never understand,' he resumed after a moment, 'why you, my child, should be her companion. You don't belong to the Orthodox Church.'

'No, but she trusts me not to talk to everyone about her private affairs. Oh, Papa, I hate the whole business, it's grotesque and degrading, and Alesha detests it, and I loathe leaving him and the children, but when I've suggested to the Czarina that she might have a more suitable companion, she—she—'

'She becomes hysterical,' said Father shortly.

'She says desperately her other ladies-in-waiting are all "false wicked cats", ready to betray her and gossip about her.'

'What a typically English *bourgeois* schoolgirl expression—"false wicked cats"—yet Victoria's grand-daughter who says this goes on pilgrimages of a wholly medieval nature to pray for a son! I take it that this Seraphim is famed for being helpful in such cases?'

'To be perfectly frank,' said Father, 'he's chiefly famed for something that should make any normal member of the Imperial Family run a mile at the sound of his name. He died seventy years ago, leaving in his cell a quantity of manuscripts that were burned by order of the Holy

Synod. One sheet escaped destruction, a page of prophecies. Seraphim wrote that he will be canonised at Sarov in the presence of the last Czar and his family—'

'*Last* Czar!'

'—and shortly after this disaster will come to Russia, torrents of blood will flow, God will permit all kinds of calamities in order to purify the Russian people. Millions will die, millions more will be dispersed to far countries, where by their exemplary faith and resignation they'll save the rest of the world.'

'That's hard luck on Russia, providing the awful example,' said Uncle Raoul. 'One understands why the rest of Seraphim's literary remains were destroyed. I take it that besides being a Jeremiah, he's something of a miracle-worker—cures at his tomb, and so on?'

'Such things have been reported,' said Father, 'and in the last year his powers have been cried up by various Russian clergy eager that the Imperial interest—and patronage—should be diverted from foreigners. And in the highest circles it's been decided that Seraphim must be canonised—a commission's been set up already—so that in gratitude he'll prevail upon Heaven to send the Czarina an Heir; they call it horse-trading in the United States, I believe.'

'For heaven's sake, let's change the conversation,' said Mother desperately. 'How did it all start? Oh, I know, the ball! Let's talk about that. It's a costume ball, seventeenth century—'

'I hope this isn't reported in highest circles,' said Father piously. 'What—Avoye Hamilton deliberately switched the discussion from spiritual matters to a topic of frivolity? She's no better than the rest of the Russian girls—nothing in her head but officers!'

'I take it that's another quotation from the Imperial repertoire,' said Grandfather.

'Word for word,' said Father, 'only I can't do it properly—I can't get the self-righteousness, the primness, the pursing-up of the lips. It's uncanny how the moment she becomes disapproving she loses that classical beauty and looks just like her horrible old grandmother.'

The Imperial party appeared at a Court Ball at nine in the evening; the guests were expected to assemble at half-past eight. We were allowed to inspect our parents; Mother was gorgeous—I don't use the word lightly—in old rose satin and gold tissue; she wore a *kokoshnik* of gold and pearls that set off her beauty to perfection—it isn't the most becoming kind of head-dress for Russian women because they tend to have wide cheekbones which this particular style emphasises. But Mother was enchanting.

Father looked magnificent in sapphire-blue velvet and sables.

'Oh!' said Alix. 'It's all wrong that your own children can only look at you for minutes and other people can stare at you for hours!'

Father came to a decision. 'They can come as far as the Palace Square,' he said. 'If they wrap up well and are brought straight home after we've been deposited there's no danger of their catching cold or losing much sleep. After all, these functions are becoming rarer and rarer—it may very well be their last chance to catch even a glimpse of what a Court Ball can be like.'

So we bundled into the carriage with them, the carriage very much prepared for a great occasion, harness glittering with gold and silver trappings, rugs of sable and ermine to wrap about the passengers. There were long lines of sleighs and carriages gliding towards the Winter Palace, which was blazing with lights. Immense braziers burned around the great granite monolith of the Alexander Column in the middle of the Palace Square; you could just, coming up, make out the dim silhouette of the archangel on the top. Most of the guests arrived in carriages, but the more dashing officers, who wanted to display their contempt for the cold, came in open sledges, having taken the precaution of erecting a kind of screen of blue netting so that snow would not blow into their faces. We saw Mother, huddled in furs, going up the snow-covered steps, surrounded by her escort of three tall men, and then the coachman was turning, to get us back home as soon as possible so that he could get back to the Palace Square and secure a good place by the fires.

'What did Papa mean by saying this might be our last chance to see a Court Ball?' Alix asked me before we parted for the night.

'The Czarina doesn't care for this sort of thing.'

But on this occasion the unique miracle happened.

'She was really enjoying herself,' Mother was saying when Alix and I interrupted the late breakfast next morning.

'Enjoyment is scarcely the word I'd use,' said Grandfather, 'but, from the stunned comments I heard, she was decidedly more gracious than usual. Undoubtedly she looked magnificent.'

'She was wearing a dress weighing over seventy pounds,' said Father precisely. 'Over it a cloth-of-gold cloak fastened with a clasp of enormous rubies. She must have felt damned uncomfortable.'

73

'Why the graciousness, then?'

'Oh,' said Father, exploding, 'it's all part of this lunatic cult of Alexei, the second Romanov, Peter the Great's father. One of the sure ways of forwarding your career these days is to subscribe with loud enthusiasm to the idea that this reign was the Golden Age of Russia—before the introduction of western ideas, you see! If you want to get on, all you have to do is laud and eulogise "the Most Tranquil Czar" for his piety. Believe it or not he'd start every morning by bowing down before the holy images, striking his forehead against the cold stone floor one thousand five hundred times. And his devotion to his family—not least the fact that he gave his beautiful and virtuous wife Natalia a place in all his councils. And who were the Czar and *his* beautiful and virtuous wife masquerading as last night? Alexei and Natalia, of course! That's why for once she was happy—she could imagine she was back in the good old days, surrounded by obsequious, pious, obedient-minded boyars.'

'Oh, my God,' said Grandfather in disgust. 'More of the little boy who's never grown up and has to be kept amused with fairy tales! Oh, I believe you, Alesha, if only because of an incredible conversation I had last night with the Czar. As you know, we had the honour of being summoned to the Imperial side for a few words, and were actually given a lecture on Czar Alexei more or less on the lines you've suggested. I was rather taken aback, and tried to cover my confusion by saying that, of course, I didn't know much about Alexei, because his reign was so much overshadowed by that of his son. I might as well have detonated a mine beneath the Imperial feet. "Peter," said His Imperial Majesty, "is the ancestor who appeals to me least of all." "He had far too much admiration for what he thought was European culture," said Her Imperial Majesty. "A mania for change, transition—all so un-Russian." "I should dearly love," said His Imperial Majesty, "to abolish all the modern uniforms of court officials and replace them by copies of the costumes of the boyars." I gazed around me. "The sort of costume you see now, sir? But wouldn't that be ruinously expensive—these furs, these festoons of diamonds?" After a moment I gained reluctant Imperial agreement to this.'

'You were lucky,' said Father. 'He has no idea of the value of money.'

'I might have known. And the conversation ended as it began— fresh denunciations of Peter, now on the grounds that he'd founded St Petersburg—"this bog", the Czar called it.'

'That's his usual way of referring to it,' said Father.

Grandfather left a week later; Uncle Raoul stayed on longer, until he had seen the way in which Easter was celebrated in Russia. And so he stood at midnight in the Nevsky Prospekt and saw the stream of worshippers, each shading a tiny candle-flame with his hand, come from the Kazan Cathedral to meet the great river of people flowing from St Isaac's, until it seemed the whole square was filled with flickering sparks. He was deeply impressed.

'Fortunately,' said Father, 'you won't be seeing the lunatic charade to be perpetrated at Sarov in July.'

Neither did Father himself. Politicians in Paris might dislike Uncle Raoul and all that he stood for, but among soldiers he had good friends. In the late Spring, therefore, Father received an invitation to attend some artillery tests that summer. 'I see Raoul's hand in all this,' he said, 'but I'll go. It'll save my sanity. If as much zeal and energy were shown in vital matters of state as are being displayed in this canonisation project, Russia would be transformed overnight.'

Mother said she must stay, to be in attendance on the Czarina; 'If I came with you, Alesha, she'd feel betrayed, grow hysterical. But you go, and take the children with you. I'd like them to see Papa celebrating the fourteenth of July.'

Grandfather, like all his immediate ancestors, celebrated Bastille Day by simply drawing the blinds and sitting in stuffy discomfort. He thought it all a great bore, but the villagers expected him to go into mourning for the *Ancien Régime*, and we couldn't disappoint them.

'You'll find no one more frenziedly devoted to Throne and Altar than a Breton,' said Grandfather. 'The other day I was telling one of them that the Holy Father himself had had a few kind words to say about the Paris government. "Indeed, Monseigneur," he said ferociously. "Then the sooner we get a Breton Pope the better." '

Mother's letters to us described what Grandfather called the tomfoolery going on in Russia. Although she did not say as much, clearly the journey to Sarov was completely exhausting, because of the July heat. After leaving the train, there was a long journey by *troika*, along narrow, winding roads and through clouds of blinding, choking dust. The Czar and Czarina were in the first carriage, the Czar's mother and younger sister in the second, the Grand Duke Serge and his wife, the Grand Duchess Elizabeth, the Czarina's elder sister, in the third. Mother had thought that the drive in the terrific heat would leave the Czarina in a state of collapse. 'You know how easily she gets tired, and how the mere prospect of public functions and crowds makes her ill. Those drawn blinds when we travel by train! At every stop I looked anxiously for the tell-tale signs—the fixed stare, the set, unnatural smile, the rigid, constrained posture. But they weren't there. Her face was expressive, not mask-like, all fervour and expectancy. She showed no sign of tiredness, none of that dreadful pallor one knows so well. It was *I* who felt worn out, and could have called out in joy when at last, after driving through a seemingly endless pine forest in the heat and dust, we saw the gold domes and spire of the monastery.

'That evening I was in attendance on the Czarina in the Abbot's lodging. It was a heartbreaking repetition of what I'd seen and heard so many times before—*this* was the real thing, at last. She *knew*. God wouldn't have given her this mood of exaltation otherwise.'

'You were quite right not to go,' Grandfather said to Father. '*I* couldn't have endured it, either. But women seem to be able to suffer fools more gladly—'

'Oh, yes, Avoye will stay sane and sweet in that medieval madhouse. I feel a brute deserting her but if I'd gone—'

'If you'd gone, you would have lost your temper and spoken your mind, and a good cool breeze is never welcomed in the artificial atmosphere of a hothouse.'

On the second day of the visit the remains of the new saint were taken from their grave in the abbey cemetery and carried inside the gold-domed cathedral erected solely to be a shrine. The Czar and Grand Dukes acted as bearers. That night there was a gala banquet; after this Mother followed the Czarina into the garden, where a few old priests awaited them. First, long, silent prayers at the grave of the saint; then bathing in the waters of the river.

'One doesn't know whether to laugh or curse,' said Father, when he heard of it.

When Mother rejoined us in Brittany at the end of the summer she said little of the pilgrimage to Sarov except that she had been glad to have the opportunity of spending some time in the company of the Grand Duchess Elizabeth, the Czarina's elder sister, an angel of beauty and goodness. 'She asked after you, Papa—so did the Grand Duke Serge.'

'I always find it incredible that two sisters can be so different in the

76

matter of *sense*. And what did Her Imperial Highness' husband think of that vaudeville performance of a pilgrimage?'

'He's worried by it all—he's been worried for a long time. He said he was sorry you weren't there, Alesha, because he can talk frankly to you—he gave that rare smile of his and said, "Your husband, like a lot of people, doesn't share my political ideas, but, unlike most, he believes I can differ from him politically, yet still retain a certain amount of honesty." '

Grandfather was interested. 'The most reactionary of the Grand Dukes! I didn't know you and he ever got as far as discussing politics, Alesha.'

'He's always been friendly—it all began, I think, because *my* father died saving his. He adored Alexander II, and that, of course, is why he loathes the revolutionaries who murdered him.'

'From what he's said to me,' said Mother softly, 'I think it would not have been so bad for him if he'd been in Russia when it happened, but he was in Italy, being delicate.'

'And I don't suppose the story of death by high explosive lost anything in the telling,' said Grandfather.

'His isn't a blind, unreasoning hatred of reform,' said Father. 'In the first place, he said to me once that if change comes, the Czar must take the lead, as in his father's reign. "There's all the difference in the world between a free and generous gift from a sympathetic ruler and a grudging concession wrung from a weak man terrified by threatened revolution," he told me.'

Mother laughed. 'He doesn't think much of women's intelligence, does he? When he was trying to tell me that Russia wasn't ready for change, he solemnly recounted how one arranged a child's diet. "Bread and milk, not *bortsch*," he said.'

'I think he was *lucky* being in Italy when his father was killed,' whispered Alix. 'He's the very tall one who keeps twisting the ring on his little finger, isn't he?'

I nodded, momentarily puzzled by a hazy idea that I'd seen a portrait of the Grand Duke doing precisely that, unlikely though it seemed. It was only years later that I realised I'd been thinking of someone else with the same characteristic. Another poor, maligned devil. Richard III.

After this conversation the pilgrimage to Sarov was never discussed in the remaining weeks of our stay in Brittany. Mother and Grandmère were fully occupied with preparations for Grandmère's winter stay in

Egypt. If it was successful it would be repeated in the following year, and then Alix might go too, as Petersburg winters often gave her a bad chest. The men frequently talked of territories further to the east. It looked as if there might be some kind of trouble between Russia and Japan.

8

'All is quiet on the Sha-Ho'

General Kuropatkin to the Czar

THE SPRING of 1914 was to find me in Paris. Uncle Raoul was carrying out one of his usual forays along the *quais* in search of books on military affairs; I accompanied him, and came across a new English textbook on European history. And there, at the commencement of the chapter on the Russo-Japanese War, were listed the causes, so neatly tabulated, so succinct, so definite! How fortunate to be a teacher of history—in particular a writer of history textbooks. All is so tidy, then.

I, who lived through it, and lost by it, can't be donnishly dogmatic about the causes of the war with Japan, except to say that there would never have been a war if Alexander III had lived, for if ever a war was caused by lack of financial integrity, this was it.

God knows what final verdict historians will pass on the reign of the last Czar; possibly among the more lurid aspects, the fact that it was a reign of much financial speculation will receive scant notice. Yet it was significant enough. The Japanese War would not have been fought but for the Yalu concessions granted to a group of adventurers. And speculation didn't end with the war against Japan; between 1914 and 1917 the pace grew even more fast and furious.

Even so, the wish of dubious adventurers to bring about a last great landgrabbing expedition in Manchuria in the old manner, regardless of Japanese interests, would have got nowhere without the concurrence of the government—and of the Czar. For, disastrously for us all, one of his few real interests at the time was the Far East.

I can remember Father pacing up and down in Mother's boudoir, throwing out angry, jerky phrases.

'He's travelled there, he tells me a dozen times a day, and this is propitious. I clamp down a rigid control and don't reply, *And you were nearly assassinated in Japan, sir; is this equally propitious?* He talks endlessly about his work as Chairman of the Trans-Siberian Railway Committee. Of course, that was his first and only experience of Russian administration before becoming Czar. He was never anything more than a—a dummy chairman, but, even so, he sat in on meetings, and couldn't help catching words, grasping arguments if they were heard frequently enough. And now, amid so much that he finds difficult and boring, these names, these old arguments have a dear familiarity. Add to this the fact that his own ministers encourage him to think of himself as *the* Far Eastern expert in this country. One old fool said to me today, "It gives him some outlet for personal ideas," meaning that they think it safe to let him loose in a field of lesser importance, where he can't do much damage.'

'But you think he can,' said Mother.

Father shrugged. 'He told me one day it was his ambition to be the mainstay of European peace. But if you're conscious of weakness in yourself, you're afraid to follow any policy that can't be classified as firm.'

'But with the Council of Ministers to check him—'

'They don't. It almost makes one believe against all medical evidence that lunacy's contagious. There's a catch-phrase going round at present —Korea must become to Russia what Bokhara is. We are also going to do to Manchuria what the British have done to India. Our little bureaucrats sit at their desks in a Petersburg pea-souper, and think of themselves as the spiritual descendants of Clive and Hastings. Enter that gloomy fool Hamilton. "If we want war," he says morosely, "we'd better start building the second track of the Trans-Siberian Railway, we'd better concentrate troops in Eastern Siberia, we'd better launch a few modern battleships." They scoff at the buffoon—who isn't even amusing. I continue that the mass of the people are quite indifferent to all that's going on, except that certain sections'll pray for defeats leading to trouble at home, and a clown in a high office grins and says, "We have not forgotten that, but the quickest way of dealing with discontent at home is diverting it by a short, successful war." '

Mother recorded all this in a letter to her parents, and ended wryly, 'He's not exaggerating. I was in attendance on the Czarina last week. It was all as Alesha said. The Czar doesn't want war, but Russia cannot draw back and if war *does* come—well, assuredly God will not allow Holy Russia to be defeated by heathen Japanese—someone has told her they're no better than ape-men.

'I believe that war will come—but no one will be able to give an intelligent account of how we came to stumble into it.

'All this, of course, is not to be repeated. The next piece of information is even more confidential, if possible. The Czarina is rumoured to be expecting another child. She says it is all thanks to St Seraphim. I am waiting for the appropriate time to tell Alesha.'

At the beginning of 1904, Grandmother Hamilton died peacefully in her sleep. To me this seemed far more important than the fact that in the same week there began war with Japan, a war containing nothing remotely edifying as far as Russia was concerned. Its genesis was squalid and clumsy; its outcome catastrophic; wherever one looked there was no relief. The intellectuals, it is true, had opposed our entry—all credit to them—yet I think it little to their credit that afterwards they were to be seen exulting whenever news came of a Russian defeat. True, it was the army that had given its allegiance to the Czar that was being decimated in Manchuria, but those poor victims were their own countrymen. Perhaps I lack the wider vision, but I see in their joy only a criminal lack of patriotism and, to say the least, a kind of moral incoherence.

When Mother left Russia for the last time, she carried with her, as always, Father's last diary. I have it before me now; a few extracts will give a better idea of the crass confusion of the period than any amount of official histories of the war.

'We in the Chevaliers Gardes have drawn lots as to who is to go to the front. I "lost"—Serge Revashov's commiserations were particularly loud and sincere. I was missing the "picnic". His only fear was that the war would be won before he could get to Manchuria. Can one blame him when already, in the first days of the war, a set of regulations has been published "to govern the administration of the Japanese territory which will be occupied by Russian forces"?

'God help Russia. This war will be fought according to the textbooks, our textbooks, those textbooks that left Raoul half-amused, half-aghast. It is against the rules of war to kneel or crawl when approaching the enemy; any attempt to hide yourself is shameful. The soldier must meet death boldly—and in an upright position.

'Our tactics are all wrong. They show no advance on 1812, and then it was the Russian winter, and not the Russian army which conquered Napoleon. We will take up the same open positions that we assumed then, and our men will be mown down by camouflaged Japs who will make use of masked guns. *Our* guns—such as we have—are military antiques—'

'I went down to see off some of my people. The train was—inevitably —late. The troopers muttered at this, but the sergeant told them they couldn't have everything—they'd been seen off from their quarters with proper ceremony, hadn't they? They said rather glumly, Yes, they'd had the all-important blessing, but—But what? I wanted to know. Well, it wasn't the blessing they were used to—and then they were all crowding round me, full of grievance. It wasn't St Nicholas' ikon. It had always been St Nicholas' ikon. For three hundred years he'd seen the Fatherland through—and now he was being cold-shouldered. The face on the ikon was strange to them—they wanted St Nicholas, not this saint they didn't know, and it stood to reason, didn't it, that the prayers of a well-established saint would carry more weight in Heaven than—

' "Good God!" I said to the sergeant. "This saint—is it St Seraphim?"

' "That's him, Your Excellency. St Seraphim Sarovsky, that one the Czar had canonised last year to help his wife to have a son. Well, he doesn't mean anything to us, you see, and if he's got all his work cut out interceding for an Heir he won't have much time to spare for us, will he?"

'My sergeant had asked me wistfully if I could get them some ikons of St Nicholas, and I've done my best. I met Vladimir Ostrogorsky crossing the Palace Square, and told him what I'd been doing. He said bitterly, "I wish to God you could send the poor devils long-range guns. You can't fight battles with ikons." '

'Vladimir Ostrogorsky again—he says we should cheer up. According to his brother Vassily, who's stationed at Kronstadt, there's even greater chaos in the Baltic Fleet than there is in the army. His particular squadron, commanded by Nebogatov, is known as *Staryia Galoshi*— Old Galoshes.

'Vladimir says it seems as if the government's going to give way to the public clamour in the newspapers to send the Baltic Fleet to the East, although the naval specialists point out the insanity of sending the Baltic shallow-draught vessels to circumnavigate the world before arriving in the North China Seas.

'Rozhdestvensky, the Admiral, has no hope of winning a victory even if he gets so far, but he has said gloomily, "I am willing to make a supreme sacrifice. Something should be done to satisfy the public demand." Vladimir says this, for some reason, has evoked admiration, but he thinks it lamentable, and so do I. It's one thing for the Admiral himself to have a suicidal mentality, quite another to sacrifice the lives of thousands of sailors—to satisfy the public.'

'A letter from Feodor Soloviev. "If in the old days it was bad enough to charge at an enemy drawn up for all to see, believe me, Alesha, it's a million times worse to advance on an invisible enemy when you suspect they might be anywhere. And then, though the ground ahead still seems absolutely empty, the air's full of bullets. It saps the nerve. Of course, if we listened to our superiors, bullets can be disregarded. They actually keep quoting Suvorov—'The bullet's a mad thing, only the bayonet knows what it's doing.' "

'I knew from Feodor's letters that fighting is going on all along the front, fierce fighting too. Against this fact, the despatches being sent to the Czar are quite incredible. "I have received no report of serious fighting. All is quiet on the Sha-Ho. General Baron Meyendorff fell from his horse on the 10th inst. and broke his collarbone—"

'Our Baltic Fleet is to proceed to the Pacific after all. The part played in all this by the Czar is significant. For a fortnight he was against the whole idea. Then he changed his mind—the Baltic Fleet was to go. He himself set sail for Kronstadt to wish the Fleet God-speed—and, presumably, bestow fresh ikons of Seraphim—and then, on the Imperial yacht, he changed his mind. He said he'd made an "irrevocable decision" not to send the Fleet. This lasted for ten days. The Fleet has gone.'

And finally:
'Seraphim has earned his canonisation, even if he's not winning the war for us. Yesterday, July 30, the Czarina gave birth to a son. He is to be called Alexei, which does not surprise me.

'I wish I could rejoice, but, knowing the Czar as I do, I can only think that this event will make what's happening in Manchuria slip from his consciousness altogether.

'I almost wish I had drawn the lot to go to the front. I had flattered

83

myself I might be of more use here, and was absolutely wrong. I have achieved nothing.

'As far as I am concerned, I think, my military career is drawing to a close. Ever since I came back from South Africa, and tried to talk to the Czar, and he spurred away, I realise I've been labelled *unsafe*.'

9

'A kind of Socialist priest called Gapon'

Czar Nicholas II

AGAINST such a background the christening of the Heir seemed grotesque to those who, like Father, realised that to the Czar and Czarina this possessed more substance than what was happening in Manchuria.

Mother wrote to France, 'Alesha is so angry because the Czar talks about the birth of his son as if it's the turning-point in modern Russian history.' Some years later, Grandfather wrote in the margin, 'For once Alesha was wrong. It *was* the turning-point—but who was to know?'

Certainly no one at the baptism in August when the Heir was twelve days old.

He was taken to the ceremony in a gilt carriage drawn by eight horses. He had for his godfathers the King of England, the German Kaiser—and the Russian Army.

Everyone commented what a big healthy baby he was. Everyone commented on the various good omens accompanying the ceremony— it was raining, which was supposed to be lucky, he cried loudly, also lucky. Above all, when he was being anointed for the first time, he raised his hand and extended his fingers 'As if he were pronouncing a blessing,' it was reported back to his parents. 'Oh, it shows he will be a true father to his people!'

It is not the custom in the Russian Church for parents to attend a christening. The child's sisters were there, though, enchanting in Russian court costume of blue satin, braided in silver, with head-dresses of blue velvet embroidered with pearls. Olga whispered to me afterwards, 'We're delighted with him! Isn't he beautiful? Mamma and Papa keep showing him to people. "Have you ever seen such a *strong* baby?" they keep saying.'

The only nervous fear was that shown by the old lady, Princess

Galitzine, who carried the child on a pillow of cloth of gold. She was terrified of the slippery floors, so had rubber soles put on her shoes.

But otherwise—all glory and splendour. Alix, who was going with Grandmère to Egypt in October, was ecstatic. A gold and glass coach, snow-white horses, grooms in white and scarlet livery with powdered wigs. An escort of soldiers.

Well, the escort of soldiers remained constant to the end.

Early in December, 1904, four workmen had been dismissed from the Putilov Ironworks in Petersburg. There had been indignation among their fellow workers, who had held a meeting and decided to send a delegation to the management asking for the reinstatement of the workmen and the dismissal of the foreman who had got rid of them. The delegation was to report back on January 2, but before this a priest, Gapon, had taken charge.

He is a figure of mystery, Gapon. In the years that have passed since that Sunday in January there have been so many rumours about him—he was in the pay of the revolutionaries, he was in the pay of the Secret Police who used him as an *agent provocateur*. At the time the general impression was that he was a dreamer with no grasp of reality, but with a gift of eloquence that could make simple working-men clay in his hands. It was also said that he was intolerably vain, had ambitions to cut a great figure in the world. He said once, betrayingly, that a priest, Philaret, had been the adviser of the first Romanov Czar, three hundred years before.

On January 2, 1905, the delegation duly reported back on the management's response, which was simply that, of the four men in question, only one had been dismissed—for faulty work. One had left of his own accord, another was still employed at the works, the fourth had been under notice for unauthorised absence but he had promised it wouldn't happen again, and so was kept on. And this was all the management would discuss.

But by this time the workers were bemused by Gapon's rhetoric, which abounded in such terms as 'martyrs', 'sacred cause', 'persecutors' —possibly because of his clerical background. He proposed a strike. Some workers demurred—this would be breaking the law. Gapon told them they could break the law and still be loyal, pious subjects of the Czar, and they accepted his word. He was a priest. He knew.

86

It was on the afternoon of January 6 that Gapon began to talk politics as well as economics. They should now demand the reinstatement of the four workmen, the dismissal of the hated foreman, an eight-hour day, a basic wage of a rouble a day—and they should do this in a petition to the Czar himself, in which he would also be asked to summon a constituent assembly and to end the war in Manchuria.

Friday and Saturday were spent by Gapon in working out a complicated scheme by which tens of thousands of workmen and their families would take part in a march through the city on Sunday, different columns, walking from different assembly points at different times, but all converging in the square before the Winter Palace at two o'clock in the afternoon for the presentation of their petition to the Czar. He left his planning only to dart off to address more workers. They, of course, were entranced. It was a fairy tale, a dream come true. The Little Father would accept the petition; how gratefully they would kneel before him as he granted their requests! January 9 would be the greatest day in their lives, the day when the people breached the wall of lies keeping them from their Little Father, preventing him from knowing their needs, from carrying out his proper rôle of protecting them from wicked employers.

If they were unworldly, so was Gapon. He seemed to think the Czar would welcome this confrontation with his subjects; he eagerly sent the Petersburg authorities full details, times and routes of the projected march. One could guess what the happy ending would be for *him*—he and the Czar would stand together on the balcony overlooking the square, smiling down at the sea of rapt, adoring faces—

So full information was given to the authorities—not that there was much authority in Sviatopolk-Mirsky, the Minister of the Interior, or Fullon, the Prefect of St Petersburg. They were pleasant, educated, well-bred men, completely lacking in strength of character.

But someone was taking fright. Troops were pouring into Petersburg, from as far afield as Reval and Pskov. And on Saturday evening Sviatopolk-Mirsky and Fullon in desperation summoned a meeting of civilian and military officials to discuss what should be done. Father was one of them.

His advice was simple. The Czar must receive Gapon. Above all, bloodshed must be avoided. He was supported by the Procurator of the St Petersburg Superior Court who said that if the Czar himself didn't receive Gapon, he must depute another member of the Imperial Family to do so.

But the Minister of the Interior and the others only replied that unauthorised marches were illegal activities and must be treated as such.

'Which means using force, if necessary?' said Father.

'Yes. Really the points raised by you and the Procurator are quite irrelevant. This meeting is to decide on the tactics to be used to prevent the march tomorrow—'

'And effectively to prevent such marches in future,' added another official.

Father stared about him, saw frightened faces everywhere he looked. He said slowly, 'Let's be honest. This talk of preventing future marches means only one thing to me. Intimidation. Tomorrow those men—and women and children—are to be treated in such a way—'

'We cannot allow a precedent of such illegal activity to be established—'

'—by the greatest shedding of blood—'

'My dear Prince, you must allow us to get on with our planning—'

And ignoring him, they bent over the large-scale map of Petersburg spread out on the table.

That damned map, thought Father, it's half the trouble. Peter Romanov'd done it, putting the government of his successor in this panic because of the way he'd built his capital, with broad avenues like spokes on a wheel reaching into the Winter Palace Square. Along these avenues the workers would march in a golden haze of exaltation; they would meet the Little Father face to face, he would understand—as God's representative, he would understand—how his people, his children, were treated by employers and especially by wicked foremen—

And the Little Father would have them shot down.

Here were his ministers now, talking feverishly—'Standard procedure—mounted police and cavalry using the flats of their swords—won't meet this emergency. It must be warning volleys first, and then firing direct into the crowds—'

He said desperately, 'For God's sake, don't let us—and even more important, the Czar—forget that these people are protesting against the conditions of their employment, they have no quarrel at all with *him*—'

'By God, you're forgetting yourself, aren't you? No quarrel with the Czar? That's good!'

But Father persisted. 'All the poor fools really want is to know that they *can* get through to the Czar, that he's not intolerably remote, inaccessible, that he cares about them. He doesn't need to commit himself, he only has to meet them. He needn't even make empty promises, he doesn't even need to *say* anything—let him just appear on the balcony with Gapon—or even receive Gapon—and the Reds can say goodbye to any idea of—'

He stopped breathlessly, inwardly asking God to forgive him for the cynicism he had expressed. It was in a good cause, He knew.

Shocked faces stared owlishly at him. 'A monstrous suggestion—As if the Czar would lower himself to such an extent—'

One voice, louder than the others, said, 'What's the point of letting Gapon get to the Palace, in any case? The Czar won't be there.'

'He won't be there?'

'He's going out to Czarskoe, of course.'

Again the struggle to be calm, to suppress the first incredulous, *The grandson of the Czar-Liberator?* 'Is that wise? Won't it be interpreted as running away? Let's look at it from the revolutionary point of view, what propaganda they'll make of it. The Czar speaks always of the love and loyalty of his people—he knows it's a lie, or he wouldn't be afraid to meet them—'

'Again, we must ask you not to interrupt the preparations we're making to deal with the emergency.'

'There are only two sure alternatives open to you—to advise the Czar to be in the Winter Palace tomorrow, or to persuade Gapon to call off the march. Since you won't do the first, I'm going to try to do the second.'

It was bitterly cold and raw outside. Light snow fell, driven on by the biting wind. Father hesitated on the icy pavement; he had not changed his mind, but the truth was he had no idea where to find Gapon, who was flitting about like a frantic bumblebee. A voice spoke politely, with an undercurrent of anxiety, beside him. 'Your Excellency, is the meeting breaking up?'

'I shouldn't think so,' said Father.

'Your pardon,' said the elderly policeman, 'but if all the sleighs are needed—'

Father said, 'You can answer me this. Where have I the best chance of catching Gapon?' He saw the man stiffen and added hastily, 'I'm not going to arrest him—I'd hardly go off single-handed to the Narva District to do that. I just want to talk to him.'

'The best place to go to is the Narva Hall, Excellency.'

'How do I get there? Can you tell my coachman?'

'I know it well, Excellency, it used to be a cheap tavern, *The Old Tashkent*. With permission, I'll tell your coachman the way.'

His directions were so lucid that Father said, 'You know that Quarter well.'

'I was born there, Excellency,' the policeman said simply. 'My brothers live there still.' He hesitated for a moment then continued, 'They work at the Neva Spinning Mill, which came out on strike in sympathy with the Putilov men, and they'll be marching tomorrow, but the Lord God knows, Excellency, they'd cut off their right hands rather than do anything disloyal.'

'Did they sign the petition?'

'Good God, Excellency, the fools didn't know what they were doing! I was talking to them about it last night—them and their constituent assembly, they've as much knowledge of what it means as one of your horses there! Well, in God's name, I asked them, why did they sign—make their marks, rather? They said Georgei Appolonovitch* kept on at them that if they had faith in him, they'd sign, even if they didn't understand, and I don't suppose one should blame them, Excellency, they're simple folk, and if you've ever heard him speak— You haven't? Well, with him every other sentence is, "*Ne tak li, tovarischi?*" (Right, Comrades?) and they get like sheep. I will be frank, it's because I'm worried about the whole business I was bold enough to ask you if the meeting were over.'

'I am going to try to get Gapon to call the march off.'

'God go with you, Excellency, but he's a vain cockerel of a man. He's got so far by having the gift of the gab, and he thinks talk will get him anywhere. Not that he plans harm—otherwise he wouldn't let people know all about tomorrow, would he? He thinks that since the humble folk listen to him, people like the Prefect will be wax in his hands—'

'The fool doesn't seem to realise that the Prefect won't accept his assurances that it's a peaceful affair.'

'I swear he's honest there, sir. Why, my two eldest brothers are

* Gapon.

90

carrying big portraits of the Czar and Czarina, and the youngest's carrying an ikon, and his little lad, just ten on Innocents' Day, is marching beside him—they're all like little lads themselves, because they say tomorrow they'll see the Czar.'

The only danger Father met was the slipperiness of the hard-packed ice under the light covering of snow in the ill-lit streets outside the Narva Hall. If, before leaving the sleigh, he borrowed one of the coachman's many coats to cover his uniform, it was only because he realised that in the wildly hopeful, exalted expectancy at Gapon's headquarters, the appearance of an Imperial ADC would lead to a wild outburst of rejoicing—the Little Father had sent word to them. This thought he found unendurable.

Gapon was tall, good-looking, black-bearded. If only, thought Father, he were not good-looking, he wouldn't be so influential. Others wouldn't listen to him so readily; he wouldn't always be seeing himself as the hero in a fairy story.

Gapon would not abandon his happy ending to the fairy story. Useless to tell him that the Czar would not be at the Winter Palace. The Czar was aware of his loyalty—and the loyalty of his followers. Why, policemen had told him what favourable reports they were sending about his meetings—how socialist agitators, students usually, sometimes Jews—were thrown out by force, while, more recently, when leaflets had been distributed urging the workers to 'reduce the Autocracy to dust' Gapon had publicly ordered his followers to tear up these evil documents. 'The audacity of the idea!' said Gapon indignantly.

It was quite impossible to convince him that the Czar might not want the march to take place.

'If the bureaucracy lie to him about our aims, he will immediately see through their falsehoods!' said Gapon triumphantly. 'Was it not for this very purpose that I sent him this letter today?'

He proudly produced a copy.

'Sire,

Do not believe the Ministers! They are cheating Thee in regard to the real state of affairs. The people believe in Thee. They have made up their minds to gather at the Winter Palace tomorrow at 2 p.m. to lay their needs before Thee—Do not fear anything. Stand tomorrow before the party, and accept our humblest petition. I, the representative of the working men, and my comrades, guarantee the inviolability of Thy person.

Gapon'

Then, not waiting for any comment from Father, the priest was laying before him the petition the Czar would assuredly accept the next day.

'Lord,
We workers, our children, our wives, and our old, helpless parents have come, Lord, to seek truth and protection from you—'

Father could say nothing. The pathetic *naïveté* caught at his throat. Gapon, interpreting his silence as that of absolute conviction, admiration even, chattered on happily.

'How can our motives be misunderstood when I've given the government ample details of what we intend to do, especially the places at which, the different columns having converged, the final advance is to be made on Palace Square?'

Remembrance of what the policeman had said, the brothers, the little nephew carrying Imperial portraits and holy images, made Father interject harshly, 'Don't you think the way in which the whole march is planned to converge on the Palace will impress the authorities in the wrong way? They'll be scared. Some will be so scared they may even see it as an attempt to storm the Palace—'

'Storm the Winter Palace with the Czar there!'

'I tell you, the Czar will not be there.'

Gapon swept on unheeding, 'And *he* will know why we come, *he* will not be afraid, so what does it matter what the fools and liars of ministers say?'

Father spoke with the parade-ground rasp of command in his voice. 'Georgei Appolonovitch, that march tomorrow must not be allowed to take place! I tell you, there will be bloodshed.'

Gapon said bewilderedly, 'How can there be? I've told my people there must be no violence, I'll see to it they carry no weapons, not so much as a stone—'

'You fool, can the violence come only from your side?'

Gapon said disbelievingly, 'You mean—from the Czar? Violence from the Czar to his people? Never! He knows we come in peace, with love and loyalty in our hearts.'

Father got up to go.

'I beg of you,' said Gapon, 'not to speak to my people as you've spoken to me. They're peaceable by nature, but if they heard you saying such things about His Majesty, I couldn't guarantee your safety.'

'I wish to God,' said Father, 'I could guarantee theirs.'

He drove back home. What else was there to do? As he climbed wearily from the sleigh, a man came saluting across the courtyard, begging his pardon, but when he'd come off duty half an hour ago he'd taken the liberty to come across to wait for His Excellency's return—

'To see if I'd any luck? You're a good fellow, I wish your wait could be rewarded by good news. But I might as well never have gone.'

After a moment the policeman said, 'I never really had much hope. Reasonable argument's never been much use with him, conceited as he is, you can never tell him anything, and now—well, he has this dream, hasn't he? He's going to meet the Czar and in half an hour that persuasive tongue of his'll set right everything that's wrong with Russia, *and* bring the war to an end. We'll all live happily ever after, thanks to Georgei Gapon—'

'Bullets will rouse him from that dream,' said Father, grimacing.

The policeman said, 'My sergeant's given us our orders for tomorrow —not that there'll be much for us to do, he says, with twenty thousand troops and eight major-generals taking a hand.'

'My God, you'd think the Japs were coming up the Nevsky!'

'I've asked to be put on duty escorting the march from the Narva Quarter along the Peterhof Chaussée—that's Gapon's own column.'

Father impulsively put out his hand. The policeman took it gingerly. 'My mate Peter has volunteered with me. We want to stop trouble if possible,' he said, 'but if I can't, and anything happens to my brothers, I want it to happen to me, too. I've had the advantages—the priest taught me my letters, and I've got on. They've never begrudged me anything.'

'What is your name, my friend?'

'Lavrentiev, Your Excellency.'

'When it's over come to see me. Here. Or if it's not possible, get word to me, and I'll come to see you.'

Lavrentiev saluted. 'I expect you know the name they give the police, Excellency—the Pharaohs. Let's hope the poor folk will know tomorrow that we don't all harden our hearts.'

Inside the house, Mother was waiting. She listened without interruption to all Father had to say, and then she said, 'Alesha, the Chevaliers Gardes will be protecting the Winter Palace itself, I suppose. Andrei and I will come to stand in the Square. Whatever happens, we must see it.'

'My dearest, you don't know what you're saying.'

'Indeed I do. We must see what happens, and—' in a lower voice, '—you can't deny to us the right claimed by that good policeman—the right of sharing.'

'My own true love,' said Father, and kissed her hand. 'Thank God for giving you to me. Without you, I couldn't go on.'

'No more illusions left?' she asked pitifully.

'In 1831,' said Father, 'there were riots here because of an outbreak of cholera. The Czar's great-grandfather, Nicholas I, went out quite alone to face a raging, terrified mob. He talked—without an army behind him—and the people listened. No one is asking the present Czar to do as much. He has only to remain in his palace, possibly come out on to a balcony—to hear his people, kneeling, sing *God Save the Czar*— and they would call down blessings on his head. But he's gone out of Petersburg, on ministerial advice, I know, but his predecessors wouldn't take that advice. He's also agreed to the use of force. By this time tomorrow no power on earth will be able to restore him to the position he holds in his people's hearts today.' They had been talking in French, but he ended with a Russian word. 'They will all know that he is *nespescovnie*.'

'That's one of the Russian words I don't know, Alesha.'

'It means unfit to rule,' said Father.

10

'A painful day'

Czar Nicholas II

SNOW was still falling thinly next morning from a sky of lead that pressed down heavily on a city that seemed completely lifeless.

Father was standing at the window staring out as I joined my parents for breakfast.

'Andrei, you know what your mother intends to do today? Have you anything to say about it?'

'Yes, Papa. When do we start off?'

He smiled suddenly. 'Is that really all?'

'I *do* know it's dangerous.'

'Danger isn't fun, Andrei. Never make that mistake.'

'No, sir. Maman didn't say so, but I know we may be killed. But if you and Maman are going to die, I'd much rather die with you, please. When do we go?'

'Gapon's column assembles at ten o'clock for prayers and hymns. They move off at noon, and will be outside the Palace at two. It will be a long wait for you both, I'm afraid, and bitterly cold—And please God it will be for nothing at all.'

The wait was indeed a long one. Crack units were holding the Palace Square. They were drawn up before the Palace itself, and before the other important buildings in the Square—the Imperial Archives, the General Staff Buildings, the Foreign Office, the Admiralty. The Chevaliers Gardes were on the left side of the Palace, sitting erect in their saddles, two rows of men and horses like statues. There were only two breaks in the immobility—first when Father sent a message across to us. 'Nothing will happen here. We're the second line of defence— the orders are that the march is to be stopped much further out. Gapon's column isn't to get beyond the Narva Gate. Why don't you go home?'

95

'What do you say, Andrei?' asked Mother.

'We'll go when Papa goes.'

I could see Father smiling as he scribbled his reply. 'Heaven knows when that will be, so I can't accept such a proposal. Will you go at dusk —I mean just before it gets really dark?'

Mother agreed to this, watched him with a kind of proud wistfulness as he faced us across the Square. We settled down to wait. It was a long wait.

Two o'clock struck, but no marchers appeared.

Three o'clock, and still no marchers.

'They *must* have been turned back,' said Mother in a low voice, 'but if so, why haven't the troops here been dismissed?'

Another message from Father. 'God knows what's happening. If they haven't been turned back, they'd be here now, but, believe it or not, we haven't the faintest idea what's happened at the Narva Gate, for a start.'

'Most people seem to assume the danger's over,' replied Mother. 'Remember how everyone seemed to be expecting trouble when we came along—houses shuttered, no one on the streets. Look at all these people coming through from Alexander Park now—they're not marchers, are they?'

A final note, the despatch accompanied by a distant, smiling salute. 'Curious citizens, who've plucked up the courage to come out to discover what's happened. A sprinkling of students. Well, my darling, give it another half-hour and get home. Gapon or the COs on the spot have shown sense, after all, and history hasn't been made today. I've been a melodramatic fool, and tonight I'll abase myself before you, and Andrei shall drink about a thimbleful of champagne in celebration, and you'll wear my favourite dress, that velvet the colour of pansies—'

People kept on coming into the Square from Alexander Park. It was the most obvious thing in the world that there was nothing remotely organised in their arrival, they were in small groups, differing widely one from the other; noisily curious students, respectable middle-class citizens consciously bold in venturing out to discover what, if anything, had happened.

Mother said, 'I think we'll go now, darling. Nothing's going to happen, and I think we'd better get off before it's too crowded to move. Look how they're still pouring in—there must be thousands here now!'

She raised her gloved hand and waved to Father. He smiled, raised his hand in salute. We turned away—dusk was falling, I remember, and then I saw them.

'Maman!'

'What, my darling? We shouldn't stop now.'

'People—with blood on them. Look—coming from Alexander Park.'

'Dear God!' said Mother. 'There are women among them. Andrei, they may talk to you where they wouldn't talk to me. Ask them what's happened. I'll go back near Papa—come and tell us.'

Three men, two women, with blood on them. No, they were saying, they weren't hurt, it was the other people's blood, but they'd all been lying there in the road. They'd managed to get away—made their way here—had to find out what had happened—

I know now they were all five in a state of shock. I asked, 'Please, were you with Father Gapon's group?'

Their eyes didn't seem to focus. The younger woman said suddenly, 'Don't say anything. Don't trust anyone. *We* trusted—'

'Please!' Gratefully I remembered the name of the policeman. 'We're friends of the Lavrentievs—'

'They were in front. They went down first.'

'Then you *were* with Gapon's group?'

'Yes, till we came to the Narva Gate. It happened then.'

Choking back my tears, I fought my way back to Mother. She hadn't reached Father yet. She was intercepting a mounted messenger. 'You know me—the Commanding Officer's wife. What orders did you take him?'

It would have taken a more determined man than the young lieutenant to refuse to answer Mother in that mood—the only time when you suddenly saw in her any physical resemblance to Grandfather.

'Prince Vasilchikov, Your Excellency, says the area must be cleared.'

'But these people aren't dangerous, they're just innocent onlookers. They're not even simple working folk hoping to see the Czar!' Mother flared.

The ADC said, fiery-faced with embarrassment, 'The general anticipates the possibility of mob action, Your Excellency, and the endangering of property we've been ordered to protect.'

'Maman, they shot down the marchers at the Narva Gate, the people say they can't trust anyone now—'

'We must tell your father,' said Mother distractedly, 'he doesn't know—'

Father sat erect on his horse before the two lines of Gardes.

'Alesha, they shot down the marchers at the Narva Gate—Are you going to obey *your* orders?'

'Clear my part of the square, Avoye?' said Father, never looking down. 'Yes, it can be managed easily enough. I'll do it my way—quite efficiently, and no harm done, and it'll keep other units from being ordered up to do the job—differently. Get away to the end of our line, my darling.'

He raised his voice. 'Listen to me, everyone. We have been given orders to clear the Square. I give you five minutes to get out, then I'm going to give the signal to charge—'

'Oh, God, what does he mean?'

'Maman, they *can't* charge properly! It's too slippery! Papa knows what he's doing.'

'Yes, my darling, forgive me!'

'—If by any chance you can't get away—and want to—sit down. Five minutes, then.'

The crowd immediately before us began to hurry away. There were cries of, 'Thank you, Your Excellency.' Father was talking earnestly to his men, who listened as seriously, nodding.

The five minutes were up. Father turned to the trumpeter, raised his hand. The result was the oddest little whinny of sound; with fifteen degrees of frost, the trumpet had frozen. The soldiers laughed, so did the crowd who remained within earshot. Some of them, however, didn't—couldn't—hear the miserable travesty of a call, and so were unprepared for the advance, and when they did sit down, sat down so hurriedly that the horses stopped dead or skidded so abruptly that their riders nearly came off, shooting on to their horses' necks. The second line could scarcely sit in their own saddles for laughter.

'Right,' called Father. 'Now, lads, wheel your horses—I know it's tricky because of the slippery ground—and back them on to the crowd, and help them out that way. Nothing like a horse's hindquarters for getting rid of an unwelcome visitor!'

More laughter from cavalry and crowd, cheerful, good-natured pushing from all concerned.

But from the other side of the Square, the side where the Preobraz-hensky Regiment was stationed, there came the sound of shots.

'They're firing into the air,' said Mother. 'Warning shots. *They must be warning shots!*'

We could see nothing with the cavalry before us, but we could hear the sudden dreadful clamour, and then, as Father's command, grinning, saw off the last remnants of the crowd that had been opposite it, we could stare across to the other side of the Square, and there they were, men, women, children, running, stumbling, crawling, lying still, and every-where there was red blood on the close-packed snow.

The commanding officer of the Preobrazhensky, shakily lighting a cigarette, said to Father, 'It was rather an unpleasant experience, giving the order to fire at an unarmed crowd.'

Father said, 'Did you think the crowd found it any more enjoyable?' and turned on his heel.

Now Petersburg became a city of nightmare. We struggled out of the Palace Square, quite quiet now, tenanted only by the dead and the dying, but the Nevsky Prospekt was the same, worse even, for it was always crowded on a Sunday afternoon, people brought their families out for walks. The open area outside the Kazan Cathedral was especially bad.

'Try not to look,' said Mother. 'Later on you mustn't forget that this was done to living people, but till we get home think of it as unreal —like a painting.'

A painting in black, white, red.

My teeth were chattering. 'It's the cold,' I said. 'When will Father be home?'

'I don't know. Soon, I hope.'

But she herself delayed his return. At ten o'clock she sent him a scrawled message that was brought to our house. The policeman Lavrentiev was asking for His Excellency. The policeman Lavrentiev was badly hurt—

The doctor at the Litovsky Castle Infirmary, the hospital of the biggest gaol in the city, said, 'Yes, he's still alive, he's kept himself alive by willpower. It's a miracle. I know our police have the strength of bulls—and precious little else—but that this man should stay alive—conscious—'

Lavrentiev's eyes were fixed on the door of the ward. 'He's been like that since we said we'd send the message. Yes, let him talk as much as he likes, or is able. Nothing can hurt him now.'

And then Lavrentiev's last report:

'There were several thousand of them at the Hall at ten o'clock. Men, women, children. Prayers till noon. Then they brought out the ikons and the banners and standards and the march began, Peter and me at the head of it, yes, right in front, clearing the way. *Excellency, let that be known. It wasn't the police who did the shooting.* And all along the march the police took off their caps, because it was a Procession of the Cross, clergy, the people carrying ikons, singing hymns—*"Our Father"*, and *"Save, O Lord, Thy People"*, but of course we all sang the Czar's Hymn as the march started. Gapon got very angry because one or two of the younger fellows, more for devilment than anything else, sang 'Save Georgei Appolonovitch' instead of 'Save Nicholas Alexandrovitch'. He shouted at them for their wickedness, got in a real state about it, kept saying to us we mustn't take any notice, this was a loyal, peaceful procession. Well, we'd had that from him all the morning—at one time Peter said to me, "Lord God, next minute the man'll be asking us to search every one of the folk here to make sure the women haven't a bodkin in their pockets or the kids a couple of marbles." He said now, "Georgei Appolonovitch, we *know* it's a peaceful procession, and we'll say so in our reports. Loyal, restrained enthusiasm, we'll say." Gapon was pleased then, he started striding out with a self-satisfied look on his face. "There he goes, the damned fool," said Peter under his breath. "Saviour of the Nation, isn't he?"'

'Still, it was very pleasant. The singing, everybody happy, the crowds bowing. My people, in the front row, looked as if the good God had taken them up to heaven already. There was Pavel holding his big portrait of the Czar, and Ivan with his portrait of the Czarina, Kyril with his ikon and the little lad running beside them with his lantern. It was a grey day, you see, so he carried the lantern for people to see the Imperial portraits quite clearly. And there were the banners and the ikons, and the national flag, and everybody in their Sunday best singing hymns, and the children, hundreds of them, running along on each side.

'Well, that was the first mile and a half. A lot of the crowds watching had joined in, too. *Excellency, remember two things—we'd been given no order we were not to march—it was an orderly procession, we police were clearing the way for it*—Oh, my God, they'll think we knew what was coming, that we did it all to trap them—'

'For God's sake,' said Father, 'is there nothing we can give him? This is frightful.'

The doctor had his fingers on Lavrentiev's wrist. 'Lavrentiev. It's all right. Good God, weren't *you* shot down?'

'I'm glad of it, glad of it—'

'Lavrentiev, my friend, you must tell me. People will have to believe what *you* say.'

'We were coming to the Narva Gate,* and then we saw the troops. Riflemen—the Irkutsk Rifles—and Horse Grenadiers. And the Grenadiers charged.

'There wasn't time to think, let alone make plans or give orders. I remember thinking, "So there's going to be a massacre after all," but it didn't seem to have much meaning. Peter kept his wits better—he didn't have people in the crowd behind. "Open up!" he shouted. "Move over to the left and right. Let them through!" It was amazing how many heard him, with all the shouts and screams. He said to me, "We go on, old friend. Perhaps they haven't noticed that the police are *with* the procession."

'But the charge went on just the same. They rode on down the lane left behind us, striking on both sides. People were going down like logs of wood. It was bad towards the back because they hadn't been able to hear us shouting to open up the ranks. And then the cavalry turned and cut their way back again, rode to the Gate and the infantry let them through. I shouted to Gapon, "Make the people halt! I'll go forward and say it's a peaceful procession!" but I don't think he heard me. I don't think he'd have heard me even if there hadn't been the moans and the shrieks. Gapon kept saying, "We must go on! It'll be all right—once they see the flags and the banners and the Czar's portrait, it'll be all right." I think he was trying to convince himself more than anything else, but people heard him, and obeyed. God pity us, they still believed in his fairy tale, though *he* was beginning to realise it was turning into a nightmare. And so—though it's hard to believe—they formed rank again, those who could, and they went on singing. They were singing the National Anthem.'

Tears were running down Father's face.

'They were singing it so loud, they didn't hear the bugle blowing.

* A triumphal arch erected by Alexander I to commemorate the victories over Napoleon.

Even if they had, of course, they wouldn't have known what it meant. Walking in front, being only thirty yards from the soldiers, with just the bridge over the Tarakanovsky Canal between us, I actually saw the bugler raising his bugle, but even after the charge, I didn't guess what was coming. *I didn't think they'd shoot down the people as they came forward singing "God Save the Czar".* That's how it had started, and that's how it ended.'

The doctor's lips were moving soundlessly. 'He can't last much longer.'

'We heard the rifle shots, though. I turned, and there was Pavel going down. Ivan caught the Czar's portrait as it fell from Pavel's hands—he was still singing—he was carrying it with the Czarina's. He called to his boy to lift up the lantern so that everybody could see the portraits. Ivan went down with the next volley. As he went down he shouted, "I may die, but I will see the Czar!"

'I turned back to the soldiers, shouting things that made no sense. "What are you doing? How dare you fire upon the portrait of the Czar?" Peter was near me. He was shouting to the crowd to lie down flat. They wouldn't at first, they knelt down and went on singing. "Lie down flat!" Peter shouted. "Hide your heads!" Then they shot him. They'd gone mad, I think. They were shooting into the courtyards of houses where people were trying to hide.

'I saw our little lad go down. He tried to get up again, but then another bullet got him in the face and he was down, his arms stretched out, with Ivan and Pavel and Kyril, and there was the blood all over the ikons and banners and the Imperial portraits, and I thought, looking down at the Czar's portrait, "And this is all your work, our Little Father," and I just waited for the bullets to get me too—and was glad of it.'

'He's going,' signalled the doctor.

Lavrentiev said, 'In my job, I'm used to corpses. But what was so bad about these, lying on the snow, was the—shock on their faces. They hadn't expected it.'

Father said to the doctor, 'How many people have died—have you any idea?'

'There are about a hundred dead in the hospitals, three times that number wounded. I'd say that ten times that number were carried away by friends and relatives—we'll never know the correct figure.' He took a few paces, then said abruptly, 'I entered the prison service for idealistic purposes, you know. I believed in the essential nobility of man. It doesn't apply in government circles. I've heard of your actions this afternoon, that's why I'm talking to you in this way. Supposing you commanded, not cavalry, but—well, let's say that in place of Captain von Hein you were commanding a detachment of the 93rd Irkutsk Rifle Regiment. You're confronting an advancing mob. What do you do?'

'I first give them a warning. Then, if they advance in a menacing manner, I tell the men to shoot in the air. If the advance still continues, I give orders to open fire—'

'Yes, but you'd add something.'

'Of course. I'd say, *Aim at their legs.*'

'Precisely. Captain von Hein had before him a peaceable crowd of men, women and children, escorted by police, and singing *God Save the Czar*. I've been dealing with the results. Like Lavrentiev I was struck by the horror on the dead faces. All that the poor wounded devils have said is, "Why did the Czar have his people killed? We didn't throw stones, or break windows. We only wanted to see him—" All the wounds, you know, were in the head and body. I'm glad Lavrentiev was spared that knowledge.'

'Thank God he was spared other knowledge too,' said Father. 'Casualty lists must be issued. The fact that two policemen were killed can't be hidden. But they'll not only appear as casualties on the government side, they're going to provide the justification for what happened. Can't you see it—"Units of the Rifle Regiment opened fire *after two policemen had been shot by the marchers*"? Goodnight.'

I I

'The perpetrator of a bad comedy'

FATHER SLOWLY made his way home. Men were washing the Palace Square, just as no doubt they were washing the approach to the Narva Gate and other spots. He spoke to two officers that he knew—the first, elderly, very senior, showed no hesitation or misgivings in discussing the day's events. 'Complete success from our point of view, of course. *We prevented the assemblage!*' The other, younger, spoke in a low voice with little satisfaction. 'The older people here talk as if everything's finished, Alesha. It's not—it's only beginning—and it's beginning something new. God knows where it'll end.'

Mother, waiting up for him, guessing the mood in which he would return, had put on his favourite dress, the velvet he called the colour of pansies. She read, and walked up and down, she started to write to her father, but mostly she prayed.

And then from time to time she would go to pull back the ivory velvet curtains and stare out into the freezing night.

When she saw the sleigh she thought Father was returning, and ran out to the head of the staircase, down the two flights of stairs. But then she saw, in the light of the open door a member of the Imperial Family coming into the house—and she could think of only one reason.

'My husband?' she entreated. 'Something has happened to my husband?'

Light-coloured eyes stared petulantly from beneath puffy lids. 'He's not here, then? So that incredible story is true—he *did* go out to the prison hospital.'

One of the Grand Dukes, holding, because he *was* a Grand Duke, a nominal command in the Army. A man of bad reputation, public and private. A man completely lacking in physical and moral courage, who had dabbled in Korean concessions, and had done his best to involve us in the war. Implacably opposed to Father.

Mother took a deep breath, swept him an exquisite curtsey, then said, 'I apologise for my stupidity. If anything had happened to my husband, I do not for a moment think Your Imperial Highness could have come to take me to him. Please do me the honour of coming into one of the reception rooms.'

They stood in the greatest reception room, with the diamond-like chandeliers of Venetian crystal and the Clouet drawing of Mary Queen of Scots as a bride in France, and the golds and sea-greens of the Canalettos, and the Goya and, in its own special place, the Cimabue Madonna.

'I have brought your husband, Princess, a letter from Czarskoe Selo. From His Majesty himself.'

She knew then, of course. The Czar who could never dismiss a person verbally, who always sent written messages. Who had given way to constant pressure from such as the man before her now.

'I should have thought,' said Mother, holding her hand out steadily, 'that your Imperial Highness had so much needing his attention that to act as messenger boy—Please leave it with me! I may be trusted, I think, to pass it on to my husband. I may also be trusted not to open it myself, for I know what is inside it. And my only personal regret—'

They heard doors opening, closing, voices, footfalls coming in a slow, unhurried stride.

'He has returned,' said Mother. She did not alter her expression of vigilance, but there was a softening, a glow of warmth in every line of her face.

Father came in, stood to attention, saluted. Mother went quickly across to stand beside him.

'You're tired, my dear one,' she said, as if the visitor did not exist. Father took her hand and kissed it, and kept it in his.

'My God!' said the Grand Duke. 'You reek of prison infirmaries.'

'There are worse smells,' said Father.

'His Imperial Highness has come from Czarskoe, Alesha. He has a letter from His Majesty.'

'The Princess wanted me to leave it with her. When you came in, I was about to say I preferred to hand it over to you personally—'

'I must beg leave to correct your Imperial Highness. *I* was about to express personal regret—'

105

The Grand Duke smiled. 'You're right. By all means let's hear this personal regret, madame.'

'My only personal regret,' said Mother, 'is that Your Imperial Highness is the sole witness of what I say now. That I have always loved and admired my husband, otherwise, of course, I shouldn't have married him, but I have never loved or respected him more than today, and at this moment.'

This was so unlike anything expected that the Grand Duke gaped foolishly for a moment. Then he said, 'I think you're under a misapprehension, madame. This afternoon your husband made his regiment a laughing stock to the mob. This letter is His Majesty's dismissal of—'

Mother laughed, clear ringing laughter. 'Your Imperial Highness! Do you think I said I was proud of Alesha because I thought he'd been officially commended for what he's done today? As if I didn't know that all his words and actions for the past years have stuck in the throats of certain people in high places! But, as for me, I thank God for giving me such a husband!'

'Now, my darling,' said Father, 'we mustn't detain His Imperial Highness any longer. I shall, sir, write to His Majesty acknowledging the receipt of his letter, and thanking him and Her Majesty for the kindness they have shown my family and myself.'

'Is that all you have to say? You're not as voluble as madame here.'

'She is French,' explained Father, smiling, 'so has a natural gift for *panache*. As for me—all I can say is that I'd prefer to be remembered as the perpetrator of a bad comedy than as the author of a successful tragedy.'

And then another message came for Father.

It came one evening when I was in his study just before dinner. Father was reading to me a short story by H. G. Wells, *The Inexperienced Ghost*. The servants would never normally disturb us at this time, when Father read from an English novel to me, and while Mother was still changing, and the fact that the letter was brought in was enough to tell me that it was from someone extremely important. In fact, I immediately began to have wonderful visions—the Czar begging Father to come back, making him Commander-in-Chief, Governor-General of Petersburg at least. I actually asked in an excited whisper, 'Is it from the Czar, Father?'

I had to ask him again before he replied. Then he finished reading, put the note down carefully, and said, 'No, it's from the Grand Duke Serge.' Then he did something I had never seen him do before. He always kept cognac in his study—it was a good thing to offer any caller who came in chilled from the icy streets—but he drank little himself. Certainly I had never seen him act as he did now. He went across, poured cognac, gulped it down.

But then—so a child's mind works—my attention was diverted. When he put his glass down, very abruptly, there should have been a click. Instead there was no sound at all. So instead of asking frightenedly if anything was wrong, I demanded, 'Why didn't the glass make a noise when you put it down, Papa?'

And my Father, who had just received a request he interpreted as an invitation to suicide, explained that this particular table was glass-topped, and when he had poured the cognac he had done it hurriedly, so a little had been spilled. 'The glass I drank from has a concave bottom—do you see?—and this formed what they called a suction cushion—Andrei, will you finish reading the story yourself? I must see your mother.'

I sat in his chair, and finished the story. I had just reached the unnerving ending, and was resolving never again to gesticulate thoughtlessly when Vassily came in to say dinner was ready. He looked very blank at finding me alone.

'He's with Maman,' I said. 'I'll go and tell them.'

I ran upstairs, and gave my own particular knock at Mother's door. I heard her saying something. It didn't sound like 'Come in,' but I'd heard her voice, and I couldn't imagine that, after hearing me at the door, she'd tell me to stay out, so I went in—to discover that she and Father were so absorbed in their discussion that neither of them had heard me at all.

In winter there was always a great screen of cream embroidered Chinese silk just inside the door of Mother's boudoir. As I stood hesitating behind it, I couldn't see them directly, but I caught them both reflected in the tall Venetian mirror hanging opposite, Father standing before the fireplace, his long legs astride, looking very strong, very alive. The light shone brightly on his head; I suddenly remembered the family joke of how, when he'd first visited Brittany after becoming engaged to Mother, one of the old women in the village had stopped Grandfather and said, 'We're not worrying now, Monseigneur, he must be a Christian after all with that hair the colour of yellow apples.'

And there was Mother, leaning forward in her chair, the light bright on her face too, the face I knew and loved so dearly. But she looked oddly different. I had never seen her look like this—as a loving woman looks who has made a fruitless appeal, and is left defenceless.

When Father spoke, I was shocked again. Unless I'd seen it, I should never have believed it was Father speaking, for there was such violence in his voice.

'I must go,' he said.

'I shall, of course, go with you,' Mother said, after a moment.

'No,' he replied, even more violently.

'The Grand Duchess is there, isn't she? Believe me, my darling, it would be far worse for me to be parted from you in these circumstances.'

I went forward, and stood between them. 'I knocked, Maman, but you didn't hear me. You will let me come too, won't you?'

After a little hesitation, Mother nodded.

'Oh, this is lunacy!' said Father.

'It's sense. Of course I go with you, and naturally Andrei will want to come with me.'

'What is your father going to say?'

'We shall be in Moscow by the time he knows our plans.'

'Are we going to Moscow, Maman?'

Father sat down. 'Listen, Andrei. The Grand Duke Serge has been the Governor-General of Moscow throughout the Czar's reign, but he is now resigning.'

'Why, Papa?'

'The Czar may agree to certain reforms, and the Grand Duke thinks them dangerous. Do you remember how he told your mother the people are unfit for self-government, they can't digest it yet, just as a child can't cope with an adult diet? Within the next few weeks he will have a tremendous amount of work to do, and he has asked me if I will go to him as equerry until the job's done.'

'Why did he ask *you*, Papa? I know you'll be a tremendous help, but he could find somebody he'd agree with more, couldn't he? As far as politics are concerned.'

Mother said quickly, 'The Grand Duke dislikes reform, but he's an honourable man. He loathes the underhand manner of your father's dismissal. It's his idea of the *amende honorable*.'

'Yes,' said Father. 'That's it. He says in his letter, "I am making my views clear on paper, but if you come I assure you your nose—and mine —will be applied so relentlessly to the grindstone there will be no time for political dialogues." He thinks I'm a wrong-headed fool, but even wrong-headed fools can be treated badly, so here's one member of the Imperial Family who's making an open gesture.'

'Why don't you want Maman to go to Moscow?'

'Because it's dangerous,' said Father. 'There is going to be trouble throughout Russia after what's happened here, and the Grand Duke will be one of the first targets. He's always spoken openly of his hatred for the revolutionaries.'

'Why are you going to him, Papa?'

'Your Father is going,' said Mother, 'because, without any desire on his part, he's become something of a public figure since Sunday. And he believes that if he's with the Grand Duke, he'll be a protection.'

That seemed sensible to me, and I said as much. Then I added hastily, 'Vassily told me dinner was ready—that's what I came up to tell you.'

'Go and wash quickly—you needn't change,' said Mother. 'Then straight to the dining-room.'

Years later she told me that when the door had closed behind me, she looked at Father and said, 'Oh, my dear, if only you could convince me as easily as you've convinced Andrei.'

'Meaning what?'

'The child was quite radiant. Everybody knows *you* wouldn't take part in a massacre, and as a result you've been dismissed. You are popular with the workers, no one will raise a hand against you, anyone plotting violence against the Grand Duke will give up the idea when he sees *you* with him—'

'Whereas?'

'It's not the workers who plot assassination, Alesha.' She took his hand and pressed it to her cheek. '*I can't say it!* But when Andrei says his prayers tonight—'

'An extra prayer tonight, Andrei. Psalm 91.'

Since I am writing in English, it is easier for me—in more ways than one—to use the most familiar version in that language.

'—I will say of the Lord, He is my refuge and my fortress: my God, in him will I trust—

109

'—He shall cover thee with his feathers, and under his wings shalt thou trust: his truth shall be thy shield and buckler.

'Thou shalt not be afraid for the terror by night, nor for the arrow that flieth by day.

'Nor for the pestilence that walketh in darkness, nor for the destruction that wasteth at noonday—

'For he shall give his angels charge over thee—'

Father knelt at my left hand, Mother at my right. Therefore he did not hear, but I did, the verse from another psalm that she whispered before rising to kiss me goodnight.

'Deliver my soul from the sword, my darling from the power of the dog.'

I did not know at the time, but she was expecting her third child.

12

The Crows of Moscow

THIS WAS my third visit to Moscow. Of the first visit, at the time of the Coronation, I remembered crowds of people, lines of soldiers, a pale Czar, two distant, tiny, crowned figures—and final horror. We had paid a brief visit again in 1902. I'd retained a jumble of impressions of this, an ugly city, featureless streets of two- or three-storey buildings, with here and there incense floating from a tiny old church. But, above all, I remembered the captive birds of Trubnaya Square; doves, chiefly, in cramped little baskets, brought there for sale every Sunday morning. People bargained with the birdcatchers, bought a dove and freed it, opening the cage to let the bird fly away. I remember the joy with which I had watched the little white thing go fluttering away up into the sky towards the Petrovsky Boulevard. It was years later that I learned the freedom was all an illusion, a cruel trick, that these were doves so tamed and docile that they would soon settle on the ground again, folding their wings and meekly waiting for recapture. I have often thought of this since leaving Russia.

I didn't see any doves on my third visit to Moscow, it wasn't safe to leave the Kremlin. With the expectation of revolution throughout the country, we were the prisoners now. The only birds I saw in Moscow were the grey-headed crows of the Kremlin, perching on St John's steeple. Before they roosted every evening, the red winter sky echoed with their raucous cries. I think I hated them particularly because servants told me that when they flocked in from the countryside everyone knew winter was at hand; and there was a dreadful grey monotony about Moscow winters, there was never the hope you had in Petersburg, of a wind from the sea bringing a change. 'Does the winter never end in Moscow?' I asked a maid one day, and she said, 'Oh, indeed it does—once we get to the middle of February we know that the worst of the cold is over.'

Grandfather travelled through the bitter weather to try to persuade his daughter to come to France until the trouble was over. His greeting was typical. 'My child,' he said, embracing her, and gazing disapprovingly about him, 'I insist you leave these surroundings so redolent of bad melodrama—second-rate Grand Guignol stuff, in fact.'

But she refused to leave Father and the Grand Duchess. 'Ah, well,' said Grandfather, more philosophically than she had anticipated, 'I suppose that if you'd lowered your colours I'd have been secretly a little disappointed. In that case I'll come and join the garrison, if their Imperial Highnesses will have me.'

Grandfather arrived in the second week of February. There were twenty-eight days in February; I almost counted the hours to the fourteenth, when the weather would change—as change it did. The mid-day sky was blue, instead of a dirty white. There were even apricot-coloured clouds that afternoon, prophesying another fine day to follow.

February 17 was brilliantly fine, and, since the snow still muffled all noises from the city, one had a feeling of peace, serenity. Mother, to celebrate the coming of spring, wore a new dress, the bright green of a new beech leaf. In the afternoon she planned to go sick-visiting with the Grand Duchess. As usual, Father would be driving out by the Spassky Gate with the Grand Duke to work at the Governor-General's palace. I hated the Kremlin by this time, was dreading being left to myself in our little suite of rooms as the short, though brilliant winter's day drew to a close. To my infinite relief at lunch Grandfather said we'd keep each other company, and would both write letters to Grandmère. So I began to scribble away:

'Dearest Grandmère,

I wonder who will write the longer letter to you, Grandfather or I? After we have finished, he's going to read *The Last Days of Pompeii* to me—'

There was a sudden sullen roar. The windows rattled as if in a gale. The door of the room banged open, then shut again as if someone, leaving us abruptly, had slammed it behind him.

'An earthquake!' I exclaimed, with Pompeii in mind.

'An—Yes, probably you're right,' said Grandfather, speaking more rapidly than I had ever heard him talk before. 'I've no doubt one of these old towers has collapsed—'

'I must see!' I said rapturously, beginning to run across to the window, but—'No!' said Grandfather strongly, and dragged me back.

All I could see from where he held me, was the big spire of St John's across the Square, with frightened crows wheeling madly about it, the grey-headed crows whose appearance spelt winter.

'Go to your room, Andrei,' said Grandfather. 'Stay there. If—' He faltered for a moment, '—a tower has collapsed, you can't help much, so—'

He was breathing hard, as if he had been running. He seemed to have difficulty in forming words. The bone ridges showed pale and distinct through his taut skin.

'Go to your room,' he repeated.

A servant ran in; his face was frightened. He stammered out something—in Russian, of course. 'God pity us,' said Grandfather harshly, 'you will have to translate, my child.'

'He—he says something about the Grand Duke, sir.' I gave a sudden sob. 'That means Father! And—Mother running out into the snow. *You can't hold me back now!'*

'Mother of God!' said Grandfather, turning, breaking into a run. I ran after him.

We were too late to see the worst, but there were great pools of blood on the snow—everywhere—a mass of fragments eight to ten inches high where the horses had been, Rudinkin, the coachman, trying to crawl like a bloodied, sick baby, writhing all the time, and my father motionless, and he had only half a face. Mother knelt beside him, and as we came up she lifted him very gently, so that the marred face was hidden against her breast.

God had granted Grandfather's prayer, had pity on me. I stood there in a state of shock, cushioned from reality, not appalled, not even very surprised. But suddenly I was angry, furiously angry. The staring crowds kept their hats on. I shouted at them, 'Aren't you ashamed, staring there? That's my father, he must be dead, half his face is gone! Go away! Go away! We don't want you!'

They did not go away, but they took their hats off, slowly.

'Avoye,' came Grandfather's voice, very clearly, 'my dear little girl—'

'I am better off than the Grand Duchess, Papa. I can—put my arms about him still. There was scarcely anything left of the Grand Duke. He was quite shattered.'

Grandfather bent over her. 'Come, my darling,' he said, 'we must take Alesha away, too.'

113

'He hated the war,' said Mother. 'He said it was all blood and mess. Moscow—isn't much better, is it? I suppose we must take him to the Chudov Monastery. The Grand Duchess is already there.'

They sent for a stretcher. Somewhere, from the Chudov Monastery, the Monastery of the Miracle, a bell was tolling. The crows were still wheeling above us.

'Papa, help me—'

'Yes, my darling—'

'I don't really want him taken to the Monastery; I want him safe in the chapel at home. Help me to think we are there, that will make it easier for me to pray, I think. I can't here. It is so cold. If I could hear the waves and see the first snowdrops under the statue of Notre Dame de Bon Secours—'

He talked to her softly with a gentleness and simplicity I had never heard from him before, as he had talked years before to his adored baby daughter as she walked uncertainly beside him, clasping trustfully at his hand, with a posy of flowers for the small gracious figure with the Child in her arms and grave pity in her eyes. So he took Mother back to Brittany, and love and peace were about her. I don't think she was conscious of the confusion at the back of the crowd as the assassin was dragged off, but I saw it, can still see quite clearly that figure in the blue coat, the red scarf about his neck, the exultation on the pallid, bleeding face. He was shouting something confused about avenging the people.

Mother said, 'I must not let myself be angry with God—or doubt that there is such a thing as a God of Mercy and Love.'

'No, my child,' and now his voice had the harsh note of command. 'Now you must submit to the most terrible of disciplines.'

'I think I can pray now, Papa. You must still help me, please. *Eternal rest grant unto him, O Lord.*'

'*And let perpetual light shine upon him,*' said Grandfather.

There were soldiers, with a stretcher. Mother supported Father's head as his body was lifted. She said to Grandfather, 'Aren't you glad now that I wouldn't listen to you and let him die alone? I hope I shall be able to bear this; I don't think I could have done so if I had been away from him.'

Inside the monastery the Grand Duchess was kneeling before another stretcher covered by a soldier's greatcoat. I could not bear to look at her face; I could only stare at the right sleeve of her pretty grey dress, stained with blood, and the interlocked, imploring hands that slowly unclasped and were extended towards us.

'Avoye, come to me.'

Dry-eyed, they embraced.

'Pray with me, Avoye.'

A fool of an official, eyes goggling like a fish, face the colour of the underbelly of a dead fish, said to Grandfather, 'There are differences in religion, you know.'

Grandfather's fingers caught my shoulder in a bruising grasp. In a controlled voice he replied, 'Any father knows his children can show their love for him in different ways.'

I looked at the bent fair head, the bent dark head, the bloodsoaked dresses of grey and green the colour of a young beech leaf; I bent my cheek suddenly, briefly, to Grandfather's restraining hand. 'I hate Russia,' I whispered. 'We don't have to go on living here, do we?'

He replied—and his eyes, too, were fixed on the bowed heads before us—'Remember that you are a soldier's son.' I thought he had misheard what I said.

We re-entered the palace we had left in another life, it seemed. No one but Grandfather seemed capable of any ordered activity. 'Your Imperial Highness,' he said to the Grand Duchess, 'tell me what's to be done, and I'll do it.' But she was determined to play her part, wrote telegrams, the first to the Czarina, telling her she must not come to Moscow. 'She is nursing her baby, and the risks are too great.'

After a moment, Grandfather asked, 'And His Imperial Majesty?'

She shook her head. 'He mustn't come, either. The danger must be stressed.'

Her voice never broke, but sometimes she would seem lost in a dream of horror. For her own sake he would rouse her gently by speaking to her, and then she would give him a blind look so tragic and desolate that his words died away.

And Mother?

They had told her she must rest; she had agreed to go to her room and there she changed her dress, but after this she sat staring out of the window, where the steeple of St John's made a blacker bar against the gathering darkness of the sky. All the while her right hand kept passing over the table on which Father had left a little pile of small change when he had put on his full-dress uniform to attend the Grand Duke. For hour after hour the searching fingers continued to move, probing like those of a blind woman.

People talked, tried to move her; she did not hear them. She sat there in an impenetrable silence, a frozen, dead silence, the empty silence of winter, listening only for another voice. Yet she was not entirely remote from us. If anyone came in, she would look round with a start, as if seeking the one face that could assure her that the nightmare of pain was over.

'Please God,' I prayed soundlessly, 'never let me love anyone as Mother loves Father.'

It would be endurable only if grief could kill. But grief alone cannot kill, alas.

But shock can.

Grandfather had brought me to Mother; I knelt beside her with my head in her lap, and at last the blind groping ended, she began to stroke my hair. 'Such bright hair,' she whispered. 'Hair the colour of a yellow apple—'

Grandfather drew up a chair and sat beside her. 'My darling, I'm not asking you to go to bed, but if you'd lie on the sofa for—'

Someone was talking in a high carrying whisper in the corridor outside, '—if he'll go back to Her Imperial Highness when he can. The first interrogation—'

The loving hand was stilled. Mother turned her head.

'Kaliaiev—a terrorist, of course—standing for weeks by the Chapel of the Iverskaia Virgin—the coloured picture in the glass frame reflects the road—said, "I could have killed him before, but not when the women were in the party." '

Mother stared up at her father: 'So he spared us, the women,' she whispered. 'Wouldn't it have been more merciful to kill us together?'

I had raised my head, and I cried out now as I saw the look on her face. Grandfather managed to catch her as she fell sideways.

They hurried me off, and kept me away from Mother for the next two days. When I could, I crept along to hang about in the corridor outside her room. If the door opened, the smell of antiseptic came out, and Mother's room had always been fragrant with flowers. Grandfather kept me with him as much as he could, but one morning he had a visitor, and went off, leaving unfinished a letter he was writing to Uncle Raoul. Unashamedly, I read it:

'—stayed his hand to spare the women. Nevertheless, he nearly did for Avoye as he did for Alesha, and the baby's gone—'

Grandfather, meanwhile, was talking with an attaché from the Austrian Embassy. 'I'm going back to Vienna, sir, and His Excellency sent me to ask for news of the Princess so that—' His voice faltered wretchedly.

'Yes,' said Grandfather, 'they'll be grateful to you at Hohenems if you can take back word.'

'At the Hofburg, too.'

Grandfather nodded. 'My humble duty to the Emperor. His goddaughter is alive—just.'

As the grim-faced visitor left, Grandfather pulled himself together, tried to remember the ordinary usages of courtesy. 'Thank you for coming. How did you manage it?'

The attaché stared. 'Why, by the usual train.'

'I imagined they'd hold up all other traffic until the Imperial train got through, and since that never exceeds twenty miles an hour—'

'The Imperial train? But the Czar's not coming, is he?'

'We're expecting a telegram any moment—*Not coming?*'

The attaché became red in the face. 'We tried at the Embassy to get some guidance. We were told that the Grand Duchess had sent a telegram—'

'Telling him not to come because it was too dangerous! I know—I sent it for her. But—my God, do you mean he's accepted this?'

'We were told definitely he's not coming.'

'What species of an animal is he? His sister-in-law, who's just picked up the—the débris of her husband, tells him not to come—it's dangerous. The greatest poltroon in the world, if he wanted to claim there was an atom of manhood remaining in him, would have disregarded that telegram. My God, the Czarina's other sister, Princess Victoria of Battenburg, is coming from *England* despite the danger! And the Czar not coming! Is there *nothing* to him? Does he mean to go on skulking at Czarskoe for the rest of his reign, dissolving into fear whenever—'

The attaché said in sudden bitter scorn, 'It would not appear that his chief emotion is fear.'

'What is it, then?'

In the tone of a police inspector giving evidence, the attaché reported what he had been told by a foreign prince whose veracity could not be doubted. 'Besides, who could invent such a thing? He dined with the Czar the evening after the news had come from Moscow. The Czar made no reference to it whatsoever; after dinner he and his brother-in-law, the Grand Duke Alexander, amused themselves by sitting on a long, narrow sofa, and trying to push each other off.'

I was half-frightened when at last they let me go to Mother, but the moment I entered her room she opened her arms to me, and I ran across to her.

'Maman, you will—you will—'

'Yes, my darling, I'll get better. I'm just tired now, but that will soon go. Andrei, they won't let me write letters yet—will you write one for me?'

'To Alix?'

'How did you know?'

'You said once that it was worse for—the Grand Duke, because he wasn't in Russia when—his father was killed.'

Mother said, 'What I am saying to you now, you must tell Alix. That the most important thing is that God was supremely good to us in giving us Papa, and letting us love him as he loved us. We must not grieve for Papa—for *his* sake. He is more in the loving hands of Christ than ever before, death can't separate anyone from the love of God, it can only bring him closer.'

'But other love?'

'Other love doesn't die. It's only a—a temporary parting, and each day is lessening it. I'm not saying this to comfort you or myself, darling, I believe it with all my heart.'

After a moment.

'I shan't tell her—exactly what I saw, Maman.'

'No, my darling, it's enough for her to know that Papa died—suddenly—in the course of duty. Andrei, there's something else I want you to do—later. When the man who—who did this thing is brought to trial, I want you to read what he says. You must try to understand why he did it.'

'But afterwards we can go away, can't we, out of Russia, and never come back?'

Another moment's silence. Then:

'When Papa asked me to marry him, I said of course I would, but we shouldn't have to live in Russia, should we? I was young and thoughtless then, remember. No, he said, he could never leave Russia. In the first place, it had given his ancestors sanctuary when they were homeless fugitives. In the second place, though he didn't claim to be a saint or a genius he was convinced that the ideas and beliefs he held were needed in Russia today. "So even if it means losing you, I can't leave Russia." I said something about danger. "I can't desert my post in battle simply because it's become dangerous," he said.'

'That was what Grandfather meant when he told me to remember I was a soldier's son.'

'Of course,' said Mother, 'he believed that serving the Czar wasn't just a matter of being a loyal soldier. One must serve *intelligently*— never be a courtier, never flatter, never tell him merely what he wants to hear. The Czar's best servant is the man who tries to tell him the truth, who shows him reality.'

'Don't bombs do that?' asked Grandfather, coming in quietly.

'Oh, no, Papa. An isolated fanatic, he'll say, and go on to talk of the great heart of Russia.'

It might have been Father speaking.

At his trial Kaliaiev said to the judges, 'We are two warring camps, two worlds in furious collision.'

Later he called out, 'Learn to look the advancing revolution straight in the eye!'

With Mother, I read his words. Grandfather, looking on, wondered if the Czar was bothering to do as much and, if he were, whether what he read left any lasting impression on his mind.

Only once did I see Mother weep. We had gone back to Petersburg to make hurried preparations for our departure to France—for a year, if Grandfather could persuade Mother. He was in a fever to get us away. The news from Manchuria grew steadily worse, anything could happen when the inevitable defeat was admitted.

The servants moved red-eyed about the house, pathetically searching in their minds for some action that might help Mother a little. And Vassily, the butler, had what seemed an inspiration; he sent a footman down to Wolff's in the Nevsky to buy up a great bundle of French and English newspapers. 'They'll take her mind off things.'

Eager hands rushed the papers upstairs.

Those who brought the bundle to Mother could not know that they were bringing her the first Western accounts of what had happened in

Moscow. And so Mother, opening the bundle with a grateful smile, found herself staring down at the complacent comment in an English Liberal paper on the bomb-throwing that had killed her husband. 'Heroic young men and women, members of freedom movements, are now driven to extremes—'

Grandfather, sitting with us, saw the life draining out of her face, but when he called her, the tone of her response was conversational. 'They should see what bombs can do at close range. We should—tell them some of the details, Papa. Do you remember them? I wish I didn't—remember.'

She put her arms across the opened newspaper on the table, and rested her face against them. And then great rending, shuddering sobs which she tried to check. Sobs without a tear.

The Grand Duchess, for her part, had not merely read the report of the trial, she had visited her husband's murderer in prison and talked with him. She said to Grandfather afterwards, 'He claims he acted as he did because of the condition of the people.'

Grandfather said nothing, waited.

'He's a murderer,' said the Grand Duchess, 'but that doesn't necessarily make him a liar as well.'

'No.'

'I've always kept out of politics, but I have eyes and ears. In Russia there is ignorance and poverty and disease—'

'Yes,' said Grandfather. 'It is frightful.'

'In such a vast Empire, I can do very little, but I must do what I can —under God's direction.' She caught his startled expression, and smiled at it. 'Oh, be assured, there'll be no melodramatic disappearance from the palace by night, followed by a reappearance a few weeks later clad in rags in Siberia!'

Emboldened by the smile, Grandfather replied, 'It seems to be the way matters are arranged in Russia.'

'I know—this is one of the things telling me that, much as I love Russia and would identify myself with her, I can't do everything in a Russian way. I have made up my mind to become a nun, but I know the purely contemplative life is not for me, I'm not a mystic, my talents, such as they are, will always be practical, I'm one of the Marthas of this world. Yet there is no such thing as a nursing order in the Russian Church—and there is need enough!'

'Your Imperial Highness is then intending to start something entirely new? Do you realise,' said Grandfather gravely, 'that you will meet suspicion, even hostility, in attempting this? Established authority has never liked innovation.'

'But it will all be done unobtrusively!' she protested. 'And gradually! I must travel, study nursing orders in Western Europe—'

Grandfather, not wishing to distress her prematurely by describing the very real opposition she might have to face, replied promptly, 'Then I beg that when Your Imperial Highness comes to France you will honour my home by regarding it as your own.'

Some years later the Grand Duchess did indeed honour the house in Paris. She was still trying to obtain consent for her plans; Mother, meeting her, had been dismayed by her look of desperate fatigue, and had persuaded her to postpone for a few days her visits to French nursing orders. So, one afternoon, following the Grand Duchess' arrival, they had driven out to Fontainebleau, the sun had streamed in pale golden pools about them, a smile had come into the Grand Duchess' tired eyes, and she had discussed certain of her problems with deprecating humour—the Holy Synod, for example, was outraged because she wanted her nuns to be known as the Order of Martha and Mary—Martha first.

But later that evening she was more hesitant.

'Avoye, you don't think that what I am doing is simply self-dramatisation, do you?'

Mother flared, 'That is exactly the spiteful criticism to be expected from society fools who can't forgive Your Imperial Highness for turning your back on them.'

And finally, after moments of complete silence, even more hesitantly: 'Avoye, be frank with me. Do you think that what I hope to do will—lower the dignity of the throne?'

'*Lower!*' At first Mother was speechless, then, thinking this was the echo of further brainless society backbiting, she said, raging, 'Your Imperial Highness' conduct would enhance any throne on earth! What stupid, wilful—'

'Be careful, my dear,' came the quiet voice. 'Don't say anything else. I am to blame. I should never have introduced the subject.'

Mother realised then who had been the critic. She remained silent, though her anger, if anything, increased.

The Grand Duchess said suddenly, as if to herself, 'I thank God that

I'm practical, not a mystic. Complicated mysticism can be—dangerous.'
And then she deftly changed the subject.

Eventually the long battle ended, the Grand Duchess was allowed to found her order. The tall, slim figure in the sweeping grey robes went as a matter of course into Moscow slums where the police dared not go, undertook the nursing of cases too bad for any hospital to handle. Except for very important Imperial functions—and they decreased each year—she did not visit Petersburg. The rift between her and the Czarina deepened—now because a fresh threat to the monarchy had appeared, a threat more dangerous than any bomb-throwing terrorist. It had appeared in Czarskoe itself—and to the Czarina it symbolised salvation.

13

No Statue for M. Netzlin

GRANDFATHER WROTE to Grandmère, 'I won't let her go back to that criminal madhouse for a year at least. She mustn't see another snow-covered Russian square so soon. From the way things are going, there may not be any Russia left in a year's time, the damned country seems to be falling apart.'

The reek of death crept out of Russia throughout that dreadful year. The wretched Baltic Fleet, which had left northern waters in August 1904, reached the China Sea nine months later and was annihilated in a defeat with nothing to redeem it. The news reached Petersburg on the ninth anniversary of the Czar's coronation. Worse still, there was the smell of blood nearer home. Throughout the country there were peasant risings, landlords murdered in atrocious circumstances. What remained of a Baltic Fleet rose at Kronstadt, murdered its officers. There was mutiny in the Black Sea Fleet, street fighting in Petersburg and Moscow.

We reached Brittany in the late spring; Uncle Raoul joined us at Paris. Later he would go to Marseilles to escort Grandmère and Alix home.

Mother did not drive straight to the château; with Uncle Raoul she broke her journey on the outskirts of the village, at the tiny grey church where Father le Guerric, who had baptised her and married her to Father twelve years before, was waiting for her.

Grandfather said to me, 'Wash and change, then come down to the library. I want to talk to you.' But I disobeyed him. First I stole along to the rooms always occupied by my parents. Two years ago Father had come here alone, Mother had stayed in Russia to go to Sarov, and the Grand Duke Serge had simply been a name mentioned in a letter.

I wanted to see what possessions of Father still remained in the rooms; if Mother found them . . .

Grandfather had had the same idea; he came into Father's dressing-room five minutes later and found me clutching an old favourite dressing-gown Father had left behind, dumbly rubbing my face against the warm, worn stuff, not crying, my eyes were too hot and aching for tears. He put an arm about my shoulders, and said after a few minutes, 'You'll have to help me to help *her*.'

'She doesn't need *help*,' I said.

'No, I was stupid using that word, but you know what I mean. But someone else really needs help—that's what I want to talk to you about. Let's sit on the window-seat.'

Still holding Father's dressing-gown, I heard about Alix.

Alix, who had adored Father, had reacted to the news of his death by absolutely refusing to speak of him. When Grandmère had broken the news to her, she had listened intently, and then asked, 'May I go to my room, please?' 'Shall I come with you, my darling?' Alix had shaken her head, then hesitated in the doorway. 'You're sure Maman and Andrei are safe? And Grandpère?' Grandmère had nodded; Alix, head high, had gone away, to emerge later tearless, bright-eyed—and never speaking of Father.

'The tears are there,' said Grandfather, 'but it is as if she has sobbed, screamed, in her mind only. Doctors, Père le Guerric, all say the same thing—her life, hitherto so protected, has received such a blow, a shock, that it has been—how can I put it?—dislocated, smashed almost—'

'Is she trying to run away from everything, pretend it hasn't happened?'

'In a way—and we mustn't force her to accept reality. Sooner or later, she'll stop running—talk of her own accord about your father. It will be to your mother, I think. And you mustn't think her a baby for acting in this way. I only wish to God you too had been spared having to accept a nightmare as reality.'

There was the sound of hooves below.

'We haven't decided about Father's things,' I said in panic.

Grandfather looked out of the window. The carriage was coming past the gatehouse into the forecourt. The sun shone on Mother's face. He said, 'We both insulted your mother by taking it upon ourselves to make decisions for her. Leave everything here.' And then, in a whisper, 'But I wish to God that she too might have been shielded from reality a little longer.'

Alix returned with Grandmère. There was colour in her cheeks, her eyes were bright, she was as loving as ever to all of us—and she never mentioned Father, although she chattered endlessly on other topics, even the prevalent troubles in Russia.

Uncle Raoul went back to Paris, but some weeks later wrote to say that he would be coming home for a few days—he had news from the Russian Embassy.

When he arrived, Mother was in the church with Father le Guerric, and Alix and I, having weeded the Father's garden and drawn water from the well, were dusting his books—actually, we had left the task half-done to argue about our own tastes in literature. Egypt had been full of English people, and Alix had made friends who had introduced her to the books of an E. Nesbit ('A woman, I *think*,' said Alix), about which she was always talking. I looked down my nose at this, having started reading Conan Doyle and Jerome K. Jerome.

We were having a kind of medieval disputation when someone came along the cliff-path whistling Gretry's *O Richard, O mon roi*. Uncle Raoul. We ran out to meet him. 'He has such *raʒorish* good looks,' panted Alix appreciatively.

'Ah,' said Uncle Raoul, 'my much-travelled niece! I suppose that after all the Italian churches our poor little specimen seems—'

'Horrible Italian churches!' said Alix hotly. 'Do you know, Uncle Raoul, in Campania there was one dedicated to the most awful saint you could imagine—a St Elmo. Do you know about him?'

'No,' said Uncle Raoul. 'Enlarge the boundaries of my knowledge.'

'Well,' said Alix, 'there were these horrid pictures all over the walls. He was having his *bowels* wound out of him on a—wait a moment, they told me the word—yes, a *windlass*. All like *worms*—and he was looking so pleased about it. There was this dreadful fat, greasy priest who kept saying weren't they beautiful pictures, and I said no, they made me sick, and in any case I didn't believe a word of it, because the Romans were practical people, and if they'd wanted to massacre thousands of Christians, they wouldn't waste time thinking up elaborate ways like winding bowels out on windlasses—there were *yards* of them—and the priest was shocked and Grandmère was trying not to laugh—Uncle Raoul, you're laughing at me!'

'Not at you, my child. Of course I've heard of St Elmo, he's one of the Fourteen Holy Helpers, you know, the saints most likely to come to your assistance. And he's supposed to be particularly helpful to—' Uncle Raoul began to roar with laughter, '—people with upset stomachs.'

We walked along the cliff to the church. The sea-breeze was strong; it flattened my hair, but made a wild confusion of Alix's dark curls as she skipped along at Uncle Raoul's side, swinging her leghorn straw hat. There were ribbon bows on it that matched exactly the peacock-blue sash on her white muslin dress. Strange how easy it is to remember that moment, Uncle Raoul with Alix, the fluttering white of her dress, the smell of gorse, the high cries of the seabirds, the sea itself making flickers of white at the base of the ribbed cliff face.

Alix said suddenly, 'Some of the English people were saying there'd be a revolution in Russia. There won't, will there?'

But you could tell from the way she said it that she saw nothing really frightening in the word 'revolution'—I don't suppose I should have done if I hadn't spent February in Moscow. To Alix a revolution was something exciting, but not half as real as the adventures of the children in the Nesbit book she was reading.

'The news from Russia must wait until I can tell your mother and grandfather together; I refuse to run into various editions like a news-paper. But I've brought something else from Paris. A parcel of books from England—'

We tore home, fell on the parcel like tigers. Alix started waving books under my nose. '*The Treasure-Seekers*—that's what the English girls said I must read first—and then *The Wouldbegoods*—here it is—and—Ah!—*The Phoenix and the Carpet*!'

As for me, I was gripping *The Adventures of Sherlock Holmes* and the two *Jungle Books*. We scarcely noticed Mother and Uncle Raoul come past us to join Grandfather in the library.

But eventually even we realised that there had been a great deal of discussion in the room behind us. Sitting reading on the terrace outside from time to time we heard rather mystifying talk about a French group of bankers. Mother and Uncle Raoul seemed so excited over this that Alix suddenly whispered to me, 'I think all our money's gone.'

'What on earth are you talking about?'

'All our money—or Grandfather's. It very often happens. In this book *The Treasure-Seekers*—'

'Which you haven't read yet.'

'It's all here in the first chapter,' said Alix indignantly. 'The father had a wicked partner who ran away with all the money. And there was another *wonderful* book by somebody else called *A Little Princess* about a girl whose father thought he'd lost all his money and died of the shock, and she had to become a servant in an awful school—'

'These English fathers don't seem to choose their business partners very well, do they?' I remarked.

Yet, by the time Alix had rattled on with further details of gullible parents who'd Lost Their All—which, it appeared, was the essential first chapter in all her English literature—for all I might say, I was secretly becoming worried.

Eventually we went and lurked in a little room overlooking the forecourt which also commanded a good view of the library, and wondered what was the most tactful way of asking Mother if we were ruined. But when it came to the point, there was no need to rack our brains. When Mother and Grandfather and Uncle Raoul left the library, we came into the hall to meet them with such odd expressions on our faces that they broke into a torrent of questions, of which Grandfather's was the most audible. 'You have been eating unripe apples again!' he said.

'Oh, no!' cried Alix indignantly. 'Truly we haven't, Grandfather! We wouldn't do it in any case, and particularly now all the money's gone!'

'Money! What money? What on earth are you talking about?'

'Alix!' I groaned. 'If only you'd leave it to me!'

But she plunged on. 'You've been talking all the afternoon about these bankers—we didn't mean to listen, but couldn't help it—and there was something about not giving a loan without security—'

They all three burst out laughing. 'Oh, come and have tea in Grandmère's room,' said Grandfather, 'and there you shall hear the full story, provided there's not a single interruption.'

The true story came as something of an anti-climax. In the first place it had nothing to do with our own financial situation at all. The Russian Finance Minister, M. Kokovtsev, was trying to get a French loan to Russia, and M. Netzlin, the head of a group of French bankers, had gone to St Petersburg. M. Netzlin, alarmed by the disorder in Russia, had told first the Finance Minister and then the Czar himself that unless there were more security in the country—best achieved, he said, by co-operation between Czar and people—the loan was not likely to be forthcoming. The Czar had listened graciously—and promptly issued a manifesto saying that autocracy would be maintained and all loyal citizens should rally to the throne. Appalled by this, Kokovtsev approached the Czar again, and another manifesto was issued, giving a concession greater than any granted by a Russian Czar—there was to be a National Assembly called the Imperial Duma consisting of 'the best men invested with the confidence of the population'. And then came a third document, ordering the Minister of the Interior to welcome any opinions from the population as to the form the Assembly should take.

It was sad, said Uncle Raoul, that only a very few people knew how M. Netzlin had started the ball rolling, so he was unlikely to be hailed as the Father of Russian Parliaments and have statues to him erected all over Russia.

Mother had said nothing during all this. It was now time for Grandmère and Alix to lie down before dinner; Mother turned to the rest of us, and suggested we should go to sit in the garden under the great lime tree.

The shadows were lengthening over the soft green grass, and the air was very sweet from Grandmère's beloved tall white lilies. Cooing white doves fluttered about us; above, from the fragrant lime boughs, came the ecstatic hum of rapturous bees, and from the distance came the soft swishing noise of the gardener's scythe. Mother, the rays of the dying sun on her pale face and dark hair, said, 'I told Père le Guerric, Papa, that I must go back to Russia next spring, and now I am telling you you must not worry about me.'

'My dear child—'

'In the hours after Alesha's murder,' said Mother, 'I seemed to move in a darkness that seemed more intense than any I have ever known, but I think it helped me to see things clearly in my mind. It seemed as if I were looking into a telescope the wrong way. There—receding at the far end—was a dwindling little creature, myself, the creature that had run out into the snow that afternoon. That creature had run out into the snow and right out of the world she had always known. She had never returned to the Kremlin; I was quite a different creature now.'

'We know that, Avoye,' came Uncle Raoul's steady voice.

'Then—you won't go on worrying about me, will you? How often I've come into a room and I've known a conversation about me has been cut off, I've come to know so well that odd, surprised expression on your faces, you look sometimes like people suddenly realising their photograph is being taken! But you mustn't feel anxiety for me any more. *I can endure.*'

14

A Mass for Travellers

WE LEFT BRITTANY in the autumn for Austria. Our last act was to
attend a special Mass, the Votive Mass for Travellers. Every villager, I
think, was in the little church.

At Vienna we were met by my great-grandfather, who had come to
escort us on the final stage of the journey. But first we must stay for one
day in Vienna, for Mother's godfather (who was also Grandmère's
godfather) wished to see her.

Not in the official reception room, not even in the study with the
great desk with the red-shaded lamp, and the portrait of the beautiful
dead wife on the wall. Directly underneath the western end of the
palace was the private garden to which only the Family had access,
and there the erect figure came quickly to raise Mother as she sank in
the most profound of curtseys, and in a voice of contained tenderness
said, 'My dear child—'

And then they talked together, those two who, in that phrase of
Grandfather's I'd never forgotten since February, had learned the most
terrible of disciplines, my mother, and her godfather, the Emperor
Franz Josef.

Uncle Raoul had come with us as far as Vienna. Before he returned to
France, he went, of course, to visit Great-great-uncle Stefan, old,
incredibly frail, but, to use Alix's rather useful adjective for Uncle
Raoul himself, still 'razorish'.

'If Avoye returns to Petersburg,' said Great-great-uncle Stefan,
'I'm convinced tremendous pressure will be put on her to join the
Russian Church.'

'There's always been pressure,' said Uncle Raoul.

'Chiefly the Czarina, I suppose. The zeal of the convert—Well, my
son, how will Avoye react?'

'She will not succumb, especially if urged by the Czarina. She would find nothing congenial in wild volubility of protestation and emotional floridity—like her daughter,' said Uncle Raoul with a sudden smile, and proceeded to tell the story of the disgust aroused in Alix by contemplation of St Elmo's entrails.

Great-great-uncle Stefan waved a thin hand. 'These Italians!' he said. 'Unable ever to rise above vulgarity. Sometimes they act as if they see the Holy Father himself as nothing better than a tourist attraction.'

He was so delighted with Alix's inborn good taste that he presented her with a fat dachshund puppy.

In the peaceful countryside Russia seemed on another planet. What news reached us, however, proved quite clearly that the Czar's eventual reaction to pressure from a French banker had not brought peace to a distracted country.

Great-grandfather, who had been a young man when the Austrian Empire was threatened by the 1848 revolutions, would take me walking in the snow and comment on the latest news from Petersburg. 'I am amazed,' he said one day. 'It seems that there is no limit to the meekness, the passivity of the respectable Russian citizens.'

I said, raging, 'They're a spineless set of idiots!'

'I dislike being impolite to your fellow-countrymen, my boy, but it must be conceded they're acting as if they're nothing more than experimental frogs, allowing themselves to be vivisected.'

I asked in a subdued voice, 'Do you think there'll be a revolution—like the one in France?'

'No,' said Great-grandfather. 'Not this time. Because the Army's largely loyal—in particular, the garrison in the capital. Agitators have tried to get at the soldiers, but the moment they set foot in the barracks they've been arrested by sergeants of long service. Always remember the importance of the NCOs, Andrei; they've been the cement holding all armies together since the centurions were the backbones of the legions.'

'I'll ask Mr Bruce to talk to me about centurions,' I said.

Great-grandfather's expressive eyebrows arched. '*Herrgott!* If your knowledge of the classics is good enough for you to be tackling Greek, it's odd you don't know much about centurions! But it's gratifying that you seek out your tutor instead of trying to avoid him as we thought you might.'

'I like Mr Bruce,' I said.

'That is obvious, even if you are more reserved than your sister in showing admiration—she hurls herself at him like an ecstatic puppy when she's not demanding fresh information concerning her heroine, the Queen of Scots. Still, there's nothing wrong with admiration for a person who's admirable.'

Mr Bruce, who had come to be my tutor, was very tall, very thin, a little stooped, face faintly careworn, eyes the kindliest in the world. He was, of course, a Scot; his father had been an Episcopalian clergyman whose hero had been Mr Gladstone. Mr Bruce, accordingly, had been christened William Ewart.

'My father,' announced Mr Bruce at the first dinner he had with us, 'never ceased to lament that Disraeli, and not Gladstone, was in power at the time of the Bulgarian Atrocities. A word from Britain would have stopped the massacres—the Turks would never dare to defy their patron. As it was, Disraeli's blind, insensate hatred of Russia saved from disaster that negation of God erected into the form of a government— to borrow Mr Gladstone's description of another despotism.'

'My Russian grandmother—who was really a Scot—loved Mr Gladstone too,' said Alix. 'Oh, Mr Bruce, we are so glad to have you with us and not only because Olga is having a tutor too, so I'm keeping up with her.'

I explained hastily that we had just heard that a Swiss, M. Gilliard, had been appointed tutor to the Imperial children.

But even Olga's letters had little significance as the year ended. 'I think Austria's the best country in the world for Christmas,' Alix said enthusiastically. 'I wish we'd been here before.'

I agreed. We were just returning from the blessing of the Christmas crib, carved by the villagers decades before. It was a big crib, about the area of Great-grandfather's desk, and the details were so marvellous that it was only with difficulty that our elders had dragged us away. Here to the left were two unregenerate rams taking advantage of the shepherds' absence to fight; here tiny lambs fed busily from complacent-looking ewes. To the right, two of the Kings were making their entrance on extraordinary-looking camels bearing a strong resemblance to dachshunds, the third King riding an even odder-looking elephant. The three monarchs were escorted by dapper eighteenth-century Jäger troops. A cow tried to lick the Child, a bleating ewe ran into the stable after the first of the shepherds, who had come in such a hurry he was still carrying on his shoulders her own newborn infant. All the pilgrims were directed by tremendously businesslike angels standing with feet firmly planted on the ground and ordering the considerable traffic about Bethlehem in a manner which irresistibly reminded one of policemen on point duty. And all this, of course, against a completely Tyrolean background—pines, soaring peaks, and an inn with pots of geraniums on its balconies.

I had always believed that Austria was at its best in spring, with the cowbells tinkling from meadows greener than anywhere else in the world, but now at Christmas, with snow creeping down from the mountain tops to give the loveliest of palls to the graves in the little churchyard where all Grandmère's ancestors lay, it showed us a new world. Can one talk of a beauty wild, without savagery? Winter here was not overpowering as it was in Russia—just as the mountains that soared above us never seemed to threaten the village below on the narrow valley floor.

Alix charged furiously about in the snow, fell half a dozen times, and caught a cold, so she was kept in bed for two days. We all gathered in her room for Christmas tea; it's still much the same, that turret room, with the thick soft blue rugs on the floor, the white fur rug before the fire, the little sofa in the corner, piled with cushions, where Alix lay curled up, a snoring dachshund at her feet, a pile of E. Nesbit books on a shelf she could reach without rising. I can remember the rose-coloured shade on the lamp, the rose silk coverlet on the bed, the great crucifix on the wall, the bed and furniture brightly painted with flowers and Biblical scenes, the blue and white stove, the hyacinths in pots, the photographs of Mother, Father, myself, all the family, and, quite as conspicuous, photographs of every dachshund we had ever possessed. (Uncle Raoul had once remarked that Alix dated her life with the names of dachshunds just as the Romans had dated their years by the names of consuls.) We were warm, snug, safe.

Alix yawned and said, 'I think God takes special care of the Tyrol, don't you? I always feel *here* that the angels are flying so low, you can almost hope to see them.'

But then the spring was on us. A last service in the little church, and then down through the pines and flowering meadows, past the deep blue of the lake, a last prayer at a wayside shrine, and we were on the high road.

We spent two days in Vienna. On the evening before we left for Russia, Mother said we must go to bed early for we had some tiring days before us; as always she went first to Alix's room to hear her prayers, and then came on to mine. She was smiling as she came in for we could both hear Alix creeping out to transfer the puppy from basket to bed, but she was very grave when she said, after prayers were over, 'Andrei, my darling, I'm going to talk to you a little about the changes we may find in Russia. First, the reason I feel we must get back before the end of April—the Russian April—is that the first Duma, this new Parliament, will be opened by the Czar on the 26th. I should like to be there in any case, for your Father would have wanted it, but from letters I've had from her, the Czarina wishes me to be in attendance, although as yet she hasn't liked to ask me.'

'Grandfather doesn't think much of the Duma, Maman. He calls it *une être factice* created by threats on one hand and indecision on the other.'

'Yet he hopes he's wrong in being pessimistic—how he hopes!' said Mother. 'So do I—and that's why we must be there.'

Grandfather, as a distinguished foreign visitor, was invited to be present at the opening of the first Duma. He did not expect to be favourably impressed. As he put it, 'The people at the top have never shown much flair for public occasions, and they're not exactly brimming over with goodwill towards the new institution.'

He was, much to his surprise, received by the Czarina at Czarskoe. She said, 'I suppose everyone's talking about a new era, as they are here. They're all wrong, of course. Nothing can impair the autocracy of the Czar which was given him by God. These people won't *do* anything, they'll merely talk and talk.'

'Granted,' said Grandfather, startled, 'that's what most Parliaments appear to do, but the power is there, however they may fritter it away.'

'Oh no,' said Victoria's grand-daughter. 'You are quite wrong.' She then proceeded to give him a stiff, prim little lecture on Parliaments. They met solely to hear the views of the monarch, after which they humbly endorsed them.

Mother was less communicative about happenings and conversations at Czarskoe, although she did let drop that after one mention of the political changes, she'd decided never to raise the subject again. 'Oh, you've been listening to talk in Petersburg,' said the Czarina. 'It's a rotten place—not an atom Russian. And the rest of the country doesn't know what it's talking about.'

'What is the *baby* like?' demanded Alix.

'A very beautiful child,' said Mother. 'Enormous blue eyes. But one doesn't see much of him.'

'Strange,' said Grandfather, frowning. 'One would have thought that the long-awaited Heir would be on perpetual show. I can't—' He was abruptly silent.

'I expect the Czarina still says it's *her* family, and doesn't belong to the country,' said Alix.

Everyone had been watching her closely since our return to Petersburg. 'It's here that the shock will hit her,' Grandfather had said to Mr Bruce. 'The house without her father—'

But she still seemed to be running away successfully enough. Reality did not touch her. I was sick with envy.

15

'Many of the peasants should have looked neater'

Nicholas II on the opening of the first Duma

THERE WERE so many troops in Petersburg you would have thought that the war hadn't ended in a humiliating peace, and that the Japs were laying siege to the city. There were patrols day and night, every bridge was heavily guarded—the servants said there were guns in every back-yard within a mile of the Winter Palace. No one was allowed to loiter —even children—because of what the authorities euphemistically called 'a single unlucky chance'.

April 26 was a radiantly beautiful day. In Russia the Spring comes so quickly; suddenly you have the kind of day that really symbolises awakening after the long winter's sleep, and in 1906 this fell on April 26.

Mother had to leave very early in the morning to get to Peterhof, where the Czar and Czarina would board their yacht; Grandfather had only to get to the Throne Room of the Winter Palace, but with the Governor-General and the Chief of Police trying to outdo each other in officiousness, and this mania for security descending through every rank of army and police, it would probably take hours for him to penetrate so far. Before he left he said to Mr Bruce, 'Get the children out into the sunshine. God knows how long it will be before we're back, and it won't do them any good to mope about indoors.'

'Where shall we go?' asked Mr Bruce.

'Let's go to the Palace Square,' said Alix.

'Or the Palace Quay to see them coming off the yacht. It will be something to remember, won't it, sir?'

'Please let's go to *one* of them,' said Alix. 'Andrei was in Moscow for the Coronation but I wasn't, and it wouldn't be polite to the Czar to say I hope there'll be another coronation soon, so I must have *something* to remember. And my angel likes the Quay.' She referred to the dachshund puppy.

We could not have presented a more innocent picture—a tall, scholarly man, unmistakably British, a boy of thirteen, a girl of eleven in a muslin dress hugging a fat puppy, but we weren't allowed to get to either Palace Quay or Square. The police turned us back. No, we couldn't go any further—didn't we know the Czar and Czarina were coming?

'Of course we do,' I said. 'That's why we want to *go* there.'

They were sorry, but we couldn't pass. Why didn't we go and play in the Summer Garden—the refreshment kiosk was open there.

'But we want to see the Czar and Czarina,' I argued. 'We can't see them if we're sitting in the Summer Garden!'

Alix took a hand. 'It's the stupidest thing I've ever heard of. The way you're keeping us from going where we want to go, anyone would think that either we were criminals wanting to harm the Czar or Czarina or that they were—a—a kind of ogre who'd hurt us!'

The puppy with an air of self-congratulation abruptly made a puddle. 'Is that why you won't let us pass?' asked Alix eagerly. 'You're afraid she'd do it in the Palace Square just when the Czar passed? I don't think she would—after all she's done it *now*, so she wouldn't *need* to—and the Imperial Family have dogs of their own, and they'd *understand*!'

But it was no use. Disconsolately we retreated from the cordon; sulkily we sat in the Summer Garden.

A sound of cannon. 'The Imperial salute?' asked Mr Bruce.

'Must be, sir,' I said in an odd choking voice. I was suddenly thinking, there was that awful thing that happened at his Coronation, and last year a peaceful demonstration became a massacre. Please, God, don't let anything go wrong this time. Give Russia a chance.

And this time no disaster occurred, though the occasion could hardly be called a happy one. At first, thought Grandfather, making his way through the great rooms of the Winter Palace, there seemed nothing out of the ordinary in the occasion. These groups of high-ranking officers and government officials, thousands of them, resplendent in multicoloured uniforms, glittering with gold and silver lace, covered with decorations, the gorgeously-dressed court ladies not in actual attendance on the Czarina—all these were perfectly suited to the great mirrors and chandeliers, the inlaid parquet floor, the painted ceiling, the gold hangings, the brilliance and splendour. As at any court function, they were marshalled into two dazzling hedges, between which the Imperial procession would come. Then a harassed official said, 'No, no, *we* stand on the right; *they* take up the space to the left!'

'They?' asked Grandfather, staring.

'The deputies of the Duma,' said the official impatiently. 'They'll be arriving at any moment.'

'A pity,' said Grandfather in a low voice to an elderly general whose boots were obviously too tight for him; 'an error in judgment to separate the goats from the sheep in so positive a manner. On the right those members of the bureaucracy who've failed in their task of giving the country an efficient government—on the left the fellows who think the job's theirs now.'

The general fanned himself; his feet might hurt him but otherwise he seemed easy enough in mind. 'Precisely, my dear sir, the Russia of Yesterday meets the Russia of Tomorrow.'

'If I may say so, you're accepting the situation with admirable *sang froid*.'

'Ah,' said the general, 'but I'm over seventy; if real trouble starts, it won't start in my lifetime. Louis XV's doctrine of *After me, the deluge* may not be heroic or altruistic, but, by God, it's comforting! In any case, I don't think real trouble will ever come from these fellows—all pen-and-ink men from the sound of them, and I would say that's the general impression. I—'

He stopped abruptly. Before the ranks of glittering notables a more sombre procession was making its way.

Grandfather said in a low voice, 'Some months ago my son abruptly became prophetic. The Japanese would never enter the Winter Palace, he said; the Russian people might very well do so. But until this moment, when you actually see it happening—'

'I know,' said the general slowly. 'One can't—shrug it off now.' And he stared with painful intentness as, very slowly, the people for the first time entered the palace which had been the setting for the most sumptuous court in Europe.

The deputies, of course, came from different classes. There were landlords, lawyers, doctors in evening dress, even the occasional uniform, but they were hardly noticed; the attention of all those already assembled was on the few peasants in their long caftans, the cotton-bloused factory workers.

Eventually they were all assembled. The sombre and the brilliant groups confronted each other, the vacant throne between them. But the essential difference between them lay deeper than mere contrast in dress. On the right there was consternation, anger. As the general had said, you couldn't shrug off the fact that there *was* a Duma—now that you saw its members, and caught their glances. Some of the peasants looked completely bewildered, but most of the deputies showed only triumph or hatred.

'Precious little chance of co-operation there,' said the general, unconsciously squaring his shoulders. 'Oh, for God's sake, why doesn't someone shut up those fools of women?' Some of the court ladies, through boldness or stupidity, were chattering shrilly, making a great show of not appearing to notice the deputies, who began to mutter together, looking scornfully towards the women. Eventually the sheer hostility of the muttering and glances made even the most foolish fall silent.

It was in this silence, of consternation and alarm on one side, of sullen hostility on the other, that the stick of the Master of Ceremonies could be heard making its peremptory knocks. The Czar and Czarina, waiting in their private apartments, had been told that the Council of Empire and the Duma had assembled, and the Imperial procession was on its way.

'I should like to think,' said the general as if to himself, 'that all is not lost. The Speech from the Throne will contain such sentiments, will be delivered in such a manner, that the gap will be bridged, the old wounds healed, the—'

'St Seraphim,' said an official on the other side of him, 'will have to work another miracle in that case!'

The Imperial procession appeared. A short figure, plainly nervous, twisting his white military gloves. No stranger would ever suspect that it was he who had called all present together with resounding phrases, 'We, Czar of all the Russias, Thrones, Dominations, Princedoms, Virtues, Powers—hear Our decree which unrevoked shall stand—' The Czarina in white, with pearls, seeming as cold and disdainful as ever. There was grief and anxiety in the dark eyes of the Czar's mother as she looked about her. Nothing escaped her, Grandfather thought—the deliberately slouching postures that never stiffened into attention, the failure to acknowledge the Czar's bow from the throne, the bold stares of open hostility as he made his speech. Where there was no open hostility, there was at best only sullen indifference.

The Czarina stood tall, expressionless, rigid until the end of the Czar's speech when he asked God to bless their labours; she bent her head then.

'In a fervour of piety?' muttered the old general to himself. 'Or because she wishes to hide her expression? As always, a most unfortunate public manner.'

At the end of the Czar's speech, tremendous applause—but only from the right side of the hall. As the Imperial procession made its way out, again an outburst of cheering—from the right. The silence on the left could not have been more marked.

Grandfather eventually made his way home. He had found the ceremony anything but reassuring. So this was the great event for which Avoye had resolved to return to Russia! If the prosperity and happiness of the Russian people depended on the Duma, the sooner Avoye and the children left for France the better. He was worried too about her attendance at Czarskoe. She was far too reticent about it. And why were the children so rarely invited to visit the Imperial nurseries? They'd been guests often enough before Alesha had started making himself unpopular; one would have thought that *now* there was even more reason for inviting them.

The Imperial children were damnably cut off from normal life.

Luckily for his peace of mind, within a few days we had a caller who gave him some hope for the future of Russia.

I was sitting with Mr Bruce reading Greek; we had just begun to study Euripides—Grandfather on hearing this at lunch had come along that afternoon to start discussing *Alcestis*, which he and Mr Bruce found so fascinating that they soared into the realms of higher criticism, leaving me staring out of the schoolroom-window.

To see a stranger walking briskly along the sunny street. A big, black-bearded man, pale-faced, with dark, honest eyes, the most direct glance in the world, a steady, powerful gaze. The street outside our home was crowded; the tall figure made his way among the throngs of people with a sureness that would have been arrogant—aggressive, even—but for the courtesy with which he spoke to those he passed.

A big man with a sense of purposefulness, a big man in a hurry.

'Andrei!' said Grandfather. 'Don't day-dream!'

'I'm sorry, sir.'

I bent over my Euripides again, returned to the mournful palace, and then—

I shall always remember how I heard the ringing voice of Father's friend, just as I read how the great voice of Hercules, the incarnation of abundant life, sounded through the grief-stricken home of Alcestis.

He was talking to Mother in her little sitting-room. 'A visitor!' said Grandfather, head on one side. 'Wonder who it is? I've heard that voice somewhere.'

I said, 'I think it's the big man I saw in the street outside, Grandfather!'

The butler was on the threshold. Mother had a visitor—would we please come? It was Peter Arkadievitch—

'Stolypin!' said Grandfather. 'I haven't seen him for years, but I remembered the voice.'

Mother said, 'My father you know, of course, but I don't think you've ever set eyes on Andrei before!'

'No,' he said. 'So this is Alesha's son!'

'Finish your lesson,' said Mother gently, 'and then come back to us.'

So I met the man who represented Russia's last chance.

They are forgotten years now, that time between 1906 and 1911, overshadowed by war in 1914 and Revolution in 1917. Yet God knows they were important enough, for they were our last chance of peaceful change. The country was never so prosperous, the budget was balanced, even showing a surplus, the railway network was expanded, private trade boomed. It seems incredible now, but from all over the Western world firms like Singer's Sewing Machines and International Harvesters began to set up factories in Russia, yes, hardheaded foreign businessmen felt Russia had a safe, predictable future, and were ready to invest in that future. There were good harvests, heavy industries like mining broke all records in production. Strikes and terrorist activities dwindled steadily—above all, democracy was given a fair trial. I don't pretend it was a Golden Age, but it was the best Russia had ever known, and there was hope for the future. Things were going to improve. And it was all due to one man—Peter Stolypin.

By birth and relationship he belonged to Petersburg's highest society. He first showed signs of originality when, instead of entering the Army or the Civil Service as young men of his class usually did, he retired to his property in one of the western provinces to lead the life of a country gentleman. After some time, he accepted the post of Marshal of the Nobility of his district. This meant not merely safeguarding the interests of the local nobles, but entailed considerable administrative functions. In these he showed so much talent and energy that the Government offered him the post of Governor of Saratov, a province where revolutionary feeling ran high. After some thought, he accepted the post; he had little ambition, but a strong feeling of duty towards Czar and country. In the past months he had shown tremendous coolness and courage, travelling endlessly round his province restoring order by his extraordinary personality.

Grandfather had a wonderful time interrogating our visitor: 'And what's this about your seizing and disarming singlehanded a revolutionary who'd fired at you?'

'No, no,' came the even voice, accompanied by the rare smile. 'All that happened was this. A certain area of the town was threatened with revolution. The leader was an ex-soldier. I found out what I could about him—he'd been an officer's batman. I went to the scene of the trouble—'

'Unsupported?'

'No troops to spare, in any case I thought I could and should deal with the matter myself. Well, there was the mob, with the ex-batman at the head. So I walked up to him, and, without uttering a word, took off my cloak and tossed it to him. Instinctively, he took it, folded it neatly, put it over his arm. "Well, my lads!" I said. "Is this the fellow who gives you orders?" There was a great roar of laughter—he dropped my cloak as if it were suddenly red-hot, but it was too late now, of course. One instinctive reaction, and he'd lost all prestige.'

'As you relate it,' said Mother, 'it sounds the easiest thing in the world, but you took a tremendous risk, admit it.'

'A little resolution, that's all that's needed in both private and public affairs of this kind. Order has to be restored. Then the Government can, then the Government *must*, contemplate reform.'

'Ah!' said Mother. 'And keep peace abroad too!'

The even voice roughened. 'That above all. For the success of any revolution in Russia, war is essential; without war the revolutionaries could do nothing. Those who drag the country into war are the grave-diggers of the Russian state.'

Grandfather asked, 'And where's the Government coming from—the Government that's going to do all this?'

'From outside that narrow circle of bureaucracy. The Czar should look to the provincial gentry. Then perhaps we'll have a Government that can and will *govern*.'

Grandfather looked across towards the big, quiet man at the window. 'I think they'll soon make you one of the Council of Ministers,' he said. 'They'll have to. But God help you.'

There was a stir outside, then the door was flung open and in ran Alix, straight from her dancing lesson. She checked herself for a moment on seeing a stranger and then she gave a smile, and dropped three deep curtseys—to Mother, Grandfather and the visitor.

'Do you like it, Maman? I learned it today. They said I must keep practising it, because one day I'll wear a long red velvet dress and be a Maid of Honour. That's *ages* away, but I mustn't let my joints get stiff, must I?'

'Come and let me present you to M. Stolypin, Alix,' said Mother. 'He will be living in Petersburg, and I hope he will visit us a great deal, for he was Father's close friend.'

'And the visits must be returned, for my daughter, Natalia, is very much Alix's age and is only waiting for the chance to invite friends to our summer villa.'

'Of course!' said Mother. 'You have that delightful house on Apothecary Island, haven't you?'

Apothecary Island is one of about a hundred in the delta of the Neva. They were marvellous places for summer villas, being like green parks set down in the water.

Next day Alix and I went out to the Stolypin villa for the first time. It was about half an hour's journey before one reached the little island where Peter the Great had laid out Imperial Botanical Gardens for the cultivation of medicinal herbs. We came to know the journey well, Alix better than I, because she and Natalia were much the same age.

Mother was very glad of their friendship; it couldn't have come at a better time, she said to Grandfather, because Alix was not summoned much to play with Olga these days. Czarskoe wasn't far away, but for all one saw of the Imperial Family they might as well have been at the other side of the Equator.

'From what one hears, that's going to be the unvarying pattern in future,' said Grandfather. 'The Winter Palace will soon be nothing better than a series of superior lumber rooms. One should give their Imperial Majesties credit—they never fail in their unerring choice of the line of conduct most calculated to make them unpopular. Still, I suppose that someone like the Czarina—German romanticism grafted on to English Puritanism—rather glories in unpopularity.'

Mother turned away from the window, where she had been watching the evening sky, a threatening one with ragged black clouds, and then rain, with the wind whipping up waves on the Neva.

'Papa,' she said slowly, 'I don't think I've told you what she said after the opening of the Duma. The Dowager was frankly appalled, and said so. "They looked at us as if they hated us!" she repeated. There were tears in her eyes. Not a word from the Czarina, who went on staring ahead as if she were a statue—austere face, humourless eyes, you know the look. But then, when we were alone, just before the Czar joined us, she began to talk in a low, repressed voice, almost as if to herself. "This knowledge of unpopularity is new to her, but she will have to live with it, as one has to learn to live with pain. People dislike me! I can't help it—I don't suppose I even object to it, seeing the kind of people they are in Petersburg—but I'm not made of stone, I don't *welcome* unpopularity!" And then the Czar came in.'

'And what did he have to say about the historical event in which he'd participated?'

'His only comment was that many of the peasants should have looked neater. Some of their caftans were not new.'

Before the end of April, we were hearing more of the Czar's reactions —or, rather, the lack of them. All day there had been a clear sky the blue of a robin's egg, and inside Mother's boudoir all was spring too, pale yellow silk curtains, mimosa and irises in crystal vases matching the crystal candelabra, a last gleam of sunshine striking on Mother's favourite Fragonard, the beautiful shallow mouldings of the furniture. Mother in grey silk. Alix and I tickling the stomach of Malenkaia, the dachshund, as she sprawled on her back in inelegant but blissful ease in another patch of dying sunlight on the Chinese carpet.

And Peter Stolypin, staring out of the far window, and telling Mother what the Czar had said that morning.

'He said quite calmly that he succeeds in nothing he undertakes, he's bound to be unlucky, and not only because the human will's so powerless.

'I protested vigorously. He replied, "Have you read *The Lives of the Saints?*" I replied cautiously that I had read some—if I remembered rightly, they ran to some twenty volumes.

' "Do you know what day my birthday is?"

' "Of course, sire, May 6."

' "What Saint's Day is it?"

' "Forgive me, sire; I'm afraid I've forgotten."

' "The Patriarch Job."

' "Then God be praised; Your Majesty's reign will end gloriously, for Job, after piously enduring the most cruel tests of his faith, found blessings and rewards showered upon his head!"

'But he only replied that he had a presentiment—no, more than a presentiment, a conviction—that, like Job, he was destined for terrible trials, but would have no earthly reward at the end. And he ended by quoting Job's own words—"*Hardly have I entertained a fear than it comes to pass and all the evils I foresee descend upon my head.*" '

'He sounds quite complacent,' said Mother.

'It was appalling. This fatalism—indifference—passive inertia—'

'I'm not appalled by this exhibition—I'm angry. Think of the old Emperor at Vienna—if there's one man who might complain of misfortune it's he, twice the Czar's age, too; every time I've talked with him, I've felt my heart would break, for he's secretly prepared for new hurts, yet he doesn't sit in the Hofburg inertly blaming the day he was born!'

'I owe Isvolsky at the Foreign Office* an apology. I'd never really believed his account of *his* audience with the Czar when it was touch and go with the Kronstadt Mutiny last year. Do you know it? He was making his weekly report at Peterhof, and with the Czar was sitting at a little table in a window overlooking the Gulf of Finland; they could see the island and the fortifications only fifteen kilometres away, and they could hear the gunfire—it was, in fact, growing louder every minute. But the Czar showed not the slightest flicker of emotion.

' "Some might call that admirable," I said.

' "Admirable?" said Isvolsky. "It was damnable! Such complete lack of feeling was horrifying, as if something had atrophied within him. I wanted to shout, 'If the mutineers hold on to the fortress, it's all up with you, sire! Can't you see it's not merely—as you might put it—a question of the control of your capital city? Your family's in danger, man—the guns of Kronstadt could stop any escape by sea.' At the same time, I had the feeling that if I *had* bawled all this, not a muscle would have moved in his face, so I saved my breath, and got on with my report, and when I finished he went on sitting at that open window,

* Outwitted by the Austrians in 1908, Isvolsky resigned to become Russian Ambassador in Paris, where he worked for revenge.

144

calmly looking across to the horizon. 'Good God!' I thought. 'Is he admiring the view?' And then I couldn't help it—I blurted out something, I can't remember exactly what, about my amazement at seeing him listening so unmoved to the sound of the gunfire. And he looked at me and said that what was to happen—to himself, to his family, to Russia—was all in the hands of God, and he would always submit himself utterly to God's will." '

It was dusk now; Mother called for candles, so much more pleasant on a spring evening.

'M. Isvolsky's the funny little man who always smells of violets,' whispered Alix. She began to giggle.

'You're not to talk about this outside,' I muttered.

'*Cela va sans dire*,' said Alix. She was going through a phase of working expressions to death. 'Malenkaia's getting fat; Mr Bruce gave her a Scottish kind of look the other day and called her a pamperrrred voluptuarrrry. I think that's horrid, but when I go to stay with Natalia on Apothecary Island I might take her so that she could run about a bit. Then if Maman lets us take her to Brittany with us, she can run for miles—'

Mother said, 'Yet this story doesn't depress me as it would have a month ago—because *you* are governing Russia now.'

True enough. As Chairman of the Council of Ministers Peter Stolypin tried to transform the Russian autocracy into a constitutional monarchy. He gave the peasants land, and there is nothing like a sense of property to produce an instinct for public order, to give a business-like, purposeful energy. No money was spared to consolidate and increase what might well be called a new class created by him.

He had a desperate fight in order to get money for public education. The Czarina told Mother he didn't realise the danger of what he was doing, children might pick up the most foolish and revolting ideas. There was safety only in church schools, she said vehemently. Yet in May 1908, Uncle Peter managed to get a law passed giving all children primary education for four years. Large money grants were made available for this. It was the first great attempt to end the illiteracy of the Russian peasant, but Uncle Peter felt little triumph. 'Pray God it doesn't come too late,' he said. 'Land and literacy—those are the two essentials, but if we're too late—'

One can, of course, regard it from another angle. His reforms did not come too late; the 1914 war came too soon—that was Russia's tragedy.

And the man who achieved so much—was his mood one of satisfaction? He told Mother one day that his strongest feeling was one of fear, not fear for his own fate—he was convinced he would die by violence—but fear that he would die before he could carry out his work of saving Russia.

I remember him saying this. It was August 1906. He had come to say goodbye to Grandfather, leaving next day for France. We were to follow him a week later. Alix and I were out on the balcony, watching a remarkably fine sunset.

I heard what Stolypin said, but Alix didn't—she was saying goodbye to Malenkaia for the dozenth time; it had been thought more convenient for Grandfather to take the dachshund with him.

'Isn't Uncle Peter marvellous? I'm sure he invited me to spend Saturday with Natalia because he knows I'll be missing my angel—and Grandfather, of course!' she added hastily. Still rather embarrassed by the puppy's precedence, she began to talk hurriedly of the sunset. As a matter of fact, the sunset that evening *was* glorious. There was a blazing glow of piled-up red and gold clouds, with delicate rose-coloured streaks as if flocks of pink flamingoes were streaming across the sky.

Beneath us in the changing, splendid light, Petersburg glowed with rich colour. Behind us Peter Stolypin talked of violent death. Beside me Alix's clear voice said, 'Oh, hurry up, Saturday! Hurry, hurry up!'

16

'Ne criez pas!'

THAT SATURDAY in mid-August the weather was lovely enough in Petersburg itself; it would be glorious in the summer villa on the island in the estuary with its beautiful garden, and the dense foliage reflected in the clear surface of the river. I envied Alix at Natalia's party. Still, I was immensely proud that Mother had chosen me to escort her in her last-minute shopping.

We were coming out of Fabergé's, where Mother had bought a cigarette-case for Uncle Raoul; it was between half-past two and three o'clock in the afternoon. We had come out between the shop's huge granite pillars when we heard what we thought was the sound of a distant gun. Mother stopped with one foot on the carriage step and said to the manager who had escorted us, 'Did you hear that? What was it?'

Yes, he had heard it. It was probably routine military practice near the powder magazines.

It was a lovely day. The sun poured down. No one was worried.

It was too fine to go back home immediately, Mother said. She dismissed the carriage on a sudden impulse, said we would stroll along the pink granite quays, and then I could have an ice or some cakes at a restaurant. Yes, I could choose the restaurant for myself.

'Can we go to the Peasant Shop first, please? Alix wants some wooden toys for presents.'

So we bought quaint wooden toys and some lacquer boxes to put them in, and then at Eliseiev's Café Mother, suddenly gay, said, 'Andrei, it will cause many raised eyebrows, but I'll bring the two of you out for a celebration dinner tonight. Where would you like to come?'

It was a problem. Alix, I imagined, would think it dashing beyond words to go to the Medved and eat at a table under the trees, with Goulesco's Roumanian gipsy band playing. I should prefer the Europa, where one dined on the roof in summer and swifts whistled through the air as they did in Venice.

Basely I said, 'Do you think Alix will feel up to coming out tonight? After the party, I mean—'

Mother laughed. 'After the way you're wolfing cream tarts I can't see you being in a much better case. Anyhow, think about it, darling; we've hours yet—'

'Why,' I said, 'there's Mr Bruce!'

She had her back to the door, and the place was noisy. 'Druce?' she said bewilderedly. 'No, we needn't go to Druce's, darling—I don't think Grandmère really wants English soap or clothes.'

'No, Mother. It's Mr Bruce. I—I think he's looking for us.'

'Oh, not some stupid little complication at this last moment!' said Mother, turning.

Her expression did not change, but her face grew almost as white as her dress. No, whatever the cause of his search, it was not a petty thing; his expression told us that.

'Princess,' he said quickly. 'Will you come home, please?'

She said in a whisper, 'That noise—just before three o'clock. Was it an explosion?' She spoke as if there were a stiffness about her mouth.

'Yes.'

'On the island—on Apothecary Island? I should have known,' said Mother with sudden dreadful stony calm. 'Oh, quickly, let's go there.'

'We don't know anything definite—simply that an attempt has been made on M. Stolypin's life.'

'*Alix?*'

'We simply don't know. Part of the villa has been damaged, they say.'

'Quickly,' said Mother.

'I've brought the motor,' said Mr Bruce.

'Andrei must go back home in the carriage.'

I caught her hand tightly. 'No, Maman, you must let me come with you. Grandfather's not here now, and—and I know what to expect. I have seen all this before—'

'My poor one,' she said, a single tear rolling down her cheek. After a moment she whispered, 'But it was winter then.'

'Without the snow,' I stammered wildly, stupidly, 'it won't be—so bad. And, to be selfish, if someone tried to kill Uncle Peter, that shouldn't mean Alix was in danger. She'd be playing with Natalia, she wouldn't be with Uncle Peter, as Father—Father was with the Grand Duke.'

I had to stop then, for on that blazing afternoon my teeth were chattering. And Mother turned her pale face to me, her eyes the only things alive in that face, and said, 'Oh, no, Andrei. The terrorists discriminate between rich and poor, powerful and weak no more than a mad dog would do.' After this she was silent, not a muscle moving in her face but her hands—oh, God, there was movement enough in those hands that, without any volition on her part, slowly but methodically tore her white kid gloves to shreds.

God knows why we had all dismissed the sound of the explosion so lightly. It had carried loudly enough on the still summer air, and the force of it had shattered all the window-panes in the houses on the opposite shore. The trees along the bank of the Neva were uprooted.

There was a police cordon. They tried to stop us. 'You must let us through,' began Mr Bruce. 'This is Princess—'

But Mother merely said, 'I am the mother of a child in that house. You cannot stop me,' and it was her voice that made them draw back, saluting.

Just behind us near the great Red Cross motors, came the noise of a scuffle.

'Your pardon,' said the police sergeant awkwardly. 'A foreign reporter—trying to slip in with your party.'

Mother turned for a moment to gaze incuriously at the would-be intruder. 'But you should let him in,' she said in a high, remote voice. 'Encourage him to take photographs. Let him see what I expect to see —the shattered body of my child. Let him in! I want the world to know what the heroic freedom-fighters have done—they're killing the children now!'

Once you left the quay you stepped into a nightmare mist, for the dust of the explosion still hung upon the air, and through the fog stumbled the blurred, seeking figures of stretcher-bearers.

One came to the stretch of roadway immediately before the entrance. There lay a shapeless mass of wood and twisted iron, the remnants of a carriage—a landau—and the pitiful wreckage of the two horses that had drawn it.

The front wall of the house had fallen, exposing to view the large vestibule and the little reception room we had come to know so well. The ceilings of both these rooms had crashed in and had carried with them the furniture of the two rooms above.

These were the rooms where Natalia and her friends would be playing, there or on the little wooden balcony. Now they were beams, and wreckage, and people lying buried beneath them. We could hear moans, cries for help.

Mother fell on her knees, tore at the heap of plaster and splinters. She had not seen two little heaps covered with a stained tablecloth, a tattered counterpane, but Mr Bruce had, and he went quickly across to raise the bloodsoaked material, and stare down for a moment.

'Alix?' I whispered with a sob.

'No,' he said. 'The two nurses. Dead, of course.'

'The nurses? But they were big women—those heaps are so small,' and then I crouched beside Mother in silence, mindlessly burrowing and tearing at the débris.

With Grandfather thousands of miles away, only Uncle Peter's voice could have roused me. He was telling me that Alix was alive.

It took longer for his voice to penetrate Mother's stunned consciousness. She kept repeating, 'I don't believe you. You are only saying this to be kind. I don't need kindness. I schooled myself to do without it when Alesha died—'

'Avoye, I swear to you that she is alive. Look at me . . . You have heart and mind enough to know when a lie is being told.'

She raised her head slowly, looked up and then, incredibly, laughed. 'Oh, Peter, Peter!' she said. 'You're all covered with ink!'

He was indeed, forehead, neck, back of head all smeared. 'I was at my desk,' he said. 'I was thrown to the floor, and the inkpot fell on me. I suppose I had better wash.'

He helped Mother to her feet. 'Natalia?' she asked. 'And your little one? Are they both safe?'

'I found the boy myself, in that very pile of débris before you. We'd found Natalia fifteen minutes before.' He hesitated for a moment. 'Both legs and feet are crushed: she's suffering badly. We're waiting for Doctor Pavlov. He may give us better news; the doctors who've already seen her talk of amputation.'

A high-ranking police officer escorted us to the neighbour's house where Alix had been taken. He told us as many details as he knew. Saturday was Uncle Peter's reception-day, and despite frequent warnings of assassination plots, he insisted on being accessible to the public —with as little formality as possible. Anyone could come without invitation or credentials, anyone who needed help. Callers did not have to identify themselves—'It will have to be different in future.'

There were a few policemen on duty in the hall, and in the ante-room sat General Zamiatine and other ministry officials taking the names of the arrivals and asking why they had come. Next the callers were allowed into the official waiting-room adjoining Uncle Peter's study, running at right angles, and adjoining the garden. On the floor above were the children's rooms.

Nothing now remained of the first three rooms.

People had begun to arrive at two o'clock. Within half an hour there were about forty sitting in the official waiting-room, and others passing through the hall and the ante-room. All kinds of people, from high officials to widows of employees in search of help, and peasants sent by their communes to lay their needs before the Minister. There was one very pretty young woman, whose husband, some kind of working-man, had been killed two months before. She was expecting a baby soon. She had been telling people about it, laughing and crying there in the outer hall, when the assassins arrived. Yes, they could not have missed seeing her, or her condition. If it came to that they could not have missed seeing the girls on the balcony above, and the little boy, four or five years old, peering over the parapet.

They had come at half-past two in a hired landau. They wore uniform—everyone was so shocked and confused it could not be said with certainty whether they were disguised as soldiers or police. They ran up the steps and into the hall. The officer on duty there must have seen something suspicious, for he stopped them at the door into the room where names and particulars were taken. At this one of them threw on to the marble floor the portfolio he was carrying; it was packed with bombs.

All the people in the hall were killed outright, together with the terrorists, who were never identified. There were heavy casualties in the second room, and in the next one-third of the occupants were killed and the rest injured. These three rooms, together with those above, were, as we had seen, completely shattered; the rest of the building was standing because it was a wooden house, and therefore the framework was more elastic than stone would have been.

The door between the writing-room and Uncle Peter's study had been blown off its hinges and he, talking to a caller, was thrown to the ground, but escaped with bruises.

As far as they knew, twenty-five people had been killed and thirty badly injured. Most of them were poor petitioners. The young woman expecting a child—the police officer hesitated for a moment then said clumsily, 'She was only a few feet away from the bombs, you see.'

Alix lay on a sofa, still unconscious, seemingly uninjured except for the great bruise on her forehead, though strange, ugly noises came from her mouth. Beyond was a bedroom where the other two children had been taken; one could hear the little boy whimpering like a hurt puppy, but Natalia's stifled cries brought the sweat out on your forehead.

Mother turned to me. 'I'll stay here until Doctor Pavlov comes. Find Mr Bruce, my darling, and ask him to take you home; then, if he'll be good enough to come back, I'll have had Doctor Pavlov's verdict, and he can telegraph Grandfather.'

In the event Mr Bruce sent two telegrams. Grandfather showed me them silently seven years later.

The first was dictated by Mother that evening.

'Alix hurt, but not dangerously, thank God. Our journey will have to be postponed for a time.'

The second was sent the following morning.

'On M. Stolypin's authority, I beg you to come immediately, monseigneur. The injuries are worse than the Princess believes.'

There are certain internal injuries not immediately discernible to even the most gifted doctor, I suppose, though I myself think that Doctor Pavlov realised soon enough what was wrong, but compassionately did not break the news to Mother until her parents were with her.

Her first reaction, Grandfather told me later, was to ask tonelessly, 'When?'

'She might live for some months, until the spring.'

'I must take her away from here,' said Mother. 'I don't want her to die in Russia. Can I take her to France? We were going to France.'

The doctor explained gently that such a journey was impossible.

'I don't want her to die in the cold,' said Mother desolately.

Grandfather, almost unable to bear the glance of the great empty dark eyes, had an inspiration.

'My dear,' he said, 'it should be possible to take her to the Crimea. A special carriage attached to the train—'

Mother said, 'Oh, yes, yes! Let her have the sun and flowers, some kindness and warmth from this horrible country.'

The Imperial Family came to stay at Livadia, and visited us frequently. The Czarina sat for hours beside Alix's bed—Alix, of course, was her godchild—and after the last visit she went away with tears pouring down her cheeks. Olga was very good, prattling endlessly about her baby brother. 'We might have had a baby brother, too,' whispered Alix. 'I wish we had—it would have helped Maman.'

A few hours before Alix's death, Grandfather received a telegram which brought him searching for me. Mr Bruce and I were to take the carriage to Sebastopol and wait there for Father le Guerric.

I gazed at him in bewilderment. 'Father le Guerric? From the village?'

'Yes, and don't ask me how he's managing to turn up in the Crimea; bar his time at the seminary he's never been out of Brittany. If your Uncle Raoul hadn't seen the saintly imbecile blundering about the railway station in Paris he'd as like as not been in Constantinople by this time. But he's due to arrive on the morning train, so off you go to get him.'

And there he stood, screwing up his short-sighted eyes in the strong sunshine, a little crumpled figure. No doubt St Francis had not looked more impressive. In his arms he clasped Malenkaia.

Our wonder seemed to surprise him. Had we not expected him long before Uncle Raoul's telegram? But of course he had planned to come from the moment he had heard the dreadful news, and if the thought hadn't entered his head, his people would have given him no peace until he was on his way—once they'd raised the money, of course. That had taken some time, for it was quite a long way, wasn't it? The Marquis had shouted at him at the railway station in Paris, 'But, *mon père*, why didn't you *ask*?' But for once the Marquis wasn't being very intelligent, though, of course, he'd understood later, and apologised. The people had to do this themselves, send their priest to Mademoiselle Avoye, who had such great need of him. He'd had to obtain permission from the Bishop, of course, but Monseigneur, it scarcely needed saying, saw the point at once, and was arranging that the parish should be looked after during his absence. He would stay as long as Mademoiselle had need of him—the people insisted on this. And he had brought flowers from Mademoiselle's old garden, and some sea pinks, which he had first put before the statue of Our Lady.

Grandfather had timed the moment of our arrival, and had persuaded Mother to come out on to the terrace to take the air. So she was there when we arrived, and I caught the first words after the look of incredulous joy, the quick rush down the steps like a girl, the kissing of the old worn hand, 'Oh, *mon père, mon père*, I wanted to take her home, but now you've brought home to me!' And then, at last, after months of anguish, the flood of saving tears.

Grandfather drew me away then, but when, half an hour later, he and Grandmère went to greet Father le Guerric, they, too, knelt to kiss the hand of the old priest as if he were a prince of the Church.

Alix, aged twelve, had for months been afraid to admit that Father was dead. Now, opening her eyes, she smiled in greeting, and whispered, 'I am glad you have come to help me, *mon père*, help me to die—does that sound silly, but you know what I mean, don't you?—I wish I were cleverer and not so young—I can't say things very well.'

There was a choking sob—from Mr Bruce, of all people. Alix gave him the ghost of her old mischievous look. '*Ne criez pas; j'ai promis pour vous*,' she quoted. 'That's what Mary Queen of Scots said, wasn't it? There! I did remember some of your lessons, so I wasn't such an un—unrewarding pupil, was I?' But she was all gravity when she turned again to Father le Guerric. 'I'm not afraid,' she said simply. 'Papa's there, waiting for me. Maman and I have talked about it. He went just a little way ahead, and he's waiting. He always used to do that when we had a difficult journey to make—he'd go ahead to—to make things easy for us, and then he'd be waiting for us. Maman said she always used to laugh—he was so tall, and he'd take my hand and—and how did you put it, Maman?'

'He would—restrain his long stride, my darling,' said Mother, as steady as God's mercy.

'Yes, that's it, because I could take only little steps, and they weren't very sure, but there'd be Papa's hand, so strong, to hold on to.'

I clung to this picture—Father waiting, hand outstretched—a few hours later amid the terrible finality of the Church's farewell to one of her children. 'Go forth, O Christian soul, out of this world, in the name of God the Father who created thee, in the name of God the Son who suffered for thee—'

Within minutes Alix would be dead. It couldn't happen. Not to Alix. Even though in the past months I'd heard so often whispers of the one word, constantly recurrent, 'Tragic—' I still couldn't relate it to Alix. 'Tragic' didn't mean Alix, my sister, who read E. Nesbit books and spoiled Malenkaia the dachshund so horribly; the nearest Alix got to tragedy was when she had borrowed Grandmother's black velvet dress to be Mary Queen of Scots.

She was half-lying, half-sitting in Mother's arms. Mother knelt beside her, had been kneeling beside her for hours. I knelt on the other side of the bed.

'—When your soul shall leave your body—'

I cried out then, I think, and my sister put out a hand to me, and, God forgive me, *I* clung to her for strength.

'—may angels in their splendour come to welcome you—'

'No,' came the whispered, loving heresy. 'Just Papa.'

'May the Apostles rise from their twelve thrones to meet you; may the triumphant army of martyrs give you greeting—'

'Dear God, just Papa, please. All those people would frighten me.'

'—May Mary the Virgin, Mother of God, kind comforter of all in distress, be to you at this moment a true mother—'

'Ah, *yes*! Until you come too, Maman—Now kiss me—'

Mother kissed her. Alix said, 'She will be like you, I think—God won't think that wicked,' and then her head dropped on Mother's breast.

Mother went on holding her in her arms. After a time she said steadily, 'Will you take Andrei out, Mr Bruce? He should try to sleep now.'

I kissed Alix's forehead, Mother's hand. They gave me a sedative, and Mr Bruce put me to bed. At some time he carried in Malenkaia, and put her, whimpering, beside me. I clung to the warm, trembling little body, and eventually went to sleep. I don't know when they persuaded Mother to leave Alix.

I wish I could end it there, but before we left the Crimea the future touched and tarnished our grief.

It was the day of final farewell. In the house Father le Guerric had read his own valediction:

'To every thing there is a season, and a time to every purpose under the heaven: a time to be born, and a time to die; a time to plant, and a time to pluck up that which is planted.'

The Czar and Czarina with Olga were already in the church; they had entered the side chapel by another door. When the little coffin was carried out, they took their places behind Mother, walking between her parents, the Czarina for once waiving formality. And behind them Olga walked with me.

'Of course I had to come,' she said simply. 'I promised Alix the last time I saw her I'd stay with you.'

The village people had strewn the road with green boughs and pink and white roses, and now they followed us, carrying white jasmine, great bunches of magnolia, branches of cherry blossom. White doves, so tame that they could scarcely take the trouble to get out of our way, fluttered up about us to perch, cooing, in the trees. But I really had eyes for no one and nothing but Mother, walking with a firm step, ramrod in her spine. Mother—what had they called her once?—the charming, feckless little French girl, now all the Roman, her face the waxen pallor of a lily, blue shadows under the great dark eyes, dry-eyed, still not beaten down by sorrow and horror. Her hands were clasped, and between the delicate fingers was a faded posy of Breton flowers.

'Father says,' Olga whispered suddenly, 'that your mother and my Aunt Elizabeth are the two bravest people he knows.'

'That is what I think, too,' I agreed.

'Mamma says that if I cry for Alix I am only being selfish and sorry for myself because I shall miss her so much.'

'She's not being hurt now,' I said, keeping my eyes fixed on Mother. 'It was always bad, but worse when the doctors came, because they had to hurt her.'

'Mamma said it must have helped your mother a great deal, though, knowing how the people in her village loved her so much that they sent their priest here. Mamma says that's the thing that always helps most—knowing how much the people love you.'

'Yes.'

'Mamma did say, though, that it was a pity *your* Mamma is a Roman Catholic, because if only she had belonged to our Church she would have believed that the Holy Man could do so much for her—' And then she flushed and said hurriedly, 'But she said I wasn't to talk to anyone about him, because people wouldn't appreciate his holiness and value.'

'No Holy Man—whoever he might be—could do more than Père le Guerric has done!' I flared.

'I know,' said Olga quickly. Eager to change the subject, she said, 'I hope Alix can see how everyone loves her—all the lovely roses, and people crying, and the—the tenderness.'

Ashamed of my spurt of anger, I said sincerely, 'It would be exactly the same if *you* died!'

'I hope so,' said Olga seriously. 'I hope I die in the spring or summer. One has such a *pretty* funeral in summer.'

Let us leave it there. Let me think only of Alix, kissed as she was gently laid to rest, the faded flowers in her hands now, the hands lovingly folded in prayer, and above her a stone with the simple inscription, 'Here lies Alexandra Hamilton, an innocent being who died young.' And beneath: 'It is impossible but that offences will come: but woe unto him, through whom they come! It were better for him that a millstone were hanged about his neck, and he be cast into the sea, than that he should offend one of these little ones.'

Three days later we set out for France, travelling by sea as far as Venice. And at last we were among the sudden little hills, and the bent trees and the grey stones of church and village and château. Uncle Raoul had some leave, and took me riding along the sand before breakfast, so early, in fact, that we had time to go to Mass before returning home.

I told him how Father le Guerric had helped Mother, asked him if he could identify for me what the Father had said about a time to die.

'Odd,' said Uncle Raoul. 'I wonder why he chose that—wonderfully fitting, of course, but rather out of the way.' And he went on quoting, '*A time to embrace, and a time to refrain from embracing—a time to love, and a time to hate; a time of war and a time of peace—I said in mine heart, God shall judge the righteous and the wicked—*'

At breakfast he described how he had seen Father le Guerric at the railway station in Paris, and Mother, wonderfully, laughed. But the thought of that meek, shabby figure, starting off on that tremendous journey had a healing power all of its own. '*No* one could have done more!' I said, struck with a sudden memory. '*No* one!'

Grandfather said in stern reproof, 'Has anyone suggested that?'

I said, flushing, 'Olga told me her mother had suggested it, but then she wanted it forgotten. The Czarina had talked about a Holy Man, and what a pity Mother's a Catholic because otherwise he could have helped her—'

'My God, no!' said Mother with sudden violence.

'My dear child!' cried Grandmère, hurrying to bend over her. 'What is wrong?'

Mother was silent for a moment; I had a strange but strong impression that she would say she could not understand what I was talking about, but then she seemed to reach a decision, and said, 'The Czarina made the same suggestion to Peter Stolypin, about Natalia.'

'But, although belonging to her church, he refused!' said Uncle Raoul, his straight brows bent in a frown.

'How do you know he refused?' Mother asked quickly.

'If he'd accepted, if the man had been of any use, he'd have told you, of course, and you would have accepted the man's help. Who is he, Avoye?'

Still the odd, uncharacteristic reluctance to answer freely and fully, especially uncharacteristic because she was with those dearest and closest in the world to her. Neither was my presence the reason. One of her exceptional qualities was that she never treated me as if I belonged to another generation; there was a complete understanding between us.

Now she merely said after a moment, 'I haven't met him.'

'Has Peter Stolypin?' Grandfather asked suddenly.

Mother said carefully, 'When the Czarina made the suggestion, Peter'd only heard of—this man. He met him a few weeks later.'

'And?'

'He was repelled. He actually called him vermin.'

'Because he was dirty?' I asked.

'Yes, but—there was more to it than that. The man tried to hypnotise Peter.'

'Hypnotise Peter Stolypin—Stolypin of the iron will!' Grandfather roared with laughter. 'What a fool!'

The soft Breton sunshine, so different from the sunshine of the Crimea, flooded the little room where we had breakfast. Mother stood up suddenly, and went to stand before Grandfather. 'Peter was more scared than I've ever seen him in all my life,' she said simply.

'Peter Stolypin afraid—and showing it! Incredible!'

'Peter said, *He's dangerous—he must go.* But the Czarina won't allow it, of course.'

'Well,' said Grandfather easily, 'what's the name of the latest of this pitiable procession of fakes and impostors who've fooled an over-credulous woman?'

'His name is Gregory. I don't know much. Peter said, "If you are commanded to Czarskoe so that he can meet you there, there is nothing to be done, but as your friend, and Alesha's friend, I command you—

and I deliberately choose the verb—never to receive him into your own home, and never to be left alone with him." That is all I know—except that the man comes from Siberia. Peter wouldn't tell me anything else.'

'But,' said her brother, 'you've heard stories?'

'Which I prefer not to believe,' said Mother. 'And all the coffee's cold, and the rolls aren't much better! Andrei, what are you going to do when your lessons have finished for the day?'

Grandfather knew what he was going to do the moment he left the breakfast table—he was going to write to Peter Stolypin asking about the new insanity at that Byzantine madhouse of a court, and get the letter taken by a French attaché returning to the Petersburg embassy. The reply—if Stolypin were to answer frankly—must come the same way.

The reply came within a month. Grandfather showed it to me years later, when I was twenty and staying in Paris in May 1914. Picture me, then, sitting surrounded by the clean, living scent of limes and lilacs and reading what a dead man had written—of the beginning of an evil which at that time was still only too much alive.

'The person known to the Imperial Family as the New Man, the Holy Man, or, more lately, Our Friend, is Gregory Efimovitch, a Siberian peasant about forty years old from Pokrovskoe, near Tobolsk. His face is coarse and pock-marked, his hair is long and unkempt, as is his beard. His eyes are small, of a curious light colour. His voice is loud, harsh—a typical peasant's voice. But he can be the most dangerous and unwholesome influence in all Russia today. I am not afraid of the terrorists; I fear what this animal may do.

'He came from Siberia with the reputation of working miracles, and soon became a tremendous success with bored society women. They were convinced God revealed himself in the Siberiak, they awaited his appearance in a kind of suffocating, hysterical excitement, received his kisses as a religious experience.

'Monsieur le Duc, Avoye, you say, has told you how this foul wretch tried to hypnotise me. It was almost laughable. The small, furtive eyes in the great coarse face—ah, it was grotesque. But, my God, monsieur, picture the corrupting influence of the same process directed at an impressionable, suggestible woman.

'Of his influence at Czarskoe I can say little definitely. It is as if there is a conspiracy of silence among the Imperial Family—never to mention him beyond their own little circle. You will remember that when the

Grand Duchess Olga spoke of him to Andrei, she added that the children were told never to speak of him to outsiders. All that I am certain of is this; that he was first summoned to the Palace when the Heir was ill, and was brought to a side entrance. The children's nurse brought him secretly up the back stair. The Heir's health improved, since when the Siberiak greets the Czar and Czarina with smacking kisses, and *she*, God help us, kisses his dirty hand. She is convinced that here is the new friend and protector foretold by the charlatan Philippe Vachot before he was kicked out of Russia; he will even be of more assistance than Philippe, for he is a genuine Russian, a peasant, sent from God to interpret the wishes of the people to the Czar.

'I speak of him as an evil and foul thing. You might argue, "Now, Peter Stolypin, you've said yourself that the man is a typical peasant —isn't this the heart of the matter? What you might describe as shocking behaviour may be perfectly natural and acceptable ' to the man's own people." But it is not. To the Imperial Family, he is the man of God; to the peasants of his own village, he is Rasputin—best translated, perhaps, as the debauchee.

'I have been told that he is a close friend of the Tibetan quack doctor Badmaev. Whether this has any bearing on the "miraculous cures" I cannot say.'

And there was a postscript.

'I think you will understand the significance of what I write now. When the Czarina—with uncharacteristic animation—suggested this man of God should see my child, I refused, of course; immediately the unfamiliar friendliness vanished, and I was dismissed with the comment, "Others will have more affection for their children." I went straight from Czarskoe to Avoye's home; not knowing at the time how she, still stupefied with shock, would react to the Czarina's suggestion, I took it upon myself to order her servants never to admit the Siberiak into the house. I expected some difficulty here, but, on the contrary, after I had said only a sentence or two the old butler crossed himself, and then interrupted me in the most respectful and earnest manner. I reproduce his exact words. "No need to give us warning, sir, though Christ and His Mother bless you for doing it. We've heard of this Siberiak and how at Czarskoe Selo he's governing her that governs him who in name governs us all, God help us, and I guessed *she'd* try to send him here." Then he looked me straight in the eyes, and said, "Don't worry, sir, he shan't see the mistress. More. I don't know what you've been told about him, but every soul in the household knows what to do if he ever crosses the threshold—no refreshment of any kind to be offered to him, and he's not going to have any chance of touching anything belonging personally to the mistress or the little ones. Not that they needed any telling from me."

'Monsieur le Duc, every Russian peasant knows about witchcraft.'

17

'God has forsaken me'

GRANDFATHER NEVER showed the letter to his wife but at the first opportunity he gave it to his son to read.

'No!' said Uncle Raoul. 'This is the twentieth century. Motor-cars and planes and telephones don't go with witchcraft.'

Grandfather stood silent for a moment. Then he asked, 'Do you believe in the Devil?'

'Of course, what else can one do as a Christian? If one believes in absolute goodness—God—one must also believe in absolute evil.'

'For which reason I say we must never dismiss all this as absurd rubbish.'

'Have you talked to Avoye?'

'For only a moment. She said she would prefer to tell us together.'

'She could have done that when Andrei let the cat out of the bag.'

'But she didn't. Evasion's so foreign to her nature that I immediately suspected something shocking. But she'll tell us tonight, when your mother and the children—Oh, my God!' said Grandfather, 'still one talks of *the children*!'

Later on, in the library, when Grandmère dozed fitfully and I slept heavily upstairs, Mother at last talked freely.

She said, 'You must let me explain things in my own way, Papa, even if I do it badly. You see, it's the first time I've spoken of certain matters —except to Peter Stolypin, and he knew so much he could interpret what I was saying.

'First, the background. You don't know Czarskoe very well, do you? The town itself is little, dim, provincial. There's no distinction about it—'

'Forgive me for interrupting,' said Grandfather, 'but that's only fitting. I think the most striking feature of the Imperial Court at present is the complete lack of distinction in its setting—pictures, furniture, all redolent of Victorian England—and in its courtiers. All is humdrum, ordinary. Not for a moment does it strike anyone as the court of a nation with any culture, for no man of distinction is ever invited there. This, of course, is what Alesha used to say, and how you would flail him with your tongue!'

'I hadn't grown up properly then, I saw everything in terms of personalities. I'm still sorry for *her*—even more sorry than I was three years ago—but I'm still more sorry for Russia. Dear God, Papa, if you knew the atmosphere at Czarskoe! All dampness, dimness, clutter, muted colours (chiefly mauve), drawn curtains, shut windows, a kind of old-fashioned sickroom atmosphere—fresh air's unhealthy, so keep it out, let the air always be stuffy, let all sounds from the outer world be muffled! Papa, you leave the Palace and in winter the air's crisp, exciting, in summer the sun is glowing, but there's never any clear, fresh atmosphere in the court itself. Just this clogging mixture of sick-room and hothouse.'

She hesitated then, not knowing what to say next. Grandfather helped her. He went across and put his arm about her. 'It *is* a sickroom now, isn't it?' he said. '*Bolezn Gessenskikh.*'

Mother's hand was at her mouth. 'How did you know?' she whispered.

Grandfather poured himself cognac. 'On the day this reign began, I talked to an elderly Russian general whose name I never knew. He first mentioned the term, although I think all his anxieties were about the effects on the women of the family, the hysteria, the way in which they repel and estrange all who don't blindly accept their domination and prejudice. Later on I went into the matter myself, and found that males of the family were afflicted in a different way. The Czarina had a brother—and there are the sons of the sister who married the German Emperor's brother. So it's come out in the Heir, has it? Already?' There was silence, then Uncle Raoul said, 'And after it seemed as if the miracle had happened at last!'

'The birth of a son had always spelt *security* for her,' said Mother slowly. 'She used to keep saying to me that the Czar wasn't strong. Once, when they were in the Crimea, he was so ill with typhoid that the whole Imperial Family met together and decided that in the event of his death, his brother Michael would be proclaimed Czar, even though the Czarina was actually expecting a child at the time. She's never forgotten this. She knew that she was so unpopular she might very well be asked to leave Russia. She's hated Michael ever since. And therefore the birth of a son, you see, meant security to her at last, whereas—Oh, God help us,' cried Mother, tears suddenly rolling unchecked down her cheeks, 'it may be the last blow as far as the monarchy is concerned. They were wild with delight; there were all the disasters in Manchuria, but *this* was far more important. And he was such a beautiful baby, Papa, the finest child in the world, it seemed, blue-eyed, sweet-tempered—'

'How long before they suspected he was a haemophiliac?' asked Grandfather curtly.

'About six weeks after the christening.'

'Poor devils,' said Uncle Raoul. 'It's a thinness of the blood, isn't it, preventing clotting?'

'Yes,' said Mother. 'So—one bleeds to death. The veins are brittle, too. The slightest knock—which doesn't even mark the skin, can set up an internal swelling, and most agonising pain. And there is no cure.'

'Poor devils,' said Uncle Raoul again.

'It is, of course, worse for her,' said Mother. 'I'm not thinking of security of position now—she adores the child, he's her life, and she knows he's inherited from her the disease that's going to kill him one day and will give him untold agony before that.'

Uncle Raoul stubbed out his cigarette and went to stare out of the window. 'Of course,' he said softly. 'Women don't get the bleeding sickness, but only they can pass it on. My God, what a tragedy!'

Mother sat with her hands covering her eyes. 'My dear,' said Grandfather gently, 'we know that this is all most difficult and painful, and now, I think, you're reaching the hardest part of all, but having come so far, you must go on.'

'I was thinking of the Czar,' said Mother. 'One day I couldn't bear the stuffiness any longer, and I made an excuse and went out into the park to look at the lilac. It was just after lunch—you know the Czar always takes a walk then—and I met him. He said to me, "I have been thinking of Alesha, Avoye." And then I was even more *bouleversée* because he went on with that mixture of—of simplicity and weakness that can be so terrifying, "He used to tell me of his plans for Andrei. Next year he shall have a pony—a bicycle. In ten years the Army— When I look at my boy I dare not plan ahead for him for the next twenty-four hours." But that was not as dreadful to hear as what the

Czarina had said before I came out. She was beginning to think that God had deserted her, you see. She said to me, "I've often felt myself to be abandoned by the world, but now I think that God Himself has forsaken me." I said no, never that, and she must never give up hope. Surely there were doctors—"Doctors!" she sobbed. "I know doctors! Surrounded by doctors my mother died, my sister! If I believed in doctors I should believe my child's death is inevitable, but I won't believe it, I can't believe it! God is just—He wouldn't abandon me like this, play with me like a cat playing with a mouse, making me think all my prayers were answered, only to have *this*—this!"

'But even that was better than the look of frozen despair. She was like a drowning woman.'

'And then this Siberiak appeared,' said Grandfather.

'A drowning woman would clutch at any hand outstretched to help,' said Mother. 'A drowning woman would believe that any helper was sent by God.'

Her voice died away. Uncle Raoul prompted her gently, 'Who first brought him to the Czarina?'

She started. 'Anna Vyroubova. You don't know her, Papa, though Raoul has met her. Again, it's the—the awful lack of distinction about everything. She's the daughter of the Chief of the Imperial Chancery. She was a chubby, rosy-faced child with those wide eyes which are merely stupid when the owner grows older.'

'She *is* stupid,' said Uncle Raoul. 'Phenomenally so. A middle-class neurotic prig, delighting in gossip, a liar, full of self-pity. *Poor little me, poor little orphan me, adrift in the world,* she cries.'

Grandfather turned slowly to look at him. 'This is the first time I've ever heard of you talk of a woman in this way—'

'She's the most dangerous kind of fool, sir!'

'She was very ill once,' said Mother. 'The Czarina visited her at the turning point; Anna hailed the visit as her salvation and began this dog-like devotion—no, I'm wrong, not doglike, dogs are sensible, practical animals, and this awful sentimentality is so cloying, so—'

'Nevertheless,' said Grandfather grimly, 'I'm sure the Czarina wallows in it. It's just what she wants—completely uncritical, submissive.'

'A new kind of favourite!' said Uncle Raoul. 'You should see her, sir—stout, with a puffy, shiny face, not an ounce of charm. Stupid, yet crafty and sly. Appallingly dressed—'

Again Grandfather stared at him. '*You* to start talking about women's clothes!'

'It's the pose of humility I can't endure. She dresses badly to exhibit the poverty she's always talking about.'

Mother said. 'She wears only one evening dress—to show how poor she is, to gain sympathy. She doesn't get sympathy because the dress is so incredibly ugly it antagonises anyone who sees it. It's a dreadful kind of tomato-red plush. The first time Andrei saw her it was at a children's party, and he said quite seriously to me, "Who's the lady who looks like an over-stuffed armchair?" '

Grandfather and Uncle Raoul exploded into laughter. Mother said, 'It was cruel but terribly accurate.'

Grandfather wiped his eyes. 'Out of the mouths of babes and sucklings—' he said.

'She has a little cottage not far from the Palace at Czarskoe. The Czarina goes there every day. It's a primitive little place, terribly cold because the house has no proper foundations. And it's here that the affairs of Russia are decided. "Such a long talk!" says Anna. "And the floor's so cold that we have to sit drinking tea with our legs drawn up!" '

'How are the mighty fallen!' said Grandfather. 'My God, it does offend one's sense of good taste! Do you mean that it's here the Siberiak meets the Czarina?'

'Nearly always. He's not often at the Palace itself—it would be quite impossible to keep his visits secret. Also—'

'Out with it, child!'

'I don't think he's won over the Czar as yet.'

'Then why in the name of sanity does he permit this obscene charade to continue?'

Uncle Raoul spoke from the shadows. 'He will have to act. He's not completely lacking in intelligence.'

'No, but he's utterly lacking in strength of purpose. Do you realise that the only time he ever asserted himself, made an independent decision and stuck to it, was when he stood out against his parents and insisted on marrying the woman of his choice? It's as if in that one action he exhausted all his reserves of will-power.'

'Are you scared, Avoye?' asked Uncle Raoul.

'Scared, Raoul? I don't know, but certainly I'm obsessed by it all. In such silly ways too. I sit in a train and we pass a German garden

166

where an old woman's knitting. And I think of all the strands going to make up one thread of wool, and there in the next house the kitchen door's open, it's a hot day, and I can see the cook measuring out ingredients for some kind of recipe or another, and I can't escape the same stupid thought, all the—the ingredients of the Czarina's character combining to bring us to this—'

'Catastrophe?' said Grandfather. 'It can't come to that! Even that mass of meek shiftiness who's her husband must resent his wife's domination by a scoundrel with the morals of an ape and the physical rankness of a goat—'

'But he won't act. As for her, I believe that now in her strange black and white world people's goodness or wickedness will be judged by their attitude towards this—this—'

'Let us be moderate, let us be calm, my child. Let us merely call him a faith-healer.'

'No, she thinks he's more than that, far more. She told me one day that he had been chosen by God to be a link between Him and humanity. I couldn't say anything, but my face must have been eloquent. She said, "So you've heard all the slanders about him—well even if they were true, didn't Christ Himself seek out sinners, weren't several of His disciples the dregs of the earth?" And then she flared out, as if she'd never set foot west of the frontier with Poland, "You Westerners! So—so *sanitary* in your religious ideas!" '

Grandfather began to say, 'That she should speak to you like that when—when Alix—'

'Papa,' said Mother quietly, 'she will have to endure far more than *I* had to. I knew what was going to happen to my darling, and God helped me to accept it. *She* can't accept the truth about her child. There's a dreadful alternation between hope and despair, and this will wear her down mentally and physically. She will tell herself feverishly that each new attack will be the last. She will make frantic plans for the boy's future—'

'Good God!' said Uncle Raoul. 'Do you mean she seriously envisages her son—this child with the frightful double legacy of an unworkable autocracy from his father and an incurable disease from his mother—she sees her son as the future Czar?'

'I think it will be the obsession of her life. You see, *he* must retrieve the situation, she said to me one day.'

'What situation?'

'His father broke his Coronation Oath. When he summoned the Duma, he was abandoning the charge given him by God. Alexei must inherit an autocracy untainted by—'

'A boy suffering from a killing disease!' exploded Grandfather. 'I've never heard such lunacy! The woman ought to be locked up!'

'Looking coldbloodedly at the whole situation, the child's illness will win a little sympathy for his mother—' Uncle Raoul was beginning, but Mother interrupted him.

'It's to be kept a secret. A state secret.'

'Lunacy piled upon lunacy!'

'Partly it's the Russian tradition. Didn't you know that officially all Czars are marvellously well—strong to the point of immortality—until they die? But chiefly it's this—this possessiveness of hers. Alexei is *her* child, his illness is *her* personal business, *her* private sorrow, and she'll fight like a tigress to keep it *hers* alone.'

There was a brief silence, and then Mother said, 'When we—originally planned to come to you last summer—'

'Yes, my dear one.'

'The day before—it happened—I went out to Czarskoe to take my official leave of the Czarina. The Czarevitch was well. He is a beautiful child, with magnificent blue eyes—they were shining with happiness, and he was laughing—Olga was playing with him. It seemed impossible that he should be suffering from an incurable disease that might carry him off at any moment. He played there in the sunny room, his mother watching him, and you could see her heart filling with hope. She actually said to me, "God has heard me. He has pitied my sorrow at last."

'This is where the danger lies, Papa. The pain and the prospect of death will recur. The miracle hasn't happened, after all. And so she turns to Rasputin. His prayers alone can save.

'Now that in itself is a thought terrifying enough, but I brought away with me another memory that scares. As I rose to go I said something about being glad to leave her looking so happy. Her expression changed then. She drew me to the window so that we were out of earshot and said, "I feel wicked to be so happy, Avoye. I mustn't let myself forget everything except private happiness." And then she began to talk very agitatedly. She realised the Czar's prestige was shattered—because he'd summoned the Duma. Because of her devotion to him—and to the baby Heir—*she* must begin to retrieve the fortunes of the dynasty, and take an active part in the work of government.

'I made the obvious reply. His Majesty had a most loyal body of ministers, one of whom, Peter Stolypin, was able enough to—

'She interrupted me impatiently. Couldn't I see that the government was betraying the monarchy to its enemies? *She* could—clearly enough —and she was doing her best to make the Czar share her indignation. She would remain firm, be absolutely relentless in her opposition to what was being attempted.

'I said in panic, "Oh, Your Majesty, the danger—"

'She replied, "There is only one possible opinion, and I'll hold fast to that no matter how unpopular it makes me in St Petersburg society. And one day, Avoye, the people will thank me for refusing to compromise, they'll thank me for having kept the Czar *steady*, for having opposed those who wanted to make him do the wrong thing, to be weak!"'

'All this doesn't bode well for Peter Stolypin, does it?' remarked Uncle Raoul.

18

Gala Performance

AND SO Peter Stolypin and all he stood for were in jeopardy. Not only did he 'betray' the monarchy because he loyally accepted the Constitution of 1905, and would not sabotage or over-ride it; he was to gain the Czarina's implacable enmity because he tried to rid the monarchy of the disease that was Rasputin.

It must suffice here to say that in 1908 we returned to Russia, that Mother was summoned back to be in attendance at Court, while I was occasionally invited to Czarskoe. By this time Petersburg was alive with rumours about the influence of the Siberiak over the Imperial Family, some of the vilest stories even an unhealthy, feverish mind could fabricate. Yet Mother never heard the Czarina speak of him again, and I never heard him mentioned by the children. He did not come merely to Vyroubova's little house now, he came by a side entrance into the Palace, to Alexei's bedroom, to bless the Grand Duchesses before they got into bed, to receive the Czarina's grateful kiss on his dirty hand, but if the capital seethed with stories of him, at the highest level on the surface it was as if he did not exist.

I was fourteen when we returned to Russia. The day before we left France, Grandfather told me about Rasputin. The Czarina was desperate because of Alexei's illness, couldn't judge people properly. 'He's an unpleasant individual,' said Grandfather, 'like the quack doctors you get at country fairs. He's also like an animal with unpleasing personal habits—very dirty ones. Avoid him in every possible way.'

'You say he's dirty, sir. Is he dangerous, too?'

'Not to you. He couldn't hurt you. But he could hurt Russia. Russia's a country convalescing after a bad sickness. She needs a sane doctor like Peter Stolypin—as I said, Rasputin's a quack.'

So forewarned I came to Czarskoe—and never saw Rasputin, never heard him mentioned—until one day when the four-year-old Alexei prattled something about a story of a legless rider and an eyeless rider.

'That's a Siberian story,' I said slowly. 'Who's been telling you Siberian stories?'

The little boy bit his lip, went red, turned away. Olga said, 'You used to tell us Siberian stories.'

'Not that one,' I said, and then, incredulously, 'That was almost a lie! *You* to tell an untruth!'

Her honest eyes filled with tears. 'Oh, no!' she said. 'It wasn't a lie.'

'It was. You tried to give me a false impression—you!' In the shock I forgot all Mother's quiet words of caution. 'It's that man, isn't it?' I said. 'The man you talked about at Alix's funeral. Would you tell lies to Alix too?'

She looked at me imploringly. 'I mustn't talk about him—don't make me, Andrei. Mamma has forbidden us to talk about him to anyone and—and—'

'And especially to me or my mother?' I finished angrily when her voice faltered.

She looked away and said in a muffled voice, 'She loves you both but she says that your mother is French and you're both Catholics and you'd never understand. Please don't make me say anything more, Andrei.'

When Mother and I were at home, I told her what had happened. 'I might have guessed,' she said. 'The Czarina has ordered her family not to mention his name. The chief courtiers are equally discreet, if they want to keep their places. Nobody likes the situation, but they either pretend it doesn't exist or are trying to win Rasputin's favour. Darling, don't mention him again, and don't quarrel with Olga. Apologise, if you can, but don't raise the subject.'

But we, of course, talked among ourselves—especially when Grandfather came to stay, and Uncle Peter dined with us.

Grandfather was always angrily incredulous that still the Czar did nothing. Uncle Peter said, 'If anyone speaks to him of the dangers of the situation, he cuts short the conversation with, "These are my private affairs, and they are nobody's concern but mine." '

'Spoken like a good well-trained parrot,' said Grandfather. 'And suppose a man is bold enough to persist?'

'It has been known to happen. Rasputin during his drunken bouts makes obscene boasts that, to say the least, discredit the monarchy. He is also beginning to meddle in affairs of state. He gives his favourites little notes of commendation to be taken to officials. There's a cross at the top, and then an illiterate scrawl, "My dear chap, fix it up for him [or, more frequently, her]. He [she] is all right. Gregory."

'I assure you that such things have been brought to His Majesty's notice.'

'And?'

'Useless, of course. He stubbornly maintains that these topics are unwarrantable intrusions into his private life. But let me add this. I believe he has tried to remonstrate with the Czarina and has met with such frenzy that he could never bear to have such a scene again—better to tolerate Rasputin.'

'I believe that, too,' said Mother. 'Someone heard her screaming. She said he was a father who did not care if his son died. And one old general who was a friend of his father told me *he* tried to broach the subject again just after this had happened. The Czar was at breaking point. He said, "I prefer five Gregorys to one hysterical woman!" and walked away.'

'You know,' said Uncle Peter, 'before his marriage he was a sociable man, he liked company, friends. Now for years the only company he's known is that of people approved of by his wife, there's been no real contact with his subjects. He's aware of the danger of this; he's often said to me how much he wants to know what those "who are particularly devoted to the throne" are saying.'

'Meaning the peasants?'

'Meaning the peasants. And the damnable irony of the situation is that Rasputin, who, as a miracle-worker, seemed to meet all the needs of a Czarina despairing of getting help from orthodox medicine, as a "typical peasant"—God help us!—fills the gap of which the Czar has been conscious.'

'The Czarina has been aware of it, too, Peter. She keeps saying they must keep in touch with the peasants—the real Russia.'

'I know. I've lived on my estates, and I've governed provinces, but *she* knows the Russian peasant, and I don't—this meek, sentimental, kind-hearted, religious fellow—above all, ultra-loyal and quite satisfied with life. "The people who made trouble three years ago were the city workmen and students, all demoralised by Western ideas. But the peasants—ah, that's a different story!" '

He stood up. 'I think Rasputin's nothing more than a cunning peasant and a cheap charlatan—the police reports, incidentally, say he's taking lessons in hypnotism!—but nevertheless he must go. He fouls the throne with his proximity. I believe the foreign papers are full of stories about the scandals of his private life—'

'The Berlin papers, in particular.'

'Yes, the whole affair would appeal to them. Sooner or later something will appear in our own press. I must take decisive action before that happens.'

'How?'

'Police reports,' said Uncle Peter. 'Detailed circumstantial reports of the bestialities he perpetrates. The Czar cannot disregard such evidence.'

As we turned to go into dinner, the late evening sun came out. It had been a strange day as far as weather was concerned, with a darkly livid sky. Even now, with the sun penetrating the clouds, it came in such errant shafts of lurid light that they might also have been lightning.

'As God is my judge,' said Uncle Peter, 'I can't make up my mind as to what Rasputin symbolises. When I'm optimistic—which is not frequent—I think of him as the *reductio ad absurdum* to which Czardom has come. He's nothing more than a rogue of a peasant, and stupid with it. He has no real aims, ambition. There's a story of a Ukrainian who said one day, "I'd love to be Czar. I know damned well what I'd do then—I'd steal a hundred roubles, and from morning to night I'd feed on fat bacon!" And I try to persuade myself that's all there is to Rasputin. But there are other times when I become afraid. Last night I began thinking of him as a disease in himself, but by midnight I thought of him as a symptom of disease, and by the small hours I was thinking of him as the phosphorescence you have emanating from the surface of something dead and rotten. Fanciful, perhaps, but I was tired.'

And it was not only the strange light that made him look so haggard now.

It took months to collect that evidence, months more to persuade the Czar to study it. At the end of 1910, Uncle Peter said abruptly one evening, as he and his wife, Aunt Olga, were about to leave, 'I talked to the Czar about Rasputin today.'

'He let you?'

'His attitude today was strange—an odd mixture of dislike and fear as he spoke of the man. Finally he said he authorised me to collect evidence to back up the charges I brought.'

'Peter, this is wonderful!'

'Yes, but will he *act* on the evidence? Even as he spoke his eyes were flickering, kept shifting uneasily, you could tell he felt guilty towards the Czarina in going behind her back like this. Still, I'll give him the evidence. From what's been collected already, he *must* take action. No more shrugging it off with, "My dear fellow, you're taking too black a view! Don't worry—I know quite well what to make of Gregory!" '

At the beginning of 1911, the police evidence was presented to the Czar. It was vile, it was damning, it could not be disregarded, however much the Czarina might rage. Unhappily the Czar agreed; Rasputin must be ordered to return to his native Siberia.

The Czar himself made the request—not an order—in the most conciliatory way. Rasputin agreed, told the Czar and Czarina that 'evil men' were trying to rob him of their love; they must not pay any heed to these wicked councillors. In any case, if Rasputin were ever permanently parted from the Family, they would lose their crown within six months.

The Czar said this was, of course, only a temporary parting. To Uncle Peter his manner was chilling. As for the Czarina, she was now his declared mortal enemy. For this last offence there was no forgiveness.

And then Mother heard news that took her out to the Stolypins' new house on Elagin Island one evening in the summer.

'Vyroubova's going to Siberia, Peter. When she left she was boasting that she'd bring him back with her.'

Uncle Peter said, 'Each week I become more aware of the—the hopelessness of struggling against these influences.' He sounded unutterably tired and depressed; for all his great courage he was losing heart. Every day brought fresh calls on his resolution, and he was not well. He said, gazing out at the pale sky, 'Sometimes it's almost like a bad joke—so incongruous. This unclean brute from Siberia, rank as a goat, and this—this stiff German-governess type. She should find him unspeakably repulsive—'

He was drawn and ill, a shadow of himself, yet there was more vitality in this husk of the real Stolypin than there would ever be in the Czar at his most forceful. 'You can't stay in Petersburg throughout the summer,' said Mother suddenly. 'You're sick, Peter.'

He made a little gesture of dissent. 'Tired, perhaps, and not very hopeful. As far as hope's concerned, I'm living on capital now, from day to day.'

They stood side by side looking out at the lilacs and, behind them, the pink twilight. Then Uncle Peter said abruptly, 'Shall I tell you the moment I realised what precisely I was up against? Last autumn, on November 1, I had to go out to Czarskoe—something unexpected had turned up. By chance I saw the Czarina; she was dressed as for a festival, was transformed, eyes shining, face animated. I couldn't conceal my amazement. It was apparent enough for even the stupid Vyroubova to notice. "But of course she's happy!" she said. "It's the anniversary!" I stared at her in even greater wonder. You see, Avoye, it was the *anniversary of the Constitutional Manifesto.* And then she chattered, "It's the anniversary of *his* coming to the Palace; of course we remember the exact date, His Majesty told us he set it down in his diary, *We have got to know a Man of God—Gregory—from the Tobolsk province.*" And, Avoye, to the Imperial Family, this is the most important event of 1905—probably the most important event of the reign.'

'The most important event of the reign is your ministry!'

'Or the ending of it. Do you know how I believe that will happen?' As she listened incredulously, he told her.

Austria and France when we visited them that summer were like different worlds. Grandfather plied Mother with questions about Stolypin. Would he resign?

Perhaps, she said. He was exhausted by the ceaseless intrigues of Petersburg, by the hostility that surrounded him. All the privileged officials, nobles whose interests he was challenging. The ceaseless effort of trying to win the Czar's support—'It's like trying to build a house on a quicksand.'

'At any rate,' said Grandfather, 'the bomb-throwing seems to have stopped.'

Mother replied, 'He still believes he will be assassinated, Papa.'

'But the bomb-throwing's stopped! He's tamed the revolutionaries.'

Mother answered, 'He doesn't think he will be assassinated by a revolutionary, Papa; he says it will be a police agent.'

I want that to stand on record. Peter Stolypin believed he would be murdered by a police agent.

He looked better when we saw him again at the end of August. He was more relaxed, his face was suntanned, his eyes bright. He had lost his stoop, had regained his ringing voice.

The Imperial Family paid a visit of one week to Kiev, *en route* for the Crimea. A statue was to be unveiled. There were all the other inevitable minor incidents of an Imperial visit—pageants, parades, processions, the local boys' school was to be promoted from gymnasium status to that of a *lycée*. On September 1 there was to be a gala performance at the Opera—Rimsky-Korsakov's *Tsar Sultan*—on September 2 there would be a review of the troops, and then the Imperial Family would leave the charming pale-blue Nicholas Palace, to go by boat to Chernigov and thence to the Crimea.

It was very hot. There was dust everywhere. The anthem crashed out (rather raggedly) time and again. There were constant repetitions of, 'We wish Your Imperial Majesty good health.' Mother remarked it would have been more to the point if they'd wished His Imperial Majesty a little more interest, for he looked tired and bored. He also looked insignificant. That was, in a way, the drawback to being out of Russia for any length of time—you returned to see the situation afresh, you didn't accept it, you looked for the Autocrat of all the Russias and you saw someone absolutely unimposing, surrounded by towering generals, insignificant not so much because of his lack of stature but because of that extraordinary air of indecision, uncertainty, almost awkwardness, that strange but significant characteristic of looking back over his shoulder as if to receive guidance in what to do, like a timid, reluctant child, which Grandfather had noted on the day of Alexander III's funeral. That backward glance had lost nothing in significance now, because behind him there was usually the Czarina.

It also recalled irresistibly Uncle Peter's almost involuntary description of her—the German-governess type. She seemed thinner and taller than ever now, and it was painfully clear that she detested every moment of the public appearances. The four girls—Alexei did not appear—had obviously been told to show little animation. They looked like little dolls. Shy girls made shyer by their mother's orders. One felt that, if she could, she would have taken away their prettiness and left them plain.

'A pity,' whispered Mother. 'Such a pity.'

I wrote a few moments ago that the Czar seemed insignificant surrounded by his glittering generals; the impression of his being dwarfed, overshadowed—in every sense of the words—was even stronger on the occasions when he talked with Uncle Peter. I remember thinking that if I had never set eyes on them before, and knew only that one of the two was a great ruler, I should have immediately chosen Peter Stolypin, with his enormous warm vitality, his personality—

Not that he was often with the Czar. The court, in fact, went out of its way to ignore him; no place was ever provided for him in a court carriage during the stay in Kiev, there was no place for him on the Imperial boat for the trip to Chernigov. Worse. It was blatantly obvious that though the secret police and the Chief of the Palace Guards, Spiridovitch, were taking most elaborate precautions for the safety of the Imperial Family, Stolypin was left completely unguarded.

We had a brief conversation with him in the Marinsky Park, near the Palace. Mother and I had gone there after lunch for a breath of fresh air, and a little quiet; to our surprise there was Uncle Peter, walking alone.

'Good heavens!' said Mother. 'I never dreamed to see you here, Peter.'

He shrugged. 'I'm not wanted,' he said.

She shot a quick glance about her. Strollers, idlers, children playing. 'But—alone! Unprotected!'

'My dear,' he said gently, 'is it not only too obvious that I am quite superfluous?'

It was a beautiful park, the Marinsky. It stretched along the top of the red cliffs overlooking the Dnieper. There was a fountain playing; in the background came music from the orchestra, and once or twice a steamer hooted from the river below. But Mother's face, in the shade of her parasol, showed little enough of peace or enjoyment.

'Peter!' she said. 'I'm glad I've seen you. Did you know *he's* here— actually in Kiev? Vyroubova *has* brought him back.'

Uncle Peter stood quite still and silent for a moment. And then he said in a low voice, 'So it needs more strength of will than the Czar of all the Russias possesses to get rid of a Siberian horse-thief! He meant that banishment to be final, but obviously he can't withstand a woman's hysteria. As you can see, I didn't know.'

'How much longer must you stay here?'

He shrugged. 'My presence isn't wanted, but my absence—for form's sake—might be resented. When do you leave?'

'We stay for the gala opera performance tonight, and leave tomorrow.'

'Oh, yes, the Rimsky-Korsakov.'

'*Tsar Sultan*. We'll see you then.'

He kissed Mother's hand, clapped me on the shoulder, turned away.

'Let us walk part of the way with you!' Mother called abruptly. Suddenly she was running after him. 'Peter! Let us walk part of the way with you!'

177

He turned and looked at her steadily. 'My dear Avoye, that is what Olga is always saying—and for the same reason. And it's useless. A woman beside me wouldn't protect me when children couldn't.'

Mother bent her head. 'God bless you both!' he said, and went on his way with long strides.

Mother's knuckles were pressed against her lips. Her shattered composure—her sudden loss of poise, the wild steps taken after him—all terrified me. 'Maman!' I whispered. 'Maman! What's happened? Why are you suddenly so frightened for him? Is it because Rasputin has come to Kiev?'

Mother gave a sudden enormous shudder, and opened her eyes. 'Come and sit down,' I said. We sat on a seat. Some children were brought into the park by their nurses and began to play close to us. Mother said, 'You know I was invited out to lunch today and went.'

'Yes, you told me I could make up an excuse not to go—I'd be bored. That's why I thought you were so quiet when you came back—it had been dull.'

'It was dull, but just as we were finishing, Anna Vyroubova turned up. She's a close friend of these people, which was another reason I didn't want you with me. They might have said something to make you lose your temper. Well, she came in babbling about the journey—so hot in August, to Tyumen by rail, then to Tobolsk by boat, but at last here she was back with Our Friend—yes, they'd reached Kiev only this morning, at the very moment of the Imperial procession in fact. And then she started giggling, Andrei, because they sat there and watched the Czar pass and then the courtiers, and then, at the end of the procession, and designedly so, Peter, and then—and now she was giggling harder than ever, Andrei—Rasputin began to call, "Death is after him! Death is driving after him!" '

It was as cool in the park as anywhere in Kiev, but there was bitter sweat in my mouth and eyes, and my scalp prickled, was too thick, too hot, too tight for my head.

At eight o'clock that evening it was appallingly hot in the theatre, so hot that even the diamonds on women's heads and throats seemed to lack lustre through exhaustion. Elderly generals were purple in the face. The performance was as routine as any gala performance commanded by royalty.

In the first intermission we were summoned to the sitting-room at the back of the Imperial box. Olga and Tatiana were with the Czar; the Czarina was too tired to attend the performance.

Even here it was abominably hot. The conversation was anything but sparkling. The Czar condoled with us on returning to Petersburg; why weren't we sensible and travelling on to the Crimea?

Olga looked grave. As we took our leave she whispered to me, 'I know why your mother never wants to go to the Crimea now; Papa's forgotten for the moment.'

'But in any case,' I replied in the same tone, 'Petersburg is a marvellous place. If only you could get to *know* it—to walk along the quays and—'

'Olga!' Tatiana in her governessish mood. Odd how Tatiana was the only one of the four to be fiercely conscious of her rank. Not so odd in the circumstances that Tatiana was her mother's favourite daughter.

We regained our places. The music recommenced. It was quite unbearably hot. I sat thinking that if we were in Petersburg, we would walk along the quays—if only Olga could walk along the quays one night! All that she knew of reality was the glimpse she could catch of a street corner from her room at Czarskoe.

The performance ended, for the second intermission. 'Fond as I am of music, I feel this has gone on long enough,' said Mother, stifling a yawn. She fanned herself.

'You don't *look* at all hot,' I said enviously. 'I—hullo, here's Uncle Peter!'

'I'll do my best to say goodbye properly tomorrow,' he said, 'but in case anything unforeseen turns up, God be with you both. I wish I could come with you!'

'I wish we could take you with us, Peter.'

'I shouldn't be missed here. Now I suppose I'd better make polite conversation.'

He kissed Mother's hand, and went back towards the front of the theatre. In a low, furious voice Mother began to talk of the despicable treatment given him, and then, through the hum of conversation, we heard two sharp cracks. 'Some idiot is letting off fireworks,' she said. 'How stupid and dangerous!'

A woman screamed. I jumped up. 'Stay here,' I said. 'Don't move!'

Up the left aisle, past us, as we struggled out, went a thin man in a tailcoat, not very quickly, with no appearance of haste. But I had no attention for him, I was forcing my way forward towards the railing separating the front row of stalls from the orchestra pit. More women were screaming now, but I could hear Mother saying behind me (for of course she followed me), 'It's Peter.'

There were curses and shouts behind us; an officer jumped from the first tier to seize the assassin; more shouts from the direction of the Imperial box, where a fool of a general stood with drawn sword—as if a dress sword could keep off bombs and bullets! But we had eyes only for the scene before us, where in a little island of silence, it seemed, and in dreadful isolation Uncle Peter stood, turning unsteadily to face the Imperial box, re-entered now by the pallid Czar, making, very slowly, the sign of the Cross towards it with his left hand, for his right hand was covered with blood, as was the front of his uniform, a widening crimson stain. And then, very slowly, he collapsed in a chair, and began to fumble at his tunic.

Observations after this became disjointed and incoherent. A child—such as I had been at the time of my father's murder and my sister's maiming—sees things with a brilliant, objective clarity—more adult bitterness blunts, doesn't sharpen the edges of memory. They carried him out against a babel of voices, women screaming still, men shouting. Somehow we—Mother and I—were outside the auditorium. As the door closed behind us, the orchestra struck up the Anthem. Everything was confusion; we wanted to go to Uncle Peter's side, but suddenly there were swarms of school-children about us; the boys' and girls' high schools had sent their upper forms to the gala performance and some fool of a police officer had cleared the gallery.

In the confusion Mother said, 'You're taller than I am—did you see who did it?'

'A youngish man in evening dress. They have him.'

'You know what *he* said once—that he'd be killed by a police agent.'

I said stupidly, 'This man didn't look like a policeman.'

We stood looking out at the brightly-lit square, quite empty, because the mounted police had dispersed the crowd in front of the theatre; we could see them shepherding the people away up the side streets.

'I could see *him*,' said Mother. 'He's so tall. I saw him fall, but I couldn't see the wound. Was it bad?'

'Yes,' I said. 'Mother—did you see him making the sign of the Cross in the direction of the Imperial box?'

'Why are you surprised? He's always been a good Christian, trying to follow Christ's example. Christ would have blessed and forgiven Judas himself. Are they bringing him out yet?'

'No, but they won't until the ambulance comes.'

'Is that it? I can hear horses.'

'It's the mounted police backing up the side streets.'

Mother said precisely, 'I don't think the police have organised this murder, but they will have done nothing to prevent it. They've invited it by leaving him unguarded ever since he came to Kiev. I wonder that they didn't let the crowd lynch the man who did it—or why he wasn't cut down resisting arrest. *And why did he shoot Peter Stolypin, and not the Czar?*'

There was the sound of a bugle; the ambulance appeared, orderlies sprang out and ran up the theatre steps, carrying a stretcher.

'Now!' said Mother.

A pallid face, and blood soaking through the blankets. I thought, 'No one could lose so much blood and live.'

'We couldn't get through to you, Peter.'

He gasped, 'Tell Olga. I know you will break the news—as gently as possible.'

'Yes, Peter.'

'Prepare her for the worst—They've done for me.'

The ambulance dashed away down Vladimir Street, towards Doctor Makovsky's clinic, someone told us. Now that he was, in his own words, done for, they gave him a strong police escort.

I found our carriage, took Mother back to the hotel, then came out again in search of further news. There was straw lying in the street before the clinic. The bullet was lodged in his back, but they would not try to remove it until the morning. He was conscious, but in great pain.

I telephoned Mother; from her voice she had not cried as yet. She told me what to put in the telegram to Aunt Olga. Then I went in search of the Post Office through a panic-stricken Kiev. The mood of the people was ugly. They had learned the name of the assassin, Bogrov, and that he was a Jew. There was fear of reprisals. Already long lines of Jews were pushing handcarts towards the station. I went back to the hotel. Mother was sitting at the open window. Her hands were very cold. I ordered coffee and a little brandy, and made her drink. 'Poor darling,' she said. 'Not yet eighteen, and having to cope.'

'You've had to cope in the past; now I take over.'

'It's not like the other times, though, is it? Because this crime's tolerated—at least—by people in high places. In a way it makes things worse.'

I said uneasily, 'They know the name of the assassin. He's Bogrov —a Jewish revolutionary.'

But she went on as if I hadn't spoken. 'They didn't know how to get rid of him. He had such a reputation both here and abroad that they dared not remove him without a good reason. There was even some ridiculous talk for a while of making him Viceroy of Siberia—'

'Don't talk too much, Maman; you'll never sleep—'

'So many enemies among the bureaucrats and the people at court. And he'd ordered an inspection of the secret funds of the Police Department—did you know that, Andrei? I believe that the police discovered a fresh attempt on his life was planned, and decided not to intervene.'

She talked in this way for about half an hour more, then agreed to go to bed. She did not mention the Czar. I think that when she had referred obliquely to him outside the theatre she had not realised she was talking aloud.

At seven o'clock the following morning I was back at the clinic. One could get little fresh news. Kiev had quietened down now; there was no fear of reprisals with the reassuring sight of Cossacks clattering past.

The weather continued splendid. At noon we went to a solemn Mass at the Michael Cathedral, where prayers for his recovery were offered up. The church was crowded with ordinary folk, but no member of the Imperial Family was there, and no courtier really close to the little inner circle.

Mother always turned very pale when she was angry; white as a ghost she drove to the Palace after leaving the Cathedral.

She went in search of the general on duty. I remember that she was looking extraordinarily beautiful. Her pallor made her eyes shine like jewels. She was wearing a rose silk dress. The general smiled at her appreciatively.

'General, I beg you, get His Majesty to visit the hospital. If not for Peter Stolypin's peace of mind—his body won't know peace till death comes to him—for the sake of His Majesty's own reputation. Doesn't he realise how bitterly he'll be criticised for heartlessness and ingratitude if he stays away?'

She looked very beautiful, as I said, and so she was successful with the general.

The Czar called at the hospital, but did not see the dying man.

There were more prayers for recovery; no one from the court attended these either. The sun went on pouring down. Magnificent butterflies fluttered in the park.

The Czar went to Chernigov, as planned, on September 4. Uncle Peter died in great pain on the 5th. The Czar returned on the 6th, paid his respects to the body, offered stilted condolences to Aunt Olga, would not stay for the funeral. He was in a hurry to get off to the Crimea.

Mother was with Aunt Olga when he arrived; stood curtseying in the next room as he left.

'This is a terrible business,' he said. There was a slight twitch in his cheek.

'Your Majesty, what will become of us and the country now?' retorted Mother.

He only gave his slight smile; she found it shocking at this moment, although she realised it was meaningless.

In October, Mother was received by the Czarina.

'You are not looking well, Avoye.' The tone was reproving.

Mother, who was wearing black—no comment had been made on this—said that she supposed she was still suffering from the shock of Uncle Peter's murder. 'Not merely because he was a close personal friend,' she said hardily, 'but because one wonders what will become of Russia.'

The tell-tale red spots flared in the Czarina's cheeks. 'Really, you're exaggerating the man and his activities out of all proportion.'

'His Majesty never had an abler, more loyal servant.'

'Loyal! Well, perhaps being French you can't understand how wrong he was to look for support in political parties, which are of no account in Russia, instead of relying wholly upon the confidence of the Czar. If he'd done that, God would never have ceased to help him. As it is, he died to make room for worthier successors, and that's for the good of Russia!'

'Don't argue,' Mother said to herself. 'One cannot argue with a madwoman.'

She was to learn later that, if anything, the Czarina had been restrained in talking to her. To a close colleague and friend of Uncle Peter, she had said, 'Don't mention that man to me!' When he had spoken of fine, faithful service to the Czar, she had cried, 'Served him! *He overshadowed him!*'

And so, presumably, God had struck him dead.

Before this conversation took place, Bogrov, the murderer, had been hanged—trial and execution being a hurried business, carried through before the arrival in Kiev of Senator Trusevitch, appointed to investigate the murder. Bogrov, a revolutionary, had also been a police informer. He had given elaborate false details of a plot to murder the Czar—and they had given him a special police ticket of admission to the gala performance. Easy enough then to walk up and shoot an unprotected man in the back at point-blank range.

Even the authorities could not wholly ignore the indignant demands for an official enquiry—to say the least, the police had been unpardonably negligent. So there was a Commission of Investigation, and the Commission demanded that the Assistant Minister of the Interior, who controlled the police, should be put on trial.

The Commission's report was taken to the Czar, who was smiling and gay. Alexei was just recovering from another bout of illness; he was so happy he could not think of punishing anyone!

One did not need to know the dead man's prophecy that he would be killed by a police agent to talk with bitter anger of covering up a murder planned, or at least condoned, in high places.

It was late in that same year, 1911, that the Russian newspapers for the first time mentioned Rasputin. But any comment now was too late; the chief obstacle had been removed from his path.

19

'All will be ready by 1917'

General Sukhomlinov

FROM THE SUBLIME to the ridiculous—while Peter Stolypin was almost saving Russia from disaster, I was growing up. By the time he died, I was finishing my preliminary military education at the Corps des Pages.

One joined the Corps at the age of twelve or thirteen—I had been due to join in the autumn of 1905, but because of Father's death this was postponed for a year, and Mr Bruce came to be my tutor. Foreign acquaintances of my family—English soldiers, in particular—thought the kind of liberal education Mr Bruce gave me was an odd kind of preparation for a military academy, but the Corps des Pages' curriculum was anything but narrow. We had the best professors, not only on military matters, but men who were brilliant teachers of music, art, politics, and anyone of exceptional talent who visited Petersburg was asked to give us a lecture.

I eventually joined the Corps six months after Alix's death. Mr Bruce stayed on to catalogue the English section of our library and then returned to Scotland to become a professor of Russian literature and history. He wrote to us constantly after leaving us; his letters were always especially lengthy on the anniversaries of Alix's injury and death.

I wore a gold-trimmed coat, black, red-striped trousers, cap pulled over one eye—and realised with a sudden shock that after this I'd never be out of uniform except when I went abroad. In Russia officers and cadets alike were never allowed to wear civilian clothes; life was one long, endless parade.

In the summer I'd often walk part of the way to or from school; I close my eyes and can remember coming down the Nevsky in a rush, from the direction of Peter and Paul, turning right at the Public Library; usually when I went home in the evenings I'd find time to go into the main hall of the Library to pay my respects to Glass Case No. 4, which showed the Prayer Book of Mary Queen of Scots, in front of which Alix had stood the day before she had gone out to Apothecary Island for the last time; I always felt close to her there.

The school building was a deep red. It looked rather like uncooked beef in summer, but in winter, with snow on the ground and a pale blue sky above, it was quite beautiful.

Sometimes on a Sunday we would be summoned to Czarskoe. The Czar showed even more interest than his children in hearing about my education—'Papa wishes he were a boy again,' said Olga shrewdly. The girls were chiefly interested in hearing the details of my State uniform—black and gold tunic, white trousers, a torture-of-the-damned stiff red collar and a helmet topped with both a white horse tail and a gold double eagle. ('What sort of mythological beast are you supposed to be?' demanded Grandfather, when he first saw my headgear.)

At eighteen I was promoted to the senior section of the Corps des Pages.* As I was now considered to be on active service, ordinary education gave way to what was called specialised military training. This seemed to be endless drill, interspersed with standing to attention for hours.

I disliked it. It was boring, it was pointless; the only benefit obtained from this odd, artificial life was a physical toughening—otherwise I could see only disadvantages. The aim seemed to be the reduction of individuals to mere creatures of an extremely limited routine, fit only for army life, absolutely unadapted to anything outside fighting.

We still had lectures, of course. Elderly voices endlessly expounded fixed military rules as to what should be done in certain circumstances. In a letter to Uncle Raoul I demanded, 'But how can circumstances be *certain*? Surely in war the only thing you can expect is the unexpected? If the enemy's any good, he's out to surprise you.'

Then there were lectures on languages (but with my mixed ancestry I already spoke English, French and German as well as I spoke Russian), topography, fortifications, military history and law. We were all so bored that at one time we were reduced to daring each other to take forbidden sips of tap water from the sewage-laden Neva. God was kind, and no young fool got the typhoid he deserved.

The long winter months were hideously trying; we rarely went out, and had to do most of our mounted routine work in indoor riding-

* The Russian Sandhurst.

schools. The tremendous relief when, after rain and mist, the wind suddenly blew warm, snow water flooded the Neva, and it was Spring again! In those long winter months of confinement and boredom we used to sneak off to our horses when we could and, under cover of the compulsory grooming and feeding, talk endlessly to them, or lie in wait for the veterinary instructor, the only expert, with the blacksmith, I really paid heed to. A horse's ills and a horse's hooves hadn't changed overnight with the appearance of immense munition factories; the age-old ideas and techniques still held good here. But as for the other teachers—well, the tactics they laid down as Holy Writ were the kind cadets heard in 1812—and even then it was the sheer vast expanse of Russia, with her climate, that had beaten Napoleon. Now, a century later, the size of Russia might be Russia's ruin rather than salvation. She was too big and poorly organised for modern war. But if I tried to discuss this in lectures, I was told to hold my tongue; after one such occasion, in the corridor afterwards I heard two instructors talking none too quietly about me. 'His father . . .' said one. 'That unfortunate fellow, Hamilton.'

In the circumstances it was perhaps surprising that I was accepted for the Chevaliers Gardes. I had a little note of congratulation from the Czar. 'A great honour, my boy—*the* crack regiment. Even I can't get an officer accepted if the regiment doesn't want him.'

I was particularly glad of the last sentence, which removed a nagging worry from my mind.

So I put on my black tunic, blue breeches, sword, spurs, helmet and clanked along to the Gardes' regimental headquarters on the Zaharievskaia. It often struck me as odd that they never spruced up our barracks, a huge brick building painted white—the paint was always flaking away.

Most mornings I was up at six and on my way to the barracks where I worked and trained until the evenings. Those were the good days; the times I detested were those when we had to be ornamental rather than useful. The year 1912 being the anniversary of the repulse of Napoleon, and 1913 being the tercentenary of the Romanov dynasty, we had more than our fair share of ceremonial and gala occasions—even the Czarina's hatred of public functions couldn't prevent this—and so there were excruciating vigils in high patent leather boots and tight white leather breeches—so tight that most men had to wet their bare legs with water to get them on. Sitting was impossible; if the occasion went on for too long even standing was real agony. Mother proved my salvation; she went out and bought the largest silk stockings possible, and I slipped these on first.

There was guard duty at Czarskoe and at the Winter Palace. For Winter Palace duty I marched my twenty men in their long grey coats for three miles along the Neva, and changed in the guardroom at the Palace into the white tunics and bepigeoned* helmets we wore for our vigil of twenty-four hours.

Duty at the Winter Palace could be unnerving at night. The place, scarcely used, was an empty shell of vast, echoing corridors and halls. Highly-strung soldiers hated being on guard near the bedroom of Alexander II, left unaltered since the day of his murder, even to the bloodstained bed. At Czarskoe things were different—the Czar sent Abyssinian servants with coffee every few hours, which helped you to keep awake, and he himself often came out of his study to have a chat. It must have looked a little odd—the lieutenant like an *émigré* from Bayreuth, and the Czar in his simple grey *toujourka*.† The irrepressible Anastasia was always making excuses to appear; nine times out of ten Tatiana would come in pursuit, and bear her off, Anastasia making hideous grimaces all the while.

Odd what memories are strongest of that period. Riding on the frozen Neva in the winter, special nails screwed to the shoes of our horses, the outdoor life in the summer months, with the hot sun bringing out the scent of the pinewoods and clover and the smell of lilac in the gardens. Christmas Eve in the white regimental church, bells of churches in wild competition outside. Dark-faced ikons. Glittering ikonostasis. And white-tunicked fairhaired giants carefully lighting candles. The men of the Chevaliers Gardes.

My own men were all Ukrainians, who became the best soldiers in Russia. As recruits they were the best physical types, most of them immensely tall, but all peasants, most of whom saw the inside of a train for the first time when they were brought to the Army early in October. They came wearing peasant clothes, they were longhaired, illiterate, bewildered, terrified of Petersburg and, in most cases, acutely depressed because they had been assigned to cavalry. In the first place, this meant three years' service, half as much again as you had in the infantry; in the second place, it meant harder work—in the infantry you didn't have

* Young officers referred to the double eagle as 'the pigeon'.
† The everyday military tunic—from the French *toujours*.

to feed a horse three times a day, clean it twice, and learn to ride it.

They had no idea of distance—or even of the directions of their homes, north, south, east or west. If you asked one where he came from, he would scratch his head, and say: 'A long way away, *barin*.' It was the most difficult thing in the world to teach them to use a map —in any case, you had to teach them the alphabet first, and then, very slowly, to read.

These bewildered, terrified giants were physically as brave as lions, but for at least the first six months of service they would follow their officers like sheep. They moaned with terror if you suggested they should have a look round Petersburg; it often took them a year to venture out—I don't exaggerate. I got mine out after three months, and this was considered something of a miracle, but, then, I lured them out to a circus—they loved circuses. Even so, they kept clutching at me during the performance, and begging for reassurance that I wouldn't desert them.

There is an idea prevalent outside Russia that the discipline in the Imperial Army out-Prussianed the Prussian, that officers feared and hated their men and men feared and hated their officers. This was not the case in the old Imperial Army, whatever happened after 1914, when the old Army ceased to exist.

It is hard to describe that relationship; no other Army had anything like it. Except when we were actually giving orders, we officers never used a military rasp—we talked confidentially, often using Christian names. We knew all about their families, and we called them '*bratzi*— little brother.' They told us all their worries, and they gave us their entire devotion. We tried to repay it.

I remember going to see Mother in an absolutely triumphant mood because at last all my recruits were using their metal plates; hitherto they'd been quite unused to individual eating, families always eating from a single bowl. I remember the trials and tribulations of trying to teach them muscular co-ordination. It was the most difficult thing in the world to get them to shut one eye at a time, to use their fingers independently, so that there were moments when you felt that they would never learn to use a rifle.

I already knew something—and was to know even more—of conditions in the French Army, and nothing could be more extraordinary than the difference between the ordinary soldiers of the two countries. The Russians were ready to fight for God and the Little Father;

politics, and a political reason for fighting, meant nothing to them. The Frenchmen, articulate, politically conscious individuals to a fault, all had their own point of view. They would have spat with outrage at being treated like children, whereas the bewildered batches of Russian recruits would have been terrified if given any other treatment. You explained everything very carefully to them; they were scared into dumbness if confronted by an individual problem, simply gave up.

I was worried over all this, tried to talk to fellow-officers about it, eventually, like the recruits, gave up and relapsed into silence. 'You're a mongrel,' people would say. 'All this French passion for logic and the critical approach, English mania for self-reliance! Remember you're in the Russian Army.'

No, I have never forgotten.

The huge Christmas tree after the service—the music and dancing in the regimental school, with a gift for every man from the officers.

Sunset at Krassnoe with the men's deep voices singing the evening hymn.

Their oath-taking a month after their arrival. The entire regiment paraded, and the adjutant read out the Army regulations, which must have been largely incomprehensible to them since language and regulations alike had scarcely changed since Peter the Great had issued them. God knows why there had been no revision; it was a little odd to stand there hearing how much reward we'd get if we captured a Turkish pasha.

But they understood the oath.

First the chaplain read it slowly to them, then, in unison, right hands raised, they repeated it, phrase by phrase, after him.

'I promise and swear in the name of the Almighty God and in the presence of the Holy Evangel that I wish to and must serve His Imperial Majesty the Autocrat of all the Russias and His Imperial Highness the Heir to the Russian throne, loyally and truthfully, without sparing my life, to the last drop of my blood.'

Then each in turn went forward, kissed the Cross, and regimental standard, and said again: 'I swear.'

By 1917 most of my tall, fair brothers were dead, and conscription had swept a new type into the barracks.

There is one more general Western misconception concerning the old Imperial Army, the idea that the officers were all idle aristocrats spending their time in a series of luxurious orgies with gypsy dancers and ballerinas. The truth is that of all the classes that served the State none was so down-trodden, so forlorn or ill-provided as the lower officers. Their rights and self-esteem were disregarded or trampled upon by the senior officers. They were wretchedly paid; even if they reached the rank of colonel, if they had no private means, retirement and old age meant semi-starvation. As for the life of luxury during actual service, the fact of the matter was that, since our railway system was so bad, it was felt best to keep most of the Army in frontier posts even in peacetime so that days, even weeks, would not be lost in strategic concentrations. You don't find many ballerinas in frontier posts. The life of the average officer was, in fact, one of deadly monotony, not helped by the fact that daily you had to cope with an avalanche of paper work. You were a bureaucrat before you were a soldier.

So when one reads of the brilliant show of officers on formal occasions*—Hussars in white and gold with scarlet, fur-trimmed dolmans, Tirailleurs in magenta shirts, fur-trimmed dark green coats, my own regiment in silver breastplates—remember the reality of life; grey monotony in a dull frontier town, with an even bleaker prospect on retirement.

There are other factors, too, to be remembered in the general degradation

Sukhomlinov, for example.

A short, fat man with heavy-lidded eyes, and oddly pale lips. He was always heavily scented, had soft white hands, and wore golden bracelets on his podgy wrists.

He was, to say the least, a man utterly without principle. He was corrupt—he had a young wife with expensive tastes—and he was stupid. He was utterly lacking in moral courage; he would never admit the truth if it would be unwelcome and thus make him unpopular— so much easier to fall back on the old myth of Russian invincibility.

He had graduated from the Staff College in 1874, since when he informed people—proudly—he had made no attempt to keep up with military theory.

This did not prevent him from becoming War Minister thirty-five years after graduating.

His appointment was a savage blow to the Army, which had suffered enough during the war against Japan and afterwards, when many of the

* Of which there were far too many in Petersburg. What with ceremonial parades and guards, a soldier got real training for only about a third of his service.

191

better officers had resigned in sheer disgust from that atmosphere of diseased rottenness. Then had come a glimpse of hope. The Czar's cousin, the Grand Duke Nicholas, had been appointed President of the Council of National Defence. He was tremendously popular and universally respected, within the Army and without, physically and morally courageous. He pointed out how wretchedly unprepared the Army had been, insisted on the necessity of strenuous work and study. He set in train a whole series of important reforms—and then Sukhomlinov became War Minister and the General Staff came under his control.

In the late summer of 1912, Uncle Raoul was sent to Russia as one of the members of a special military mission. He now existed in a unique kind of limbo—the French government was frantically eager to strengthen all links with Russia, and therefore the knowledge that he was very much *persona grata* in the eyes of the Imperial Family at last outweighed the facts of his birth, religion and education. 'They are kind—they ignore the fact that I'm a Breton, Catholic, a *Postard*, rather as if I've been suffering from some rather shameful disease not mentioned in polite society. And I have to thank that convenient attack of measles for all this!'

'Oh, not entirely, surely!' said Mother, flushed with indignation on his behalf. 'Even the French government can't go on ignoring people of your calibre indefinitely!'

'It's certainly true they can't very well afford to pick and choose these days,' he agreed. 'Do you know, Avoye, between 1900 and 1911 the number of applications for St Cyr dropped from 1,875 to 871, and quality dropped with quantity?'

'That is a dreadful state of demoralisation,' said Mother. She went on, after some hesitation: 'But, according to Andrei, affairs are quite as bad here.'

'So he has more than hinted in his letters. You're going out to Czarskoe, Avoye? Then Andrei and I will take a walk along the quays and he'll probably tell me a great deal more than I'll learn from that quite obscene lump of suet, the Minister of War. That Russia should endure him . . . '

'He keeps changing Chiefs of Staff!'* I exclaimed, at the same time

* There were four Russian Chiefs of Staff between 1908 and 1914. In Germany there were precisely the same number between 1861 (the great Moltke) and 1914—fifty-three years.

that Mother said, 'But he suits the Czar so perfectly, you see. No unpleasantness. Constant optimism. A fund of funny stories.'

We walked along the quays. The cranes were flying southwards into the sun. 'That means winter's close,' I said, staring up at the white shapes floating overhead. Nevertheless it was a golden day; the leaves, the gilded domes and the bright sun's reflections in the river vied with each other.

'The winter of our discontent,' said Uncle Raoul. 'Do you know why I'm here? Because of the condition of your artillery. Apparently your Bellona's bridegroom—' (when he was angry he always became very Shakespearean)'—doesn't believe much in guns.'

'Even he can't *abolish* artillery!' I said.

'Oh no, but he certainly shows several varieties of slug-like cunning in cutting it down as much as possible. I will give you an account of my forays into the files of your War Ministry in search of the artillery, and the reasoned excuses given when I discover it to be practically non-existent.

'One. The patriotic. "Ah, my dear Marquis, after 1908 we decided to place no more orders for guns and munitions in Germany—for obvious reasons. But it's so hard to make a break with routine, isn't it? After dealing with Krupp for so many years, it's difficult to get into the hang of negotiating with strangers!"

' "Difficult to place orders with Russian heavy industry?" I demand incredulously.

' "Such as it is!" says Sukhomlinov, simpering. "And it's nearly all German-controlled; so, you see . . . "

' "I see muddle, delay and precious little done!" I retort.

'This wounds him so much he has to retire and lie on a sofa. A few hours later, refreshed by the rest, and more perfume dabbed behind his ears, he receives me again. This time he's thought up a new excuse—there's no artillery because the department is staffed entirely by perfectionists.

' "Shell fuses," I snap, "are obviously most desperately needed."

' "Yes, yes, my dear Marquis, but, you see, the Artillery Department will not consider even starting to buy until the most exhaustive tests have proved conclusively that this is the *ideal* fuse."

' "This new mania for perfection could not be worse-timed," I begin, but here he glances at his ornate little clock, gives a cry of anguish —"the Grand Duke!"—and waddles out for a non-existent telephone conversation. I sit on grimly. Various subordinates peer in, tell me His Excellency may be engaged for a long time. I reply, unmoved, that I have come a long way to see His Excellency, a wait of a few hours doesn't matter to me. Sukhomlinov, who was probably listening outside the door, gives up at this, and comes back in. Rage makes him look more than ever like something that's crawled out from under a stone. But his time has not altogether been wasted—he has a new excuse. There's no artillery because the Russian Army's so up-to-date—positively forward-thinking. "The war with Japan taught us so much! Heavy guns were scarcely used—nothing above three inches. So we've learned our lesson. Waste not!" said Sukhomlinov, in arch English. "Want not!"

'In actual fact, my dear Andrei, what I've discovered in my peregrinations round the Palace Square is this—your munition stores in the west were plundered in 1904 for the Army in Manchuria, though whether the guns got through, God knows. Your Artillery Department has done nothing to make good the depletion; as a matter of fact it seems to have no idea where the rest of these stores are to be found.'

They still didn't know in 1914.

A few weeks after Uncle Raoul's visit, Grandmère's last illness began. Mother left for France the moment the news came; a few days later I was on duty at Czarskoe, and the Czar came out of his study—for the usual kind of chat, I thought erroneously. Actually it was to tell me that he had suggested to the War Ministry that I should be sent to France on some kind of course. I said, rather startled, I didn't know of any course. 'Ah, my dear Andrei,' he said. 'If you're attached to your Uncle with orders to keep close to him and observe him, that's course enough.'

Stumblingly, I began to thank him.

God forgive me if I have given the impression that he never performed acts of quite extraordinary delicacy and kindness.

So, 'attached' to Uncle Raoul, I began to observe the workings of the French Army at close quarters. 'It's not a waste of time,' he remarked, 'though not in the way the Czar thinks. You Russians show a perverted genius for copying our most abysmal follies.'

Such as the mania for *élan*.

Until 1905, France had possessed the finest defensive system in Europe, a line of fortresses—Toul, Belfort, Verdun and so on—constructed by a military engineer of genius, General Séré de Rivière.

194

The idea was to let the Germans invade the 'slots' between the fortresses, and then shatter them by a carefully prepared flank attack. Then in 1905 came the Military Revolution. The General Staff was still desperately trying to establish the reasons for the *débacle* of 1870, and in an unhappy hour they heard that the Germans had formulated their basic strategy by intensive study of Napoleon's campaigns. Napoleon's successors belatedly began to follow suit and discovered what seemed to be the secret of success—the offensive. The French soldier was invincible in attack. It would seem they had never heard of Waterloo.

There was also the rediscovery of Colonel Charles Ardant du Picq, killed in 1870 but not, unfortunately, before he had made a careful study of the experiences of French soldiers in the Crimean War and in the brief Italian campaign of 1859. He had tracked down the officers who had taken part in these battles, and had questioned these veterans closely as to precisely what had happened at the moment they had made contact with the enemy. Their accounts were made public in a posthumous work, *Etudes sur le Combat,* and made amazing reading; the officers had affirmed that they had never made real contact with the enemy, that hand-to-hand combat virtually never existed, *because when well-led attackers collided (as it were) with defending troops, the defenders broke and ran.* The vast majority of bayonet wounds suffered by troops in battle were in the back.

I have Uncle Raoul's copy of the slim little book that played such havoc with French military thinking, and so much else. He has written in the margin at this point: *Have we therefore evolved for future wars a new breed of troops immune from the effects of high explosive?*

Ergo, concluded Ardant du Picq triumphantly, to win battles it is necessary only to develop the *spirit* of the troops to the point where they will allow themselves to be led in a furious and utterly determined charge . . .

True, perhaps, in the days of the phalanx, wrote Uncle Raoul, *and possible in the days of the musket. But in the age of Krupp?*

They would, of course, be reassured by the knowledge that no enemy would be waiting for them if they advanced with sufficient determination and that *no* one stands his ground before a bayonet charge.

Possibly not stand. But one might lie at rest with a rifle—or machine gun. One might even stand with something bigger. If it were a clash of

195

rival patron saints, I'd back Saint Krupp every time against Saints Elan and Bayonet. Even Saints Elan and Bayonet accompanied by military bands, as our Staff idiots prescribe in all seriousness. But really I insult the heavenly hierarchy to speak of saints—the way in which people at the War College talk of élan smacks more of witchcraft. One is reminded of the savages of Africa and their belief in Juju. In the Sudan the dervishes believed no rifle bullet could hurt them—and our unhumorous clowns are heirs to them rather than to Napoleon, who from the start showed the utmost trust in the efficacy of a whiff of grapeshot. Fighting to them is a state of mind. A battle is lost only if you confess yourself to be beaten. You stand erect among the corpses of those who charged with élan towards the enemy that was so militarily illiterate it hadn't read Ardant du Picq, and believed in a defensive position with well-sited guns, and the enemy emerges unscathed from its defensive position, but you're the victor. But what if these illiterate fellows in their tens of thousands don't realise it?

It was unfortunate that Ardant du Picq ever wrote his little book; since he had written his little book, it was doubly unfortunate that he had died in 1870, before he wrote down further reflections inspired by the sight of Prussian guns tearing great holes in the ranks of French infantrymen long before the Prussians came within range of *chassepôt* or *mitrailleuse*—far less the bayonet—and the knowledge that Sedan was won by five kilometres of Prussian artillery. True, the Elan Dogma made its disciples economical as far as armaments were concerned, but, my God, it made them spendthrifts in blood.

And the Russian Army, the army known to be the most immobile in Europe because of lack of modern equipment and insufficient training? Why, inevitably, because of our feeling of inferiority to the French, we aped them slavishly. From 1905 onwards, our Staff, too, insisted on the spirit of the offensive.

Insanity had not always reigned at our War Ministry. Alexander III, despite his hatred of war, had seen to it that Russia was in a position of strength. His War Minister, Vannovsky, gave particular attention to the defence of our Western Front. Fortresses were built, and garrisons organised, reliable troops who knew their own zones.

And then came Sukhomlinov, to abandon the idea of garrison troops who knew their own territory, to abandon the fortresses, too.

No trench mortars or hand-grenades—unnecessary in a war of movement in open country. We kept the rifle of 1891.

By the end of Uncle Raoul's 1912 visit, Sukhomlinov was reduced to making wild promises to him. 'I assure you, all will be ready by 1917.'

He said this again, pettishly, in 1914.

By 1917 something else was ready.

20

To the Ipatiev Monastery

SOMETIMES when I was in France Russia appeared to be even more remote mentally than it was geographically. The little artificial world at Czarskoe, for example, so unreal, enclosed. One constantly met people who had never been to Russia, who talked wonderingly of the splendour of the Russian monarchy, the great palace, surrounded by guards on constant patrol. No one who had not experienced it could have any idea of the dull self-sufficiency of that enclosed—stiflingly enclosed —family life.

Above all, moving about, meeting people, making my bow to dozens of mothers who led forward marriageable daughters with maternal cluckings and cooing, I developed almost a feeling of outrage about the upbringing of the Grand Duchesses. Now I realised as never before why Mother became so agitated on the subject, and how right she was to call it dangerous and cruel. The Czarina kept them in complete ignorance of all reality, in a strange half-world all illusions and false conceptions. She would argue that she had preserved for them the happiness of innocence, but it wasn't innocence, it was ignorance, and the happiness of ignorance is a stupid happiness, and dangerous, as Mother had seen. One might say that the Czarina had blinded her children to reality, except that blind people don't advance so unhesitatingly, with such self-confidence.

It was a caged innocence. Caged innocence is not true innocence.

They wrote to me quite frequently. Olga's were the only letters with any real originality—the other letters were all incredibly stereotyped, with certain basic conceptions underlying everything. That everybody else had the same tastes, beliefs, way of life, that theirs was a typical family, that all other girls had their kind of education, and pastimes, that all mothers had *their* mother's attitude towards religion, politics, everything, and that everyone adored and revered the Imperial Family with its indisputable rights.

So physically healthy, fresh, charming; so mentally credulous, simple, completely unprepared for the realities of life, the ordinary realities of life.

There could, of course, be no preparation for the reality which eventually came to them.

In the autumn of 1912 the Imperial Family went to Spala, the ancient hunting seat of the Kings of Poland. The lodge where they stayed was wooden, poky, dark, so dark the lights had to be left burning all day.

In one of her daily letters from Brittany, in mid-October, Mother wrote, 'I've been told that Alexei's ill, and they've sent for Professor Fedorov. Have you heard anything?'

I replied, 'No, I had a letter today, but it was all about the acting—Marie and Anastasia did two scenes from *Le Bourgeois Gentilhomme* in the dining-room before their parents and the guests. There are plenty of Polish guests there all the time, and shooting parties every day—there can't be anything seriously wrong.'

Away from Russia one tended to forget the incredible secrecy with which Alexei and his illness were surrounded.

Even when, eventually, it was believed the boy was dying, and Russia had to be prepared for news of his death, the nature of his illness was never disclosed. Abroad, one heard the wildest rumours. In France I was told in all solemnity that everyone knew that the boy had been born with too few layers of skin.

In mid-November, I received a letter from Olga. It was mostly about her father, who had played tennis, walked in the woods, taken Vyroubova out in a boat which hit a rock and almost capsized. It ended:

'Mamma is not well. She is in a very nervous state; her heart, she thinks, is affected.'

Not a word about Alexei.

I wrote back, 'I am shocked to hear of Her Majesty's nervous state. *Is it because of Alexei's illness?*'

The reply came from Czarskoe. 'We arrived back later than we expected because the train moved at the rate of fifteen miles an hour.' A paragraph about settling in again at Czarskoe, and then:

'Yes, Mamma's nervous state is bad, very bad. And it's not merely because of Alexei's illness—it's because of the strain of pretending that nothing serious is wrong.' And then—I imagine she was, for a wonder, alone as she wrote—she told me what had happened in Poland.

The damage had been done before they reached Spala, during the short visit they'd paid to another Polish hunting lodge, Bielowieza.

'The weather was perfect; Papa and I went for wonderful long rides, and the poor Little One fretted so much because he was not allowed to ride that finally Papa said he might be taken for a row on the lake. Poor darling, he was so excited he jumped about, and fell against the side of the boat. Doctor Botkin examined him, found a small swelling on his leg, and kept him in bed for a few days. The swelling went down, and people stopped worrying. Even so, when we came to Spala, Doctor Botkin said the Little One must go on resting, but, of course, he hated it, the house is so dark and you feel *cramped* all the time you're inside it, and he knew the weather was still beautiful outside. Eventually Mamma decided to take him for a carriage-ride; Anna went too. He started off so bright and cheerful, but then, of course, the carriage began to jolt—it's an awful road, nothing more than a sandy track. Every time the carriage lurched, the Little One cried out; Mamma, of course, ordered the carriage to return immediately, and the driver did his best to avoid rough patches, but by the time they were back at the Lodge, the Little One was almost unconscious with pain.

'There had been a severe haemorrhage. Doctor Botkin sent telegrams to Petersburg—doctor after doctor came, but nothing could stop the haemorrhage. His leg drew right up against his chest—the doctors said that this was to give the blood a larger socket to fill. Part of the time the Little One was delirious, but we were almost glad of this, because when he was conscious there was pain, such pain, Andrei, pain unending, he couldn't sleep with it, he screamed day and night, people put cotton-wool in their ears to stifle the noise—his body was contorted, his eyes were rolled back in his head, we prayed for the screaming to stop, but when it did, what followed was worse, because the pain hadn't stopped, he wasn't screaming only because he was so exhausted, he was making a dreadful hoarse wailing, a little mewing noise, like a sick cat, and, when he could talk, he was praying to die. *At eight, Andrei, he was praying to die.* "When I'm dead, it won't hurt any more, will it?" he said once, and, again, "When I'm dead, let me be buried in the light—in the forest." But more often he just groaned, "Mamma, Mamma, help me!" For eleven days Mamma never undressed, never lay down. She would leave him only for a brief moment each evening. Papa at times was so overcome he couldn't stay in the room; there was one evening when the Little One cried, "Papa, Papa, why is it that you, the most important person in the world, can't stop this pain in my leg?"

'Mamma's hair is beginning to go grey now. Imagine the strain on her poor nerves of having to dress in the evening and go to talk to her guests as if nothing seriously were wrong! I wrote to you about the French play Marie and Anastasia put on, didn't I? They did it awfully well, everyone was laughing, talking at the tops of their voices between scenes, and Mother was there, smiling, in the front row, saying what good fun it all was—but once or twice she'd make an excuse, and move slowly to the door, and once out of sight she'd pick up that long, awkward train and run to Alexei's room, just for a moment, and then she'd go back.

'Father couldn't leave, so he'd stand where he could see her face when she came in again—just for the one moment before she made herself smile, and talk to the guests—'

I showed the letter to Mother when she paid a brief visit to Paris. 'It's not brave, it's not self-sacrificing—it's *stupid*! If the worst part is pretending that nothing's wrong—well, why keep up the pretence, for God's sake?'

'They would reply,' said Mother, tears running down her face, 'that they are safeguarding Alexei's future. If people knew he were so ill—'

'But *hiding* his illness won't cure it! If they let the truth be known, they'd be spared all this strain that's brought the Czarina to the verge of a breakdown, and they'd gain the sympathy of all Russia. Don't they realise what incredible rumours are circulating?'

Mother said, 'I don't think you can have heard the most incredible story of all. How does Olga describe Alexei's recovery?'

'It's odd,' I replied slowly. 'She just gives this last paragraph to it. On October 10 he was given the last sacrament—they'd given up all hope. And then, quite suddenly, the haemorrhage stopped, the fever left him, he fell into a sound sleep. It was like a miracle, because the doctors hadn't seen any chance of improvement—'

'But the Czarina suddenly had?'

I stared at her. 'How did you know? Yes, see for yourself: *Mamma had said in the morning that she was no longer afraid. She even managed to smile—a real smile.*'

'I want to go out!' said Mother suddenly. 'Let's get into the fresh air, for God's sake. We'll go to the park.'

It was a golden late October morning, too early for the fashionable world to be abroad. Gardeners made bonfires of fallen leaves; children played, dogs barked and bounded.

'I, too, had a letter from Spala—from Anna Vyroubova,' said Mother.

'From Vyroubova! But I thought you'd stopped being on speaking terms for ages—because you were blasphemous enough to denounce Rasputin.'

Mother said precisely, 'But Anna is reluctant to abandon the *rôle* of missionary. Whenever she thinks there is a chance of effecting a conversion, she seeks out the hard of heart—'

'Maman, dearest, whatever in the frightful business at Spala was likely to make you change your mind about a filthy swine who was hundreds of miles away?'

'Only the fact that Anna—like the Czarina—considers that Rasputin saved the boy's life.'

'But this is absurd! He wasn't there! It's a small, poky place—they couldn't smuggle him in!'

'He sent a telegram,' said Mother, 'and Alexei recovered. That is what the Czarina explicitly believes.'

After a moment I said, 'You'd better let me have the details.'

A ball bounced at her feet. I threw it back to a chubby little girl who threw it to a younger brother. He fell down twice in getting to it, getting entangled with the family pug who wanted it as well. The mother, watching, laughed.

If it were Alexei, and Alexei fell, the Czarina couldn't laugh.

'They had given up all hope, the child had been given the last sacrament, and the bulletin sent to St Petersburg was worded so that the following one could be a death announcement. And the Czarina asked Anna to send a telegram to Siberia, to Rasputin's home—even he'd felt it wiser to retire there for a time after a new frightful scandal. The telegram asked for his prayers. He telegraphed back that Alexei would not die. *That's* why the Czarina was suddenly calm—Olga said that, didn't she? What she didn't say was that her mother told them she'd had a telegram from Rasputin—"I'm not a bit anxious now," she told everyone.'

'Vyroubova's lying. Olga doesn't mention it.'

'*Would* Olga mention it—Olga who's ashamed of her mother's attitude to Rasputin, but dare not challenge it openly? And you're the last person she'd tell—she knows how you feel about him. If, as seems almost certain, the episode has strengthened the Czarina's belief in Rasputin, all the more reason for Olga keeping silent.'

'It's a coincidence,' I said. 'Or a fraud.'

'Coincidence or fraud, *how* the cure came about doesn't matter,' said Mother. 'The really significant thing is that the Czarina doesn't think it was fraud or coincidence, it was the action of God working through His chosen instrument, Gregory. Nothing will ever shake Rasputin's hold, now. He has been proved to be the Man of God.'

The little boy rolled about on the grass, his arms round the obliging pug.

'You will make your clothes so dirty!' called his mother.

Fortunate mother, the worst that can happen is that he'll get grass stains on his clothes.

'It began to snow before we left Spala,' Olga had ended her letter. 'Mamma sat with the Little One all the time.'

The Czarina sitting watching the snow falling, turning back again to gaze at the waxen little face on the pillow, the twisted little body—it would be months before Alexei's leg would straighten. But he was alive; they had all given him up for dead, but then there had been a sign from heaven. A sign, and a warning. Only Rasputin's prayers could keep Alexei alive.

I left France again for Russia at the beginning of 1913; in February the Romanov tercentenary celebrations were due to commence.

The Post Office issued a special stamp bearing the Czar's head— but not for long. Bishops denounced the *lèse-majesté* of putting a can- cellation-mark over the Imperial features; this scared most Post Office employees into scarcely touching the stamp at all, so they could be used again. The government decided to issue no more celebration stamps.

Two commemorative gestures in particular were confidently expected of the Czar—some stupendous work of charity, and a wide political amnesty. 'Not both, surely?' Mother had said, before I left France. 'Both,' I replied. 'God knows there's room enough for both.'

'Well, if it's a choice, I hope the Czar decides for charity—a great building of schools and hospitals. Surely there's an Imperial adviser sensible—or cynical—enough to see that this would make the monarch popular, and that popularity's badly needed?'

'I know, but an amnesty would produce even better results—if old scores are wiped off, old grievances can be forgotten, and there's a chance that we can start writing an entirely new page of Russian history.'

'You'll both be wrong,' said Grandfather, joining in. 'Remember your Imperial mentality—he believes all the *giving* should come from the people. For him the tercentenary will be nothing more than a flow of gifts and loyal addresses in his direction. The only effort he'll make is to admire the decorations.'

All that actually happened was that there was a partial amnesty, partial in the wrong direction. All criminals were freed, but not political prisoners. And the press was graciously 'pardoned' for past misdeeds.

No concessions were given to the Duma—that had been another hopeful idea.

Perhaps the greatest concession made to the people was this—for the first time since 1905 the Imperial Family took up residence in the Winter Palace. For three days.

March 6 arrived—the three-hundredth anniversary of the day when a deputation of the boyars, headed by the Patriarch of Moscow, had gone to Kostroma to offer the crown of Rurik to Michael Romanov.

Early in the morning there was a salute of thirty-one guns. It was bleak and wet; as the day wore on, the rain fell more and more heavily until, at the time of the Imperial procession, it was coming down in torrents, drenching the magnificent decorations, leaving sodden flags hanging dismally along the route lined by troops. But I was glad that the weather was so vile; it excused the thinness of the crowds. A fine day would have made it embarrassingly clear how little public enthusiasm there was for the tercentenary; after all, what was there for the public to celebrate?

I had been told off to act as an usher in the Kazan Cathedral; I clanked about in full-dress uniform, feeling several kinds of a fool, since I'd been given no very precise orders. Dozens of officials were making last-minute preparations; the only fact one could be sure of was that the places for the Imperial Family were beneath the crimson canopy erected opposite the altar, facing the miraculous image of Our Lady of Kazan. '*They* will sit,' said a flurried little man weighed down with gold braid, 'and so will foreign ambassadors and members of the government.'

'What about the Duma?'

'The Duma?' He stared at me as if I were standing there beneath the golden dome of the cathedral saying something in particularly bad taste. 'They stand!

'*Where?* At the back, of course.'

He turned away, shaking his head over my stupidity.

Gold of ikons and candle-flames, flash of jewels. A figure coming towards me looking as if a saint had stepped down from a painting. I kissed the hand of the Grand Duchess Elizabeth and she gave me her blessing. She wore her simple grey robes, and the other women's jewellery and finery became irrelevant.

'Come to see me before I go back to Moscow; I want all your news.'

A sudden commotion at the rear. People were smiling, looking across with real satisfaction. Rodzianko, the President of the Duma, a giant of a man, well known to my family, was protesting loudly over the treatment given to the Duma. '*One*—the Duma should be at the front. *Two*—members must be seated!' Sympathy was so obviously with him that eventually the flustered Master of Ceremonies gave way. Rodzianko, taking no chances, brought in a kind of posse of Duma sergeants-at-arms. He grinned at me like a good-humoured bear. 'Ah, young Andrei Alexandrovitch, it's years since I put off *my* Chevalier Garde uniform, but I still remember a few of the lectures they gave us. Never neglect to fortify a newly-occupied position, eh?'

And very pleased with himself, he went off to snatch a breath of fresh air in the porch.

The Imperial procession would start at noon, coming out from under the archway of the General Staff building; trumpeters, Cossacks of the Guard, then the carriages—

Please God all would pass off well.

To compose myself, I stood looking at the Grand Duchess.

She had been standing with her head bent in prayer. Suddenly, to my amazement, she started—her head jerked up, and she stared around her half-dazedly. She was pale to the lips. I hurried across. 'Your Imperial Highness—are you unwell? Please sit down, and I'll—'

She looked at me with real anguish. 'Andrei—*I cannot pray.*'

'You're tired, Your Imperial Highness. If you sit—'

'It's not something within me, Andrei, it's something external. Something evil has come here—' Her voice died away. For a moment we stared at each other wordlessly. Then I said, '*He* has come.' She nodded. 'Yes, I think it must be he. Andrei, for the love of God get him away, he mustn't be allowed to desecrate the celebration for—

for—' Her voice was so low I could not hear her last words with any distinctness, but I believe they were, 'the monarchy he has done so much to ruin.'

I kissed her hand and saluted, turned and for the first time saw Rasputin.

He stood in front of the space reserved for the Duma. He wore a crimson silk tunic, baggy black trousers, boots with patent-leather tops. He wore a gold pectoral cross on a gold chain—everyone knew about that cross, a gift from the Czarina. Probably the tunic was another gift of hers—she delighted in making and embroidering blouses for this greasy-haired animal who stank like a goat. That was my first impression of him—the coarseness and the sheer animal smell of him. I began to think confusedly as I made my way towards him, 'How *can* she?'

And then, with a furious stride that resounded through the cathedral, Rodzianko was back, Rodzianko practically berserk with rage; the space he'd won for his beloved Duma being usurped by *this* filth!

'What are you doing here?'

Rasputin stared at him insolently. 'What's that got to do with you?' He used the familiar *thou*.

'If you address me like that, I'll drag you from the cathedral by the beard. Don't you know I'm the President of the Duma?'

Rasputin stared at him. His eyes were pale, very small; they narrowed now to glittering pinpoints. I thought, incredulously, My God, he's trying to hypnotise Rodzianko—*here!*

But he had chosen the wrong man. If his own eyes were narrowing, Rodzianko's seemed about to start from his head. He towered over the Siberiak. 'Clear out at once, you heretic, there is no room for you in this sacred place.'

An invitation card was flourished. 'I was invited here at the wish of persons more highly placed than you.'

'Clear out at once!'

Rasputin fell on his knees and began to pray, bowing to the ground. The enraged Rodzianko said, 'Enough of this tomfoolery. Clear out at once, or I'll order my sergeants-at-arms to carry you out!'

With a heavy groan, a loud, 'Oh, Lord, forgive him such a sin!' and a look that scarcely testified to the sincerity of the prayer, Rasputin lurched to his feet and walked clumsily away. I followed him to the West Door, saw him helped into a sable-lined coat by a Court Cossack, drive away in a luxurious motor-car.

How could she? How *could* she? No one with a grain of sense would accept the obscene accounts of the relationship, but Mother knew that this animal greeted the Czarina with loud smacking kisses—and that she accounted it a privilege to kiss his hand. His hands were filthy, the nails were black with grime. And the animal stink of him. The odour of sanctity?

The Czarina who filled her boudoir with flowers, lilac, lilies, hyacinths.

Her mania for white wood and bright chintzes for the children's rooms.

This animal.

No, worse than an animal. I recalled the ugly look he'd given Rodzianko as he slunk out—and suddenly it was with the greatest difficulty that I suppressed a violent shudder. It was more than uneasiness, disquiet. I was suddenly convinced that something very horrible had passed close to me, something of stupefying evil and malevolence. My first reaction had been sheer physical repulsion, now came mental loathing.

No wonder even the Grand Duchess had been unable to pray.

I started, and went back to her. The whole cathedral was alive with whispers now; I wondered wretchedly how much the affair would snowball as it was recounted throughout Petersburg.

'He's gone,' said the Grand Duchess. 'I knew it—the oppression lifted, and I could pray.' She looked at me anxiously. 'I was selfish, Andrei—I shouldn't have sent you to—'

'Rodzianko, the Duma President, got to him first, Your Imperial Highness.'

'Thank God. Rodzianko's well able to look after himself; if, through me, you'd spoken to—to *him*, I should never have forgiven myself. But, Andrei, that he should *be* here!'

'He had an invitation,' I said awkwardly.

After this episode, the arrival of the Imperial party, and the actual service made little impression on me. Only three memories recur with any vividness. Alexei being carried in by a Cossack. His face was pinched, waxen. A kind of rage within me. 'They shouldn't have brought him, they shouldn't have brought him!' Couldn't they see the bitter irony of it—this poor sick child represented the future of the dynasty whose tercentenary we were supposed to be celebrating?

The Czarina, wearing white, with the blue ribbon of St Andrew across her shoulder. She seemed as remote as ever.

The sheer lack of warmth in the cathedral. A cold scrutiny, curiosity, soon the criticisms would come—that was all. Half-hearted actors taking part in a play they had little faith in.

And the atmosphere didn't improve. In the evening there was a gala performance at the Marinsky—inevitably Glinka's *A Life for the Czar*. It would be poetic licence to say the boxes blazed with jewels, but they certainly scintillated. The stalls were crammed with court officials. And everywhere the same unfriendly curiosity so palpable at the *Te Deum* in the morning. This time the question being asked was, 'Will she last it out? It's the first time for years she's come with him to the theatre.'

She didn't last it out.

She wore white velvet, a turquoise tiara, again the blue St Andrew ribbon. No smile at the cheers at the end of the Anthem; her face became expressive only when she sat down, leaned back out of view. The old familiar expression of relief because an unpleasant duty was over.

Behind me two women were laying bets with each other—would the Czarina stick it out until the end of the first act?

'Give her credit for one thing, though—she's not deceitful. She doesn't care how clear she makes the fact that she detests the lot of us!'

She had a beautiful fan of white eagles' feathers—that was all you could see of her.

Soon it was shaking convulsively.

I sat there like a fool willing her to stay. 'Just a little longer— twenty minutes, ten minutes, then there'll be an interval. It won't be so bad if you at least wait for the interval—and don't come back afterwards.'

But she didn't wait for the interval. She bent across, whispered to the Czar, had gone. He must have caught the muttering that went round the theatre, must have seen the even more eloquent shrugs of the shoulder.

'I've won! I've won! I *said* she wouldn't stick it out until the end of the first act! You'll come with me to Fabergé's tomorrow—'

Next night there was the ball given by the nobility of St Petersburg in honour of their sovereigns. The Czarina, eyes downcast, lips unsmiling, danced the first dance with the Czar—the ceremonial polonaise—and then left. Resentment was bitter, and outspoken.

'*They're* not giving a ball at all—' (incredible, but true), '—and she's slighting the function we're courteous enough to give them!'

'In any case,' said one of Mother's friends to me, 'she should have stayed for her daughter's sake! To leave like this at the child's first public appearance in society!'

Olga wore a pale pink chiffon dress. There was a silver ribbon threaded in her hair, which shone as if it had been burnished. She stood on the steps leading down from the gallery to the floor of the ballroom, and she was laughing. Three of her Grand Ducal cousins were claiming the next dance. She was laughing but her blue eyes had an expression familiar to me—it was the expression I'd seen when I'd found her in the cornfield all those years ago—and never forgotten. She waved to me. 'Andrei! Andrei! Andrei Alexandrovitch,' (more formally) 'I'm sure this dance is with you!'

And a few minutes later, 'It isn't, I know—'

'No fault of mine, but I thought I didn't stand a chance—'

'Andrei, will you dance with me again? I hate telling lies—begging favours like this—'

'You know it's not begging favours, but don't you think that your cousins should—'

She panicked. 'I'm afraid. I'm so stupid. I don't know how to talk to anyone except Papa and Mamma and the Little One and the others. And you and your family because of Alix. Why are you looking so furious? Have I said anything *unutterably* silly?'

I couldn't say, 'So your mother leaves you, having relegated you to the background, utterly unprepared to take your proper place in the world?'

I said, 'You've always had a remarkably quick brain.'

'Once, perhaps, but not now. It worries me. I plod where I used to run.'

'It's the deadly life you lead,' I said.

'*Deadly?*'

'Seclusion. No friends, no entertainments, no contacts outside the family circle.'

Olgar said slowly, deliberately, 'I—don't—complain!'

'Because you don't know anything better.'

'I'm perfectly satisfied!'

'With a life that would drive any other girl to despair or revolt. Good God, you haven't even a room of your own! You're one of the

greatest heiresses in the world, and you haven't a room of your own!'
'You'll be shouting soon,' she said, 'and I wish I hadn't asked you—'
'I saw a letter you'd written to Mother—she'd dropped it and I
picked it up and couldn't help seeing the postscript. You said you would
love to have a manicure set, but daren't suggest you might have so
luxurious an article. And you were being serious! Oh, God!' I raged on,
'I'm spoiling your first public appearance, and it's the last thing I
wanted to do. What can I do to make amends? Start—clumsily—
flogging myself within an inch of my life, having cut off my right hand
first?'

'You'll be returning to Paris soon,' said Olga. 'Do you think you
could bring us back some perfume in the autumn?'

Grandmère died just after Easter; at Easter the Czar gave the Czarina
a Fabergé egg covered with miniature portraits of all the Romanov
Czars and Czarinas, framed in double eagles. Inside was a globe with
the Russian Empire inset in gold. There were delegations of peasants
in carefully-prepared costumes who offered loyal congratulations in
carefully-prepared words.

'Be sure that our lives belong to thee,' said a ninety-year-old village
elder. 'Be sure that at the first call we shall place ourselves before thee
like a wall and sacrifice ourselves, like Ivan Susanin, for thy dear life,
thy house—'

It was as unreal as the Easter egg, but not to the Czar and the Czarina.
Her letter of sympathy to Mother ended with, 'We were so sorry you
could not be in Russia for the celebrations. The stupid ministers have
been proved utterly wrong, the Czar can do anything he wants, for the
love and loyalty of the people is unbounded.'

The Imperial Family visited Nizhni Novgorod, Moscow, Kostroma.
At Moscow once again Alexei had to be carried by a Cossack; the
lasting impression left on most spectators was not of the might of the
dynasty, but of the pathetic helplessness of the dynasty's heir. In the
towns the feeling was the same as that in Petersburg, not enthusiasm,
but curiosity, and curiosity of a cold, shallow kind. Outside the towns
it might have been different—at Nizhni the Imperial Family sailed up the
river, and all along the Volga banks gaily decorated landing-stages
were set up at places where the Imperial boat would stop. Crowds of
peasants gathered here, dressed in their best, hoping to see the Czar,
but he did not appear—there was a bitterly cold wind—and the steamer

did not even stop, but went on steadily until it reached Kostroma.

It was almost as if day by day the Czar became more and more withdrawn from his people; 'He seems,' a minister wrote in despair to Mother, 'to have lost all interest in the celebrations. *We* thought it would be a superb opportunity to win over the people, but all it has done is to underline the remoteness and unpopularity of the dynasty. And, most tragic of all, *they don't see it.*'

Indeed they did not. Mother received another letter from the Czarina. 'What cowards the ministers are, and how they misrepresent the true nature of things! Don't they realise that *they* are the barrier between Czar and people? All this senseless talk of "changed conditions", not to mention that even more wicked lie about the threat of revolution! Perhaps we'll hear less of this now that they've seen for themselves that we need merely to show ourselves and the people are ours, body and soul!'

'Oh, dear God!' cried Mother in despair. 'She must know that they *don't* show themselves—that's the whole point!'

'*He* followed them, I've been told.'

'Who? Rasputin?'

'Yes. He couldn't be smuggled on to the ship, but it was arranged that he should follow them. He had all the necessary permits and was seen in churches along the route—Kostroma, for one.'

'The Czarina wasn't at Kostroma. She was so exhausted by the Moscow celebrations that the Czar's sister had to take her place.'

'That was unfortunate.'

For Kostroma, the terraced town situated above the Volga, was the cradle of the Romanov dynasty. A little over a mile from the centre of the city stands the monastery where in March 1613 the boy Michael Romanov had received the deputation which offered him the crown. In 1613 the monastery was more of a fortress, where Michael had taken refuge from his enemies; it was well suited for this, having strong stone walls dating back to the fourteenth century when the founder of the Godunov family built it on the spot where he had had a vision of the Virgin accompanied by a saint. The monastery had been given the name of the saint—Ipatiev.

When we returned to Russia in the autumn, the Imperial Family's withdrawal from public life was receiving more bitter criticism than ever. '*She*, of course, is like her grandmother, Victoria—Doesn't she realise what she's doing to her daughters, cutting them off from all outside contacts?' 'Oh, my dear, but then she thinks any outside contacts would contaminate them!'

But few people really considered the girls themselves—their isolation was used as another stick to beat the Czarina. Few people wondered if they ever rebelled against the monotony of life at Czarskoe, the lack of gaiety, if they ever wondered *why* they lived in such isolation. It had grown worse, of course, since Alexei's birth. Before that they had occasionally mixed with the children of officers of the Guard, court officials. But no longer—now if Alexei were allowed to play with anyone, it must be the children of Derevenko, his sailor attendant. It seemed the easiest way. If he were ill, an order was enough—'The children must not come to the palace.' Derevenko would simply accept it. You could not do that with other people. As for the girls, there was never any question of inviting young people for *their* sake; 'There are four of them—they can amuse themselves.'

But for a short time, in the autumn and winter of 1913-14, the Czarina relaxed the restrictions. She was happier, more confident because of the way in which she believed the tercentenary celebrations had confirmed her convictions about the people's love and loyalty, so a few concerts, even a dance, might be permitted. Not in Petersburg, of course, but during the autumn stay in the Crimea, where Alexei was having hot mud-bath treatments for his leg. The pretence that little was wrong was still maintained; official photographs taken that year always showed him seated, so that the bent left leg was not noticeable.

Mother, on returning from France, always went almost immediately down to the south to Alix's grave, and I, whenever I could, went with her. Olga sent a little note; would it be considered heartless if Mother were invited to a dance that was being given at the palace at Livadia? Mother's reply was prompt; nothing could give her greater pleasure.

It was a new palace now, the old one had been pulled down and a new building planned by the Czarina took its place. It was in the Italian style, and its creatress tried to reproduce much of what she had seen during her girlhood visits to Venice and Florence. The scenery, of course, was magnificent, olives, cypresses, roses covering the great mountain on the slope of which the palace was built. Almost every room had a view of the sea, sapphire-blue.

And the Grand Duchesses had a brief glimpse of the life led by so many young girls of their age.

The Cossacks of the Escort had sung, the balalaika orchestra from the *Standart* had played. Now the Imperial orchestra was playing, music by Strauss, from *A Thousand and One Nights*.

'It was when this was being played for the first time that my grandfather and grandmother met,' I said to Olga.

'Will it distress your mother?' she asked instantly.

'No—it wouldn't distress Grandfather either, if he were here. He misses Grandmère horribly, of course, but it's like what Mother said after Father was killed—you don't rage against God because you've lost them, you can't find words to thank Him sufficiently for letting you have them.'

Yet the bitter-sweet music was influencing my mood, and it was a glorious night, the wind carrying down from the higher slopes of the mountain the scent of innumerable flowers and herbs, ruffling the waters of the sea below us. The moon silvered the silhouettes of the cypresses.

Olga wore white, a very simple dress, and a single string of pearls. 'I wish it weren't so beautiful,' she said. 'Too beautiful.'

'Are you happy?'

'Yes. *Positively* happy. I'm such a coward. I half wish I weren't—it can't last.'

'Why not?'

'Because soon we have to go back to Petersburg.'

'But you can go on being happy there!'

'Dances, you mean? Well, Grandmamma's going to give one for Tatiana and me—'

'You'd be happier walking along the Neva quays.'

'You've said that before. Is that the best thing you can wish for me, Andrei?'

'No. I'd like you to see Brittany; walk along the path along the cliffs. And I wish you could see the Tyrol when the spring flowers are just beginning.'

'But I never want to leave Russia!'

'You may have to one day.'

'Marriage, you mean? I couldn't bear to leave my country.'

'My mother did.'

'Oh, but she was coming to Russia!'

'Yes,' said Mother later that night, 'I had quite a long talk with the Czarina. She was watching you and Olga talking together. "Olga is

213

growing up fast," she said. "Pray God there is a long and happy life before her," I said. "Avoye," she said, with a sudden warmth and softness that one sees so rarely nowadays, "I know how devoted you are to Olga—she and your poor darling were so close, weren't they? It's because of Alix and for fear of hurting you that I've rarely talked about the girls to you—"

'I said I should like nothing better than to talk about Olga.

' "When she looks as pretty and sparkling as she does now, I can't go on avoiding the fact that soon we must be thinking of her marriage. We have no fixed ideas, of course, except one—that she must marry for love, as we did. Of course, it goes without saying that she mustn't make any kind of marriage that could weaken the monarchy." '

'Those ideas might cancel each other out,' I said.

'Meaning that a love match with a commoner will never be considered?' Mother's eyes met mine. 'Yes. But there is another obstacle to Olga's marriage which the Czarina can't or won't see. Olga might give her children the disease which makes her brother's life a martyrdom.'

When the Imperial Family returned to Petersburg that winter the Dowager-Czarina gave a ball at the Anitchkov Palace for her granddaughters. Mother said it followed the old pattern—the Czarina left early. The Czar, however, stayed on until the small hours so that his daughters' pleasure would not be cut short.

I received an invitation, but was unable to accept, as within a few days I was returning to France for my final period of duty; I should be back in Russia for good in the summer of 1914. Instead I sent a music-box I had found in Vienna some years before; it was ivory and mother-of-pearl and tinkled out music from *A Thousand and One Nights*.

21

'The best seasons . . .'

'The best seasons for a tour in Bosnia-Herzegovina
are the months of May, June and September . . .'
Baedeker's *Austria-Hungary* (1914)

TO WRITE OBJECTIVELY of that spring and summer is now impossible. One records that the weather was glorious—and remembers all the while that the same brilliant sun was beating down on the white houses, poplars and plum blossom of an obscure Balkan town where the road runs along the quay of a river that almost dries up in summer, so that dozens of little boys stand in its bed, fishing for minnows.

Mother and I spent the April of 1914 in Paris with Grandfather and Uncle Raoul. Spring is anywhere the most miraculous time of the year, but in Paris there is a peculiar wonderment in the air. We would drive down the long Avenue des Champs Elysées, Elysian enough, with the sun warm on the face, flower-sellers holding out bunches of pale primroses as we passed, and all the chestnut trees were just bursting into bud—yes, the chestnut candles were being lit for the dead who would die from the high summer onwards.

One could understand the envious Germans saying, '*As happy as God in Paris,*' I remarked one late evening to Mother as we stood before an open window in Uncle's study gazing out at the dark garden, from which came a scent of violets and early lilac so vivid and strong you might almost swear you could see and touch it.

'That,' said Uncle Raoul, looking up from a letter he was writing, 'is a typically gross Teutonic view of the Deity. Does one assume He takes pleasure in the good food and bad women which Paris means to *them?*'

'Now all your Jesuit hackles are up,' said Mother.

'Come, Avoye, should I tolerate a—a blasphemous conception of a —a guzzling Godhead—'

It was then that Michel brought in the telegram with the news that in Austria my great-grandfather was dangerously ill. So on a moonlit night of black and ivory and silver I took my last view of a Paris that was sane, and have always been glad that it was so. I hadn't been there long enough, the season wasn't far enough advanced, for me to be bored or irritated by the vapidity of fashionable life; the milling crowds at the Auteuil and Longchamps races in June, the mass exodus a week later to Deauville or Biarritz or Le Touquet, the more idiotic women discussing only the decree of Poiret, the dictator of fashion, 'Let the bust be liberated and the legs be fettered!'

My great-grandfather died two days after we reached him. Thank God for it. Had he lived until August he would have seen his only grandson serving in one enemy army, his only great-grandson fighting in another. Better that he should be at rest in the little church beside the clear stream leaping down to join the Inn, the church in the flowering upland meadows beneath the white crags of his beloved Tyrol.

Years before, the Austrian Emperor, in recognition of Great-grandfather's services, had given him the Order of the Golden Fleece. It was now the duty of Uncle Raoul and myself, as his sole descendants, to return in person that Order to the Emperor.

So we paid our last visit to a sane Vienna, caught the scent of the lindens, and the appleblossom, rode in the sun in the Ringstrasse, past the double line of trees like green lace, and everywhere there was music, bells from the churches, violins from the cafés, the surge of waltzes, and laughter in the light, fragrant dusk.

There was not a tremendous amount of ceremony involved in our visit to Schönbrunn. We were taken to the first floor where we were received in audience in the Emperor's study.

The Emperor, wearing general's uniform, white tunic, scarlet trousers, his own Golden Fleece about his neck, received us standing, with his left hand resting on the hilt of his dress sword. He was eighty-four then, but straight as ever, his movements giving no indication of physical weakness; he had, he said, just come in from a brisk stroll in the gardens, and was looking forward to his summer visit to Bad Ischl and the rather nondescript yellow two-storey villa there where, for a few hours each day, he could be happy, getting up before dawn, putting on an old felt hat, the well-worn Tyrolean *lederhosen* (allegedly worn by his valet for several years to break them in), creeping downstairs so that he would not disturb his daughter and grandchildren, out on the

216

mountains, a gamekeeper his only companion, until eleven o'clock and then back to his desk till the end of the day.

He spoke to us now slowly, but finely, of Great-grandfather's long life of loyalty and service. We had expected restraint and gentleness from him, the greatest gentleman it has ever been my privilege to meet, melancholy too, for to any man over eighty each fresh report of death must have personal significance; what we had not been prepared for was the curious intimacy of the conversation. For example, after we had described the funeral, he said, 'I expect you know what happens at an Emperor's funeral? The coffin is taken to rest in the Capuchin church in the Neuemarkt, that small plain-looking building, and the Chamberlain knocks with his golden staff at the closed door. "Admission for His Apostolic Majesty the Emperor," he demands, and from behind the door a monk replies he knows nothing of His Apostolic Majesty. It is only when admission is begged for a brother, a miserable sinner, that the door is opened—Yes,' said the Emperor, as if to himself, 'he ceases to be an Emperor, and is admitted as a poor ordinary sinner—relieved, at last, of all his burdens—though God knows, Emperor or not, one tries to humble oneself before Heaven, and its decrees.'

After a brief silence, which we would have died rather than break, he went on more animatedly, 'Your great-grandfather, you know, was with me at the beginning of it all, when it was decided that I should become Emperor. When you reach my age, in some ways the remote past's clearer than more recent years, and I can recall very vividly indeed how in the Archbishop's palace in Olmutz in Moravia, I knelt before my uncle, the Emperor who was abdicating, to ask his blessing, and he embraced me and whispered, "God bless you. Be brave, God will protect you!" And then, when I kissed his hand, he said, "You won't find it too bad, Franzi!"'

Then a smile in his blue eyes, he began to question me kindly about myself, and about Mother, who was back in Petersburg. I remember particularly how he used one adjective to describe her—'vortrefflichste', the incomparable one.

He offered us his hand, and the audience was over. It had taken more than half an hour; we had not expected it would last half that time. We were so moved that for a good ten minutes after leaving the palace we were quite silent, then, 'Well!' said Uncle Raoul. 'That's grandeur for you. Strange that one straight-backed old man standing alone in a rather small room can give you a greater feeling of majesty than any amount of state banquets. Not to mention a greater feeling of safety.'

'Safety, Uncle?'

'Oh, yes. Those great blazing chandeliers at the Hofburg, they're always crashing down, there's a real casualty rate at those state affairs. You keep squinting up all the time, fearing a blow from heaven, and at the same time trying to eat like fury. The Emperor doesn't believe in wasting time over food, and detests small-talk, and he's trained the palace staff to serve and clear a twelve-course dinner in less than an hour. With a new course being served the moment the Emperor clears *his* plate, if you're at the bottom of the table you keep getting *your* plate whisked away before you've taken a mouthful. As Milton put it, *The hungry sheep look up and are not fed.*'

The weather was magnificent in Vienna, too, that year. The foliage in the Vienna Woods had never been richer, the sun had never sparkled more brightly on the many-coloured dome of St Stephen's; even the *café-au-lait* Danube seemed less dull than usual. Uncle Raoul loved Vienna; he always found its irony, its gentle brilliance, its bitter-sweet charm far more congenial than the garish glitter of Paris. We decided to stay in Austria until early June, after which Uncle would come back with me to Russia, to help make arrangements for the state visit of the French President.

So, as we had been in Paris for the Easter of 1914, we spent Whitsun in Vienna. Was Austria planning war? If she were, only a very few men were in the secret. We visited friends in the gold and red Chancellery, sat chatting to them as the scent of lime flowers in the Volksgarten drifted in through the tall windows, but from them no whisper of war—and assuredly they would have given us some warning, no matter how oblique.

Two days before we left for St Petersburg, we went to the Prater, where teams of Austrian cavalry officers were jumping—a marvellous show. It was during the applause following one particularly good round that someone slapped me on the back, and I swung round to be hugged by Franz von Mayrhofen, the son of Great-grandfather's neighbours in the Tyrol. Next moment he was saluting Uncle Raoul in a more orthodox fashion, and I could take a good look at him. He did not exude his usual vitality, he looked worn; I said so—in fact I was so surprised the remark was almost jerked out of me.

Uncle Raoul had noticed it too. 'What in the devil have you been up to, Franzi?' he demanded, frowning.

Franz grinned ruefully. 'No need to send a sheaf of telegrams to Mother, sir,' he said. 'She knows the cause of my deplorable appearance —all incurred in the line of duty.'

He had always been one to rattle on, gesturing, changing position every half-minute, but now he was chattering away like a machine-gun.

'Obviously,' said Uncle Raoul, with his sudden smile, 'you're in attendance on someone who expects you to keep your mouth shut. No *panache* now, all discipline—Good God, you're not ADC to the Archduke Franz Ferdinand, are you?'

'For the moment, sir, but Lord knows how long it—or I'll—last.'

'But why *you?*' I demanded, and began to laugh helplessly. 'Good old insouciant Franzi, dragged at the chariot-wheels of manic efficiency and "spit-and-polish".'

'You needn't tell me; not for nothing does he wear his hair *en brosse* and a Hohenzollern moustache—it's worse than Potsdam!' He cast an agonised look behind him, 'Please come quickly—I caught sight of you two a few minutes ago, and in an excess of positively berserk courage, dared to mention it. Do come along and make your bows— he's pleased to be gracious.'

'Ah, yes, my grandfather was an associate of his,' said Uncle Raoul, 'while Andrei's nationality—'

'I keep forgetting he's pro-Russian,' said Franz.

'Half the time,' I said gloomily, 'I feel *that's* solely because contemplation of any Russian is good for his self-esteem. Compared with our unfathomable way of running things, Austrian *schlamperei** is sheer bureaucratic genius.'

'For God's sake don't mention *schlamperei*—it'll bring out all his Prussian phobia on the subject. And I have to live with him.'

A heavy face, generally mask-like, or, if it showed emotion, usually morose or arrogant. Grey-blue eyes with unusually small pupils. A stout, clumsy body in a uniform that always looked as if it fitted too tightly, a thick neck too closely confined by the high collar, a manner too often noisy, blustering—the contrast between the charmless, ungracious Heir and his uncle, the old Emperor, still spare, upright, trim, elegant, and the epitome of dignified courtesy, was almost shocking.

* Carefree inefficiency.

But on this occasion, as Franz had said, the Archduke was pleased to be gracious. More, hearing that Uncle Raoul would soon be leaving for Petersburg, he said, in the thin voice oddly high-pitched for a man of his bulk, he wanted to talk with him when there was greater time and privacy. It seemed I was included in the invitation for the following day at the Belvedere.

Later Uncle Raoul said to me, 'I was forgetting—you've never been presented to the Archduke before, have you?'

'No—Did I stare, then?'

'You weren't obviously sizing him up, if that's what you mean, but I didn't miss the veiled scrutiny.'

'I couldn't help it, Uncle; he's so unlike the Emperor, and he—he doesn't fit in with Vienna!'

'And doesn't Vienna know it, and doesn't he know that Vienna resents his lack of elegance and lack of an air of breeding, and lack of appreciation of the arts and beauty—and doesn't he hate Vienna because of it!'

We found our way back to our seats, continued our conversation in low voices to the background of a ripple of applause. The jumping was really extremely good that year.

I said cautiously, 'In his photographs he always looks overbearing and bad-tempered.'

'I know someone who saw him fly into a paroxysm of rage one day and rip the seat of a railway carriage to shreds with his sabre. I should think the uncontrollable temper is a relic of the tuberculosis he had years ago; his lungs were in such a state most people rather obviously wrote him off as a future Emperor, and as obviously weren't shedding any tears over it, either. My own idea, absurd though it may seem, is that he willed himself to live simply to cheat them of that satisfaction—and, of course, to get revenge on them one day. Only the day of revenge is slow in coming. He's frustrated, and he's brooding, and that's why Franzi's life is hell on earth.'

But next day the ogre was transformed, a family man; in fact he couldn't have been more a family man, for he received us in the company of his wife and three children.

The Duchess—his morganatic wife—was a dear. God forbid that I should appear flippant or familiar in speaking of a lady ill-used in her lifetime and shockingly done to death, but there was a sweetness, a motherliness about her that would make young men of my age describe her in this way. She was kind, and she was charming; no wonder the Archduke said that marrying her was the cleverest thing he had ever done.

She chatted to me now, while the Archduke and Uncle Raoul talked at the far end of the red salon: talking about gardens, it seemed, for I heard the Archducal sentence rising to a crescendo of '. . . plum trees!' She set me so completely at my ease that when she smiled past me and I realised the Archduke was approaching, I would not have been too scared even if he had been at his most overbearing and boorish. But to his wife and children he always showed his better side. He asked for details of my great-grandfather's funeral—a lucky beginning, because I managed to bring in something about the little church on the sunlit hillside—an unassuming little church, but I said, honestly enough, we wouldn't have it any different. Great-grandfather had always set his face resolutely against the modern craze for restoration-run-mad.

The heavy face lit up. 'Yes, he was my good ally in my work as head of the Central Commission for the Care of Monuments—I remember he told me of the church, medieval foundation, baroque above, I believe? These village priests, once they get the bits between their teeth—'

I could remember Great-grandfather, with his usual exquisite politeness, telling Grandfather carefully, 'His Imperial Highness is what you might call a strong colleague!'

When he stopped for breath I said hurriedly, 'Two activities gave my great-grandfather tremendous satisfaction in recent years, sir; his work on the Commission headed by your Royal and Imperial Highness, and the gardens of his home here in Vienna and in—'

'Ah, yes, he had very good ideas as to the massing of colour, and the use he made of the sun on that hill, and that waterfall against the pines—I am so very sorry he did not live long enough to come to Konospicht this summer; there are some new landscaping arrangements there he'd have found immensely interesting. The roses will be excellent in mid-June. The Emperor of Germany will be paying me a visit then, and afterwards I was hoping I could persuade the Prince to come. With this glorious weather, the roses should be quite outstanding—'

So on and on, very cordial, roses and old churches and, towards the end, a friendly tap on the shoulder and a gruff, 'Well, my boy, I hope you share my views that Russia and Austria should be friends, close friends!'

'Your Imperial Highness, every time I come back to Austria I wish my Jacobite ancestor had made for Vienna instead of Petersburg.'

'Good! Good!'

The audience was over, but as I kissed the Duchess's hand, the Archduke began talking vehemently to my uncle again. But only for a moment; he was, for him, relaxed and smiling as we saluted him, and he smiled even more broadly as Uncle Raoul said in a low voice, looking back to where the Duchess stood with the three charming children in a pool of sunlight, 'Your Imperial Highness, you will know it made my grandfather feel greatly honoured and gratified that every year on the anniversary of your marriage—'

'No need to remind me. He would always send an exquisite vase filled with white roses to Her Highness. I don't forget things like that.'

'We, his family, would ask Your Highness' permission to continue the custom of duty and devotion—'

'Yes, yes, by all means, but I shan't tell Her Highness, let it be an agreeable surprise for her—eh? We shan't be here, of course—you know that? We shall be visiting Bosnia.'

'Then, with Your Highness' permission, I'll ask Graf von Mayrhofen where you will be on the precise date.'

'No need—I can tell you myself. No need for me to make an effort to remember where I'll be on the 28th of June. Sarajevo. Our fourteenth anniversary.'

Genially he accompanied us to the white doorway. 'Your great-grandfather always admired the view from the terrace.'

We had looked back and saluted for the last time. The Archduke had rejoined his wife and the three children. They stood smiling in that radiant sunlight.

'It's incredible!' I whispered to Uncle Raoul as we came through the arcades, and down the flight of steps, to walk away past the fountains and clipped hedges and smiling stone sphinxes. 'The ogre of Austro-Hungary a—a pattern of bourgeois domestic felicity.'

'No!' said Uncle Raoul. 'It's more incredible still. It's still a love match. Well, you survived.'

'Indeed I did—on a conversational diet of gardens and church preservation.' After a moment I ventured, 'Did *you* ever get beyond the plum trees, sir?'

'What in the devil—' began Uncle Raoul, only to burst into sudden laughter. 'Yes, I *do* believe plum trees were mentioned—but all as part of high diplomacy.'

My turn to stare as he went on, 'I'll tell you what was said, because you may have the opportunity to pass on the message to someone in the Imperial Family, and it'll be more likely to reach the Czar that way than through official channels—that's why the Archduke talked to me. A French officer with Russian connections, he said, was probably a better intermediary than a Russian diplomat.'

'Uncle Raoul! Get back to the plum trees!'

'Ah, yes, the plum trees. Well, he wants it to be known that he personally will always be opposed to any war between Austria and Serbia if only for the reason that Austria wouldn't gain by it, or, as he put it, "All we'd get out of it would be a pack of thieves, ruffians, murderers and a few plum trees!" '

After the end of that summer, there was Allied enthusiasm soaring to fever-pitch for two Davids, Serbia and Belgium, facing the two Goliaths of Austria and Germany. The legend of 'gallant little Belgium' has foundation enough; that of Serbia rather blinded people to the fact that for a dozen years the Serbs had been regarded by the rest of Europe, as Grandfather put it once, 'As a gang of savages, Turks in everything but name.' He was speaking at the time that the King and Queen of Serbia had been murdered in circumstances so atrocious that England and Holland had broken off diplomatic relations with the new government headed by the King and Prime Minister in power in 1914. Serbia, dominated by an infamous 'secret' society, the Black Hand, symbolised treachery, violence and cruelty of another time and age; more, since the barbaric extinction of the old royal family, the new régime was showing a megalomania which threatened to set the entire Balkans alight in the name of Greater Serbia. The Serb government was not particular about the lies it told; it was always screaming that the Archduke on his accession would oppress his Slav subjects in a way which would make Turkish rule seem a miracle of enlightened tolerance—I said as much now to Uncle Raoul, who replied, 'Ah, but the Archduke's unforgivable sin, in their eyes, is that he plans to do the very opposite, he's going to shore up his empire from within, give the Slavs a status equal to that of Austrians and Hungarians, be crowned in Prague, give Serbs and Croats federal status, after which none of them will ever listen to any invitation to join Greater Serbia—'

'Of course,' I said, 'his wife's a Slav, too!'

'Exactly. You saw his affection for her; when he succeeds, she may well become Empress after all. And now, from the sublime to the ridiculous; when you do your packing, be careful with those *flaçons*—'

Which brought me back to Russia with a sudden start. 'Oh, God!' I said. 'Things are so different there and I get so irritated—'

'My good Andrei, lower your voice, you're shouting. Not that I don't agree thoroughly with your sentiments, but I don't want you to be yelling them at the top of your voice just when some *pickelhaubed* Prussian here for the jumping contest is passing by. And take care in packing those *flaçons*—since you won't let my valet do it.'

I went red and said something confusedly about the *flaçons* being special—but, after all, one mightn't be needed, so what did it matter if it got broken?

'H'm,' said Uncle Raoul. 'A pity the Jesuits didn't have the educating of you. Well, I'll see you at dinner; I must go to the Embassy first.'

The point about the *flaçons* was this—the four Grand Duchesses were, of course, brought up in the utmost simplicity. They slept on camp beds, did not have rooms of their own, their mother chose and ordered their clothes—and no frivolity was allowed. Usually they were dressed alike. They rather hurt the Czarina because they liked softening their bathwater with almond bran, Mother told me once—and they *did* love perfume, nothing musky or exotic, just pure flower essence, but, still, the Czarina didn't really approve. So remembering what Olga had said at the dance, Mother and I had bought their favourite perfumes in Paris; Coty's *Rose Thé* for Olga, Jasmin for Tatiana, Lilac for Marie, Violet for Anastasia. All had been secreted in Mother's luggage—she had, of course, come with us to be with Great-grand-father but immediately after the funeral had left for Russia since she was required in attendance. In the haste, the perfume had been left behind; I'd resignedly brought it with me to Vienna, and there was something faulty about the stopper of the bottle of Violet—a perfume I detest—and some had leaked out on to my shirts, which now reeked of it—I had to beseech giggling laundresses to scrub the smell out. However, the bottle I grumbled about chiefly was the *Rose Thé*—the biggest of the lot, for Olga's name-day fell in mid-July. It would not be needed, I kept saying resentfully, because apparently all the talk in Russia now was of an engagement between Olga and Prince Carol of Roumania.

And so I was saying sulkily to Uncle Raoul as we parted, he to go to the French Embassy nearby, I to do a little shopping in the Ringstrasse then to Stephansplatz and the Café de l'Europe, that it wasn't really proper that I should be carrying about outsize bottles of perfume for a Grand Duchess who would be engaged to a foreign princeling by the time we got home.

'Such delicacy!' he said ironically.

But when he returned, it was with news that made us forget everything else. Grandfather was so unwell that he had issued the laconic and startling announcement that in July he would be following his doctor's advice and taking a cure at Kissingen.

'Kissingen?' I'd queried incredulously.

'Deliberate choice on his doctor's part,' said Uncle Raoul. 'He won't know anyone there—not like Aix—so he'll have a dull, restful time.'

'He'll go mad, alone, surrounded by Germans.'

'Wait, here's a postcript—your mother's joining him.'

Grandfather wrote in his usual astringent way, but, as Uncle Raoul remarked, the very fact that, (a) he had listened to his doctor at all, (b) accepted the extremely unpalatable advice to visit Kissingen, showed that he was indeed feeling far from well. What he did not say, what I did not say, though we both knew it only too well, was that Grandfather was missing Grandmère dreadfully.

Franz arrived that evening to say goodbye. He reported that the Archduke's good humour had remained after we had left. 'It's because you're carrying on the Prince's custom of sending roses to the Duchess. But don't give definite orders yet about sending them to Sarajevo—'

'Why not?' asked Uncle Raoul, putting down his glass of wine. We were sitting on the balcony; soon they would be illuminating the hundred-foot fountain that played between us and the Schwarzenburg Palace.

'The trip to Bosnia might be put off.'

'Too dangerous?'

Franz laughed. '*Not* for any melodramatic reason, sir. No, do you know the country? High, arid, no trees, hellishly hot in summer. The Archduke has to take care of himself because of the state of his lungs, and too much heat, too much exhaustion won't help. That'll be the reason for a postponement if there is one, though I've no doubt people who don't like the Archduke—or Austria—will say he's scared of something else—Serbian threats, for example. Last December there was a charming article in an *émigré* Serb paper published in Chicago; the Archduke was visiting Sarajevo, it said— let all Serbs take knives, rifles, bombs, dynamite—death to the Hapsburgs —and so on.'

'Does the Archduke know about the article?'

'Oh, yes, but threats wouldn't turn him back, especially since His Majesty visited the place four years ago, aged eighty, and came away complaining there were too many police guarding the roads, keeping him from his subjects! He's wonderful, isn't he? After that, even if the Archduke were told there was a Serb assassin behind every cypress in Bosnia, he wouldn't let *that* deter him.'

'I think you're wrong there,' said Uncle Raoul. 'If he thought there was that kind of danger, he wouldn't take the Duchess, would he?'

'You're right, of course,' said Franz, after a moment. 'For her sake— and for the sake of the children. I don't mind telling you, though, I'll be damned glad when it's all over; he takes a delight in giving his bodyguard the slip if he can. Well, back I go to my duty, which at present consists of keeping the Archduke in ignorance of the more idiotic rumours floating round—like the one that the entire trip's been planned solely to give provocation to Serbia. Some Serb papers are screaming about a quarter of a million men being massed on their frontier with Bosnia, whereas they're perfectly ordinary summer manoeuvres, miles from the border. A quarter of a million men couldn't exist in that stretch of country. Then there's the story that the whole thing's been arranged so that the Duchess can be received with imperial honour. I don't doubt that the Archduke will want as respectful a reception for her as possible, but the plain fact of the matter is that Potiorek, the Bosnian military governor, planned routine summer manoeuvres months ago, and invited the Archduke to attend as Inspector General of the armed forces—'

'What kind of a man is this military governor—Potiorek, you called him?' I asked curiously, struck by a sudden thought.

'I've never met him, but from his letters I'd say he's a high opinion of himself; why do you ask?'

'Because I'd say that he's unintelligent as well as being conceited.'

'Why, Andrei?'

'He must think he has the situation in Bosnia completely in hand to arrange a State Visit by the Austrian Heir for June 28.'

'It's the Archduke's wedding anniversary, I know,' said Franz, staring, 'but—'

'The Serbs use our calendar, so it's June 15, St Vitus Day, the Vidovdan. No, it wouldn't mean much to you, but that lunatic Potiorek should know better. For centuries June 15's been the day of national mourning for the Serbs because it's the anniversary of Kossovo—*now* do you see the point?'

Franz said soberly, 'Oh, yes, 1389, and the Turkish destruction of the old Christian kingdom of Serbia.'

Uncle Raoul, who had been listening in silence, said softly, 'One should be extraordinarily tactful on such anniversaries when nerves are laid bare.'

'But surely the anniversary doesn't grate so much now?' demanded Franz, rallying. 'Turkish enslavement is no longer a *fact*; if it comes to that, the Turks have been thrashed pretty conclusively by the Serbs—'

'And aren't the Serbs cockahoop because of it, and screaming of joining Bosnia and Herzegovina to a Greater Serbia! My dear boy, even if it were an anniversary for *rejoicing*, it would mean Serbs drinking too much, and drunkenness rarely lends itself to an atmosphere of sweetness and light.'

The little French clock chimed softly from the room behind us. 'Oh, Lord!' said Franz. 'I must be off. Well, sir, I'll let you know in good time if the visit's being postponed, though I don't think it will be. And really, I'm sure there's no need to worry.'

We said goodbye in the mildness of a Viennese May dusk; the sunset sky was pink behind St Stephen's spire as we waved down from the balcony; there was just light enough to make out the black Hapsburg eagle among the coloured tiles of the roof; below they sang Vespers, and within minutes the great gleaming eagle was lost in twilight.

22

'Es ist nichts'

PETERSBURG again, and the white nights. The wide waterways and streets seemed to sleep peacefully enough, but in the industrial areas, it was whispered that there was feverish unrest.

It was dreadfully hot in Russia that summer. About Csarskoe Selo, as I went to smuggle in perfumes, the park was dusty and lifeless, not a leaf stirred. Olga was not going to marry Carol of Roumania; she had said to Mother, 'I could never leave Russia.'

In Krassnoe the heat was particularly atrocious. Every field in the flat countryside was iron-hard, and baked brown. The smell of burning was inescapable—either turf piled high on the plain, or from distant forest fires. Dust was everywhere.

Still, it was better than Petersburg, hot and suffocating, with both sun and river seeming absolutely metallic.

The heat was almost tropical on the afternoon of the Officers' Races at Krassnoe; it poured down from the sky, it seemed to scorch up from the ground. In fact, I thought as I finished riding my mare, Douchka, it was the heat that caused the sudden hush in the crowd, that people had suddenly become too weary to talk. But they started whispering again, the whispers, like the silence, all spreading from the Imperial box.

I couldn't see very clearly what had occurred; the dust had got into my eyes. Rubbing away with my handkerchief, I said, 'Uncle Raoul—did you see anything happening?'

He stood beside me, patting Douchka's neck. His voice was very quiet. 'An officer, one of the Czar's entourage, I think, has just handed him a telegram.'

It was as if the thunderclap we had been expecting all that day suddenly burst about my ears.

'My God!' I said. 'I'd forgotten. I'd been thinking only of the Russian Calendar, and in the West *today's the 28th, isn't it?* Uncle Raoul—'

Uncle Raoul said, very slowly, 'The Czar's expression hasn't changed, but he's passed the telegram to the Austrian Ambassador—who's excusing himself, I think—yes, leaving. Andrei, I'm not waiting here to listen to distorted rumours, I'm going straight to the Austrian Embassy. Try to get to your mother, she'll be very upset.'

She was upset—with reason. For not only the Archduke had been shot that morning at Sarajevo—the Duchess had been murdered at his side.

Days later two letters came from Franz, forty-eight hours separating them. The first, though written hurriedly, had a proper address and date:

Hotel Bosnia,
Ilidze.
June 27, 1914

'The whole thing's turned out much better than I dared hope. The manoeuvres have gone very well indeed—positively no *schlamperei*, in fact, the Archduke's as pleased as Punch, though he expressed his pleasure in rather an unflattering manner by saying the bearing of the troops and the intelligence of the officers surprised him. However, he made amends in his cross-grained way by sending a telegram to the Emperor praising the Fifteenth and Sixteenth Corps, and had the message read aloud by every regimental commander in the language of his regiment, so everyone's more or less glittering with pleasure.

'Still, it's been gruelling work, and since it may be as hot as the devil tomorrow, it was suggested to the Archduke after dinner tonight that the visit to Sarajevo at ten in the morning should be cancelled; after all, we'll be there for only a couple of hours, and the real purpose of the Bosnian visit was the manoeuvres. But he wouldn't hear of it, said it would give offence to the town. The Duchess was delighted with the way the shopkeepers had sent up rugs and beaten silverware and all kinds of ornaments to make the rooms we're occupying here look a little better than temporary quarters in a Bosnian hotel; she and the Archduke actually made a surprise visit to the town just before the manoeuvres started to look for antiques in the Turkish quarter, a real labyrinth, filthy narrow lanes. They were quite unprotected, and were mobbed by the crowd. Loud cries of "*Zivio!*"

'Potiorek preened himself at being proved right. No disaffection whatsoever, he keeps saying in various ways contrived to give you the idea it's all due to *his* consummate handling of matters. The situation's so excellent that Sarajevo's out of bounds to the troops, who're being kept up in the hills, though Potiorek's boring us to death with descriptions of a most hideous mustard-coloured barracks in a bastard baroque he's had built for them; we shall have the privilege of taking a good look at this atrocity tomorrow—but empty; the might of the Austrian Empire, as far as Sarajevo's concerned, is currently being manifested by 120 policemen.

'It wasn't so good at the beginning. When we were leaving South Station in Vienna last Tuesday the electricity failed. "Ah!" said the Archduke. "Another premonitory sign!" He began to roar with laughter. "Be careful, travelling with me!" he said. "I was told by an old gypsy that I'd be the cause of a world war!" It was some time before the electricity came on again; he was disgusted with the miserable candle-light. "Like in a tomb!" he kept saying. "Like in a tomb, isn't it?"

'Still, not the rage we might have expected. As I said, he roared with laughter. He's always much better away from Vienna, and, of course, he's particularly good-tempered because the whole tour has been a triumph for the Duchess. She's been visiting schools and hospitals, saying and doing just the right thing, and tonight at dinner brought off wonderfully well what might have been a tricky situation —Roman Catholic Archbishop of Sarajevo on one side of her, Orthodox Archbishop of Sarajevo on the other, mutually glaring at the beginning of the meal. At the end, she had them both eating out of her hand. She's so good and kind and intelligent; one would do anything for her.

'Just come away from Mass—they fitted up a tiny private chapel for us. Your flowers have arrived and were received with very great pleasure; the Archduke told me to open my letter to convey their thanks, after seeing a telegram was sent to the children saying Papa and Mama are well and will be home with them on Tuesday.

'Hot sunshine today; the Duchess looks lovely, white dress, big picture hat. We go down to Sarajevo by the 9.28 train—little narrow-gauge railway—then drive to the City Hall (built by us but looking remarkably like a Turkish bath-house) in a car I feel your Uncle Raoul would like, a dark green Graf and Stift 4-cylinder belonging to Franz Harrach.'

The second letter was almost illegible, scrawled so incoherently it was difficult to recognise the writing, much less make sense of it.

'It was frightful—frightful, they were dying and we didn't know it. They were sitting upright, Andrei, looking ahead so calmly, it seemed. We thought the second murderer'd missed, as the first had done. The revolver snapped twice, no more sound than blanks. There was Potiorek with his vacant face telling the driver to go back the way we'd come, and he went on reversing the car across the Lateiner Bridge in the direction of the Governor's Residence. It was only when the car was turned in the right direction and we moved forward again, picking up speed, that I saw a stream of blood spurt out of the Archduke's mouth. *She* cried out, "For heaven's sake, what's happened to you?" and crumpled up in a heap. We thought she'd fainted.

'We thought she'd only fainted, we didn't guess how badly *he* was hurt. He—with the bullet in his chest, knowing he was dying, was the only person to realise she might be hurt too. He managed to turn to her, to brace her up, whispering all the time: "Sophie! Dear Sophie! Don't die! Keep alive for our children." There was blood all down his tunic now, but he went on whispering to her.

'But she was dead, she'd been shot through the stomach. He died a moment after we reached the Residence. Harrach and I were trying to steady him and her in that awful jolting car; Harrach said something to the Archduke I couldn't catch, but I heard what the Archduke replied, "*Es ist nichts*—It's nothing." He repeated it six times, each time in a weaker voice, "It's nothing—it's nothing—it's nothing—it's nothing—it's nothing—it's nothing." I can't stop hearing him say it.

'They put them, all bloodied, on twin iron bedsteads, and I went down to the luncheon table in the banqueting hall below and grabbed all the flowers to cover them. I kept remembering how pink and pretty she'd looked this morning when the white roses came for her wedding anniversary, and wondering if the children had got the telegram saying they were well, and would be home on Tuesday.

'Andrei, whatever my shoulder was like, I should have been on the right side of them!'

Beneath was written in a precise hand, 'Graf von Mayrhofen does not mention that in the first attempt, he had received a wound in his shoulder of which he said nothing for several hours; he is now in a feverish state while also suffering badly from delayed shock. I have tried to dissuade him from writing any further to you, but he insists that at least he must be allowed to dictate to me an account of what happened, repeating, "They were right, and we were wrong." Accordingly, I thought it best to humour him.' And then came an indecipherable physician's signature followed by poor Franz's verbatim account of what happened.

'Sarajevo's a much bigger place than you imagine, quite sizable. Ninety-nine mosques, so plenty of minarets among the poplars and plum trees. A steep river gorge, but not much water at this time of year, in fact the river bed was practically dry, and there were usually some little boys fishing in the pools for minnows. When I told the Duchess this she laughed and said, "I wish we could stop and watch them."

'About ten o'clock we got into the cars near the railway station to drive to the City Hall for a reception by the Mayor, a big fat Moslem, sitting with the city police chief in the first car. In the second was the Archduke at the back on the left, the Duchess beside him. Before them Potiorek and Franz Harrach, on folding seats. They'd rolled back the top of the car to let the crowd have a good view. Three more cars with members of the entourage, a sixth car in case there was a breakdown. I was in the car following the Archduke, sitting with Potiorek's aide, von Merizzi, and the Duchess's lady-in-waiting.

'Nobody expected any trouble; things had gone so wonderfully well on the trip. One last stage, get it over, back to Vienna.

'At a quarter-past ten we were shaken out of the dream. We were driving along the embankment in glorious sunshine, just passing the Bank of Austria; it reminded me I'd have to cash a cheque the moment I got back to Vienna.

' "Look," said somebody with a giggle, "the governor's on about the mustard-coloured atrocity again." And there he was, sure enough, pointing across the river to the new barracks he'd been boring us about ever since we got to Bosnia. Just where his finger pointed, there was a gap in the crowd, only one man standing there, scrawny, youngish; he brought up his hands, I thought for a moment he was lighting a pipe, it was such a queer gesture, but then I saw he was banging something against a hydrant. God help us, I thought it was a prayer-book, it was the size and shape. An odd little sound, like a cork popping from a bottle, then this small black object sailing towards the Archduke's car, so slowly it seemed to be floating.

'The chauffeur had seen it coming, and had had enough sense to put his foot down on the accelerator. The Archduke had seen it too; he kept his head, raised his arm to protect the Duchess, who was sitting on the side nearest the embankment, and deflected the bomb so that it fell on the folded-back hood of the car. It bounced into the street, exploding just in front of us. It made a lot of noise. There was Erich von Merizzi, his face covered with blood, Countess Lanjus was wounded by a splinter, so was Boos-Waldeck, several people in the crowd. I was hit, but was so angry and excited I didn't realise it at the time.

'Well, we all spilled out of the car, and the whole avenue was boiling with confusion. I was running towards the swine who'd thrown the bomb, but he'd jumped over the parapet into the river—only, the river being more or less dried up, this hadn't helped him. I jumped over after him; there he was, retching among the boulders because he'd taken cyanide, but it hadn't worked, being old. Some policemen were there too, none too soon, for the crowd had got at him first, and had tried to lynch him. Once the police had him safe, I climbed back up on to the embankment, and to my horror the first thing I noticed were the Archduke's emerald-green ostrich plumes. When he'd realised that people in our car were wounded, he'd ordered his own car to be stopped so that we could be attended to. When I reappeared our car was being pushed off to the kerb, and Potiorek and his military geniuses were having a cosy little technical *conversazione*. The sound like a popping cork was the fuse-cap or detonator of a small bomb or hand-grenade (they did not wish to commit themselves too definitely at this point), blown off when the criminal had deliberately knocked it against the hydrant—or had it been against a lamp-post?

'It was only then that I realised two things—that someone a year or two ago had described to me a bomb or grenade the size and shape of a prayerbook, and that a splinter of the bomb must have hit me. My right arm felt very odd indeed, but a quick look told me there wasn't any blood yet, and I made up my mind to keep quiet about it for the present.

'I went over to the Archduke and the Duchess; they were incredibly brave because although, for all they knew, there were other assassins in the crowd, *they* had taken command, and were seeing to the safety of the wounded. "Sir," I blurted, "with respect, if the Emperor Alexander II hadn't stopped his carriage in order to look after the wounded—" "The fellow's a lunatic, Mayrhofen," said the Archduke, "but come on, let's get on with our programme."

'He got back into the car with the Duchess. I asked permission to stand on the running board to act as bodyguard.

' "Well!" said the Archduke. "If you must be heroic!"

'By the time we reached the City Hall my two lines of thought had developed even further. First, when you're wounded in the arm, the best course of treatment is not a ride standing on the running-board of a rapidly-moving car; secondly, I'd identified the bomb, which even Potiorek's experts had agreed seemed too complicated to be the work of local amateurs. The Serbs had used grenades like that against the Turks in the Balkan Wars—that's when I'd heard them described. That bomb had come from the Serbian National Arsenal in Belgrade.

'All the time it was becoming more difficult to hang on to the side of the car.

'Well, we reached the City Hall, went up the steps. The next happening was grotesque. The fat Mayor, as I've said, had been in the first car, and he'd no idea of what had happened. The cheering had drowned the noise of the explosion. So he began reading his speech of welcome. "Your Royal and Imperial Highness! Your Highness! Our hearts are filled with happiness over the most gracious visit—"

'The Archduke stopped being calm then—and who can blame him! "Mr Mayor—one comes here for a visit and is received with bombs! It is outrageous!"

'I thought the Mayor would faint. Someone gabbled to him a brief account of what had happened while he'd driven peacefully ahead, concentrating on his speech of welcome; some damned fat Bosnian matron behind me actually said, "Fancy being rude to the Mayor like that!" Why the hell was she so shocked that a man who'd nearly lost his life should now lose his temper—what did she expect him to do, give a vote of thanks for such interesting local customs?

'But the Archduke recovered himself almost at once. "All right," he said. "Now you may speak!"

'And the Mayor started all over again, went on reading like an idiot—"Your Highnesses can read in our faces the feelings of our love and devotion, of our unshakeable loyalty—"

'The Archduke kept his self-control. He actually smiled, Andrei, as he made a formal reply. He ended his speech with a sentence in Serbo-Croat, "May I ask you to give my cordial greeting to the inhabitants of this beautiful city, and assure you of my unchanged regard and favour."

'Immediately afterwards he told me to get a telegram sent off to the Emperor, asking him not to take too seriously any reports he might get about the bomb incident. When I came back they were in a side-room discussing what to do next. One of the most unreal aspects of it all was that Potiorek and Gerde, the Police Chief, who should have been shocked into thoughts of suicide—or at least silence—didn't seem to feel disgraced in any way. Potiorek, in fact, was as cockahoop as usual. There would be no more attempts, he was sure. There was no need to cancel the scheduled programme, the visit to the museum, the lunch at the Governor's Residence, and so on. He began to flourish a printed menu-card, to show us the joys in store for us.

'Before that, said the Archduke, he would go to the hospital to see the wounded. The Duchess said she would go with him. No, he said, she should go straight to the Governor's Residence—or, better still, back to Ilidze. While they were discussing this, there was Potiorek bleating on about the flowers specially arranged on the luncheon tables, the champagne already on ice; the lunch itself. I took his damned menu-card from him because the way he was flapping it got on my nerves, and said, "My God! Are you still going to offer them *this*?"

'One of the items was *bombe surprise*.

' "Surely, Excellency," I said, trying to be correct, "you'll have to rush down a company of troops to line the streets before their Highnesses leave the City Hall?"

' "Impossible," he said. "They're improperly dressed." And then, seeing the look on my face, he said, "What, do you think the streets of Sarajevo are full of assassins?"

'I said, "Do you think that creature stinking of bitter almonds and vomit was the only one?"

' "The Archduke himself said he was a lunatic."

' "That was a Serbian bomb."

'Franz Harrach came across from talking to the Archduke and Duchess. "She won't leave him," he said. "Still, if we go first to the hospital, it means the advertised route is changed, and that should lessen the risk, especially if we go at a hell of a rate."

' "Ah, yes, indeed," said Potiorek. "It'll mean going back the same way, along the embankment. *If* Sarajevo's full of assassins, they won't be waiting there. I'll see to everything."

'So there he was, issuing orders at the top of his voice—only it didn't occur to him to tell the chauffeur of the changed programme.

'Franz Harrach said to me, "You're not looking well."

' "I think a splinter hit my arm," I said. "Nothing to worry about, though—for God's sake don't tell anyone."

' "I'll keep quiet on one condition—I'll stand on the running-board this time—the left side he's on, isn't he, and that's the side closer to the embankment, and the attack came from that direction this morning. Right, I'll do that. You sit in my place."

' "*He* thinks there may be another attack," I said suddenly. "That's why he tried to get the Duchess to go on alone."

' "*She* thinks there'll be another attack; that's why she insists on staying with him. But it'll be all right—we'll be moving fast, along an unexpected route—*the* most unexpected route, since it's where they made their first attempt."

' "Well, let's get it over and done with," I said. "This place gets on my nerves."

'There was a dreadful awkwardness and silence among the people still waiting outside; what, after all, could one expect when they were staring at a guest who'd almost been killed, asked Harrach.

' "Some of them," I said, "may be hoping he'll still be killed."

'There was a stale smell about the place I shall never forget. I know now it was the smell of fear—sweat and dreadful anxiety. I don't know whether the smell came from them or from us.

'The Archduke and Duchess came out of the City Hall. I think he had said again that they should separate, because I heard her whisper: "All the more reason that I should stay with you."

'People had frequently sneered that, while he was obviously infatuated with her, she really cared nothing for him, and her motive for marriage had been nothing except ambition. I think that this, the last sentence but one I ever heard her say to him, gives the truth.

'Royalty must be gracious, protocol must be observed. The right acknowledgments were made, they came down the steps, and into the car.

'It was blazing hot now; but the Archduke's hand brushed against mine as I held the door open for him, and it was icy cold. I thought, "My God, he believes there'll be another attempt."

' "More of this tomfoolery on the running-board, Mayrhofen?" he asked.

' "I shall be the fool this time, sir," said Franz Harrach. "I'm better acquainted with the way my car changes gear."

'He had drawn his sword, and was ready to shield the Archduke with his body.

'I blundered into his former seat, still startled by the touch of that cold hand. I kept thinking, He believes they'll try again, and then, quite horribly, *He*, with his passion for hunting, knows what it's like to be hunted now.

'With his wife beside him.

'But we would be moving at top speed, and along a route different from that advertised.

'Only Potiorek hadn't told the driver.

'The crowd was thicker and was cheering. An old woman cried in Czech, "*Nazdar*," and the Duchess smiled. We were moving very fast, back along the Appel Quay, only a matter of minutes now before we were out of it, and then, without warning, when we reached the Lateiner Bridge, turned right, off the embankment, into Franz Josef Street. Franz Josef Street was on the route to the museum—the chauffeur hadn't been told of the change in plan.

' "Not that way, you fool!" shouted Potiorek. "Keep straight on."

'Since we'd already turned off, I thought it was better to keep going, fast, instead of trying to reverse. But Potiorek was bawling like a bull, "Wrong way! Straight along the Appel Quay!"

'Is it all clear, Andrei? We'd turned right, were now trying to reverse, very slowly. On the right-hand side of the street, just a few feet from the Duchess, was a provision store called Schiller's. Standing before it was a sallow-faced boy with a big jaw; he was standing there outside the grocer's shop, staring at us as the car backed, very slowly. Potiorek was leaning forward bawling at the chauffeur; Franz Harrach with his silly little sword dangling useless and I were both on the wrong side now, only the Duchess could do anything as he stepped from the kerb into the street. She tried to jump up, and shield her husband with her body, and one of the two shots hit her in the stomach.'

23

Morganatic Funeral

'CERTAINLY,' said Uncle Raoul, 'Austria will have to take some action to show the Serbs this kind of atrocity will not be tolerated, and however stringent her demands, they should receive general backing. It's one thing to give noisy approval to shouts for self-determination, another to back murder. Yes, I include Russia in this; Russia, most of all countries, can never afford to condone assassination.'

'People who live—or ought to live—in Winter Palaces shouldn't throw bombs, or approve of it,' I said.

Mother said, 'If Austria moves first, and with decision, no one will protest, even if she goes in and occupies Belgrade.'

'Oh, she will,' said Uncle Raoul. 'She *must*. God knows how much she's had to put up with in the last few years from Belgrade.'

'Did you say,' asked Mother, 'that you had a long conversation with Sazonov before you came back?'

Sazonov, a career diplomat, had been Russian Foreign Minister since 1910. He was a little man, with a small head, a big nose, and rather slanting eyes that gave his face an Oriental appearance. Because of his looks, people who didn't know him well thought his mind worked in a crafty, devious way, but they were completely wrong. He was a man of transparent honesty, utterly unable to conceal his feelings. We had frequently met him at the Stolypin's house, for his wife and Madame Stolypin were sisters-in-law.

'You might as well,' grumbled Uncle Raoul, 'ask directly what the conversation was. I said that Austria has a vital interest at stake, Russia hasn't. If there is fighting, Austria will aim at a localised conflict; the responsibility for preventing it from developing into a universal war will be Russia's. I said I hoped to God Russia would be sane enough to stop posing as the protector of all Slavs, no matter how hideous their conduct. It was obsolete, absurd, and appallingly dangerous.'

'You are getting like Papa,' Mother said. 'Ministers run like startled rabbits when he appears. But I'm sure there won't be *big* trouble, Raoul. Think—all the heads of state will be meeting in Vienna for the funeral, and *they* won't comdemn Austria for acting against Serbia. Most of them will be too nervously aware of their rank—good royal trade-unionists all for solidarity.'

Mother was intelligent and humane; Mother couldn't imagine the spite which was to allow what should have been at the most a frontier question involving only Austria and Serbia to develop into a race conflict, Slav against Teuton, and then into something bigger still.

Count Montenuovo was the Court Chamberlain in Vienna. He loathed the Duchess, because he himself was the descendant of a morganatic marriage (his ancestress was Marie Louise, the second wife of Napoleon, who had remarried after deserting her husband). He could not forgive the Duchess because the Archduke had fought for the right to marry her and he had believed that when the Archduke succeeded his uncle he would make his wife Empress. As for the Archduke himself—well, Montenuovo's god was court etiquette, and he knew how the Archduke had jeered at his obsession. He had been terrified of the Heir in life; in death both Archduke and Duchess were absolutely defenceless.

What might be expected after the outrage? A State funeral on the grandest scale as was indeed deserved by the dead—and which might have been extremely useful to the monarchy. It would have offered a rallying point for patriotism, and also, as Mother said, it would have provided a meeting-point for the dynasties of Europe. Family ties were strong, and no reigning house, except that of Serbia, would condone murder as a political weapon. The double funeral, the wife murdered beside her husband, would have been the most poignant of occasions, while the great reverence felt for the freshly-bereaved old Emperor must not be forgotten; Austria's wish to punish Serbia for her instigation of such brutality would in these circumstances seem understandable enough; even if all countries did not sympathise, the leaders meeting there in Vienna would have been given the opportunity of talking among themselves, of lessening tensions.

But Montenuovo did not give Europe that opportunity. There was no State funeral. There could be no state funeral, he argued, because the Archduke had left a will saying he and his wife should be buried together—and, of course; it was impossible a mere former lady-in-waiting should lie with the Hapsburgs in the Imperial vault of the Capuchin crypt.

In the brief lying-in-state in the little Hofburg chapel, the very coffins were placed at different levels.

All over the Continent members of royal houses were ready for the journey; all were put off.

A wreath cannot reason, negotiate, mediate . . .

Meanwhile in every major capital politicians sat in little groups and like the Monkey People congratulated each other on their cleverness in having made 'defensive' treaties, whereas the obligations of those treaties left them no freedom of action or manoeuvre.

I remember walking along the Neva quays one hot evening after Mother had left for Kissingen. The air was so still that you could even hear the faint clicks as two elderly men played dominoes. 'That's what it amounts to,' said Uncle Raoul, nodding in their direction. 'Do you remember how you and Alix used to balance dominoes on their sides in two straight lines and then with one flick of the finger send one collapsing against the next, each bringing down the next in turn?'

'And who starts the process?'

'Why, Russia, of course. It's all up to Russia now. If she mobilises, Germany will follow suit, and once Germany starts, France, God help us, because of dangerous lunatics of Presidents and ambassadors, will do the same. So we all topple to destruction.'

The factory chimneys across the river seemed extraordinarily clear, it was odd how rarely one really noticed them. And there was the spire of Peter and Paul. I think it was this sight which made Uncle Raoul continue as he did. 'One sees the nations of Europe as two files of marching prisoners chained together at the ankle. As the leader of each file takes a step forward, so those behind him must shuffle forward in their turn. There's Germany shackled to Austria, France shackled to Russia by the damned defensive treaties. And Russia, of course, is shackled to Serbia by something more lunatic yet—a so-called "moral obligation".'

Not that many people, even in that mid-July, had much sense of urgency. I don't mean merely the ordinary folk in England and France, setting out for a seaside holiday, or the peasants preparing for the harvest—no, the great ones, as yet seemed unflurried. The Czar was cruising in Finnish waters, in the *Standart*, holidaying like everyone. As to Germany, the Kaiser sailed in the Norwegian fiords, the Foreign Minister was away on his honeymoon, the Chief-of-Staff taking the cure at Carlsbad; Berlin was as empty as Petersburg.

As Grandfather was to remark a month later, the Archduke, unfashionable to the last, had omitted to get assassinated at the height of the social season. A month earlier, every European capital would still have been crowded with ministers, and there might have been responsible consultation. As it was, government officials persisted in taking their accustomed leisurely holidays, until, as if overnight, a frantic and confused nightmare descended upon us.

Only a few eccentrics like Uncle Raoul and myself sat queasily in quiet, empty rooms, waiting, heart in mouth, for the telephone to ring, or walked through hot, deserted streets that seemed alien, almost menacing in their stillness, discussing in low, angry voices the inadequate efforts of diplomats who would not have to fight.

The great ones eventually returned to Petersburg—for the State Visit of the French President. He travelled with a suite large enough to satisfy the most exacting autocrat; his escorting fleet, muttered Uncle Raoul as they anchored off Kronstadt and salutes thundered across the Gulf of Finland, Napoleon might have thought sufficient for the invasion of England.

National anthems played, Poincaré arrived off Peterhof at lunchtime, expressed admiration of the palace to his hosts, and greeted Uncle Raoul, now in attendance, with , 'A somewhat *fadé* replica of Versailles, *hein?*'

There were banquets, dances, a reception at the French Embassy, a command performance at the Marinsky, a luncheon on board *La France*. The Czarina did not appear much—she was too unwell.

Yet on the occasions the Czarina did appear, it would have been better if she had stayed away.

There was the official banquet when she talked for a very short time, but soon her smile became set, her breathing laboured, she bit her lips incessantly, was agonisingly, obviously, struggling with hysteria.

There was the evening review of the troops at Krassnoe, when she sat stiffly in her carriage, her face icily cold, her eyes haggard.

And there was that last evening on *La France*. That night, July 23, the French visitors left for Stockholm after a dinner given in the Czar's honour on *La France*. Uncle Raoul was there, though he was not returning with the official party, being detailed to stay on for a few extra days for conversations with the Russian Staff. I was there too, counting the minutes to the end. Poincaré, I felt, was a thorough menace to European peace. He'd done all he could to deepen the ditch dividing Europe in two, and at the reception to the Diplomatic Corps, he had been pointedly offensive to the Austrian Ambassador. Now Olga came across to me as I stood scowling on deck and asked me why I was looking like Ivan the Terrible? She was wearing a broad-brimmed hat with blue cornflowers the exact colour of her eyes. I muttered that I could not really tell her how much I disliked our guests.

'Why not? It's even more—what's the word?—*reprehensible*—in me, especially after he's given us all those presents. Gobelins, gold fittings for the car, diamond wristwatches—but I don't like Poincaré. He showers too many presents on us, gushes too much—I can't bear another fulsome compliment—and keeps making those endless speeches about undying friendship. He's too flowery, isn't he? I don't believe anything he says.'

God help her, she was to see the truth of what she said less than three years later when Poincaré's France did nothing to help the family and country he eulogised now.

'If only,' said Olga animatedly, 'all Frenchmen were like *your* family! Look, I'll go back to sit with the others, and you bring your uncle to talk to us. It's such a wonderful chance—'

I did not know then, of course, how she welcomed the opportunity of talking to any man without Rasputin knowing it.

Uncle Raoul was only too delighted to be detached from the side of Sukhomlinov, who looked shorter and fatter than ever against his lean elegance. 'I hope your grandfather never learns that your War Minister wears scent and golden bracelets,' he commented.

But he was able to discuss the poetry of Sully Prudhomme for moments only.

In the centre of the deck there had been a little group of four—the Czar and Czarina, the French President and the French Ambassador, Paléologue. Just after Uncle and I went over to the Grand Duchesses, the Czar and President went off to the latter's cabin to discuss State matters, leaving the Czarina sitting with the Ambassador in dutiful attendance. I should mention that the ship's band was playing, but not at all loudly—in fact, I could hear without difficulty Uncle Raoul's whispered, 'But see that! Is it jealousy?'

We had, of course, sprung to attention as Czar and President passed, but now Uncle was looking back along the deck. There sat the Czarina, staring after her husband; the moment he had gone, her face changed, became drawn, even pinched, her eyes were restless, her lips compressed, her fingers plucked at her dress in intense nervous agitation.

'I would not have believed it possible!' breathed Uncle.

There was no indiscretion in the remark; we might not have existed as far as the four Grand Duchesses were concerned. They had eyes only for their mother; their faces, so smiling a moment before, showed nothing now but a dreadful bleak anxiety.

The Ambassador, experienced diplomat as he was, could not entirely conceal his dismay, but he managed to go on talking. With an effort the Czarina forced a haggard smile, said a few stilted words, but then it was appallingly clear that she was physically incapable of answering him. Suddenly she put her hands to her ears, and gazed in agony at the ship's band.

Uncle Raoul whispered something under his breath and then, everyone else seeming frozen with embarrassment, he walked across, saluted and said formally, 'Her Imperial Majesty desires?'

She knew him well enough, but even to him she could not speak, could only make a clumsy gesture towards the band.

The Ambassador was on his feet. 'It exasperates Her Imperial Majesty,' he said. 'Be so good as to tell them to stop playing.'

The resultant silence was worse, we all stood still in that dreadful, awkward tableau of embarrassment, the Ambassador on his feet, not daring to look at the Czarina. Then Olga rose suddenly, walked lightly across and whispered to her mother, after a moment straightening up to say in a stilted way so unlike her usual manner, 'Her Majesty is rather tired, but she asks you to stay with her, *Monsieur l'Ambassadeur*, and to go on talking to her. She thanks you very much—' here, I think, the thought was her own, '—for your kindness in stopping the music so quickly.'

Resignedly, a martyr to duty, the unfortunate Ambassador sat down again. Silence, and a feeling of intolerable strain again for slow, crawling minutes, before he began to talk doggedly of the charm of sea-voyages. The Czarina sat silent and rigid beside him, her eyes vacant and strained, her cheeks livid, her lips motionless and swollen. They sat there for another ten minutes which must have seemed a lifetime to Paléologue.

Olga had come back with her quick graceful step, sat down again.

243

We tried to resume the conversation, but I have no idea what we talked about; the Grand Duchesses could have been no wiser, for they simply sat gazing at their mother.

Then the Czar was back on deck. Olga sprang to her feet, but there was no need for her to tell him anything. One look, and he had crossed to his wife's side, was beginning, with all kinds of excuses except the true one, to take his leave.

Beside me Uncle Raoul looked at my Czar, and whispered, 'Poor devil!'

I looked at the sick woman fighting and losing her battle against hysteria, and I thought with sudden terror, 'And *she* is trying to rule Russia!'

And at that time, of course, I had no idea of what was to confront Russia next day.

24

'The diplomats lost the art of making peace'

The Problem of Peace, Guglielmo Ferrero

THE LAST FAREWELL rockets hung for a moment in the sky, the French warships steered steadily westwards towards the Gulf of Finland, and we drove back towards the city in the summer half-light.
'Just in time,' I said. 'Any more anthems, salutes—'
'No,' said Uncle Raoul sombrely. 'Too late. The damage is done.'
I said tentatively, 'Aren't you being pessimistic, sir? Granted he—Poincaré—is dangerous. He's a war-monger, but I don't think he cut much ice with the Czar—in fact, he irritated him.'
'Let's be fair to Poincaré. He'd resent any hint that he was working for war. He describes himself merely as a practical man; he believes war is inevitable, so France must be ready.'
'My apologies to him, then, although—and he'd hate this, too—if that's his argument he's a bit of a Jesuit. But *why* is the visit harmful? He's antagonised the Imperial Family, for a start.'
'I know all that, but that's not so important as the fact that he's going back with a completely false idea about Russia's armed strength and preparedness.'
We were well away from the port now. Uncle Raoul said suddenly, 'Do you know, André, Poincaré used a most extraordinary expression to describe your army, but when I queried it, he repeated it, obviously he's proud of it, so it'll probably be the French official line now. He called it the Russian steam-roller, and your people have adopted the expression. Sukhomlinov and his cronies kept using it, grinning at each other and slapping each other on the back.'
'But what an idiotic description,' I said. 'In the first place you've only to listen to Sukhomlinov and you realise that as far as the Russian Army's concerned, the Industrial Revolution's never taken place,

while the whole idea's so *misplaced*. What's a steam-roller besides being a mechanical contrivance? Something making sober, planned, well-regulated, deliberate progress. They can't have it both ways—a steam-roller attacking with *élan!*'

I stopped the car beside the pink granite quay. The river looked almost lavender under the opal sky. It was still suffocatingly hot. 'I suppose,' said Uncle Raoul, 'the fact of the matter is that Poincaré refuses to see any weakness in Russia. I told him there were strikes in the industrial quarters. "Oh," he said lightly, "the work of German agents." "My God," I said, "doesn't that make it all the more disquieting? And do you think it's a sign of strength in an ally when the ruler is almost afraid to show himself in his capital?" He didn't even bother to reply to that.

'Shall we turn back now? God knows what fresh *coups de théâtre* await us tomorrow. I feel more and more like a schoolgirl at a play, rattling on in the interval what I think is going to happen in the next act, hoping for a happy ending, but fearing I may have come to attend a tragedy after all.'

'At any rate,' I said, as I turned the car, 'there's a little breeze—just the breath of one—coming in from the sea.'

But all over Europe behind doors and windows closed despite the burning heat, in airless rooms behind thick double doors, men were talking, telephoning, unrolling maps beneath green-shaded lamps, while peasants slept the sleep of exhaustion because the harvest was nearly in.

As we sat at breakfast next day, the latest French newspapers were brought in, but after a moment we gave up reading them. All they contained were lengthy reports of the most scandalous trial of the year, that of the wife of Caillaux, once Prime Minister, more recently Finance Minister. She was charged with the murder of a newspaper editor, and, though historians years hence may find it hard to believe, her trial went on obsessing the public to the exclusion of all else until the mobilisation notices headed *Armée de Terre et Armée de Mer* started going up.

But there was more to it than that. Because in March silly blonde Henriette Caillaux had shot the newspaper editor, her husband had to resign from the post he held at the time—Minister of Finance. There had been a general election two months later; until that afternoon in March Caillaux, an able if unpleasant politician, had stood a good chance of becoming Prime Minister again. Poincaré, heaving a sigh of relief in the Presidential Palace, must have thought benevolently of the hysterical murderess, for Caillaux as Prime Minister would have governed France himself, instead of taking orders from the President; more, he had shown in the past he was ready and able to abandon the old provocative policy of rigid hostility to Germany.

But he lost his chance—because of his fool of a wife. More. The Caillaux trial, beginning in July, was avidly reported in the press, so much so that intelligent men of discrimination simply stopped reading newspapers where page after page was given up to the same nauseating topic. Therefore they missed the paragraphs headed 'From our Foreign Correspondent' inserted where there was a little space to spare. The six bullets fired from Henriette Caillaux's Smith and Wesson revolver rang so loudly in the hearing of most Frenchmen that they were deafened to more ominous sounds.

They were a strange crew, the gravediggers of European civilisation. The haggard Serbian assassin, Montenuovo, Henriette Caillaux—

Uncle Raoul telephoned me half an hour later from the Embassy.

'The Austrians have sent an ultimatum to Serbia. You'd better telegraph your mother to come home. Then wait for me.'

'What's in the ultimatum?' I asked when he came.

'Demands for the formal condemnation of all anti-Austrian propaganda, expulsion from office of anyone fomenting it, the acceptance of the collaboration of Austrian agents in the suppression of such propaganda, legal action against the men behind the Sarajevo murders— and the investigation to be directed by Austrian agents.'

'What might have been expected,' I said, a little surprised that he had reacted so violently.

'Yes—but we didn't expect a time-limit of only forty-eight hours for the reply,' said Uncle Raoul.

'What will the Serb government do?'

'At present it's trying to dodge—somewhat ineffectively—the thunderbolt. Their Prime Minister, guessing what was coming, took himself off into the provinces to do some electioneering.'

When I began to give my opinion of Serb statesmanship, he interrupted me harshly. 'Wait! There's more to it. Waiting for me at the Embassy this morning was the reply to a letter I'd sent to a friend at our Belgrade Legation, saying how desperately anxious I was that we shouldn't support a set of bloodstained brutes. Louis more than agrees with me—all the more since our people there have ferreted out the truth about the Sarajevo murders. The Serbs were involved—up to the neck. The Chief of Intelligence of their Army—Dimitrievic—is the man behind the Black Hand.'

'Poor little damned Serbia! What a gang of gallows-birds to have as allies!'

'I don't think you know,' said Uncle Raoul conversationally, 'there's every reason to believe that Artamanov, your Military Attaché in Belgrade, was almost as deeply involved in the murder plot as that bullnecked brute at the head of Serbian Intelligence.'

I said shakily, 'If I thought our Government knew what was intended at Sarajevo—'

'What would you do? Shout denunciations outside the Winter Palace and expect the heavens to fall? But have you lost your wits? Would your Czar applaud murder? Would the moral Sazonov suddenly turn Machiavelli?'

It was so hot and close that one could only quote the old peasant saying: *Air so thick that an axe could hang on it.* Nevertheless I shivered as I rejoined, 'If there's a European war *because* Russians were involved in the murders at Sarajevo, *because* Russians back Serbia to resist Austria's demands—'

'Because Russia mobilises her troops first; that may happen at any moment.'

'There'll be a heavy reckoning for us,' I whispered, sick at heart.

25

'Against stupidity'

OUR GENERALS were demanding full mobilisation; Sazonov said a European war must be avoided, Austria must be stopped by *diplomatic* pressure. The Czar, looking very drawn, called a council, sided with Sazonov. He agreed to sign an order for partial mobilisation only, covering the Southern districts, and even this was provisional, to be put into operation only if the Austrians invaded Serbia. It would not affect Germany, only the frontier with Austria.

The generals were noisily indignant. No plans had ever been made for *partial* mobilisation—it had always been general mobilisation or nothing.

The Czar tried to placate them. He still wouldn't agree to full mobilisation. 'For once the man's showing sense,' said Uncle Raoul to me. 'Germany couldn't ignore full mobilisation. If Russia mobilises, Germany must. In God's name, why isn't England acting? Why isn't her government telling Russia *not* to mobilise—that'll be the starting point of the rush of the Gadarene swine. So far Germany hasn't behaved badly. Wilhelm's postured a bit, but I do believe he's doing his level best to localise the whole business, but, my God, if there's general mobilisation in Russia, the Germans will feel bound to follow suit.'

He repeated this to me after dinner that evening. It was a little cooler now, some mist had crept in from the sea.

I put down my coffee cup with a clatter. 'What's that?'

There was a noise coming from the west, a drumming sound, a faint, rapid, rhythmic pulsation.

'Can't you tell?' said Uncle Raoul. 'Cavalry on the move—and plenty of it.'

'From the West—from Krassnoe.'

There were people at every door, every window. And the cavalry came in from the west, the cavalry of the Guard, riding fast, urgent spectres in that half-light.

'Have they broken camp? In God's name, what's up?' Uncle Raoul seized the phone.

I could hear people's comments. 'Marvellous, thrilling—what a spectacle!' I remembered the lecture they had not let Father give in 1903: *Our Cossacks were matchless cavalry because of their extraordinary mobility; now they're an anachronism. Mechanical transport and railways —in which the Germans are infinitely our superiors—have destroyed the old ascendancy—'*

Lances gleaming dully in the twilight haze. The sharp, precise beat of trotting hooves on hard wooden roads. Cossacks, dragoons, Gardes à Cheval, Chevaliers Gardes—

'They should have stayed out at Krassnoe for another month at least,' I said aloud.

Uncle Raoul put down the telephone. 'The Czar didn't like to have the generals so upset, so he tried to please them, too. What is meant by "the Period Preparatory to War"?'

'Cancellation of all leave, manning the frontier posts, breaking up the summer camps—that's what's happening now.'

'He agreed to this being put into immediate operation. Secretly.'

'Bringing cavalry into Petersburg?'

He brought his hands together in a strange, desperate movement. 'He won't hold out—the generals will have their full mobilisation before the month's over. Then Germany'll mobilise—Today's Saturday. Your mother won't be able to leave Kissingen before Monday at the earliest—'

'You—'

'Don't worry about me. At the worst I can go across Germany to Switzerland. Wearing civilian clothes, I could pass as an Austrian.' He began to walk up and down. 'The Czar must have the guts to stand up to his generals. Wilhelm must stand up to his—Andrei, I see they stopped the trams to let the cavalry pass, but I think they'll let your motor pass, especially if you fly a very large *tricouleur*—'

'Yes, sir,' I said uncomprehendingly.

'The infantry will be coming in from Krassnoe, won't they? I'd like to see them.'

'Of course,' I said. 'They have to cover fifteen miles—if we go just beyond Peterhof we should catch them there.'

We drove through wisps of fog and the half-light past Peterhof, along a part of the road lined by pretty summer villas.

'War's like an express train,' said Uncle Raoul. 'It takes you very far, very fast, before you know it, you've crossed frontier after frontier, and you end your journey in surroundings very unlike those in which you started your travels. *If* you are one of those concluding the journey—I remember your father once quoted to me a Russian saying: "It's a wide road that leads to war, and only a narrow path that leads home again." '

I stopped the car. 'I can hear them coming. Shall we sit here?'

'No,' said Uncle Raoul. 'Let's get out.' Then, reverting to his former tone, he said, 'I don't think many of us will conclude the journey once it's begun, Andrei, and therefore I should like to take what may well be my last farewell of your army. The High Command may contain an uncommon number of fools, but in the ranks you have heroes who will be irreplaceable.'

They came on, giant guardsmen, tramping silently along the dusty road in the dim, lime-scented twilight. Uncle Raoul stood to attention and saluted them. I am glad I saw them then. They might appear no more than grey ghosts, but, looking back, there seems more reality in that last glimpse of them than in the bright artificiality of the great Imperial review in the blazing sunlight a short time before.

Something of the same thought must have been in Uncle Raoul's mind, for as the last tall grey shapes receded into the dimness, he turned to me and said, '*Worthies, away, the scene begins to cloud—*'

'*Love's Labour's Lost,*' I said.

'I saw it acted once—consummately. I wish now I hadn't; it hits the present situation off too well. The Court, all finery and glitter, and then the messengers with news of death, so black and sombre they seemed mere silhouettes. And a pause, a hush, the actors moved away, and the shadows deepened—one could swear a cold little wind had risen and was blowing across the stage, as this little breeze is coming in from the sea—and more to it than that; summer was done, soon the leaves would fall— Come, let's get back.'

He broke the silence only twice as we drove back. 'Of course,' he said, 'the summer's drawing to a close now. The harvest's coming in. No one will move until the harvest's in—watch over those precious grains of corn, but don't waste time worrying over flesh and blood.'

The second time he said, 'That's an underestimated play—some marvellous lines in it. *To move wild laughter in the throat of death—* And *The sweet war-man is dead and rotten.* Let's have some brandy when we get in.'

Next day, Uncle Raoul went to the French Embassy and the Foreign Ministry. In both places people were tranquil—there was no need for him to rush home, said Paléologue. Sazonov said, 'Monsieur le Marquis, there will be no war.'

In Kissingen Grandfather and Mother were unable to make train reservations for the next day so would have to stay on until Tuesday. It was now known that Russia had partially mobilised, but there was no excitement in Kissingen itself, although the railway clerk said he had already made some emergency bookings for Petersburg and Paris. He was extremely polite, hoped they would both have pleasant journeys, telegraphed through to the frontier to make sure there would be a *coupé* for Mother in the Russian train.

Next morning Grandfather obtained all the available newspapers and pored over them at breakfast. Mother asked if there were anything fresh.

'Only this partial mobilisation of Russia's,' said Grandfather. 'Nothing to worry about there. It's when every country starts mobilising *God* on its side that I'll begin to be really anxious.'

They were to leave next evening. In the morning to kill time they went for a stroll. 'Why won't England act?' Mother kept saying. 'She holds the key to the situation.'

'In her own interest she should be working to prevent war, because if war comes, she'll be drawn in.'

'How can you be so sure?'

'Because she's made a lot of damned silly half-promises to France, and thereby done the worst thing possible. If she'd had an out-and-out military alliance, Germany'd think twice—'

'But, Papa, there's a Liberal government in England, and they'd never dare take the country into a war because of secret undertakings to France.'

'Oh, never fear, she'll find some moral reasons. My dear girl, if Germany fights us, which way will she come? Not the hard way, the country difficult by nature and fortified by us—no, the flat, unfortified way, of course. For years now they've been lengthening the platforms along the railway lines running into Belgium. So England will come in like St George.'

Some people seemed to have no qualms about the future. A little street photographer cranked madly at his immense camera as they passed. To Mother's amazement, Grandfather stopped. 'When will it be ready?' he asked abruptly. The photographer, who had not really hoped for custom, blinked. 'By mid-day, gracious sir.'

'So. Give me your card.'

It was not a very good photograph, but Grandfather paid for it without comment. Outside the shop he said to Mother, 'Of course, you're a living example of the truth of Bacon's *The best part of beauty is that which a picture cannot express*. As for me, as far as photographs are concerned, I resemble Leo XIII.'

'This,' said Mother resignedly, 'is one of Great-uncle Stefan's stories.'

'It's a good one—and true. As you know, the Holy Father was a remarkable man, but—well, let's say it was difficult to paint a flattering portrait of him. According to Uncle Stefan, a Spaniard painted the Pope once, and asked the Pope to write a text from Scripture underneath. So the Pope wrote, *Be not afraid: it is I!* That's better, you haven't laughed for days. My dear child, I'm not very good at railway-station leave-takings, so let me say what I have to say now. If we should not meet again, remember that I have always loved you, in the past ten years have increasingly admired you, and will treasure this appalling street photograph until our next meeting.'

On the same Tuesday evening Uncle Raoul had gone reluctantly to a semi-official dinner engagement on one of the lovely islands in the Neva. His fellow guests were diplomats and Sukhomlinov. They had barely taken their places when Sukhomlinov was called to the phone; when he came back he was grinning broadly, and he called across the table to Uncle Raoul, 'Austria's declared war on Serbia, the bombardment of Belgrade's begun—warships in the Danube.'

His air of elation was so great that Uncle Raoul thought he must have misheard. 'Serbia hasn't accepted all the terms of the ultimatum,' he said, 'so—'

'So Austria's declared war,' said Sukhomlinov cheerfully. He winked. '*Cette fois nous marcherons*—never fear!'

He began gobbling away with a good appetite.

At Berlin on July 30 Mother would join the Nord Express that evening.

What she had not foreseen in the calm backwater of the little spa, was that Berlin was becoming hysterical. When she arrived at the Anhalt Station, she drove to the Continental Hotel, planning to take a room there, and rest. The streets were noisy, but the cab managed to get through, and the driver was polite. They received her effusively at the hotel—her accent, of course, was pure Austrian. But when she gave her name and nationality there was a change in the atmosphere. Not hostility, but definite uneasiness. They had not realised the gracious lady was Russian—if only they could accommodate her—but—

'But what?'

'Did you not know all the talk is that the Russians are mobilising? There is a rumour that soon the police will be arresting all the Russians they can lay hands on. Everything is moving so fast, who knows what the situation will be within a few hours? It might be better to go to the Russian Embassy.'

'I will certainly put through a telephone call.'

The voice at the other end said pettishly, 'Everyone here at the Embassy is so busy we have no time to spare for outsiders.'

'Well!' said Mother, replacing the instrument with violence.

The under-manager, hovering nervously at her elbow, said, 'If they didn't make too stringent enquiries, Your Excellency would pass as an Austrian lady, of course.'

'Oh!' said Mother. 'Thank you. May I use your telephone again?'

She rang up the Austrian Embassy. Her reception there was different; there were people who had known her as a child in Vienna. They would come for her, she could rest at the Embassy and then they would put her safely on the train. 'Don't be upset, my child—*Du verderbst deine schöne Augen*—you will spoil your beautiful eyes,' came soothingly from the most senior diplomat, who had taken her driving in the Vienna Woods when she was seven.

As she boarded the Petersburg train, she said brokenly, 'It will not come to war, will it?'

Her escort's fine sensitive face was ravaged with weariness. 'My dear, it's getting more and more out of civilian hands—the damned military are taking over in every country, and from them there are no explanations—they cannot explain the mechanics—or mysteries—of their trade to mere diplomats.'

'But, for pity's sake, they—the civilians—will assert themselves for the sake of preserving peace, won't they? They must realise that the days of wars of conquest are over!'

'Oh, yes, but there are other reasons for declaring war that civilian governments may not kick against. If, for example, they find they've mismanaged a situation to the point they don't know what to do next —well, war's a way out of their embarrassment.'

'It is the height of wickedness.'

'It's worse, it's the depth of stupidity. But—well, *Mit der Dummheit kämpfen Götter selbst vergebens*—Against stupidity even the gods fight in vain!'

The Nord Express came in. It was crowded, but oddly quiet. As it puffed slowly round Berlin, the Russian passengers spoke in hushed voices, yet all seemed to agree that war was now inevitable. 'But why?' asked Mother despairingly. Men spoke of 'upholding Russian prestige'.

'Oh!' said Mother now in real agony. 'You cannot weigh prestige against the misery of war!'

The people to whom she had been talking drew apprehensively away from her—she seemed to be the only person on that train talking in a normal voice. An elderly diplomat, returning from a visit to a daughter who had married a Bavarian, said in a wretched murmur, 'There's no avoiding it now. Public opinion—'

'Public opinion! In their hearts the ordinary people feel as I do, they loathe and fear the prospect of bloodshed. It's the politicians who prevent them from saying what they actually feel, who've been training them for years to give parrot cries of "national dignity". Where's the dignity of being shredded by high-explosive?'

'For God's sake, madame, you're overwrought.'

'I'm not, I'm realistic; I've personal knowledge of the effects of high explosive on flesh and blood. How many politicians have seen violent death?'

After that she was left alone. Next day was one of blistering heat. The train thundered across the flat countryside, cornfield after cornfield, but no men working in them. How far, she wondered, had the German mobilisation advanced? Russian mobilisation meant German mobilisation. There were two big bridges to cross, at Dirshau and Marienburg, both were strongly guarded by infantry, only a few in the new grey uniform, most of them in the old. The new uniform, the field grey, was the uniform issued to troops who would be serving away from the barracks, Mother knew, so since so few soldiers were wearing it, German mobilisation couldn't be so far advanced. She said as much aloud, and a fat, unpleasant millionaire from Moscow, began, 'Obviously the German pigs weren't so efficient after all—' only to shrink back, with his even fatter wife, into their corners as two officers started to rasp gutturally outside the carriage. Prussians from their accents. Mother leaned out of the window, and asked them if it were true that Russia had mobilised. Mobilisation was imminent, they said. 'May I ask how you know? Was there a—a public announcment in St Petersburg? Surely a government would aim at a secret mobilisation?'

It was a glorious summer day, and Mother's beauty was enhanced by her emotion, and she spoke with the soft accent North Germans affect to despise—yet always find moving. The major laughed. 'Gracious lady, you may be a Russian spy, but I don't really believe it, and in any case I'm betraying no secrets. The Russians haven't mobilised yet, but if they do, it can't be a surprise mobilisation, since they obligingly stick up red mobilisation notices which *our* frontier guards can look across to see easily enough.'

'I see, ' said Mother. 'Thank you for your courtesy.'

He saluted just as the train jerked and moved on. Mother's companions regarded her with awe. 'What a risk!' they muttered. 'He might have shot you without warning.'

'Oh, nonsense!' said Mother. 'I'm half-Austrian, half-French— two good reasons for loathing Prussia, but we can't dismiss the whole nation as bloodthirsty boors.' She told them what she had learned from the officer. 'If we're trying to keep mobilisation secret, then stick up large red notices in frontier villages, the Germans aren't the only people showing inefficiency,' she commented.

They said nothing. Every time the train stopped they pressed themselves as far back against the wall of the compartment as possible— which nature had made rather a difficult task for them.

The sun went on blazing down. The afternoon wore on.

Mother thought, 'Father should be in Paris now. How is Raoul going to get home? We haven't seen a single troop train. That means they're concentrating their troops elsewhere. Against France? But why should Germany and France fight over *Serbia?*'

Her companions broke silence. 'The frontier soon—'

'Yes, just a few miles to Virballen—'

The train halted again.

There had been so many halts in the past hour that there seemed nothing extraordinary in this latest stop. Acre after acre of corn stubble surrounded them. The sun was blistering. Railway officials stumbled up and down the track cursing in loud bitterness the heat, the delay, passengers with voices like peahens who asked asinine questions.

The engine whistled dolefully once, twice. The hot blue sky seemed solid.

Finally absolute silence fell outside, and, as it did, the uneasy hush within the train lifted. Voices were raised. 'Where are we? We've never stopped as long as *this* before! I shall complain about this disgusting inefficiency—insolence. He said, "Can't you read a newspaper?"—Dear God, this heat! I must have some tea—lemonade—Insolence—after all, when one travels on a so-called crack express, one expects certain standards—'

'I rather think,' said Mother, 'that this is as far as our crack express will take us.'

Shrieks from her companions. 'Never!'

Mother leaned out of the window, and saw the guard walking gloomily along the track. He was an elderly man, and his feet obviously hurt him.

'I take it,' said Mother, smiling, 'that now we have to get out and walk?'

'Excellency,' said the guard, 'I thank you from the bottom of my heart for addressing me as if I were a human being trying to do my best. What's happened is no fault of mine, or the driver, or the railway administration. We have been told that the train is forbidden to go any further, and that's all there is to it. Now, Excellency, my advice to you is put on a stout pair of shoes if you have one handy and walk to Virballen. They're supposed to be burning the frontier posts, but I should think you'll get across.'

Eventually all the two hundred passengers had to accept the outrageous and incredible truth. Mother had already started to walk, with two young companions, one a language student from Petersburg and the other a young doctor, who had gone only a few weeks before to begin a term of observation at one of the great German sanatoria. The doctor was in despair. 'Here were we, Germans and I, working together on the best ways of saving life, and soon it looks as if we'll be killing each other!'

The student said, 'I was going to Paris to the International Esperantist Conference opening on August 2, at the Palais Gaumont Cinema—do you know it, madame? I went a few days early because I planned to stay in Berlin first—that's how I was able to get this train. But Dr Zamenhov—you know Dr Zamenhov, of course, he invented Esperanto—he was ahead, he'll probably reach Cologne, what will become of him?'

Mother said, 'What a strange situation this is—not a soul to be seen in this immense plain, we might as well be on an uninhabited planet.'

The doctor smiled suddenly. 'And the train, with those little puffs of steam and the occasional dismal little whistle might be a dying dragon. I—oh, my God, I should have thought real laughter beyond me today, but—madame, look!'

Madame looked, and burst into a fit of giggles. Behind them— well behind them—trailed their two hundred fellow-travellers, men and women dressed in the height of fashion, limping and mincing forward in unsuitable shoes, mopping perspiring faces with expensive handkerchiefs, aiding themselves with parasols and walking sticks and—most incredible touch of all—headed by two impressive-looking gentlemen, linen, tiepins, watch-chains flashing in the sun, and carrying, precariously suspended between two very handsome walking sticks, a bedsheet obviously commandeered from an evacuated *wagon-lit.*

It was a sight so ludicrous that even the gloomy Esperantist forgot the fate of Dr Zamenhov and exploded into a loud series of guffaws. 'Terrible as an army with banners!' he choked.

Mother said, 'Uhlans!'

There they were, a German patrol appearing in the distance. 'Luckily,' said Mother, 'there's a ditch between the road and the railway, and the weather has been dry for weeks—'

'Madame,' said the Esperantist, suddenly in the wildest spirits, 'let me put down my coat for you to—er—crouch upon, but even if it means I'm going to be spitted next moment on a damned great Uhlan lance, I *must* see what the—the forlorn hope behind us does.'

Mother and the doctor got into the ditch. The Esperantist stood, observing. 'Oh, this is marvellous! They've seen the Uhlans. Consternation. Two ladies have brought parasols to the ready. The men are leaping into the ditch like rabbits. Oh, my God, it's wonderful, a fat international banker trying to look like a blade of East Prussian stubble! It's like a scene from a comic film. And the Uhlans have ridden by without taking the slightest notice. Oh, it can't be real, we've strayed into some lunatic film-making—!'

Mother came up from the ditch composed and unruffled. The forlorn hope emerged looking considerably bedraggled. Sounds of recrimination floated across the still air. Eventually the two stately banner-bearers resumed their burden—the bedsheet would never be the same—and the procession continued.

The second cavalry patrol they sighted came from a different direction. Russians.

They came galloping up, came to a halt, and saluted, looking curious.

'We're walking to Virballen,' said Mother. 'We've passed a patrol of Uhlans. For God's sake, war hasn't started, has it?'

'No, madame, but the frontier posts have been burned—give it two days, and then I can start packing my dress uniform for the Berlin victory parade,' said the lieutenant. 'It will take you another two hours to get to Virballen—you should make it before it gets dark. You can manage the distance?'

'Of course.'

'Then I'll wish you—God Almighty, what's that?'

Round a distant bend in the road came the *wagon-lit* banner.

Mother explained rapidly. The lieutenant tried to remain solemn, but as the details of the approaching column became clearer, he broke down, and one young trooper almost fell out of his saddle.

'Attention!' said the sergeant admonishingly. 'They are rich people, unused to walking. That is why they waddle like ducks in my father's farmyard.'

'God Almighty!' said the lieutenant again. 'There's old —— carrying the banner, he's quite thick with my father, same club—' He suddenly panicked (far more, thought Mother, than if the Uhlans had reappeared). 'It will be frightfully embarrassing,' he said. 'Knowing some of these people, I mean. I shall want to laugh, and they'll find it unforgivable.'

'Why don't you ride quite fast past them, staring straight ahead as if—er—scanning the horizon for a possible enemy?' suggested Mother. 'The Uhlans did that—'

'And they *must* have seen the rear elevation of your father's friend when he took to the ditch,' said the doctor. 'Ten to one that's the reason *they* stared straight ahead. Uhlans have a reputation for a stern martial bearing—if they'd started laughing like a lot of hyenas—'

'That's what we'll do, then,' said the lieutenant with an air of relief. 'The good soldier learns from the enemy, eh? Now, lads, *eyes front* until we're well past the—er—procession coming towards us.'

'If any man laughs,' said the sergeant, 'he's on a charge.'

They saluted and galloped off. Signs of excitement might be discerned to the rear of the bedsheet. Ladies levelled opera glasses at the patrol, and then produced lace-embroidered handkerchieves and waved them. A thin sound of cheering arose. The lieutenant's father's friend grounded his walking-stick and waved his free hand magisterially. 'He's trying to organise a proper cheer,' said the Esperantist, 'but the women won't wait.'

'Any minute now,' said the doctor, 'if the lieutenant has any dramatic sense he'll shade his eyes and bend forward eagerly in his saddle as he searches the landscape for the bestial foe—Ah! They've done it!'

They reached Virballen within the two hours, came wearily into the big white barracks of a hall, past the green-uniformed officers, burned candles before the great ikon of Christ behind the red lamps.

Mother managed to get a message sent saying that she was back in Russia, and would telephone for the car when she had reached Petersburg. But there was no need for her to do this. When she finally alighted at Petersburg, she had taken only a dozen steps when a voice called her, and she was in my arms.

'Maman! I didn't dream you'd get here so soon.'

'Andrei, my darling, what are you doing here?' Her face whitened. 'Are you—being sent anywhere?'

'No,' I said. 'I've been seeing Uncle Raoul off. He felt he had to go while there was time. He sent his dear love.'

26

'It is hard to decide'

ON THE 28th Sazonov had supported the Czar when he withstood the demands for mobilisation. Uncle Raoul next day congratulated him on his stand. 'Psychologically speaking, it's of the utmost importance. There is in every German mind a dread, a black horror of Russian invasion, Cossacks flooding across the eastern plains, coming to the gates of Berlin. If Russia orders full mobilisation, Germany will simply stop thinking reasonably.'

Sazonov listened attentively. The date was July 29. On July 30 Sazonov was the person who stopped thinking reasonably.

On the 29th, after his conversation with Uncle, he learned more details of the Austrian bombardment of Belgrade. This transformed his attitude. On the morning of the 30th Uncle saw him again, found him almost unrecognisable. No more striving after fair-mindedness, acknowledgment that Austria needed to secure her territory from revolutionary intrigues, and her royal house against assassins—now the murders at Sarajevo were forgotten and he could only talk of Austria's plans for Balkan domination; first she would over-run Serbia, then Bulgaria, Russia would have her there on the Black Sea—

Uncle Raoul telephoned. 'I think general mobilisation will be ordered today.'

'You'll have to talk to the Czar,' I said desperately. 'No, seriously, I was just about to ring up the Embassy when you telephoned. An invitation's come—all apologies for the shortness of the notice, but could you go to play tennis at Peterhof this afternoon?'

'*Tennis?* Talk of Nero fiddling—'

'Uncle Raoul, *he* has to sign the ukase for general mobilisation.'

'Are you included in this preposterous invitation? Yes? Then *you* can play tennis. I'll come out with you, and be sure I'll take any opportunity that comes my way, but—to whack balls across a length of netting while—! Andrei! You'll let him win, won't you? He likes to win.'

I played tennis—let the Czar win. He talked about the magnificent weather, and as I skied shots into the sky or drove them into the net, I wondered if the course of history would have been different if the weather in those weeks had not been superb, giving rise to wild optimism. If day after day there had been a steady downpour, creating depression, keeping people off the street, indoors—

We saw little of the other members of the Family; Alexei was ill again. Olga appeared for a few moments, and had a short conversation with me on my recent stay in Austria, and with Uncle Raoul on French poetry; he brightened noticeably in her presence. He had hitherto sat with a look of sheer incredulity on his face, caused by the Czar's greeting:

'My dear Marquis, such magnificent weather—if only I could enjoy it in peace, but I'm constantly being called to the telephone.'

But at the end of that long, hot afternoon, he gained a grain of satisfaction. The Czar said, 'We should like you to come out again—tomorrow, if possible. You will still be here?'

Uncle Raoul replied, 'I hope so, sir. Andrei has sent a telegram telling his mother to return home; I am praying I shall not have to go back to France before I can see Avoye again—perhaps for the last time.' For one not given to wearing his heart on his sleeve he did not do badly at all. More. He achieved the success he deserved.

'Everything possible is being done to save peace,' said the Czar. 'I will not become responsible for a monstrous slaughter.' But then he added, 'But there are overwhelming pressures, of course—'

'Let us forget for the moment that last betraying statement,' said Uncle Raoul in a low voice as we drove to the local station. 'Instead let us concentrate on two pieces of information given me by that elderly courtier who sat beside me for ten minutes or so while you were loyally slashing away. I spoke to him frankly, and he said, "Remember two things. He is in constant communication with the German Kaiser—telegram after telegram. Both want peace. Secondly, I know that the Czarina is sending a stream of telegrams to Tyumen in Siberia where Rasputin is recovering from a knife-wound given by a hysterical woman. They are all practically identical—'We are horrified at the prospect of war. Do you think it is possible? Pray for us. Help us with your counsel.' And Rasputin's replies are always the same—war must be avoided at all costs, if worse calamities are not to overtake the dynasty and Empire." Andrei, whose influence is strongest so far as the Czar and Czarina are concernd?'

'But Rasputin's not here in person,' I said. 'That's the all-important fact.'

'A pity. For once he might be the guardian angel instead of the evil genius of the monarchy.'

And still the glorious sun beat down. In the little town nurses with brightly-coloured ribbon streamers were pushing perambulators, silk-kerchiefed girls were walking arm-in-arm, small boys rode furiously on bicycles, old men sat on benches, reading newspapers or dozing. Everyone was lazy, happy— The leaves were yellowing, but had not started to fall.

'There's Sazonov driving past,' said Uncle Raoul. 'An army officer with him—I couldn't see his face.'

Later we were able to piece together what happened.

The Czar held out for a time. He was receiving frequent messages from his cousin in Berlin saying there must not be a drift to war. He was sure Wilhelm only wanted peace.

In the meantime, asked Sazonov, might he discuss general mobilisation with the War Minister?

No mention on either side of the crucial nature of general mobilisation, the first stone to roll and cause the avalanche.

Later the Czar sent a telephone message to the War Ministry; he agreed to full mobilisation.

But just before midnight, another appeal came from Germany. Wilhelm was seeing the truth now with bitter clarity, and, of course, he had never been unintelligent. He was trying to act as mediator— he warned the Czar he could not carry on if compromised by Russian military measures. Wilhelm at least realised how the Germans would react to Russian mobilisation.

At five minutes before midnight, a telephone rang, and Sukhomlinov's fat hand took the instrument from its stand. From the other end came the halting voice of a man obviously unused to telephoning for himself. The Czar said he had come downstairs to the hall in the Palace where the telephone stood so that he might countermand in person the general mobilisation. Sukhomlinov expostulated. Cancellation was impossible. He called in the Chief of Staff, who went into technicalities. The telegrams had been sent to the various military headquarters. Because of the size of the country, and the poor railways, if the men were demobilised and then it was decided they must be called up again, the disorganisation would be so great that mobilisation could not be renewed for another three weeks. A start of three weeks for Germany meant certain victory.

'The Kaiser does not want war,' said the Czar.

Sazonov requested an immediate audience. The Czar said, 'I am too busy,' but then, after a pause, said he would see Sazonov at three the following afternoon.

Uncle Raoul had gathered most of this by lunchtime the following day.

We went out to Peterhof again. The sun blazed down, the fountains played—there was no tennis. The Czar was giving an audience to Sazonov. However, we were told, the Czarina would like to see the Marquis, since she had heard he might soon be leaving Russia.

She was haggard-eyed, almost distraught. 'I'm ashamed of my German blood—I don't know what has happened to the Germany of my childhood. It's a changed country now, I've nothing in common with anyone there. Prussia has been Germany's ruin— The Hohenzollerns, so detestable, with their idiotic pride and insatiable ambitions. Even so, I don't think the Kaiser wants war, he's being dragged into it by the militarists—'

We could not reply that the same thing was happening in Russia. She turned to me. 'My poor Andrei, where is your mother now?'

'She wired from Virballen, Your Majesty, she'd got so far. God knows when she'll reach Petersburg.'

'Will you let us know the moment she arrives? We've thought of her a great deal.'

It was an odd conversation, because not one of the people taking part in it was really concentrating on it; we were all wondering what was going on in the room on the ground floor with the windows overlooking the Gulf of Finland.

We learned only too soon. By the time we had arrived back in Petersburg, to make a last call at the French Embassy, the first stone had been pushed into motion.

Paléologue had had it all by telephone from an excited Sazonov. The generals had not left Sazonov alone for a moment, they had kept telling him he must use every argument possible, both military and political. The Chief of Staff said, 'If you're successful, telephone me immediately from the Palace. I'll alter the partial into general mobilisation, after this I'll retire from sight, smash the telephone, and generally take all precautions so that I can't be found to receive any contrary orders!'

There had been a great deal of laughter and back-slapping.

Sazonov found the Czar pale and nervous. His face was lined.

There had been another telegram from the Kaiser, he said at the beginning of the audience. Sazonov replied instantly, 'I beg Your Imperial Majesty to disregard it. Germany is only trying to gain time.'

'I have been thinking it all out—talking to people. Our mobilisation will provoke German mobilisation. There will be no going back, the machine will begin to move, nothing can stop it.' He turned to stare in horror at Sazonov. 'Think of the responsibility which you are advising me to take! Think of the thousands and thousands of men who will be sent to their deaths!'

Sazonov realised there was still resistance to be overcome, had known this ever since he had been granted the audience, for he was not alone with the Czar. There in the study stood General Tatischev, whom the Czar meant to send to Berlin as a personal liaison officer with the Kaiser. So for an hour Sazonov argued. 'It is better fearlessly to bring about a war by our preparations for it, and to continue those preparations carefully, than to give an inducement for war by sheer cowardice, and be taken unaware.'

('God forgive him!' was Uncle Raoul's comment.)

An hour had passed. The Czar sat at the great mahogany desk, staring out at the grey-blue sea. He could not bring himself to speak. The silence was unbearable. Then Tatischev—there because he was going to serve as the Czar's personal link with the Kaiser—could bear it no longer. He had great affection for the Czar and could not endure the bewildered look on the lined face. He blurted out, 'Yes, it is hard to decide,' and by so doing started the decisive slide to war.

The Czar turned on him with all the irritability of a weak man who doubted himself—and therefore must assert himself.

'I am the one who decides!' he snapped. He turned back to Sazonov.

'All right, Serge Dmitrivitch—telephone the Chief of Staff that I give the order for general mobilisation.'

As soon as etiquette permitted, Sazonov was seizing the receiver. He gave the joyful news to the Chief of Staff. 'Now you can smash the telephone! Give your orders, General—and then disappear for the rest of the day!'

Uncle Raoul changed into civilian clothes. 'I bequeath to your care,' he said, 'a complete wardrobe of French uniforms. You'd better have my papers of identification, too. If you'll let me have in exchange those rather dreadful clothes you once got in Innsbruck for climbing about in the Tyrol— Oh, this book—can you send it to the Grand Duchess Olga with my humble duty? It's the poetry we were discussing yesterday—

'My dear love to your mother, Andrei. My dear boy, if war comes, for God's sake don't think of it as an adventure. It'll be a brutal, bloody business. Here's a letter to be read only if the worst happens—'

His train was there at the station.

'Thank God your grandmother's dead. This would have broken her heart.' He embraced me, and made the sign of the cross. 'Pray for me, Andrei, and I'll pray for you. Above all let's pray that the miracle will happen, and Europe won't crucify Christ again.'

And the train was gone, and I stood aimlessly on the platform until I saw Mother.

27

The Iron Dice Roll

AS WE DROVE HOME from the station, Mother said, 'The heat's not so great here.'

'I think the weather's breaking,' I said.

The air was very heavy; the red, setting sun was like fire. Then the short, light night began, a sky the colour of milk. Mother and I stayed up most of that night, talking, or merely sitting staring out of the window in silence. At intervals we prayed. The dawn was crimson, but after that the sun scarcely showed itself. It was a grey day.

We had rung up the Palace to say that Mother had arrived in St Petersburg. A message from the Czarina asked us to go out that evening.

The red mobilisation notices were going up in the Petersburg streets, in the frontier towns—where the Germans could see them. Useless to wonder whether things would have been different if Tatischev had kept quiet.

The message had been that we should join the Imperial Family after evening service. Afterwards the Czar would go to his study to receive any last-minute reports, but as soon as he could he would join us for dinner.

Since the Family was now staying at Alexandria Cottage, evensong was held in the little Alexandria Church. The Czar looked exhausted; the pouches which always appeared under his eyes when he was tired were more marked than ever. Beside him the Czarina, careworn, her face wearing the look of suffering we had hitherto associated only with Alexei's illness. Both prayed fervently, as if for deliverance from an evil dream.

It was nearly eight o'clock when we returned to the Cottage. The Czar said to Mother, 'Now, keep your story until I'm back to hear it!'

I said to Olga, 'My uncle told me to bring you this book of poetry, with his humble duty.'

'He remembered that with so much else on his mind!' she said, her face lighting up.

The Czar came into the dining-room. He was as white as a ghost, pulling the edges of his moustache with a trembling hand.

'A message has come in from Sazonov,' he said hurriedly. 'The earlier message from Berlin had given us twelve hours' time limit to demobilise. At ten past seven the German Ambassador handed him the declaration of war.'

The Czarina burst into agonised weeping. So did her three younger daughters—but chiefly, one felt, because of the Czarina's distress. Mother stood with her hands clenched, head erect, like a soldier on parade for a moment; then, slowly, she crossed herself.

There were tears in Olga's eyes but her voice was steady as she whispered to me, 'I think your mother would like your uncle's book— until she meets him again. So I'll just copy out the poem I like best, then give the book to her.'

One event at least in the reign of our last Czar was accomplished in the grand manner.

The day following the declaration of war was one of scorching heat. The Czar and Czarina came by sea from Peterhof, up the Neva to the Winter Palace. He was wearing field uniform, she was wearing a white dress and a picture hat. At the beginning of the journey, he looked worse even than he had done the evening before, his eyes were bright as if with fever. The Czarina was haggard.

She said to Mother, 'I wish Alexei could be here, but he's not well enough, his leg's still terribly painful. He's in a wretched state about it, and we're dreadfully disappointed. Always the same bad luck when he's supposed to appear in public. We don't want people to get the idea he's an invalid.'

Mother bowed her head.

The boat came along the quay so that the landing might be made near the Palace Bridge. Progress was slower than expected, for the Neva was full of craft—all kinds, from sleek yachts to fishing boats all flying flags. The river was alive with cheering, the bridge, the great square to the west of the Palace. They were calling, '*Batiushka, Batiushka*, lead us to victory!'

At three o'clock on that scorching afternoon, the Imperial party entered the white and gold St George's Hall in the Winter Palace.

The women's court dresses shimmered, the head-dresses glittered, male court functionaries were splendid as usual but the Chevaliers Gardes and Gardes à Cheval were drab figures today, wearing their service uniform.

In the centre of the hall an altar had been erected. They had brought here the miraculous Virgin of Kazan, before which Kutuzov had prayed before taking over command of the army in 1812.

The Imperial Family stood to the left of the altar. During Mass, Czar and Czarina stood in fervent silent prayer. The Czar's Manifesto to his people was read, explaining why war was inescapable. '*We are the victims of aggression.*' God was invoked as witness.

Then the Czar, going to the altar, took up the Gospel in his right hand. He swore the oath that Alexander I had taken in 1812. 'Officers of my guard here present, I salute and bless in you all my army. Solemnly I swear that I will not conclude peace as long as there is one enemy on the soil of our country.' There was a wild wave of cheering from the five thousand people in the Hall.

The Czar embraced the French Ambassador—the only foreigner present. Paléologue took the honour very complacently. There was wild cheering outside. The Czar and Czarina stepped out on to the red-draped balcony.

All Petersburg seemed to be there, with holy symbols, flags, pictures of the Czar. They sank as one to their knees, and began to sing the National Anthem.

> '*God save the Czar!*
> *Mighty and powerful, let him reign for our glory,*
> *For the confusion of our enemies, the Orthodox Czar,*
> *God save the Czar!*'

It came to an end, and then began again. The only men on their feet were priests, holding out their great crucifixes to bless the Czar.

And then I saw Mother. She was as white as death, and tears were pouring unchecked down her face. She said in a whisper, 'Oh, Andrei, Andrei, this is how it should have been nine years ago when the people came to him before, and they were shot down on those cobblestones in the square there!'

I think she was the only person to remember that other crowd; I know the contrast haunted her. 'In a way,' she said, in a low voice, 'it seems a defiance of God.'

The Family of Andrei Alexandrovitch Hamilton

The names in italics are those of characters appearing in the story

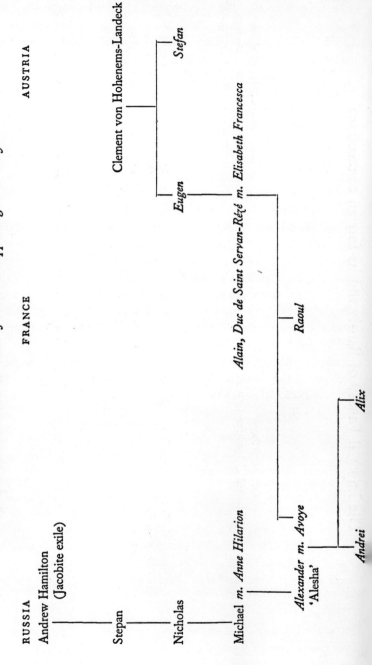

RUSSIA

FRANCE

AUSTRIA

Andrew Hamilton
(Jacobite exile)

Stepan

Nicholas

Michael *m. Anne Hilarion*

Alexander m. Avoye
'Alesha'

Clement von Hohenems-Landeck

Eugen

Stefan

Alain, Duc de Saint Servan-Rézé m. Elisabeth Francesca

Raoul

Andrei

Alix

The Imperial Family of Russia and its foreign connections

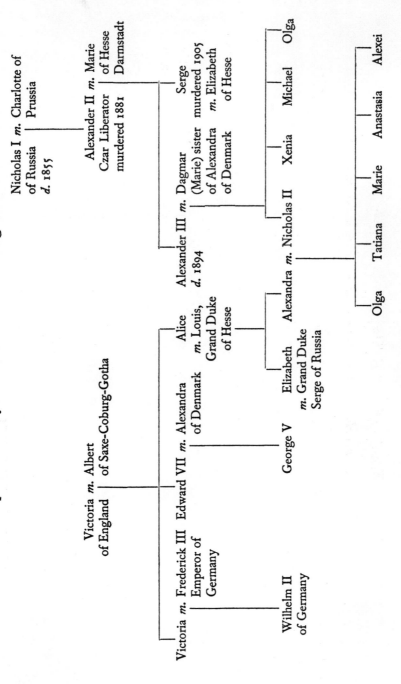